AFTER LIFE

OMNIBUS

ROBERT CHAZZ CHUTE

EX PARTE PRESS

PRAISE FOR ROBERT'S WORK

Chute sucks you in from word one and pulls you down his post apocalyptic rabbit hole! You will sleep with the lights on, covers pulled over your head and dust off the old teddy bear for comfort. Horrifically well written and engaging. There are other popular books in this genre, but after reading this there is nothing else that climbs to the heights of Chute's caliber. Chazz ranks among the top tier of our generation's storytellers. ~ Alex Kimmell, Author of *The Key to Everything*

Robert Chazz Chute is such a skilled spinner of tales that the reader is more than willing to suspend any possible disbelief to go along for the ride. ~ David Pandolfe, author of *Jump When Ready*

It's not very often one finds a writer with such a dark side that has such a great sense of humor. ~ Glenn Roberts, Amazon reviewer

The author has a definite talent with words and ideas. ~ Love to Read!, Amazon reviewer

His words lift and dance off the page, bringing the story to life. ~ Kindle Customer, Amazon reviewer

The world building is horrifically well done with twists and turns and deceit around every corner. ~ Wanda, Amazon reviewer

RCC blends characters' beliefs & worries concerning society's failures, plus vivid action scenes skillfully. ~ RMerkl, Amazon Reviewer

Nothing but sheer exhaustion could tear my eyes from the captivating dance of words choreographed by Robert Chazz Chute. ~ Halph Staph, Amazon reviewer

Wonderful action constantly holds your interest. ~ Sharon Finn, Amazon reviewer

The complexity and attention to detail throughout absolutely blow me away. ~ Kindle customer, Amazon Reviewer

Very few authors impress me with their actual writing style, it's usually always about the story. But this author paints such beautiful vivid pictures with words that I found myself not only enjoying the story but enjoying the way the words created images in my mind. I know that sounds corny, but it is true. ~ B.H., Amazon reviewer

Chute gives us story worthy of Stephen King. A read both thoughtful and fun. ~ Linda Beer Johnson, Amazon reviewer

The author does an excellent job building the characters and getting you invested and involved. ~ Michele L. Hebert, Amazon reviewer

I just can't say in words what a powerful author this is! ~ Delinda L. Calkins, Amazon reviewer

Robert Chazz Chute writes so skillfully as to make the supernatural seem perfectly logical - and terrifying! There are twists, turns and surprises galore. You will be glad you bought this book - until you lose sleep because you can't put it down. ~ johligo, Amazon reviewer

When I want to read apocalyptic books or zombie stories, those books have to also be extremely well-written and something that I could recommend with zeal and confidence to everyone I know. Robert Chazz Chute's books are exactly that. ~ Mazie Lane, Amazon reviewer

He makes the stuff that is obviously fiction, believable. ~ W. Nickels, Amazon reviewer

I am a lover of paranormal, dystopian novels and depth of story as well as intelligence in writing style, and Robert has it all. Humor, wit, depth, intelligence and an awesome way with words/writing. ~ Amazon Customer, Amazon reviewer

Thank you for purchasing the AFTER Life Omnibus. Each adventure of The NEXT Apocalypse Series is also available in paperback and ebook individually.

AFTER Life INFERNO

AFTER Life PURGATORY

AFTER Life PARADISE

Special thanks to Gari Strawn for her excellent editorial services at strawnediting.com.

Cover design by Rocking Book Covers

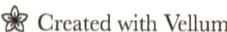 Created with Vellum

YOU MAY ALSO ENJOY

This Plague of Days, Omnibus Edition

and

Robot Planet, The Complete Series,

available in ebook and paperback.

You will find a full listing of books by this author at the
end of this box set.

AFTER LIFE

BOOK ONE

INFERNO

WELCOME TO BOOK ONE

OF AFTER LIFE

INFERNO

EPISODE 1

zombie (noun)

1. A person suffering existential angst or rage and trapped in banality, characterized by despair at interminable suboptimal life conditions and boredom, possibly escalating to violence or self-harm.

2. A ravenous cannibal, usually, though not necessarily, dead; a revenant defying death who hunts for the living to kill and feed or to convert victims to his or her kind. Origin: Voodoo religion; popularized in fiction.

    3. A person carrying the Class I or Class II Picasso agent. (See also: AFTER)

~ Notes from NEXT

1

My name is Daniel Harmon. This is my confession.

About a month into my duty on the Emergency Task Force, Steve Taylor told me about the building they called the Box. The way he talked about it sounded like a typical cop story. I told myself there might be a nugget of truth at the story's root but it was probably surrounded by a healthy dose of exaggeration. I was new to the Toronto Police Service's ETF and was wary of becoming the gullible noob who got hazed. The only reason I knew there was some truth to it was Taylor made sure I wouldn't talk to anybody outside the team about any possible mission we'd have there. I treated the Box as if it was a rumor that had gotten out of hand. Then one summer day we got the call.

"Green 32. Code Green 32 to the Box." It wasn't the regular dispatcher who gave the order. I recognized the Sergeant-Major's voice. I'd met her only twice, once when I graduated from training and again when I was interviewed to join the ETF.

As I pulled on Hazardous Materials gear, I asked Frank Barnes about the call. Frank was a sniper in the Forces before joining the ETF. He'd been promoted to Staff Sergeant two years ago. He was one of the older guys but he was friendly in a gruff way. He didn't look up as he pulled on his blue biohazard suit. "Some of the usual rules of engagement may not apply on this job."

"The guys told me bits and pieces about the Box. It's kind of an open secret, sir."

"Open secret, huh? Supposed to be only one kind of secret. What do you think you know?"

I shrugged. "I didn't think there was such a thing as a virus lab in a city. I thought they put them a thousand miles from nowhere in the bottom of abandoned salt mines or something. Then, during Hurricane Harvey, I heard there's a similar lab in Houston. It almost went down during the flood — "

Frank was more gruff than friendly this time. "We don't know shit yet and I won't know shit until I get there. You'll never know shit, clear?"

"Yessir."

He looked at me with hard, glassy eyes. "This is the deep water, Danny boy. Just watch my back and I'll do the heavy lifting." As Barnes pulled his tac belt around his waist, he moved like a man operating on automatic. His mind was elsewhere. His body was going through the motions. I'd seen him do recon, line up shots and console hostages. He was the kind of guy who wouldn't panic even as he was drowning. Still, I could tell by his face he wasn't prepared for Green 32. I'm sure now he never believed the order would ever come.

None of us really believed the rumors about the Box until we were in it. Then it was too late.

On the ride to the scene in the back of the Hazardous Materials truck, there was no chatter among the guys. I found myself revisiting the absurdity of placing a dangerous disease research lab in the middle of a city. If there is ever a hearing about how our disaster unfolded, I suspect it'll be like the Fukushima nuclear disaster inquiries. Why did they construct a nuclear reactor over a fault line? Why did they build a nuclear plant in a spot vulnerable to tsunamis?

After everything goes bad, answers to those questions are not satisfying. All we'll get is excuses, talking in circles, helpless shrugs. The tallies of the casualties climb until the media gets bored of the sensational. People keep dying but no one pays attention. If one pretty little girl disappears or is killed, they won't let that story die. Kill off a lot of people and people become casual about death.

Casual about death? Maybe that's why they're called casualties.

Maybe they built a viral research center in the middle of Toronto because they couldn't persuade the best virologists to work in Antarctica. After a hard day sweating in biohazard suits, the nice doctors studying the most dangerous bugs in history wanted to pop over to the Eaton Centre for a frozen yogurt. Perhaps the allure of Philosopher's Walk over at U of T was too much for them. I love Queen's Park in the fall, too. All well and good until somebody gets sloppy and breaches Level 4 containment. We knew the Box held the most dangerous viruses in the world. We had no idea it contained the very worst of something new and different.

None of the why of things matters much now. We're beyond the why and the how. Life's all about the next meal, finding shelter for the night and not getting bitten. We don't have a time machine to go back and stop the contagion. Just because it's too late doesn't mean we can't assign blame. The trouble is, I'm to blame for opening Pandora's Box.

The scientists froze the test tube nightmares in the deepest lab: anthrax, ebola, rabies, various poxes. The rumor was that above the elevator to Level 4 a sign read: *Abandon all hope, ye who enter here.* Somebody had a sense of humor. But it wasn't entering the Box that caused the end of the world. Getting out was the problem.

Staff Sergeant Barnes once shot a guy who took hostages on a TTC bus on Bay Street. I'd never killed before. I'd had to pull my weapon many times as a beat cop. I'd been in a lot of fights but I'd never killed anyone. I never thought I'd be put in the position of shooting people running at me in lab coats.

Once the regular uniforms had secured the perimeter, we'd go in wearing our biohazard suits. Barnes told us our job was to secure the Box and keep a lid on it. I'd hated training in our blue environmental suits. They were meant for dealing with chemical spills or "other mass casualty scenarios involving biohazards." They were bulky, the hood was heavy and they were too hot. The canned air strapped to our backs smelled sweet at first, but after a few minutes in the suit, I felt claustrophobic and sweaty.

As we pulled to a stop, I asked the Staff Sergeant, "How do we know who's infected?"

"Until further notice, assume they all are," Barnes replied. "I'll take point and do the interviewing. The rest of you hang back and control the scene."

The guys on the team threw around the term *zombie* a lot. They were trying to be funny. I've grown up around cops all my life. We all have at least a touch of gallows humor. You have to if you want to try to stay sane for all the shit you see. I've seen beaten dogs and dead babies. I've seen people in their worst moments doing the worst things imaginable. It was natural to call the infected by the z-word, just like we referred to terrorists as tangos. Killing terrorists was *slotting tangos*. We used those terms because you don't want to think of an enemy as a human being suffering any problem you might understand. Dehumanization is necessary to do our job, to stay detached, to be professional. If you got into every sob story, you couldn't police the offenders. I've got weapons of death and torture on my belt. I used to say things like, "I'm a cop, not a social worker." I said it with pride and a smile.

Things became more complicated after we got in the Box. I wanted to think what happened was the scientists' own damn fault for working there, for somehow letting the genie out of the bottle. Now, through sleepless nights, I lie very still and wonder how many mistakes led us to the apocalypse.

Barnes told us we could be dealing with a variant of rabies. People could lose their minds. They might run fast or they might walk funny and fall down a lot. They could bite and tear our suits, "compromising our barrier to possible infection." The infected might have a fever or foam at the mouth. "They might even seem fine at first," he warned us.

We should have known better. Every civilization falls eventually but this one's on me. All that death was my fault.

2

The employees who weren't trapped below Level 1 got out of the Box before we arrived. Witnesses said some ran toward the subway. Others fled into PATH, downtown Toronto's underground shopping network. The tunnels and walkways spread over thirty kilometers. It is a rabbit warren built so shoppers could avoid Toronto's punishing winter winds and multiply the number of places to buy expensive things. Each fleeing employee would have to be tracked down. People on the run always run home. Every person they talked to or touched would have to be quarantined and monitored.

On such a beautiful July day, abandoning the sunshine to work underground seemed extra sad. For us, going deep into the Box felt like running into the dragon's den. Once we arrived, it was as if a clock had been set in motion, its gears and cogs spinning, the numbers counting down to zero.

I've replayed that afternoon in my head a hundred different ways. The Box was broken from the start because the incident began with a very loud alarm. The high grating tone pulsed on and on, harsh enough to rattle eardrums. Because of that damn alarm, every scenario ends in the same shit storm. If things had gone a different way, we could have corralled all the lab's employees in short order. They could have prepared us for what waited for us in the bowels of the complex. We might even have had the wisdom to seal off the building and leave it alone.

We could hear the alarm blaring as we rolled up. Staff Sergeant Gregory "Mac" MacGonigle, the incident commander, waited for us by his truck. We piled out of the back of the Hazardous Materials van ready to roll, respirators ready and comm gear already checked.

Mac didn't look at us. He spoke only to Staff Sergeant Barnes. "Frank, the people you have to concern yourself with are in the basement levels. Anybody past the front door could be infected and should be dealt with accordingly."

Our bomb tech, Bob Lundsden, asked Mac, "Do we have the layout of the place, Staff Sergeant?"

"Your team leader has it in his head," Mac replied. "Follow his lead."

It was a good question and standard procedure to find out what we were getting ourselves into. The Staff Sergeant brushed it off as if Lundsden had asked if his mom was available for a hot date.

"All you guys need to know is there are four levels: 1, 2, 3, 4. Got it? Your orders are to secure the location."

The first principle of operational security is to recognize who needs to know what and when they need to know it. I thought at the time that sending us in blind was dumb. It didn't occur to me my superiors weren't dumb. Their tactics were calculated.

All ten of us turned to head into the Box but Mac called us back. We surrounded him, listening carefully. I hoped Mac was about to give us a wink and tell us this was a drill. Instead, Mac looked from man to man for a moment before turning to our team leader. "It's bound to be cramped quarters in there. Can you do the job with four, Frank?"

It was a question that wasn't a question. A suggestion from Mac was an order. Cramped quarters or not, we'd pulled perps out of crawlspaces and spider holes. All of us should have gone in. Barnes and Mac had served together for years and knew each other well.

Our team leader could have used that relationship to make sure the whole team tackled the task. It went the wrong way. Some silent understanding seemed to pass between them. Staff Sergeant Barnes bobbed his head and chose the insertion team. He pointed to Bob Lundsden, Steve Taylor, Patrick Davis and me.

Since bombs weren't today's issue, Lundsden shouldered the battering ram in case we needed to break down an office door. Taylor, Davis and I were assaulters. I was hoping to get into the negotiator training program but was stuck on a waiting list.

We were the youngest members on the squad. None of us had wives or children. That should have rung alarm bells in my head. I didn't think about it at the time. This was just another call and I'd worked many calls that week. I figured I'd do my job and be back to my apartment that night, maybe go for a drink at the Loose Moose, maybe meet someone. Routines can rock you to sleep. Too much of the usual can make anyone miss the important clues when the unusual is about to kick your ass. Certainly the population of Toronto — nearly six million of us — went about their daily drag with no idea killer viruses could boil out of a pit beneath our city.

Still, I was sure Barnes was the best man to lead us into Hell. A nurse I dated once told me that her IQ points went up as soon as she put on her uniform. "Once I put on my scrubs, I speak differently. I'm a professional and tons more confident."

I didn't think to question the science behind her assertion. Since then it has occurred to me that speaking confidently sure sounds smarter but maybe isn't. In my uniform, surrounded by my buddies on the ETF squad, I got dumber. We didn't stand a chance. We didn't know that yet. Nobody comes back from Hell.

This door to Hell sported an unassuming sign. In small blue letters on a white field, the sign read: *Echidna Biosystems.* It looked like any other business, maybe less so since the sign was so small. Sometimes Evil hides in plain sight. People doing shady shit enjoy a low profile.

"The rest of the team stays with me," Mac said. "Push the perimeter back another block. I don't want anybody coming out of the bank across the street or any other building within the perimeter.

Once the insertion squad is into Level 2, we'll look at evacuating the area." He pointed at the office windows in the glass cubes and towers above us. "We still got a buncha gawkers on this side but the building's being emptied out above the second floor by the fire department. We're getting them out on t'other side of the building, onto Dundas. You guys focus on securing this side. We go where the trouble is. Nobody comes out of that door until the location is secure."

I glanced up at the tower of glass and steel spiking the sky above us and wondered how long it would take to evacuate all the civilians. Did they even suspect the devils in the basement? Did they ever wonder why their building lacked a parking garage? I bet some head of an accounting firm petitioned whoever owned the building a couple of times a year to get more parking under the building. Nobody knows what they don't know.

Underneath our hoods, our respirators connected to the long, slim oxygen tanks on our backs. Barnes gave the order for us to check our meters and oxygen flow one more time. We started with one hour and five minutes of reserve under normal circumstances but, of course, normal did not apply here. We'd already spent seven minutes of that out in the sunshine.

"Harmon," the Staff Sergeant said. "You good at math? You better be because you're the squad's oxygen clock. Keep an eye on your meter and the time. We take too long on any one level, sound off. Our lives are in your hands so don't go cross-eyed on me."

I was starting to perspire standing around in the sun but the added responsibility made me sweat more. I'd never been that great at math, and if we didn't get in and out quick, we'd be floppy fish gasping on a dock. We'd turn blue and die but we'd still have plenty of time to think about the horror of our deaths before everything went black. I checked my oxygen meter a lot while I was in the Box but it turned out to be less important than expected. We're always worrying about the wrong things.

Staff Sergeant Barnes gave us the signal to saddle up. I fell in behind him and put a hand on his shoulder. Taylor put a hand on my shoulder and so on. Barnes led the way across the street with his ballistic shield up. *POLICE* was emblazoned across the middle of the shield. Above the viewport was printed the word: *INTRUDER*. It was a weird quirk of branding to use that word on a fourteen hundred dollar shield used by the ETF. Looking back, it was appropriate. We were intruders into another world we didn't understand. Give me a simple hostage situation any day and I'll know what to do. Killer germs are, as Mac would say, "a whole nother."

Each man on the squad carried the MP5A3, a kickass submachine gun that made me feel taller. The July heat scorched into my dark blue biohazard suit. I wished I'd had a drink of water before I pulled the respirator over my face. I always drank less than I needed while I worked, though. It wouldn't do to have to pee when the shit hit the ceiling fan. My nose itched but of course I couldn't scratch it. I did my best to get at the itch by contorting my face. Didn't work.

As if he read my mind, Barnes said, "If you're ever of a mind to take off your mask and get some fresh air, keep in mind that death by asphyxiation is a mercy compared to what they got in the basement. We'll get in and out with at least fifteen minutes to spare on our oxygen supply."

I wondered how many employees the Staff Sergeant intended to interview. How could he be done that quick? I contented myself with the knowledge that my superiors had a plan. On paper, somehow their plan made sense to them. But does anything important ever go according to plan?

3

I've learned a lot since we went into the Box, but I didn't believe Frank then. Asphyxiation sounded like a terrible way to go compared to dying slow on clean white sheets in a hospital somewhere. I'd take all the drugs the doctors would give me and I'd fade away. I want what everybody wants. If I can't have an easy immortality, I'd prefer the sweet, painless kind of death where you go to sleep and you never wake up.

Even that deal can go bad, of course. People say, "He went peacefully in his sleep at home." That's usually a comforting lie. When I was a beat cop, I attended to plenty of dead body calls. If the DB came in early in the morning, the results were almost predictable. Some poor Personal Support Worker, a maid or a relative would discover the dead body in bed.

If the deceased was elderly and cold, we'd call for a hearse instead of an ambulance. If the body was warm and there was no DNR order, the paramedics might arrive in time to attempt to raise the dead. Whoever discovered the body would be upset, especially if they'd never seen a body outside of a funeral home. The dead don't look peaceful. Their slack faces appear long and horsey. Their eyes look drunk.

I've lied to a lot of distraught old widows, sons and daughters. "He went peacefully in his sleep."

The deceased's clawed hands, frozen in agony, betrayed my lies. Rumpled sheets and the blankets on the floor tell a story of a painful, lonely death.

The living look for solace in the stupidest places. When people die at work, inevitably someone will say, "Well, he died with his boots on."

Weird and empty. Dying barefoot on a beach by a tropical ocean while getting laid sounds much better to me.

Another favorite is, "She died doing what she loved."

She died under her desk clutching at her chest and trying to get to the phone!

With ordinary horrors as powerful as these, why did we have to go looking for trouble in test tubes?

As we approached the building, a small woman in a lab coat appeared in the doorway to the Box. She looked about forty. Her hair was mussed and she appeared dazed. Perhaps dazzled by the sunshine, she looked up at the sky. As she turned, I saw blood had soaked through her long lab coat down her right side, from her waist to her calf. Crimson blood dripped from her mouth.

"She needs EMS," Lundsden called out from the back of our line. "Call EMS!"

Ordinarily, he wouldn't be wrong. The woman looked like the victim of a vicious attack, one that might soon bleed out. Blood makes up seven percent of our body weight, about 5.5 liters. When it ranges outside the confines of our meatbags, though — sticky and smeared and flowing everywhere — it sure looks like a lot more than that.

We advanced toward her. "Ma'am?" Frank called. "Get back inside! Back inside!"

His command seemed give the woman focus. She peered at us, unmoving for a moment. I saw no fear in her eyes. I saw no expression at all. That blank expression was what made her so scary. I'd seen that before in victims and perps. Blood loss gives people that look. Certain drugs will do it, too. Sometimes it's the crazy gaze of someone with nothing left to lose. (I have that look now, I'm certain.)

I attended a call in the Jane Finch corridor once. We'd been to the same house several times over the course of six months or so. Domestic abuse calls are rarely one and done. The abuser always keeps a key and the victim often can't afford to change the locks. After relationships go sour, somebody gets kicked out. Then they make the mistake of coming back for love or their clothes, an old CD collection or a rice cooker.

I thought I knew the man at that familiar address well. I'd already arrested him once. His wife had filed for divorce but, unfortunately, she'd lost her resolve and did the kind thing. She gave him one more chance. When I walked in, she was on the floor, bloody, crying and pleading for help. Trying to speak through broken lips, missing teeth and possible brain damage, she was nearly incoherent.

The husband had been a big talker when I arrested him the first time, but cooperative enough. He looked like an old wrestler gone to seed. I told him to turn around and put his hands on his head. My plan was to get him out of the small apartment and away from the victim. Once I'd walked him backwards and into the hall, I would get him on the ground and cuffed. He had other plans.

I was pulling out my baton as he ran at me and pinned me to the wall. Instinctively, I threw an elbow across his jaw. He didn't seem fazed. I clocked him across the jaw again but all he did was grunt. He didn't begin to go down until I got a knee in his groin and my baton in his throat.

That man stared at me the same way this woman in the lab coat stared at us. There was no passion or anger. There was nothing to see or understand in those empty gazes. If we aren't careful, anyone can end up in a situation where we act on automatic. Circumstances can too easily turn us into unthinking murder and suicide machines, dead on the inside.

The woman ignored Barnes and stepped further into the sunshine.

Over his bullhorn, Mac commanded us to flatten. The squad went down on our stomachs.

"Send it, Crenshaw," Mac said.

A shot rang out.

Behind us, someone screamed.

The woman in the lab coat opened her mouth as if to speak. More blood poured out of her mouth as her body went loose, bone-less. Before her face hit the concrete steps with a sickening wet smack, I saw the neat hole in the middle of her forehead.

I looked back. Dale Crenshaw, our team's second-best sniper, was positioned prone atop our van. He was still looking down his scope and he seemed to be staring at me.

4

The Box was an anonymous bunker at the bottom of an office building in a sea of similar edifices. Across the street, a gaggle of civilians watched from behind the glass of a Royal Bank of Canada. As we made our way toward the front door I glanced back. Bank staff and customers jockeyed for position to get a better look. Some were pressed against the glass as if the bank's atrium was an overcrowded aquarium. I had that odd sensation of being stared at by strangers. What would they think if they knew one of the most dangerous virology labs in North America sat across the street all this time? And how messed up was it that there are many such labs? Each one is one mistake away from disaster. A dropped Petri dish, a faulty freezer coupling, a broken meter, one bad hire? So many variables, so many ways to go wrong. I've never owned a single car that didn't fail me at some point.

The first thing Mac did was shut down the Toronto Transit Commission. I found that out later. It sounds mean, doesn't it? The TTC — every bus and subway in Toronto — stopped dead. Traffic tangled and snarled in minutes. We could have evacuated a lot of healthy people. Our job wasn't to serve and protect, though. The task was *containment*.

Whoever was in charge didn't want commuters to get to the GO trains. They couldn't allow millions of people pouring out of Toronto to the suburbs, out to Oakville and up to Barrie. Housing was so expensive, some even commuted from an hour or two away. Whatever happened next, the powers that be were trying to keep the disaster from going global. If we failed to contain the threat, they needed the maximum population concentration at the city center. They were prepping for a bomb drop if it was needed. I used to think people like that were cold monsters with ice for hearts. With time, I've come to believe they were not bad, just fearful. If you asked any one of them, they'd say no terrible things were done that day. When they did terrible things, or ordered others to do the unspeakable, they called it the *responsible* thing.

I was supposed to keep the situation in hand. I am guilty of doing the responsible thing. I'm so sorry. When I was a kid, fear was the last thing any boy was supposed to admit to. Lately, I've gathered a greater appreciation of fear. I understand it now that I feel it all the time.

Staff Sergeant Barnes led the way toward the entrance to the Box, shield up. "Safeties off. We may be dealing with terrorists. Assume nothing and let me do the thinking. Understood, squad?"

"Ready to rock," we chorused.

We passed the body of the dead woman. Face down on the concrete steps, what had once been the back of her head was now a messy hole.

Lundsden slowed to look. "She was wounded — "

"You'll make detective one day," Davis crowed.

"Before Crenshaw took the shot, I mean."

"The Staff Sergeant said to let him do the thinking, Lundsden."

Barnes didn't have to weigh in. Mac's command came in louder than necessary over our headphones. "Do not touch that body or you'll end up in a quarantine tent for a month."

Davis gave Lundsden a nudge and we moved on, letting Staff Sergeant Barnes set the pace.

I glanced back at Lundsden. His gaze was on the ground. His head was not in the game. The bomb tech was a valuable team member but I suspected he wasn't suited to this task. I might have saved him then if I could have spoken with the Staff Sergeant privately. I should have told him to send Lundsden back to Mac. I spared the man's feelings instead of sparing his life.

Barnes paused, his weapon trained on the entrance. He could have keyed his throat mike but his words were for the squad only. "Nobody comes out. If anybody gets past you, everybody's dead. Understand? We go in and reconnoiter, slow and cautious."

In reply, we sounded off:

"Two, go," I said.

"Three, understood." Lundsden's voice shook.

"Four, copy," Taylor said.

"Five, roger that." Davis sounded as relaxed as if we were off to visit the little zoo in High Park. *Poser.*

Our breath betrayed us. Our nervous systems were nervous and our breaths came too fast. Even with the summer heatwave bearing down on us and carrying thirty-two pounds of gear each, our breath was rapid and shallow. I took a deeper breath and let it out, long and slow between my clenched teeth as I tapped my O2 meter. Without comment, the others picked up on my cue and consciously slowed their breathing, too. It wouldn't do to let our audience see us collapse to the pavement from hyperventilation before we got inside.

I looked back toward the bank. Across the narrow street, a pretty woman watched us from behind the glass by the ATM. Her gaze seemed fixed on the fallen woman on the steps. Many faces pressed to those windows bore witness, but that tall striking woman in a white summer dress caught my eye most. Long red ringlets hung past her shoulders. She had a long, angular nose and full ruby lips. Her large eyes would make her stand out in any crowd. She also looked the most terrified.

Don't worry, pretty lady, I thought. *We'll keep the danger bottled up so you'll be home safe tonight.*

We didn't need the battering ram on Lundsden's back. Someone as large as a football player must have barreled through the front door to Echidna Biosystems. The door had been pushed so far back, the mechanism that closed it automatically was broken. The doorway to Hell yawned open in the hot breeze, welcoming us.

"Two, recon the lobby." The Staff Sergeant's voice was muffled behind his mask. Frank Barnes sounded like a haunted man.

I peered into the lobby. It looked like any other office building except for the metal detectors and two security desks instead of one. Both stood empty. I guessed that when an alarm goes off on Level 4, a private security guard making minimum wage plus overtime isn't going to stick his neck out too far. Come to think of it, the effort to save the world wasn't worth my pay grade and OT, either.

Besides a few pieces of paper on the floor that had spilled from a briefcase on the conveyor belt at the security chokepoint, there was nothing much to see. Two pairs of high heeled shoes lay orphaned on the lobby floor. Apparently, some staff ran as soon as the alarm began blaring. How many really knew all that was going on down in Level 4? Did they understand the mischief the virologists were up to? Even if they did know, a job is a job. They probably still would have worked there. The World Trade Center was a target long before 9/11. Still, thousands went to work every day until a known terrorist target became Ground Zero. We work on automatic. We operate under the blind expectation that we'll be safe.

I signaled to the Staff Sergeant that I had no news for him and he nodded. "Two by two, go."

We stepped into the lobby. The alarm was much louder than I thought. It sounded like a submarine klaxon from an old movie. It jangled my nerves and made verbal communication almost impossible. Why the hell does anyone make a siren so loud that it rumbles your eardrums and sends vibrations through your chest? The intent is to alert everyone to the danger. Instead, it's difficult to hear orders, helpful warnings or a pack of killer maniacs infected with something deadly designed to kill us all.

5

As I got deeper into the lobby, I saw the genius of the building's design. The office tower stopped at the mezzanine level above us. The skyscraper's elevators didn't go up from this lobby, only down. Somewhere above us, office workers were being ushered from their cubicles and taking the stairs. When they exited the building, they'd spill out onto Dundas a block north of the entrance to Echidna Biosystems.

Only our Staff Sergeants had trained for this task. If the powers that be had more forethought, everyone on the team would know the layout and what to expect. At the time I assumed this was some kind of oversight on Mac's part. Later, I figured out that keeping us ignorant was part of the plan.

Barnes led the way, and as soon as he crossed the threshold of the metal detector, it lit up like a Christmas tree and let out a series of loud chirps. We all froze for a moment and a grim chuckle, as cold as a death rattle, spread through the squad. It was a battlefield reaction, two parts silly and one part serious.

Barnes glanced my way and I caught his annoyed look through his hood's face shield. He waved us forward. I leaned over the counter and turned off the gateway's metal detector. One deafening klaxon was enough.

Silver elevator doors faced us, gleaming and locked. The down button flashed red. As soon as the alarm sounded, a series of auto-mated protocols shut down the elevators. I wondered if anyone might have been trapped in one or both of those elevators when the alarm sounded. The alarms would tell them the end of the world had arrived, but what then? The long wait.

In movies, if you find yourself trapped in an elevator, you can call for help using the phone in the control panel. Modern elevators have an escape hatch but it can only be opened from the outside. Some smart risk assessment lawyer came up with the bright observa-tion that nobody wants a panicky passenger losing his or her shit and crawling up into the shaft before a maintenance worker can come and free them. That knowledge wouldn't be much solace if you were trapped in that elevator in the Box. With the alarms going and the rest of staff running for their lives, you could scream your-self hoarse before you figured out you'd been left behind. No one would starve to death in there. The lack of water would kill them first. Too slowly, the prison would become a tomb.

I looked around the corner to the left. At first glance, I thought I was looking at a gleaming white hallway, but it was not straight. It was a long white ramp that stretched out a couple hundred feet before it began to spiral to the right and angle down. Aside from the alarm, there were no signs of trouble. No bodies littered the shiny floor.

If this were a movie, there'd be a bloody smeared handprint down the wall. That was to come and I'd be the one making that bloody smear.

The Staff Sergeant signaled to me to cover him. It was tempting to move fast but Frank Barnes was an experienced officer. He took his time rather than rushing into the unknown. As I sidestepped to the opposite wall, I felt exposed now that I was out from behind his ballistic shield. The ramp curved sharply so I needed to sacrifice my position to get the better angle on the shooting solution. It is bad form to shoot a fellow officer in the back. Soon, that wouldn't seem like such a bad idea.

At the bottom of the ramp, we came to our first body inside the Box.

6

The corpse blocked the door to Level 1. She lay face down, a large middle-aged woman in a dress the color of mustard. Her blood was the usual ketchup red. No plague got this one. She'd been trampled. Barnes pushed the corpse with the toe of his boot. Her eyes were open, staring into the dark forever, scouting ahead to find the way, to discover what happens after Hell erupts on Earth.

One by one, we stepped over the corpse into a small cubicle farm. Lundsden, the last in, bent beside the body. The hem of the woman's dress was ripped and her bottom was exposed. Her underwear was a pretty floral print stained with shit and blood. Using the muzzle of his weapon, the bomb tech pulled the hem of the dress down, covering the woman's bum and thighs.

"Head in the game, Noob," Davis chided.

Lundsden straightened a little faster than dignity allowed and shouldered his MP5 again. I didn't know what I was getting into then. I should have known Lundsden wasn't long for this world. The new world is an unforgiving place. Dying times don't allow for niceties.

The tidy office was lit with bright fluorescents. We could have been in any office building. Taylor, the squad's weapons tech, joined me in checking under a line of desks. No one was hiding there. I expected horrors like in the movies, maybe a damsel in distress, a cowardly bureaucrat or a corpse melting into the Berber carpet. None of the above.

I keyed my throat mike. "Nada, sir."

Barnes nodded and toggled his radio to inform Mac. "Level 1 employees bugged out. Judging by the empty desks, you might be looking for a dozen people, plus a security guard or two up top. Request we check with the security company. The emblem at the front desk said the security company was Maple." He spelled it. "Maple Security Initiatives was the contractor. Over."

"We're working on getting names and last known addresses," Mac replied. "We're working with Ottawa to get a list of employees. The last report we have puts the number of employees on Level 1 at fifteen. The date on the report is three years old, though. Over."

"We've got one dead, a female, at the top of Level 1. Looks like she was trampled. Over."

"We've got more than one DB," Lundsden said. He beckoned Barnes toward a door. "A security guard."

I moved around a line of desks to peer past the Staff Sergeant. The door led to a room that was barely bigger than a walk-in closet. An array of wires led to a modem. The slim panel of furiously blinking lights seemed like an odd electronic echo of life in the dead office. Below the modem I could see a photocopier, shelves of paper, a broom and two legs splayed out on the floor. The pants had stripes up the legs.

"Dead as shit," Barnes announced. "Movin' on."

As the Staff Sergeant backed out, Lundsden followed him so I got a better view. I wished I hadn't looked. A bald man in his mid-fifties wore a shirt that had once been white. Now it was spattered red and gray. A pistol lay in his lap and a gaping hole dripped blood where his left temple should have been.

Davis stuck his head in front of me for a quick glance. "Suicide."

"No way," Lundsden said. "That's murder."

28

Davis didn't care to be corrected. "How many suicides have you seen? That's what they look like, kid."

"Suicides don't usually drop the gun," Lundsden replied. "The angle is all wrong. The entry point is a touch too far back for the bullet to exit the skull that far forward. And most of all, who kills themselves at work next to the photocopier in a closet?"

"Suicides are either depressed, scared, stupid or fed up." Davis looked around. "That alarm would scare anyone stupid. Anybody see a way to turn it off?"

We were in the dark but Barnes knew how the Box worked. "Once the alarm goes off, the only way to shut it off is to get to the control room on Level 3. There are two locks to go through to get there. Stop playing *Murder, She Wrote* and can the chatter. Finish checking this level quick. The guard's nametag says his name was Tarique. No last name. Lundsden, call it in to Mac."

We call guys who talk too much "oxygen thieves." That thought was never more appropriate. We'd already lost too much time to the Box.

7

I spotted a small picture frame on a desk. Everything can go to shit in the time it takes to glance the wrong way.

When I was in high school, I remember walking down the hallway from history class with a textbook over my crotch. I had a rager of an erection. At sixteen, such afflictions often appear with little to no provocation. My face burning with embarrassment and sweat beading on my forehead, I made my way through a crowded corridor. If I dropped my books, I wouldn't have been able to pick them up. If any of these girls looks too closely, I'd be known for the rest of my life as the freak walking through the school with a hard-on. And if any of my buddies found out, they'd laugh and never let me forget it. For that humiliation, I would have begged my parents to let me change schools.

I got through my high school ordeal undetected, but my point is, *everything* is exactly that tenuous. For instance, I wish to God now that I hadn't seen that picture on the desk. It was the tall girl I had assumed worked for the bank, the one with the ringlets. In the picture, her ginger hair was shorter and straight. There was no denying those large eyes, though. The snap was taken at a beach. She stood in gentle surf up to mid-thigh wearing a blue tankini that made her hair look even more red. A handsome, heavily muscled guy with a wide smile stood beside her. Their arms wrapped around each other. She wore a big rock of an engagement ring. That happy couple looked like they would live forever. If I were him, I'd smile, too.

The worst part? I was working on automatic. I wasn't thinking about ramifications and consequences. My defense is common and equally amoral: "I was just doing my job."

I keyed my mic. "Two to Ops, be advised, an employee from Echidna is at the bank. Tall woman, red hair, white dress. I spotted her in the atrium by the ATM." I opened her desk drawers looking for a name. Pencils, paper clips, assorted notes and files. I saw no business cards but she had used a label maker to clearly print out her computer password. Idiotic, but understandable. Since system administrators had begun insisting passwords be renewed and different every three months, everybody started writing down their passwords and keeping them handy.

I pushed the space bar on the computer and the dark screen brightened to a login page. I didn't need a password. The screen read: *Make it a great day, Kaela!*

"Is that all, Two? Over." Mac asked.

"First name, Kaela, K-A-E-L-A. No last name evident … " Then, at the back of a drawer, I spotted an envelope addressed to her. "Hold. I got it. Last name: Santini. S-A-N-T-I-N-I. Over."

"Roger that. We'll cross-check the employee list and interview her. Over."

Frank added in, "She's got a desk on Level 1, Mac. She's probably only support staff from Level 1. Over."

Mac clicked his mic twice as shorthand for, "I got it," and there was no more from the radio. He must have been busy rounding up the onlookers to figure out who they all were.

Women like a man in uniform. That's what got me into this mess. I was glad to be on an elite team of professionals who saved lives — ordinarily our job was to *save* lives. The ETF started as an ad hoc force called out for extraordinary circumstances. That wasn't the job anymore. We broke down doors every day. When there wasn't enough of that to do, we ran drills to see how fast we could breach a plane in a hangar at Toronto International. We fired hundreds of rounds a week to stay sharp. We exercised to keep ourselves fit for the demands of duty we hoped would never come. My point is, when the regular force needed us, we were the cavalry. I miss that feeling.

I found out later that, as we checked Level 1, another team was gathering in the street. We were the probe. The JTF-2 team outside was supposed to be the solution. Joint Task Force 2 saw us as part of the problem.

It never occurred to me that I wasn't one of the good guys. I used to be so proud of this uniform.

EPISODE 2

"I pursued my enemies and destroyed them,
and did not turn back until they were consumed."
~ 2 Samuel 22:38

(Collected human artifact)

8

T he entrance to Level 2 was secured by a gate with heavy steel doors. Wire reinforced the slab of thick glass. The door's lock consisted of a heavy industrial alphanumeric keypad. I'd seen similar pads but never one built to withstand a sledge hammer blow.

"What do you see?" Barnes asked me above the din of the klaxon.

"Set up like an airlock, sir."

"Technically, it's called a decontamination chamber. We go in. With the lockdown alarm going, nobody below us can get out, not without the code." The Staff Sergeant leaned his shield against the steel door but kept his MP5 at the ready. He stepped to the keypad and pulled a lanyard from a Velcro pocket. From a laminated yellow card, he scanned a series of numbers and letters. With his left hand, Barnes keyed in: 5 - 5 - A - Z - 2 - 5 - 0 - 0 - L - 1 - 1 - V - 3 - T - P - D - Q. He tried the code twice. The lock buzzed each time but failed to click open. Slowly, he tried the sequence one more time with the same result.

"Did the silly buggers change the code?" Davis asked. "They haven't kept their staffing list up to date."

Barnes shook his head. "Couldn't change it. Nobody on this site has the code to get out after lockdown. This is the master override code. When the sensors detect some breach, the alarm goes off and everything shuts down automagically, nobody in or out. To move between the levels, we have to enter the code and crank the hatches by hand. Anything happens to me … " He waved the card at us. "Everybody got it?"

As one person, the squad said, "Yessir!"

"Then why isn't the code working, Frank?" Davis asked.

"Maybe they keep the germs out but my fingers are too fat in these damn gloves." To our horror, Barnes pulled at the duct tape around his wrist to remove his outer glove. The outer latex glove came with it so he was down to one thin layer of latex. Frank keyed in the code. The lock clicked open with one long buzz and I spun the lever to yank the door open.

Only when he turned around did the Staff Sergeant see us staring at his hand. "Don't worry, boys! Still pretty safe. When we get out I'll sterilize it with Purell and steam it for an hour. If that doesn't work, we can cut it off, burn it and bury the ashes. Big trouble for my sex life, though."

Chuckling nervously, all five of us pushed into the decontamination chamber. The heavy steel door closed behind us and high powered fans blew some kind of yellow dust onto our suits. The chamber was bigger than I expected, built not just for people but to get equipment in and out. Still, I thought of curses on tombs in sealed pyramids and a frisson of claustrophobia made me tighten my jaw as my anxiety rose another notch.

Taylor wondered aloud what was in the air blasting around us. I told him it was the latest fragrance from Paris. "It's called Apocalypse."

"Shut up, Harmon," Barnes said. "It's my mission. I'm the only one allowed to make jokes."

"No jokes at all, sir?"

"I'll let you know."

"Yes, sir, thank you, sir."

As the air cycled through the chamber, my ears popped. The others must have felt it, too. We got more fidgety.

"Should it take this long?" Davis asked.

"It takes as long as it takes," Barnes said. "It takes a little longer in the next part. This gets us to the staging area. Level 3 is the lab. Level 4 is the virus vault."

"Permission to have a brain, sir?" I asked.

"Until that far door opens, we can pretend, sure," he replied.

"But if that woman on the front step was infected with something — "

"I don't think she was infected," Lundsden put in. "She was hurt but I don't think she was sick."

"Stop that train of thought, Lundsden," Davis said. "There will be plenty of time for Monday morning quarterbacking on Monday morning."

Barnes didn't seem to mind Davis shutting Lundsden down. "Simple answer to your question, Harmon. The woman currently polluting our street by inconsiderately bleeding all over the place was probably the source of the containment breach. We don't know what we're dealing with or how long the sickness takes before it's communicable and in full effect. Remember my rules."

We did remember. Mac was a by the book sort of cop but Frank Barnes had rules of engagement nobody wrote down. Our leader had five rules. Usually he was in some high perch on overwatch scoping out a hostage taker through a window. To keep us sharp when a call became drawn out and the waiting got heavy, Frank would occasionally recite his theories of police work:

1. Bad guys are stupid. Be smarter than the bad guys.

2. There's no crying unless Frank cries and Frank don't cry.

3. Don't take your work home with you. No unhappy spouses, no drinking to excess ... or at least not because of the job.

4. Everybody goes home at the end of the shift. Death of a suspect was to be avoided when possible because of the extra paperwork it would entail. Death of a fellow officer was to be avoided because police funerals in Toronto require bagpipes. Frank hates bagpipes.

5. When one of us shoots at a suspect, we all shoot. In the expenditure of bullets, we were to spare no expense. If called upon to kill, no waiting. Details are things to sort out later.

The air finished cycling and the chem sprayers stopped. "Playtime is over, gentlemen. Follow my lead."

We pushed forward through the blowers and entered Level 2. Looking around, I wondered what this area smelled like. With my respirator plastered uncomfortably tight to my face, I had no idea. It looked like it might have that strong aroma hospitals have: industrial cleaner atop a sterile hint of mortality.

I was beginning to sweat more heavily under my hood and mask. The palms of my thick gloves were rubber so my hands wouldn't slip on my weapon. That wouldn't be much help if the lenses on my mask fogged. My hands and head felt hot but my feet were cold. I felt clumsy. Adrenaline had pushed my heart rate too high. I consciously slowed my respiration again. Lundsden picked up on what I was doing and mirrored my inhalations and exhalations. When you can't control anything else, all you can do is get hold of your breathing and wait.

I was slightly relieved to find that Level 2 appeared to be abandoned. Ghost towns crossed my mind, though. Look at any old map and compare it to a new map. You'll find places that don't exist anymore. Towns get abandoned, sometimes inexplicably. Any old village churchyard tells grim stories. Do a rubbing over barely legible gravestones and you'll find waves of deaths as influenza took all the babies, children and old people. Sometimes more than that. Little towns die. People flee burning cities.

I wondered if someday someone will look at an old map, compare it to a new map, and ask, "Anybody ever hear of a place called, 'Toronto?'"

9

Taylor shouted. "I got a DB here!"

"Coming, Steve," I replied. This level was as wide as a large house. It didn't take long for me to find Taylor near the end of a long narrow shower room, The staging area appeared to split into showers and a locker room. Empty biohazard suits hung open like deflated balloons, or maybe like dejected ghosts.

As Lundsden and I rushed to Taylor, Barnes chastised him for raising his voice. "It's a radio. You don't have to shout. You're killing my ear, dumbass."

Taylor apologized without looking up from the corpse. He stood at the curtain to a stall. It could have been a changeroom at any clothing store. The floor angled down slightly to a depression in the center of the shower area so tentacles of blood reached for the drain.

Taylor used the barrel of his weapon to pull back the curtain so Lundsden and I could take a look. The corpse was a naked man in his late thirties or early forties. He had a few gray hairs in his beard. He'd never have to worry about going grayer. Blood trickled from his mouth but it had gushed from a gaping wound that stretched from his navel down into his ruined groin. It was all a red mash.

"What virus does that?" Lundsden asked.

"Split from asshole to appetite," Taylor said absently.

Barnes didn't bother to show up. He keyed his throat mic instead. "Not interested in the dead ones, boys. Let's find some live ones. Report to the next lock to go to the lab."

I suspect we were all relieved to do as ordered.

"Maybe the rest got out," Taylor suggested.

"They didn't," Barnes said. "Levels 2, 3 and 4 go into lockdown after the contagion alarm goes off. There's no time to get out once the outbreak alarm sounds. They've only got a few seconds. I'm sure there are people trapped below."

"A few seconds, though? Why not simultaneously, sir?" Lundsden asked.

"Because you don't want those heavy doors slamming shut and cutting a lab tech in half," Barnes told him. "Blood, guts and bone might mess up the hermetic seals on the doors, don't you think?"

"Then why are we down here breaching these seals at all? Why not quarantine everybody who's trapped where they are, set up communication and figure it out from there?"

It was a decent question. When Chernobyl went up and spewed radiation across Europe, the government evacuated the people and told them never to go back. The Staff Sergeant's only answer was, "Orders."

There were reasons why we were sent in — not good ones, but reasons. There was something down in the Box that was valuable and somebody in a position to give orders wanted it. Maybe they wanted to reuse this facility. Maybe we had to secure the lab so nobody else could get out ... or in. Maybe the plan was to get hold of something before medical professionals who knew what they were looking at got down here.

I could have become a physiotherapist but my college girlfriend said I would look good in a cop's uniform. If she hadn't said that, I probably wouldn't be where I am now. That girlfriend cheated on me with a buddy from the basketball team in our senior year. They both moved to New York State. She's working in a dentist's office while he studies to become a chiropractor.

39

We do all sorts of crazy things for silly reasons. I saw people do stupid things every day in my work. Worse, we fall into things and come up with the rationale for our actions after the fact. I didn't think I made silly mistakes. I assumed everyone else was an idiot. But here I was, proceeding to Level 3.

I've had a lot of time to think since we went down into the Box. Having time to think is not always as good as it sounds.

Somebody pounded on the decontamination chamber door. Between the thickness of the door and the alarm sounding, we wouldn't have heard it if they used their fists. They smacked the door with something metal.

Barnes put a hand on the door and waited. "Dit-dit-dit, dah-dah-dah, dit-dit-dit."

"S.O.S." Lundsden declared the obvious.

Davis told him to shut up. Taylor cursed. I said nothing.

Barnes ordered Davis to close the hatch to Level 2 behind us. He did as he was told and, after a short buzz, shower nozzles blasted us with water as a red light glowed above the far door. There was surely more than water in the spray but nobody told me what chemicals we might be exposing ourselves to. Our environmental suits were supposed to protect us but they weren't quite as bulky and shapeless as a normal biohazard suit, either. We had gear on our belts and backs that did not lend itself to easy sterilization protocols.

The Staff Sergeant pulled open a small access door on the wall, apparently familiar with the controls. I thought again how we should have all been better prepared. We ran hostage scenarios at the airport three times a year. Why not have an ETF field trip into the Box when the alarms *weren't* blaring?

"I'm getting a mother of a headache," Davis said. "We gotta shut off that damn alarm."

"From the control room. Almost there." Barnes pushed a button and a screen revealed the view from a camera on the other side of the steel door. The person sending the plea for help wore a bulky biohazard suit. He or she was using the leg of a metal chair to pound on the door.

I keyed my throat mic. "Two to Ops. We have visual on a survivor, at the door to the exit of Level 3. Over."

No reply came.

"The radio won't work now that we're entering 3," Barnes said. "No cell phones, either. That's why we don't have the relatives of the employees screaming at the barricades."

As we waited to get deeper into the Box, families of these employees were still going about their day, oblivious to the danger to their loved ones. I wondered how long this breach could remain a secret and what would happen when word got out?

I tapped the oxygen indicator on my wrist. "Let's get in and out so we report to Mac in person. This place creeps me out."

As the chamber's gear finished its cycle, the water nozzles sprayed us with an orange chemical mist that gathered in thick beads. The slime rolled down our gear as quick as mercury. Finally, a blue UV light surrounded us as scanners hummed somewhere behind the wall.

Through it all, the pounding on the far door continued, a staccato metronome communicating desperation.

I stood beside the Staff Sergeant as he stared at the figure on the security cam screen. I was probably the only person who heard him. "No communication back to Earth. We're alone. We may as well be on the moon. We're moon men now. Earth rules do not apply here." Barnes might have been talking to himself.

I was already nervous. Not that panic ever helps but, when my superior officer started talking to himself, I should have picked up on the clue to freak out.

A buzzer sounded as the door to Level 3 opened. The figure in the bulky biohazard suit stepped back, still holding an office chair. "Took you long enough!"

Through her faceplate, I could see the woman's dirty blonde hair plastered across her forehead. She was sweating hard and I wondered if it was fear or the effort of pounding on the door. Or was it fever? I prayed it wasn't fever. Barnes had his shield and MP5 up and in position to do business so we all pointed our weapons at her.

"What's with the guns?"

"Identify yourself!" Barnes demanded.

"Dr. Christine Newberry. If you point your damn guns somewhere else, you can call me Chris."

The Staff Sergeant didn't exactly take his weapon off her but he let the barrel point down a couple inches. "What happened?"

"I don't know. I was about to go back to the control room when the alarm went off. Someone messed up big time."

"Okay, Chris. How many people are working today?"

"It's a skeleton crew. Three of my colleagues are at a conference. It's the first week of July, so a bunch of people are off to Cottage

Country. Between the Canada Day long weekend, the conference for the bigwigs in Aruba and summer holidays — "

"How many on Level 1?" Barnes said a little louder.

"I don't know. The people up top are support staff. I don't really know them well at all. I certainly don't know their vacation schedules. I spend all my time down here." She paused to think. "There might be ... I dunno ... nine, maybe? It could be twelve."

I had a grease pencil tucked into a compartment on my sleeve at my left shoulder. I took it out and wrote, *12* on the vinyl shell of my environmental suit. Adding up the guard under the blinking modem, the trampled woman, Kaela and the dead woman on the front steps, I added: 4. +, -, *?*

"Twelve on Level 1?" Barnes echoed. "Okay, it seems they got out."

"That's not the protocol. They're supposed to stay put. Nobody stayed up top?"

Barnes ignored her question. "How many on Level 4?"

"Four. Two docs in the vault's lab and two techs running experiments in the Box. I think ... "

"You're not sure?" Davis said.

The doctor pursed her lips. "I don't know, man! Every time we want to take a leak we have to go up to Level 2, shower and go through the whole isolation protocol again. People come up and down a lot."

"Great system." I could hear the sarcasm drip through Patrick's tone. "You guys got complacent."

"With that damn alarm going, my nerves are all jangly. Let's get out of here!"

"Everybody stays until we get this sorted out. How do we know you're not a terrorist?"

"Davis!" Barnes barked. "De-escalate."

"Yes, sir." He nodded and stepped back but Patrick Davis's voice told me he was already far away, probably thinking about crawling into his bed at home. That's what I was doing.

I'd seen Davis under stress before but this felt different. It was as if we were used to exploring caves but now we were doing the same task far underwater and encumbered by SCUBA gear we hated. I sympathized. Sweat slipped down my forehead and salt burned my eyes. My nose was itchy again but there was nothing I could do about it.

He was right, too. The lab had become complacent if they allowed employees to come and go without tracking where everyone was. I imagined no one on the International Space Station was ever so easygoing about safety protocols.

"I'm no terrorist," the doctor said. "This has got to be some kind of system failure."

Lundsden surprised me by taking the initiative after the Staff Sergeant told Davis to shut his gob. "Got anything special downstairs, Dr. Newberry?"

"There's always something special down there. The vault contains four freezer pods that hold some of the world's most deadly bugs. We've got various killer strains of the popular scary things. The latest additions are frozen tissue samples from a failed Arctic expedition from the early 1900s. We're figuring out what a team of British explorers died of."

"But you think there are typically four people working on Level 4?" Barnes pressed.

"Likely. There are only three air hoses for three suits in the main work area, max. Two are for work and one for emergencies in case anyone needs to be dragged out. You don't want a bunch of people tripping over each other down there."

"What do you think triggered the alarm?"

"I don't know. Maybe one of techs on 4 pulled the alarm or there's some kind of equipment failure that set it off. A change in air pressure could trip the sensors. Each floor from 2 down has neg air pressure — "

"To keep the germs in, not out," Barnes said.

Newberry waved her gloved hand vaguely to a door behind her. "I've got six lab techs on this level. They aren't feeling well. Could be nerves, though."

"Why do you say that?" I asked.

"I feel fine," she said. "They didn't look sick until the alarm started blaring. The power of suggestion is strong. You see some-body throw up, you want to puke, too, so — "

Barnes spoke in a calm, soothing voice I'd only heard him use on hostage takers. "Chris, listen carefully. We've got bodies on 1 and 2. This is not the power of suggestion, a drill or a mistake. Some-thing serious is happening here."

"Oh."

I could barely hear her small voice. She was so used to dealing with deadly viruses that it never occurred to her they'd turn on her one day. I went out on a call to a little house in Scarborough once. A guy kept tigers in his basement. He made the same mistake.

Side note: Don't keep tigers in your basement, but if you do, make sure they are well fed. If you don't make a lot of burgers for a predator, they'll make a burger out of you.

This bit of wisdom became important later, too.

"What were you working on today?" Barnes asked the doctor.

"Mostly? Madagascar has an outbreak of bubonic plague. It might be mutating and we're trying to figure out if there's a new vector. We've all got different projects, though."

I'd read about the Madagascar outbreak on Facebook a couple of times in the past week. Death and mayhem on the other side of the world had seemed so remote and irrelevant, it may as well have been happening on another planet. I'd become much more interested in frightening diseases in the last — I glanced at the oxygen meter on my wrist — eighteen minutes. Could it have been that long already? Between coming in too slow, moving around too fast, speaking and waiting, I suspected we'd been using more air than we should have. If we'd prepared better, been given time to run through a few practice runs …

I pushed the thought away, waved to get the Staff Sergeant's attention and tapped my wrist to urge him to move his interview process along.

He nodded and asked, "Chris, who's in the control room now?"

"I was in there but one of the techs — Cherry Gillis — called me to the lab."

"Which lab?" Barnes sounded patient, like he had all the time in the world.

She pointed vaguely at the double doors leading to the laboratory on the same level. "This one, down the hall."

"You left your post," Davis said.

She looked at him evenly and some steel came into her voice. "This is an office, not a military installation. I'm a doctor, not a soldier."

"I understand what you're saying." Barnes's reply betrayed no hint of irritation at Davis or his interview subject. He seemed to show no emotion at all, in fact. "What did this Cherry Gillis have to say?"

"We spoke about her symptoms — just a headache, no big deal. I was on my way back when the alarm went off. I need to get in there to see what's happening and to shut off this alarm! Can we please shut off the alarm? My entry code won't work!"

"Who is on Level 4?"

"Dr. Hamish Allen — he's the senior staffer on site most of the time. Also, Dr. Natalie Gignac and two lab techs, Glen and Arthur. That's who should be there, I think."

"Should be? You think?"

"They might have been on Level 2 or maybe they even went out to get a Starbucks or a Timmy's. I was up all night working and busy this morning. The senior staff have keycards so they come and go. I can't watch the surveillance cameras every minute. I've been catching up on filing before taking off on vacation. I'm not even supposed to be here today!"

Barnes shrugged. "I guess that's fine as long as everyone stays where they are. We can get into the control room to confirm who's where and then everything will be fine — "

"You can? Great! The bigwigs who have the emergency code are all at the Aruba conference. I can't call them because of the damn security protocols! The lockdown is supposed to be for our protection but so far it's screwing me up, y'know?"

"Brilliant," Davis said. "How can you people screw around with microscopes and still — "

"Don't look at me," she said. "Master codes are above my pay grade, high security and all that bullshit. I only started here in May. They don't trust me to get the Friday afternoon pizza orders right for the weekly staff meeting."

"Fine. Are the sick lab techs locked in the lab?" Barnes asked.

She nodded. "Yeah. I talked to them on the intercom a few minutes ago. If I hadn't been headed back to the control room when the lockdown happened, I'd be stuck in the Level 3 lab, too. They're in the conference room, actually. We might need an evacuation team of virologists who are used to handling hazardous materials. Or maybe all we really need is an HVAC tech who can reinstall freon in a freezer pod. If this is a simple sensor getting a false read on temperature in the vault or something, I'm going to be so pissed!"

"Thank you, Chris," the Staff Sergeant said. "Please lead the way to the control room."

She pointed to her left. The large steel door was less than ten feet away. The steel alphanumeric keypad, almost identical to the apparatus on Level 1, gleamed next to the door. The only difference was this one had a slot to swipe a keycard, as well. "The control room is right there. Get me in, quick!"

"Lead the way, Chris."

"No offense, glad you're here and all, but we don't need guys with guns. I need the door code." She beckoned us forward.

"We're here to provide security, Ma'am," Taylor said. The way he said it, I had an inkling that, when all this was over, he might ask Christine Newberry for her number. Among the youngest guys in the ETF, Steve had the reputation for being the biggest hound.

She turned and took a couple of steps. "Security? Look at all these steel doors! I feel safe enough, thanks."

"We don't provide security for you, Chris," the Staff Sergeant said. "We're here for everybody else's safety." Barnes shot her in the back of the head once at close range.

49

Dr. Christine Newberry flopped to the floor. The Staff Sergeant shot her twice more in the chest, dead center.

Barnes stepped back, careful to avoid the pool of blood spreading from the body. "You're wrong, kid. This *is* a military installation and you *were* a soldier."

That's what the Staff Sergeant meant when he said he would "do the interviewing."

13

W e all froze. We weren't supposed to freeze but it seemed all we could do was stare at the murdered woman. Barnes turned to regard each of us. "This is what securing the location looks like. We have to assume they're all infected. We erase the threat."

"Whether it's a threat or not?" Lundsden asked. He seemed to recover first and grasp the situation faster than the rest of us. "It's a hard reboot, then. 'Securing the location' sure looks like murder, doesn't it?"

"Shut up, Bobby!" Davis barked.

Taylor wasn't looking at the doctor's corpse. Steve was looking at me, *to* me. We'd gone fishing together. He was the only team member I knew well outside the job. He was waiting for me to say something but my throat had gone dry and I said nothing. Until that moment, I hadn't done much I should be ashamed of.

"Hold up. It makes sense," Davis said. "It would be worse if we didn't already have bodies upstairs. The contamination could get out of control. We're here to nip an epidemic in the bud."

"By killing doctors," Lundsden said. "I sure hope it's not what she said, a faulty sensor on a freezer."

Barnes raised his weapon and pointed it at Lundsden. I pointed my MP5 at the Staff Sergeant so Taylor did the same. Davis — who never heard an order he didn't like — pointed his submachine gun at me. The bomb tech just stood there pretending he was Switzerland.

"Everybody be cool," Barnes said. "You guys don't have to understand the order. I'll do that for you. My mission, my responsibility."

"What are we supposed to say at the inquiry?" I asked. "Am I supposed to tell some tribunal that I was only following orders? That woman wasn't even sick."

"You don't know she wasn't," he replied. "We don't know how long it takes for the bug to take over."

Take over. That seemed like an odd way to put it. I later found out that was the perfect way to put it.

"Here's what happened: An infected person met us at the front door. In a lab like this, if a bug gets out, somebody's got to go in and shut that shit down. Doing the hard stuff is what somebodies do. This is the job. You can philosophize and whine about it later but keep it to yourself around me. There isn't going to be an inquiry, Harmon. We do our job and this time next week maybe they salvage the lab. Maybe they pour concrete down here until it's a solid block. That's not our business. Now everybody stand down. *Everybody.*"

Barnes pointed his weapon at the floor first. Davis was still drawn down on me and didn't look like he wanted to ease off. The Staff Sergeant gestured for him to lower his weapon and Davis relented. Taylor and I followed suit.

"We've got bodies upstairs," Davis said. "This place is already compromised."

"Are you trying to convince us or yourself?" Lundsden asked.

"Shut it!"

"Bob's right," I said. "Glad you don't have a weapon on me anymore. Your finger shouldn't be on a trigger right now. You look shaky, Patrick."

"I can do my damn job. Can you? And I'm not shaky ... not

because ... " He pointed at the dead doctor. "I'm freaking because I don't want to get sick. Viruses and shit? You heard what she said about what they keep down here. Let's do the job and get out. I don't know about you, Harmon, but I don't want to die of plague. The plague? Jesus! They mess with that stuff, they get what they get. A bullet is a mercy compared to shitting yourself to death."

"Easy, guys," Barnes said. "If we all do our jobs and watch each other's backs, we'll all get out of here quick. Everybody take a deep breath."

I tapped my wrist meaningfully. I was twenty-four minutes into my oxygen supply.

Barnes nodded his acknowledgment. "On second thought, suck it up, buttercups. Clear this place. It shouldn't take long. We get out and we get a long vacation after this. Isolation, hazard pay and pretty nurses."

"Yeah, we'll need quite some time to tell ourselves this was all okay," Lundsden said.

The Staff Sergeant waved his objection away. "The people who sent us had lots of time to think about the right and the wrong of it. It's not up to you because it's not supposed to be. You can't make clean decisions while you're in the shit. That's why this contingency was planned ahead of time by people who are not in said shit. What we do today saves lives, lots of them. Clear, Lundsden?"

"Clear,"

"Taylor?"

"Y-yes, sir. Clear."

"Harmon?"

"Yes ... sir."

Barnes didn't even bother to ask Davis. In his whole life, Patrick never considered that he might be wrong about anything.

And so our fates were sealed. It's really easy to commit to do something stupid.

"Everything's going to be peachy!" Barnes said.

The alarm stopped so abruptly that when the Staff Sergeant said, "Going to be peachy," he was still shouting above the alarm's din.

My ears rang. I guess they'd been ringing all this time. I was relieved until the speakers in the ceiling clicked on. "You killed Christine! Do you believe in karma? Because that is what bad karma looks like."

The voice was male. His tone told me he was on the edge of hysteria. I pictured a smallish man with round glasses and frizzy hair. People's appearances rarely match their voices but it seemed a good bet that whoever spoke into the mic on the public address system could be a mad scientist sent over from Central Casting, complete with pocket protector.

Barnes twirled one hand above his head and our training kicked in again. We went back to back, weapons ready. Ahead of me was the elevator to Level 4. There was that sign I'd heard about: *All ye who enter here, abandon all hope.*

To my left stood large double doors that led to the lab. It was not a large space. We were stepping in Dr. Newberry's blood. I glanced at Barnes for a cue since he knew the layout of the place. He pointed right, toward the control room.

"This lab ... our company ... ," the disembodied voice said, "is called Echidna Biosystems. Echidna is from Greek myth. We chose it because Echidna was the mother of monsters. So it goes."

To my left, I heard a lock click and buzz from the entrance to the Level 3 lab. Monsters burst through the double doors and attacked.

The man on the PA system shouted, "Round one!"

EPISODE 3

Last night
I dreamt a gigantic wave
of perfect Picasso blue
crippled, crushed and swallowed
a sea of ships.
I felt the seduction of destruction
I knew the meaning of
terrible beauty.
I understood that any night
could be
the
last night.

(Artifact from the subconscious)

14

---

wo men in white lab coats sprinted out first. I raised my
weapon but I hesitated. I didn't open fire but it wasn't out
of mercy. I held back because I thought something might
be behind them — something terrible — chasing them out, coming
for us.

Lundsden fired first on the cannibal bearing down on me. Two
rounds caught the infected man in the shoulder, and as a crimson
flower burst across the chest of his white coat, he spun to the floor
howling like a wild animal.

The other attacker, a large bellied man with a unibrow, barreled
into us as I got one shot off. It was Christine Newberry's blood that
really brought us down. The floor was slick with her blood.
Lundsden began to fall into Davis and I reached out to catch the
bomb tech. He took me and Davis with him.

Davis, like Lundsden, had been knocked flat on his back. He
began to get up but the man with one eyebrow shoved him back to
the floor. He clawed his way atop Lundsden, pulling at his faceplate,
trying to get his hood off.

I yelled for Lundsden to watch out as I slipped to my side to grab hold of the man's collar. I worried that if I used my gun I'd shoot Davis, too. The attacker's jaws snapped at me and he bent back to close his teeth on my forearm. His eyes blazed like a rabid wolf as he bore down. He shook his head back and forth trying to get to the meat of my arm.

Still on their feet, Taylor and Barnes moved in. Taylor grabbed the man's hair and jerked his head back sharply. The Staff Sergeant did not hesitate to bring the butt of his weapon into our attacker's Adam's apple. The man's eyes rolled up and a wheezing sound creaked through his broken windpipe. Taylor still held the man's head back so Frank rammed the MP5's butt into his throat again.

Feeling clumsy in the environmental suit, I struggled to get up on my side. I didn't know if our attacker's teeth had breached my suit so I was careful to keep my forearm out of the pool of blood. Even as I got my feet under me I spotted Christine's wide eyes through her faceplate. I'd seen death before. I'd always thought the stares of the dead appeared empty but Dr. Newberry's glare was accusing.

"Is your suit torn, Harmon?" Barnes asked.

I looked up into the mouth of the Staff Sergeant's weapon.

The man with the broken throat was still struggling to breathe, clutching at his throat when Taylor tossed him aside. The dying man's heels drummed on the floor as he struggled to get air that would never come.

Taylor bent to check my suit's integrity, rotating my wrist sharply and painfully. "He's good."

"I-I'm not," Lundsden said. I could barely hear his weak voice muffled by his respirator. "My back."

When the bomb tech fell, something in his spine had gone wrong. Either his oxygen tank or the battering ram he'd slung over his shoulder had delivered a crushing blow.

"Can you move?" Barnes asked.

"Feels like my backbone is on fire but I can feel my feet. I think I can get up, but maybe I shouldn't?"

"*Can you move?*"

"Yeah … it's not that bad."

Lundsden would have been correct if that hadn't been the moment when the second wave of attackers hit us.

The mad scientist on the public address system shouted gleefully, "Round two!"

15

Two women came at us through the same double doors. Blood dripped from their gaping mouths as they howled and snarled. The way they came at us so fast — teeth bared and jaws snapping — I thought of wolves again.

I was still rising to my feet but I threw myself toward Lundsden. He screamed in pain. I managed to get us both out of their way. Barnes and Taylor didn't hesitate to open fire. They took the women down with headshots.

From a crouch, Davis rolled to his right to stay out the line of fire. If he'd rolled toward us, he would have been okay. Instead, he ended up beside the infected man Lundsden had shot. The shoulder wound wasn't enough to keep him down for good. Maybe the attacker had been playing possum. I should have put a round in his head to be sure. Had I taken that precaution, I would have saved Davis from getting his hood yanked down, then off, by the crazed screamer.

Davis's hair was plastered to his head with sweat. The straps that held his respirator in place slipped and the air mask went down to his neck. Exposed to the lab's potentially toxic environment, he panicked, scrabbling to pull the mask back up to his mouth. Though the attacker's left arm hung loose from his shoulder wound, the infected man seemed unnaturally strong and determined.

Davis finally pried his respirator from the wounded attacker's grip. He was still trying to wrestle his mask and hood back on when the Staff Sergeant shot the attacker twice in the face. The infected lab tech's head rocked back and forth as if his neck had turned to a loose spring. The man was dead before he slumped back to the floor.

Lundsden cried out from the pain.

"I'm so sorry, Bob," I said. "I had to get you out of the line of fire and away from those women."

Bob Lundsden could be an aloof know-it-all pain in the ass. Worse, sometimes he really did seem to know it all. None of that mattered. He wasn't our bomb tech anymore. He was Bob, a human being in pain. Trying to save him, I'd caused more pain. Story of my life … and death.

On the job, Steve Taylor could sometimes be a poser who thought he was G.I. Joe. Off the job, no one was more generous or funny. Hanging out with Steve, I figured out that he amped up the macho bullshit because he was the least sure of himself. He wanted to do well and to never get anything wrong. Better than doing well, he wanted to do right. When I caught his eye, even through his face-plate, his fear was obvious. We'd dealt with a lot of shit but I'd never seen him that scared.

Patrick Davis was the asshole of our squad who came off badge heavy even when he wasn't wearing the badge. He acted like he was better than the rest of us and destined to run all of the ETF one day. Moments ago, he'd pointed his weapon at me. Despite the fact that I liked Patrick least, a wave of relief washed over me when he got his respirator back on. There were still plenty of us to fight our way out of here. With Bob in agony, we were already down one man and we still had a mission.

Chest heaving, Patrick sat on his butt and took another few breaths from his respirator. He looked from the dead lab tech to Staff Sergeant Barnes and gave him a grateful nod for taking the shot. "Thanks. I'll never forget that."

Barnes shot Patrick Davis in the forehead. His head jerked back and the smacking sound of the hit startled us. Our first team member was sacrificed.

"You're welcome, Pat. I'll never forget this, either."

A bullet is a mercy compared to shitting yourself to death. Pat had said that. I guess it's better than becoming one of those screaming, mindless, infected things.

16

As I pulled Bob to his feet as gently as I could, Staff Sergeant Barnes turned his weapon on the next two attackers. These wolves were a young man and a woman of about forty. They came at us in tandem. The young man was broad and barrel-chested and came at us like a bowling ball. The woman's wet hair hung in her face so I couldn't see her eyes. She ran with the grace and speed of a gazelle.

Still recovering from shooting one of his team in the face, Barnes wasn't quite quick enough to line up the shot. Despite the close range, he missed the male attacker as he flashed by. Two of Frank's rounds chunked into the door behind my head. The projectiles spat a metallic, unyielding *bamp! Bamp!*

"Round three!" the crazed voice, so shrill and excited, knifed at us from the ceiling speakers.

Taylor didn't wait to shoulder his weapon. He fired from the hip and ripped through the male attacker's thick torso. The zombie's inertia kept him flailing forward. He clawed at Taylor as he went down and managed to grab Taylor's belt. The infected man pulled him down as Taylor punched and kicked, trying to pull away.

The attacker was in such a determined, orgiastic fugue that I spotted the whites around each bulging eye. Single-minded and seemingly starving for meat and blood, the zombie's mouth dripped with a mixture of blood and thick saliva.

The zombies seemed to know where we were most vulnerable. The infected man clutched at Taylor's faceplate and tried to pull off his hood.

Barnes turned to fire on Taylor's attacker but there was no safe shot. The Staff Sergeant spun to take the woman down by clothes-lining her with his gun butt. She surprised him by nimbly ducking his outstretched arm and joining the fray against Taylor. Maybe she went for Taylor because his struggle with the other zombie had gone to the floor. Perhaps, with the pack intelligence of wolves, she zeroed in on the prey that appeared most vulnerable in that moment.

In the fight for survival, Taylor was no longer the tough G.I. Joe-type I'd known. He was Steve, yelling for help in a high trembling voice. The floor and my boots were still slick with blood. I tried to stand Bob up but he screamed from the pain and stayed bent at the waist. With Lundsden leaning on me heavily, I had to plant my feet wide so I wouldn't go down again. I was only a few feet away but I was useless to my fishing buddy.

I left it to Staff Sergeant Barnes to do the killing. He seemed to have a taste for it I lacked.

I turned my attention to Bob and pulled on the strap to get the breaching tool off his back. I let it clang to the floor. I hoped that, with the forty-pound weight of the battering ram off him, the bomb tech might prove more useful. Instead, Bob's face twisted into a mask of misery. He dropped his MP-5 and wept.

I knew what Bob wanted most in the world. It's what I wanted, too. His eyes implored me to get him out of the Box. I punched the button to open the lock so we could get out of Level 3.

It buzzed briefly but of course the hatch didn't open. I reached out with one shaky hand to turn the handle. It wouldn't budge. I glanced at the keypad outlined in glowing red numerals. In my rush, I'd forgotten I needed the manual override code to retreat and evac-

uate the wounded. I tried to remember the code. It had started with
5 - 5 - A - Z - 2 ... beyond that I was in a fog.

"I'm sorry, Bob. I can't get you out until we clear this place."

"It's okay, Danny. We aren't getting out of here anyway. You
know that, right?"

17

The zombie under Taylor was wounded, losing the fight and beginning to lose consciousness. Steve would have been okay if not for the infected woman. She was older than Steve by at least fifteen years and he probably had seventy more pounds of muscle. As the male zombie's hands slipped from Steve's faceplate, the woman came at him at a dead run.

Coming out of a crouch in the small space, there was no time to aim and fire. Steve braced for impact, ready to be the wall so his new attacker would get knocked to the floor. Facing a much smaller opponent, I would have done the same thing. It would have worked, too, but she didn't run to collide with him. Instead, with unnatural grace and speed, the attacker yanked off his hood as she dove over him.

Steve looked to Barnes and read his expression in an instant.

"Wait! Stop!" Bob managed to yell through his pain. "He's still got his respirator on!"

True, Steve was still breathing his own air. However, his eyes and ears were exposed.

The Staff Sergeant hesitated. He shouldn't have. The woman, now behind him, reached around his head to plunge her fingers into

Steve's eye sockets as she lunged for the exposed flesh of his cheek. The zombie's eyes rolled back in ecstasy as she sank her teeth into him.

Steve let out a long keening wail that was not silenced when Barnes shot the woman in the head. With her mouth full of meat, she slumped on his shoulder and bled gore down his neck. Blinded, in pain and still thinking he was under attack, Steve yanked his pistol from his holster and the muzzle found the dead woman's skull. He pulled the trigger three times before collapsing forward, throwing her body forward atop the corpse of the bare chested attacker.

Steve was still screaming as he fired his Glock 17 three more times into the body. Two of those shots made the corpse shudder with the impact.

The last shot clipped Staff Sergeant Barnes through the shin, shattering bone and spouting a fountain of blood. He went down hard, slamming into the floor. He could have survived the wound but his suit was perforated. By his own rules, Frank Barnes had to die.

The Staff Sergeant wasn't my funny, gruff and tough superior officer anymore. Shot and in pain, he was simply Frank, now.

Steve's Glock clattered to the floor and he curled up, the heels of his hands pressed to his ruined eyes. "What's happening?"

"Your attacker is down," I said. "You did it, Steve."

Gingerly, I leaned Lundsden against the hatch to the chamber that led back to Level 2 and safety. My instinct was to get a tourniquet on Frank's wound, stanch the bleeding and somehow get the wounded out of this pit. Frank waved me away.

Bob and I looked at each other. I could tell Bob was about to tell Steve that he'd shot Frank. I shook my head hard. Bob had the good sense to shut up. My throat had gone dry. I croaked, "The Staff Sergeant is wounded, too, Steve."

"Wounded? I'm blind!" Steve groaned at what must have been monstrous pain. I would have moved to comfort him but I was the only one left who was mobile. I had to stand my ground and guard Bob. I raised my MP5 and trained it on the open doors to the lab.

Frank pulled off his hood and respirator, sucking air in and out fast. Tears cascaded down his cheeks but I don't think it was all physical pain that made him weep. "I'm sorry. I'm sorry, I'm sorry — "

"You've got nothing to be sorry about, sir," I said.

"Yeah, I do." Frank winced. "Damn, that hurts!"

I glanced down at the gaping wound.

"It burns! I didn't think a gunshot wound would burn so much, like acid and fire." He gasped for breath. "I don't think I'll feel it for much longer anyhow. Sorry I brought you guys down here."

"We go where the trouble is."

"But we aren't all here. Mac and me ... we had the training to take care of this. He should be down here. The veteran officers should be down here. Mac and I thought it would be easier ... better ... to take the youngest on the team."

"Why?" Bob asked.

"Because I've known the rest longer. They're seasoned. I came up with the others. I golf with them. I know their wives and kids."

"You took the guys without families of their own," I said. "It's understandable."

Frank managed a grim laugh. "I took the guys on the squad I like the least."

I stared in his eyes. Those few seconds seemed to drag out a long time. When I looked away, I looked to his gushing wound again. It wasn't gushing so much anymore. He was bleeding out. Frank would die but he'd have more time to think about his sins and I was glad of it.

"I should have asked for volunteers."

"Yeah, you should have," I said.

"And briefed us better," Bob added.

"Mac thought — with what we had to do — the less you knew going in, the better."

"When is that ever true?" There was more anger than pain in Bob's voice now.

"I led the mission. It's me who messed up, *all* on me. Protecting everyone on the other side of that hatch is up to you now,

Harmon." With trembling hands he fumbled for the lanyard with the yellow laminated card. "The override code is the only way out of here. Secure this location, Danny. Kill whoever's left and get the hell out. It stinks in here."

"Frank?" Steve asked.

"Yeah?"

"You brought us down here." Taylor reached for his pistol, groping blindly. He found his weapon, raised it and pointed it in our direction.

I recoiled and fell on my back, trying to avoid blind fire. No pun intended.

Crack!

As I scrambled back to my feet I saw what he'd done. Steve shot himself in the head.

You brought us down here. His last words were not eloquent. Everyone should plan their dying words. To be safe, the message has to be short and preferably wise or kind, maybe imparting wisdom, maybe a comforting lie for the living. I say it should be that way but that's another of those lies we tell ourselves. On the day you die, you're the same dumbass who got up that morning with a head full of hopes and dreams for the future. Dying doesn't make us special.

Killing? Dying? Those are the easiest things to do in the world. Looking around me, I didn't think anybody had much of a handle on how to live, either.

"How is your man, the one who shot Christine?" The man on the speakers asked. "He doesn't look good."

I glanced down at Frank. His face was very pale and his breaths came fast, like that of a man running uphill, running out of wind. His eyes were rolled back in his head. While I was distracted by all the rampant death and destruction, he must have passed out.

"I'd offer to help," the voice said, "but I'm not really that kind of doctor."

"What kind are you?" I yelled.

"A bioengineer. I work on nefarious projects for multinational corporations that manufacture bio-weapons."

"I thought doctors are supposed to help people."

"Yes, well, people aren't supposed to kill people. What they tell you and how it really is are obviously two different things. The rules are loosey-goosey. Your murders are sanctioned by the state so no big deal, I guess. All things considered, it's hard to feel sorry for you. Came to kill, got killed. I'm sure my pets come as a surprise but they have the potential to be superior killers."

"Your *pets*?"

"I'm speaking fancifully but they are a lot like you on the micro scale. You're packed full of microorganisms, you know. You've got more bugs in your guts than you have cells you think of as *you*."

I looked at Bob. "This is insane."

"You know what else? You have a lot in common with my creations."

"How's that?"

"Like you, they're only doing what they were designed to do."

Bob struggled to straighten up and gasped in pain. "Are you talking about these people or the bacteria or … what is this? Something like rabies? Is this a chemically induced psychosis?"

"Idiots talk about flying off on suicide missions to Mars but bioengineering right here is the real frontier. The parasites are alive and all they want to do is feed, reproduce and survive, like us. My work is with waterborne parasites. They take over brains. That's what Nature made them do even before I came along with some helpful tweaks."

Bob was sweating. I wasn't sure how much longer he could stand. I didn't want to have to carry him out. I tried to hurry things along. My plan was to scrub the mission and get Bob and me out after I'd gathered what information I could (as long as I could do it safely and quickly). "Brain parasites? You made brain parasites do this?"

"It would be poetic if the process wasn't so gross, don't you think?" the man replied.

"Were these people your co-workers?" I asked.

"A short time ago, yes. I'm supposed to feel bad, aren't I? The trouble is, *somebody* was going to get turned into bio-weapons. Isn't it fair that the people working so hard to develop more ways to kill people get slain by what they strove to create? Surely you don't agree that the targets should only be people who live far away? It's not nameless brown people on the news getting the shaft this time. I'm morally flexible but at least I'm not a racist, hm?"

"You're a killer," I said.

"As are you."

I hadn't killed anyone yet. I sure wanted to.

"How'd you do it?" Bob called out and it hurt him. His breath came in a wheeze. I wondered if he had a broken rib that was now poking into his lungs.

"The short answer is that I took what was and extrapolated. You wouldn't understand the long answer."

"How did you infect these people?" Bob persisted. "How did you manage any of this?"

"Are you familiar with the tongue-eating louse? It's a parasitic crustacean that infests a fish's mouth, devours the tongue and then replaces the tongue. Amazing parasite, wouldn't you say?"

"I don't see — "

"How about Scopalamine? It's also known as Devil's Breath, most popular among criminals in Columbia. It's terrifying what that drug can do. You get that powder blown in your face, and not only are you highly suggestible, you lose all memory of someone subverting your will. One dose of Devil's Breath, I could get you to help me rob your house, empty your bank accounts or shoot all your friends in the face."

"Bullshit," I said.

"Under the influence of drugs, I'm sure you're seen people do crazy things. Hurt those they love? Jump off a building?"

I had seen those things but I didn't want to admit it.

"Under stress, too, people are often surprised by what they can do. I understand. I've been under a lot of stress lately and I've surprised myself. Look around you. That's the work of weaponized parasites. They said it wasn't possible to do it to humans. My so-called superiors thought our brain chemistry was too complex to highjack."

"You must be so proud."

"They had no vision but, no matter. Nature provided my vision. *Toxoplasma gondii* is a parasite that sexually reproduces in the guts of cats. But how does it get into cat guts? The parasite alters rat brains so they aren't repelled by the scent of their predators. The rats don't run from the smell of cat urine so they get eaten. *Et voila!* More *Toxoplasma gondii* in the world. While everyone else toyed with bacteria and viruses, I spent my days weaponizing a parasite, one that turns ordinary people into the glorious demonstration you see today: Ordinary, law-abiding people attacking police. I'm good at what I do. Very good, *singularly* good."

"This is a monster factory."

"Through the magic of biological manipulation, we are defense contractors in the business of turning enemy civilian populations into soldiers."

"Killers with no souls."

"How do you feel about 'agents of chaos?'"

"Zombies, more like it."

"Not to be pedantic, but they didn't rise from the grave or anything. Though I did enjoy those old Romero movies, I made cannibals who act remarkably like zombies. That's the brain parasite seeking to feed and reproduce. Nature's a cold-hearted bitch, hm?"

"Who are you?" I asked.

"I'm an employee … or at least, I was. Human Resources probably won't want me back for my exit interview after all this. It's okay. I don't need their references."

"What happened with the bodies on Levels 1 and 2?" Bob asked.

"Got in the way, that's all. I actually liked Tarique. That was the guard's name. Brought him coffee sometimes. I gave him a bottle of sangria last Christmas. Too bad, really, but I had to access the tanks and put some sensors into maintenance mode."

"Tanks?"

"I've got a little lab set up in my apartment. Bringing in my waterborne strain to Level 2 was easy. I dosed the water tanks. The staff showered before entering the decontamination locks. Before they ever got near the clean rooms — "

Bob let out a shallow laugh. "I get it. As the staff showered on Level 2, they thought they were going through the usual decontaminating process." Bob gripped the hatch door. He looked like he was about to slide to the floor. "They were infected before they even climbed into their biohazard suits."

"Bright boy!" The man sounded jubilant. "But I prefer the term *infested*. You can be infected by a virus. We've got those down in Level 4, too, but these pets are parasites. They're like cockroaches infesting a house, hiding in the rugs and under the fridge. Stem cells cannot cross the blood brain barrier but my pets breach the barrier, carry the nanites across and take up residence in your brain folds and crevices."

Infested is such an ugly word, I thought, *even worse than infected. That word won't stick.*

I checked my oxygen meter. We hadn't been down here thirty minutes and everything had turned to shit. I didn't want to waste any more time. "What's your name?"

"His name is Hamish," Bob said. "I forget his last name but there aren't that many guys named Hamish."

"You are correct. Hamish Allen. My name is Hamish Allen."

Bob had surprised me. I asked, "How'd you know?"

"Dr. Newberry mentioned his name, said he was senior staff on site. Listen to how this guy talks. He's gotta be the guy running things. You can't talk like that and be a grunt."

"You are bright," Hamish said. "I'm the one in charge when people with more money aren't around. Are you a hazardous materials expert, sir?"

"I'm a bomb disposal specialist," Bob said.

"Ah. In a way, I guess we're both bomb disposal specialists."

A small security camera was fixed on me. I looked straight into the lens as if I could see the man in the control room. "Are you willing to come out, Hamish?"

"Sure. You're what I've been waiting for. I couldn't disable all the sensors. I need your override code to get out."

"Come out then."

"Shoot the man on the floor first."

Frank Barnes snorted and one weepy eye fluttered open. He had been listening, after all. "No."

"You want me to shoot Staff Sergeant Barnes?" I asked. "He's already down! He's no threat to you. Why on — "

"Not like this!" Frank said. His anger burbled up first, then he began to weep.

"I need to know you understand who's in control here," Hamish said. "You've got the guns. I've got something better. I've got a pock-etful of miracles and a skull packed with secrets. Shoot him or I'll unleash another bioengineered miracle. You and the bomb disposal specialist can eat each other."

"You'd be stuck down here."

"They'll send someone else along in a short while. Next time I'll try playing victim. I'll tell them I have the cure. They'll escort me out and give me a blanket. The people who own this place don't want the research to be destroyed and I've got it all in my head."

"Don't do this," Frank pleaded.

He was crying. I was, too, a little.

"He's as good as dead anyway, Dan," Bob said.

"You said it was in the shower water!" I argued. "It's in the water! We didn't go through the showers on Level 2!"

"I'm sorry. I had orders!" Frank said. "I killed the wrong people for the wrong reasons. I'm sorry!"

Before I could reply, a shot rang out.

I whirled to discover that Frank hadn't been talking to me.

Bob leaned against the wall, his pistol drawn. He'd shot Frank in the head.

"Like the man said, I'm pretty bright. I did the math in my head. At least the Staff Sergeant got a chance to apologize for being a shithead."

20

I looked down at Frank. Despite all the blood loss, it looked like he still had plenty of fluid flowing from his skull. The pool of blood expanded to join the rest of the flood smeared across the floor. They say the body is up to 60% water. Sometimes on the job we used the term *meat bags* for the dead. We are bags of blood.

"Forgive the bright boy," Hamish said over the intercom. "He knows what's up."

I looked down at the yellow card in my hand. The lanyard, once blue, was wet and dark with spray. "How should I handle this, Bob?"

"Give him the override code, Danny. I'm tired."

I couldn't think of any way to stall until a better idea came along. Our oxygen was more than half gone. Bob didn't look good. It would be bug out time soon, no matter what. I might salvage the mission if I could take Hamish out as a prisoner. "I'll tell you the code, Hamish. Key it in on the keypad on your side and open that door. Understand?"

"What's not to understand?"

I gave Bob a long look. "I'm going to get us out of here."

He could barely lift his head to look my way. "Doubtful."

I put some bass in my voice to address the doctor. "When the door buzzes, come out slowly, hands up where we can see them."

Hamish laughed. "You still think you're driving this bus?"

"Come out so we can talk and get it over with." Bob sounded exhausted. Or maybe that was the tone of a man resigned to death.

"Good lads," he said. "I'm all for getting out of here as quickly as possible. Look around you. This place isn't good for your health!"

I'd seen enough horrors today to last for this lifetime and into the next. It was the "good lads," thing that made me want to become a wolf. Hamish's arrogance made me want to become one of his weapons so I could turn on him without hesitation, without thought or consequence. I wanted to tear off his ears with my teeth as I closed my hands around his throat. I wanted to choke that smug laugh out of him. Becoming a remorseless murderer would make everything so simple … or so I thought at the time.

I'd taken an introductory course to negotiation tactics. I knew I was supposed to keep him calm. I wasn't supposed to allow the situation to escalate his fear. The trouble was, Hamish Allen didn't sound scared in the least. "Give me the code twice. Speak loud, slowly and clearly. Doctor's orders!"

You can't bluff when you don't have any cards. I did as I was told. "5 - 5 - A - Z - 2 - 5 - 0 - 0 - L - 1 - 1 - V - 3 - T - P - D - Q. 5 - 5 - A - Z - 2 - 5 - 0 - 0 - L - 1 - 1 - V - 3 - T - P - D - Q."

Hamish repeated the code back to me twice. It didn't occur to me he was stalling.

Like everybody, I've made a lot of mistakes in my life. Some highlights: I chose a university based on the fact that it had the shortest application form. I wrapped my first car around a tree when I took a corner too fast, showing off for buddies in the back seat. I first got into law enforcement because a girl who cheated on me said I'd look sexy in the uniform. I told myself I liked my job. I told myself that even if I hated it, I was committed to the Toronto Police Service for life.

Doing as Dr. Hamish Allen told me was another big mistake.

Ding!

"Here I come!" Hamish shouted.

I could have used the override code to open the control room door myself. Instead, Hamish used the code — the code *I* gave him — to raise the elevator from level 4. I didn't even know what he was really up to, yet. I didn't have time to think about that as Hell boiled up from the bottom of the Box.

EPISODE 4

AFTER (acronym)

Artificial Facilitation Therapy for Enhanced Response, a biomimetic stem cell nanotechnology with numerous health and wellness applications. The term was first coined by Chloe T. Robinson, PhD, a biomedical engineer at the University of Toronto, in 2013.

~ Notes from NEXT

21

Two men burst from the elevator followed by a large woman. Their protective hoods were off. They'd splattered green puke down the front of their white environmental suits.

Hamish, still safely behind the control room door, cackled over the PA system. "Gentlemen, meet Natalie, Glen and Arthur! *Dinnertime!*"

I stood closest to the elevator doors as they parted. The area was not a large space and the attackers came at us fast. I should have been the next to die. The infested would have attacked me if it hadn't been for Bob.

The biggest man slammed me and I went down hard. My head bounced off the floor. As my MP5 clattered to the floor and spun away, a high whine shot through my ears. Everything seemed to slow down for a moment. Like wolves, all three pounced on the easiest prey first. As they rushed to get at Bob, he slid to the floor while firing his pistol. He might have hit one of them but they soon knocked the Glock from his hand. They were too fast. Bob was too injured to defend himself.

The woman leaped atop him first, pawing at his faceplate. Her angry growling sounded borne of starvation. One of the men pinned his arms as my teammate let out a scream. His body contorted under their attack. I guessed that whatever had cracked and shifted in his spine was now grinding nerve-rich fractured bone ends together. Pain ripped through him.

One of the men got his hood off. Then the drooling killer began to rip into Bob's throat. Bob screamed until his windpipe opened.

I was trying to get to my feet when the man holding Bob's legs wheeled and jumped on top of me. He was heavy but I had one knee under me. I managed to flip him to the floor. He kept rolling. I found myself on the floor face up. I managed to wrap my right arm around the back of my attacker's neck and curl around to trap his head in my right armpit.

Biohazard suits are not ideal for hand-to-hand combat. It was slippery, awkward work. I didn't have much time to end the fight before the others would turn their murderous attention to me. I didn't want to be the object of their blood frenzy. If it came to that, I'd shoot myself first.

My sidearm was on my right hip. I tried to make a quick grab for it with my left hand. I could barely get hold of the pistol grip before my attacker grabbed my wrist.

Struggling to keep him at bay, I could see Frank's Glock out of the corner of my eye to my right, just out of reach. I tried to haul my assailant toward it but I didn't have enough leverage to budge him sideways.

I tried kicking my legs out, rocking us both upwards. I held no hope that I could stand us both up. However, I did manage to slam his face into the floor as we fell back down. The man grunted in pain. At least these monsters felt something. I had to inflict more pain, *all* the pain. I tried the same maneuver, kicking my legs up again. When he resisted, I allowed his momentum and weight to carry us back down to the tile floor. His face made a wet smack on impact.

On my next attempt, the man finally got wise and tried to twist sideways. We rolled a little closer toward Frank's Glock. If I broke my grip to reach for my own pistol, the cannibal would yank my hood off and make me more vulnerable to his teeth. I would have to take him out with my bare hands and quickly.

Then I remembered a lecture from a visiting trainer on loan from the RCMP. Exoculation is not standard procedure but one of the trainers had stuck his fingers in an attacker's eyes. "Don't hesitate and go for it if you need to," the constable had said. "If you commit, you'll go in to the second knuckle."

I let my attacker out of the headlock. As he rose up, I pushed into his eyes with my thumbs. I didn't perform the attack exactly as it had been described to me but it did the grisly job. My attacker reeled back, clutching his eyes. The man curled up. In his agony, he arched his back at an alarming angle I didn't know was possible for an overweight office worker. He let out a high screech, went rigid and collapsed to the floor, apparently unconscious.

If I were a different person, maybe I would have felt a few seconds of triumph over an enemy bent on killing me. A feeling of relief would not have been out of order. Instead, a wave of revulsion pulsed through my guts. I almost threw up into my respirator.

That's what that woman did to Steve! I'm becoming one of them!

But I wasn't infested yet. I was a man fighting off bloodthirsty monsters. I was struggling to remain a human.

They warned us about letting emotions rule us in training. "When you roll up on a scene, maintain officer neutrality. Do the same when you go home. Leave the troubles of the job at the job."

We saw people do terrible things to each other every day. A lot of cops get angry about that and they stay angry. Sometimes we take that anger out on spouses or even our kids. Maybe we start drinking and fail to figure out how to stop.

"We send you out on the streets with a whip and a chair to be lion tamers. Don't join the lions."

Another trainer added, "And if you figure out how to deal with the stress, let me know how you did it because I'm not sure, either. At some point you're going to see something that messes with your head. Your head might stay messed up. On your best days, you'll feel like you're saving the world. On your worst days, you'll feel like the world isn't worth the effort."

It was my attacker's pained screaming that got the zombies off Bob. Their heads rose from his still body. They turned to look at me. Jaws covered in blood, the man and the woman broke into broad red smiles.

I almost pissed myself. My head still buzzed and ached from my concussion. Forgetting the pistol in my holster, I panicked. I needed to create space between me and the threat. I wanted my submachine gun in my hands.

The man and woman sprang to their feet as I backpedaled toward my MP5. I would have been fine except for all the blood on the floor. Bob, Frank, Patrick, Steve and Christine Newberry fed the pool. Fresh blood on a tile floor is as slippery as soap. Crabbing backward on my heels and palms, I slipped and slid.

After the pain of being torn apart and eaten alive, what awaited me? Darkness? Nothingness? A heavenly choir and a harp? David Bowie jamming with Elvis and John Lennon? I hoped Lemmy from Motorhead would be there, too. He was more to my musical taste.

Questions about the afterlife used to be so theoretical. The answer was coming fast.

The zombies didn't step over the dead. They stepped on the bodies of Christine Newberry and Frank Barnes as they came for me.

22

Until that moment, I'd only had the bad kind of luck. However, as they stepped down from Frank's face and chest, the slick floor slowed the monsters, too. They didn't seem to mind falling much. Both of them crawled across the floor. Coming at me like that, it was impossible not to think of them as wild animals. My MP5 lay against the wall. I might get to it in time, but I might not. My hand closed on my pistol.

Everyone on the team used Glocks with rubberized pistol grips. It was supposed to be a measure against sweat. Today, it helped me avoid dropping my weapon back into the blood. The female attacker was faster than the male. At the last moment, she surprised me by leaping, apparently intent on landing atop me as she had with Bob. I raised my weapon and fired. I had no time to aim but a pink mist blossomed like a halo from the back of her exploding skull. She was dead before her body fell on my legs.

My brain already felt like a pea rattling around in a matchbox. The report of the gunshot in such a tight space made my ears whine louder.

The last attacker was a man who did not seem the least deterred by the fact that I'd taken out two of his pack. He crawled over her to get at me. He seemed to know the gun in my hand was a weapon. These zombies were not the shuffle and moan variety. There was intelligence behind his eyes. He grabbed my wrist and bashed my hand against the floor. I tried to drive a knee into his ribs but the weight of the dead woman was on my legs.

He bashed my hand against the floor and I triggered it by accident. This time the gun went off beside my right ear. A few inches the wrong way and I would have shot myself in the head. The walls seemed to vibrate with the roar of the report. My headache had been a painful throb that matched the pace of my racing heart. Now it felt like I was trying to hear my thoughts above the roar of a jet engine.

I tossed the gun so I'd have a free hand to grapple. My attacker lunged with his teeth. I punched a couple of knuckles into his sternum to make some room to move. The sternum is nerve-rich and sensitive but half-measures weren't doing the trick. He raised both fists and began beating my faceplate with whaling fists like a gorilla in one of those *Planet of the Apes* movies.

I could only try to block the man's blows. The long, slim oxygen tank on my back was digging into the space between my shoulder blades. I gritted my teeth against the pain. I was weakening. I couldn't keep him off me forever. The adrenaline raging through my bloodstream slowed my perception even further. Soon, I was sure, he'd pull my hood off. The blows rained down on my forearms like the zombie was pounding timpani.

I looked at the man's bloody maw. He'd chewed on Bob. Those same teeth could open my flesh at any moment. I gave up hope in that moment. It was almost as if I was watching my unfolding murder happen to someone else. When one relents, when a victim's death as inevitable, it is a dreamlike state.

Then a stranger thing happened. The zombie was forming words. No sound passed his lips but he was mouthing something. Even as he continued to try to kill me, he mouthed a message. I was almost sure he was trying to say, "I'm sorry, I'm sorry. I'm sorry." Not that it mattered. Each apology was accompanied by a fresh wild swing, punctuating each impact.

Exhausted and ready to die, I didn't hear the door buzz open. I didn't see who picked up Frank's Glock. I only felt the reverberation of the gunshots pound into my head as my attacker took three to the chest. The man fell back dead, adding weight to my legs, pinning me under two bodies.

Maybe I'll live.

My little flame of hope was quickly extinguished as I saw a man in a blood-spattered white coat gather weapons from the fallen and toss them though the open door to the control room. When that was done, he slammed it closed and the lock buzzed again.

"Dr. Allen, I presume?"

He pointed Frank's pistol my way. "Got that right, buddy."

I tried to get up on one elbow to get a better look at him. Hamish was medium: medium height, build and looks. I expected a sweaty maniac in a biohazard suit. Instead, he was calm and methodical, just another man, utterly unremarkable except for his ugly paisley shirt.

Hamish retrieved the yellow card from the bloody floor, stepped over me to punch the elevator button. "Stay down. I'll be right back. If you're good, I'll give you some answers to your questions. This whole thing … I know how it looks but this isn't even what you think it is. Believe it or not, I'm the good guy."

He checked the time on his phone. "We have a little time left — not much — but it's almost over."

Ding!

23

I struggled to get out from under the two bodies weighing down my legs. My head pounded. It was as if the blood in my head was squeezing past the bite of a vise at my temples. I rocked back and forth to get out from under the dead. That done, I slipped over to my side and grunted like an old man trying to get to my feet.

I have since learned that people infested with weaponized brain parasites are very sensitive to sound. Like a flock of bats, they will turn as one when they detect noise. Hearing is more important than sight. I had confirmation of this as I got to my feet. The attacker whose eyes I'd taken came at me in a rush on all fours, jaws snapping.

The zombie's ruined eyes seemed to stare at me. For a second, I was transfixed. I only had that second before his teeth closed on my calf. I stepped aside quickly and kicked him in the ribs. He grunted but seemed undeterred. I went to the edge of the room where the blood spill was most sparse. I was careful to avoid treading on Bob's body, and as I leapt over the man and woman who'd attempted to murder me, it crossed my mind that they might come back to life and join the chase.

My life is a horror movie. My death would be worthy of a horror movie.

The wolf at my heels either didn't see the corpses he climbed over or didn't mind them.

I had a moment of inspiration and stopped running. Instead, I tiptoed to the middle of the room. I took a deep breath and held it as I stepped atop Frank's body and stood still.

The zombie's jaws dripped saliva in long strings as it kept crawling in circles around the room. As suddenly as it had come at me, it stopped to sniff the air. There was such a mix of blood and gore and death, I didn't think he could track me by smell. The dead not only look drunk, as I mentioned, they're messy drunks. As soon as the sphincters loosen, they shit themselves.

I was reminded of this fact when I shifted my weight on my team leader's guts and the corpse let out a long fart. I would have laughed — grimly and bitterly — except the infested thing trying to kill me snapped his head my way. Tentatively, he crawled my way, sniffing the air.

My lungs burned for air. I glanced at the control room door to my right. What was the override code? Trying to remember the alphanumeric sequence felt like a physical strain. Of course, I was so freaked out, I'm not sure I could have come up with my sister's phone number. Jenn was an EMT in Mississauga. I would have loved to come up with the code so I could escape through the hatch and leave Hamish to deal with his creation. I could get the hell out and, in my fantasy, Jenn would be waiting for me in her ambulance. She'd drive me far away. I'd lie down in back and I'd never think of the Box again.

But what was the code? 5 - 5 - A - Z - 2 ... dammit!

My lips began to tremble. Beneath my mask, my face felt hot. Warm sweat trickled down my back. I reached for my belt searching for something useful. I had ammo mags and a first aid kit but I didn't even have my telescoping baton. Maybe I could beat on the zombie with my handcuffs but what I really wanted was my knife. I normally carried a retractable blade but orders were to leave our knives in the truck. When we trained in biohazard suits, we were told to leave our edged weapons behind. Knives slice and cut.

Serrated edges tear. They didn't want us slicing our gloves or protective suits.

In hindsight, that was a decision made by a higher-up who would never be in my situation. We had guns but they wouldn't trust us with knives if we wore our blue Hazmats? Ridiculous, but mindless bureaucracy can be as dangerous as any cannibal starving for human flesh.

My lungs were on fire now. I couldn't hold my breath any longer. I let go of the old air to suck in the new. My respirator clicked. It was enough for the eyeless monster to zero in on me. I should have broken the bastard's eardrums.

The locked control room door stood to my right. Behind me was Bob's corpse and the hatch to Level 2. To my left, the double doors leading to the Level 3 labs stood open. I almost ran that way until I noticed the one weapon Hamish had failed to lock away. Bob's body lay atop the battering ram.

As the infested man crawled forward, I stepped off Frank and bent to reach for the breaching tool. One end was a blunt hammerhead. The other end came to an edge thin enough to cram into the crack of a door. It would open the blind zombie's skull quite efficiently. However, to get at it, I'd have to turn my back to the attacker and take the time to roll Bob aside.

As I bent forward, the zombie — still on all fours and coming fast as a rabid dog — rushed forward. As soon as he came to Frank's corpse, he launched himself at me. There was no time for the battering ram. I whirled and swept my forearm up like a club. I caught the killer under the jaw. He reeled back, clutching at his throat. He landed on the floor hard. I thought he'd stay down but, shakily, he got to his feet. Hurt but still hungry, he edged forward, hands extended, coming back for more.

There was little time for the battering ram. Inspiration struck. I yanked at the straps to Bob's oxygen tank and lifted it out of its pouch. It wasn't as heavy as the ram. It was harder to hold as well. With clumsy fingers, I yanked at the hose to get enough slack to use it as a bludgeon.

The attacker was almost on me. I heard a rasp in his throat. I might have lacerated something in there, pushed the hyoid bone out of whack. The hyoid anchors the muscles of the tongue and holds the larynx open. I didn't have much slack from the air hose so I struck the attacker in the same spot. A solid throat punch can ruin anybody's day. Doing it with an oxygen tank instead of a fist was a decisive move.

Gurgling, the blind monster sank to his knees. I could bash his head now and I was motivated. He went down. I kept bashing him in the head. Blood sprayed all over my suit and faceplate until it was hard to see.

My enemy was blind. I fell into a blind rage. He stayed down but I kept pummeling him with the oxygen tank until the crunching sounds became merely wet. At that, my fury left me.

The Box taught me something about myself. You can only get so full of rage. There is a limit to how much terror you can feel. After so much gore and horror, all my emotional meters had redlined and were broken. I was too exhausted to feel more anger and fear. Moments before, I'd felt resigned to death. I still didn't want to feel pain but death sounded like a relief, like escape. Now I was too tired to care. I guess the body's system can only pump out so much adrenaline. When that was burnt out, I wanted to fall into a dreamless sleep.

Getting the override code and remembering it would have solved all my problems. Since I couldn't do that, I took it out on some guy who probably stopped at Tim Horton's that morning. He probably picked up a double double and vanilla dip donut. This morning, this killer had been just another person in a city of people going about their lives.

Once he was dead, I began to see him as the victim he really was. He wasn't an it anymore. What had his name been? Hamish had said the people in the basement were ... who were they again? Was one of them named Glen?

Sorry, Glen. Sorry, everybody. I wish you'd gone to Timmy's and left it at that.

Ding!

24

The elevator doors parted. "Wowie, man! Looks like you had a bonus round." In one hand, Hamish carried a hexagonal aluminum box about the size of a beer cooler. My Glock was in his other hand. The doctor peered down the barrel at me to take careful aim at my head. "Put it down."

I dropped the bloody oxygen tank to the floor with a clang. "Shit."

Hamish sized me up. "Yes, you'll do nicely."

"I'm Daniel," I said. "My friends call me Danny."

"Don't care. We aren't going to be going to ballgames, drinkin' Moosehead and grilling steak together."

"Talk to me for a minute."

"A smart man would ask if there is a way to stop the spread of the outbreak."

"Okay. Is there a vaccine?"

"A repellant, and," he tapped his temple, "only I know the formula for the water-borne vector. Other variations were the purview of ... well ... all these dead people and a few others."

"Other variations? You people were doing more with this stuff?"

"That is the best question you've asked. It gets to the crux of the matter." He nodded toward the control room. "They were pretty squirrelly about our research data. I crashed and smashed the server for good here. Fried the backups in the vault downstairs, too."

"That's what you were doing down there?"

"Among other things. Thanks for your help. Couldn't have done it without you."

"You seem to be the man with the plan."

"And all the answers." Hamish gestured to the bodies of his former co-workers. "Those were some brilliant researchers, a good team. They had all the answers, too. Unfortunately, their answers were very dangerous. Maybe someday we'll figure out how to neutralize our deadly creations but that day is far off. I'm telling you this so you understand that, for all of humanity to survive, you can't kill me. If you understand, say yes."

"Yes, you killed them all for insurance."

"My survival was one reason but I'm more altruistic than you give me credit for. My knowledge is quite singular, I assure you. I need to walk out of here safely. *You* need me to get out safely."

"You must have gotten to know the staff. How does that feel to know what you've done to them? To their families?"

"Necessary. It feels necessary. You undoubtedly think I'm some kind of cartoon villain. Not at all."

I glanced at the bodies surrounding us. "If you aren't a monster, I don't know what is."

"Then you don't know what is. You're confusing an ought with an is."

"What?"

"I'm saving the world, Daniel."

"How do you figure?"

"Do you even know what this place is?"

I shrugged. "You study diseases."

"We *weaponize* diseases," he huffed. "All these people you think of as victims made a living from turning nature's worst into man's worst. That's how all these nice people were paying for their lattes, their kids' private schools, their mortgages on nice homes in Rosedale — "

"You did this."

"I literally gave them a taste of their own medicine. These so-called victims were monsters before my pets went to work on them. Imagine a whole city's civilian population tearing each other apart, no missiles, no radiation. They would allow every man, woman and child to go at each other. Then they'd surround an enemy city and shoot whoever comes out. That was the operating theory anyway. Burn the bodies, clean up the blood and you've got a whole new city to occupy without knocking down a single building."

"You're describing a war crime."

"There's a lab like this one in nearly every major city. Everybody's trying to figure out how to make the next war crime happen. Did you really think all these labs were discovering something new and useful about bubonic plague? We study the deadly sins, not to cure them, but to use them in warfare."

"You worked here, too," I said. "What changed, Hamish? You get religion?"

"Thanks to emerging technologies, there was a breakthrough of sorts." He nodded to the box in his hand, the one that didn't hold my gun. "They borrowed some goodies from one of the company's medical subdivisions. The bioengineering is called AFTER. It has the potential to save the world but most likely, people being people, it will end everything. If it weren't for that, I would have left well enough alone. Believe me, AFTER's nanotech takes bio-weaponry beyond the next level."

"Nanotech?"

"This demonstration ... heh ... this *demon*-stration ... " He let out that shrill laugh again. "Demons, get it? I thought you — "

"What do you mean next level?"

"With this tech, a brilliant researcher extrapolated beyond my wildest dreams and darkest nightmares. AFTER's nano engine took my elegant, targeted solutions up to something far more sinister and harder to control. I deal in microorganisms and gene splicing. Put my waterborne brain parasites together with the little robots and you've got the marriage from Hell."

"Speak plain English."

"Organo-nanites. They put another division's nanotech together with my weaponized parasites. With my work, the outbreak is confined to one water supply. Outside a host, the little buggers die. They wanted a 70% casualty rate. If our work with rhesus monkeys is a straight correlation, they've got it. I told them 70% is still too high to shoot for."

"Why that number?"

"The military objective was to sow chaos so no defense could be mounted. They weren't satisfied with making everyone drop dead. They wanted enemy populations — civilians — to turn on each other. Make the majority killers and the uninfested will become the hunted. It's too much. If you want a dragon to defend your castle, you gotta keep that thing on a leash and make sure he's tamed so he always works for you. Somebody has to shut this madness down. I'm somebody."

"A real humanitarian."

"Better than them, man. I built them a bio-bomb, sure. My pets could turn a city inside out. The bosses weren't satisfied with that. Now we're dealing with the equivalent of a nuclear explosion that could spread around the planet. With their plan, the epidemic could spread around the planet. I voiced my concerns. I warned them this was an evil genie they couldn't stuff back in the bottle. I was ignored."

"So you decided to kill everyone you worked with plus my squad?"

"My colleagues were overconfident in their ability to control their new bio-bomb. What if the organo-robotic limits fail? They were sure they'd figure it out but, in the meantime, the nanites proved less than 100% dependable."

"This is all above my pay grade — "

"Funny," Hamish said. "When I raised my objections, that's exactly what they told me. 'Above my pay grade.' This is the end of a long, dirty road that started with turning noise into a weapon. I'm sure, in your line of work, you're familiar with sound cannons."

"LRADs, yeah. What about them?"

He blew a raspberry at me, loud and long. "LRAD, as in Long-range Acoustic Device. Makes it sound like it would be good at an outdoor concert, doesn't it?"

"It's crowd control," I said. "Better than wading into a crowd with batons and shields and cracking skulls."

"Police used the LRAD on protesters at the G-20 Summit in Pittsburgh. Sonic weapons shouldn't be used on peaceful protesters, Daniel, but deafening people and the potential for permanent damage is nowhere near the point. Maybe you got what you wanted for crowd control but here's the problem: Weapons development never ends with the least effective dose."

"What else have they got brewing?"

"For one silly instance, the military research branched into trying to turn enemy forces gay and irresistibly horny."

I let out a hollow chuckle. "Not a thing."

"The experiments were unsuccessful but they really did try to make that happen. My point is, there's nothing they won't do. Go farther down that road and you find me, down here, double double, toil and trouble."

"This is your life's work, isn't it? Why turn around now?"

"I've got kids. I see where this road leads. Somebody has to say when enough is enough. My colleagues found a way to take my work to the next level. What they made is unacceptable."

"The word, 'unacceptable,' sounds weird coming from a guy willing to wipe out a city by poisoning their water supply."

"*Airborne*, Daniel! One contained vector of disease could be a precision tool that could end a war. To give brain parasites some robotic assistance and hope the weapon won't mutate further? To place all your faith in a vaccine for your population while committing genocide against all others? They're very clever but they aren't at all smart. They don't even have that vaccine yet, just the faith they can limit the effects using the nanites."

"I don't — "

"Before the first test of the nuclear bomb there was concern among some scientists that the explosion could ignite all the oxygen in the atmosphere and kill the planet instead of a couple of Japanese cities. Do you know how they ruled out that possibility with certainty?"

"I dunno. Math?"

"Wrong. They detonated Trinity and hoped for the best. That moment right there defines the best and worst of humanity. Curious, creative, inventive and too damn stupid to be half cautious."

He lifted the box and raised his voice to a shout, "That was a nuclear weapon. I hold in my hand the end of the world, a living weapon."

"What are you going to do with it, Hamish?"

"I'm going to destroy it, of course."

"The world?"

"No, you idiot! The world is where I keep all my classic vinyl of Creedence Clearwater Revival. I'm destroying the contents of this box, the wicked research and all the evil people behind it."

"So kill it and let's call it a day."

"I have to get it out of here to kill it. There can't even be any puzzle pieces left for anyone to try to put together. I love my daughters and I love, love, love my Creedence. We gotta keep the good shit goin'. I want my daughters to live on a hospitable planet. I want them to live and grow up and, when they listen to *Bad Moon Rising*, they'll remember their dad as the man who saved the world."

I looked at Frank and wished I'd had the balls to shoot him myself. I looked at Steve and Bob and wanted to cry. Patrick was kind of a prick so I didn't feel much of anything for him. Christine seemed nice. All these others? God, what a bloodbath. It did appear to me the waterborne parasites were bad enough. Their kill ratio seemed higher than seventy percent.

"Well? Do you see where I'm coming from, Daniel?"

"Well," I admitted, "I still hate your guts but I do have some mixed emotions."

"Attaboy."

26

Hamish told me to get into the decontamination chamber to go to Level 2. He waved my Glock at me so I did as I was told. While the air cycled and the washers and sprayers hosed us down again, we stayed on opposite ends of the chamber. Hamish didn't let down his guard but he was talkative. "Can you guess what the big three bosses of this lab are doing right now?"

"Christine said they were away."

"Ah, Christine. She trained at Johns Hopkins, came here from the CDC. She was with the Epidemic Intelligence Service. She had the brains to work on curing cancer with nanotech someday. Nice woman, to all appearances."

"But?"

"Everyone has blind spots. People get sidetracked. When Christine was in high school, she wanted to win a Nobel prize. Then she heard what work in the cleanroom of a weapons manufacturer pays."

"So you decided she needed to die so you could do this."

"You lot killed her, actually. I was watching from the control room. How do you feel about that?"

"My superiors ordered me down here because of what you did. You were talking about your bosses. Where did they go?"

"Aruba, to attend a conference of thought leaders. Sam Harris is delivering the keynote and Foo Fighters will play a private concert. They'll talk about climate change and how to turn the Sahara into farmland. The thought leaders from this lab will be discussing the dangers of nanotech and Artificial Intelligence. You know what? They'll talk so earnestly, too, like kindly and concerned grandfathers. One of our company's divisions is working on perfecting drones that could swarm a city. They could search and destroy targets based on what Facebook groups they belong to. These people are psychopaths with no sense of irony."

"Sounds like you don't like your bosses much. There's a support group for that. It includes everyone who has a boss or has ever had a boss."

"But my immediate boss, as one example, is a man named Thomas Dill. He's so rich, it's sick. He collects paintings that should be in museums so anyone can see them. Art is fine but spending millions on a painting when a copy looks the same and is so cheap has never made sense to me."

"So he likes things and you like other things. That's how things work, Hamish."

"You don't understand. Thomas sees himself as a modern day Prometheus, bringing fire to mankind. He thinks overwhelming weapons will bring all our enemies to heel. We'll never have to negotiate and can do what we want because we are as gods. You can't scare people into submission, though … not for the long-term. Gods should rule by love, not fear. If we scare them enough, they'll just get hold of the same tech and use it against us. All Thomas remembers about Prometheus is he brought fire to humanity. He forgets fire also brought forged weapons and war. Prometheus literally means *foresight*. The people who run labs like this have no foresight."

As the sprayers hosed me down, I searched for some weakness I could exploit, some common ground that would get me out of the Box alive. "Sounds like we feel much the same about our bosses."

Hamish nodded. "We all want to control our fate. That's the

origin of most stress, feeling like you're out of control. Of course, nobody's really in control of much. That's what these people don't understand. They think they can let the genie out of the bottle and stuff it back in when they want? That's never been true. Once we went nuclear, we had to continue."

"Sounds like you regret loading their gun. The weapon you say you hate so much is based on your work."

"I do regret it. We're fighting the wrong wars. We created antibiotics and declared victory over microorganisms. Meanwhile, the microscopic war went on without us. The bacteria keep evolving and adapting so we're running out of effective antibiotics. You can't get a gallbladder removed without worrying the hospital stay will kill you."

"You're making me antsy about getting an ingrown toenail, Hamish."

"You should be nervous. Staph infections, MRSA, Clostridium difficile … we're so casual about the ordinary, everyday horrors. Necrotizing fasciitis is rare but it won't be rare forever. I've studied ebola in Liberia. I've seen bodies piled up in the center of a village, burned like cordwood. Here, you can live your entire life and manage to avoid seeing one dead body. We've forgotten what reality is. We lock the elderly and the dying out of sight and out of the way. We worship youth but people are young for a really short time. Death is Life, Daniel. We've blinded ourselves to reality."

I pointed to the shiny box. "But you think you're making the world safer by taking that out of containment?"

"I'm taking a loaded gun away from toddlers," he said. "A person in your profession should understand that."

"You say everyone has blind spots. What are yours? Did all these people really have to die?"

"No point in taking their weapon away if they can go make more. Besides, logistically, it was easy to get in here but it's much harder to subvert the sensors on the way out. To get out, I needed the master override code to turn off the system safeties. Anyone with clearance can get down here but walking out with this little box of horrors is a trial."

I could feel the heat in my cheeks and scalp, so hot with embarrassment that I wanted to yank off my gear then and there. Hamish subverted the lockdown with the master code I delivered into his hands. "You're such a smart guy, why not go away and work in a new lab somewhere else? Go cure cancer."

"Daniel, Daniel, Daniel. Don't you see? I'm curing cancer as we speak." He hefted the box. "*This* cancer."

My ears popped. The washers and sprayers finished their work and I opened the hatch to step into Level 2.

EPISODE 5

Breakdown (noun)

Crisis; collapse of a system (societal, technological and/or nervous) that can no longer sustain its illusions and/or delusions.

Lockdown (noun)

The attempt to contain a systemic failure and maintain illusions and/or delusions.

Fakedown (noun)

The purposeful assertion of delusions in order to install or maintain a failed system; arch. *propaganda*.

Wakedown (noun)

Succumbing to fakedown due to exhaustion or despair; the failure of proponents of hope to continue to act as if hope is not illusory.

~ Notes from NEXT

2 7

My head still throbbed with unrelenting pain. I'd had two concussions before. At 16, I was checked into the boards playing hockey. My second brain scramble laid me out after a bar fight in Chinatown West. I wanted to lie down now, go to sleep and wake up in my bed at home. I wanted all this to be a nightmare, easily dismissed, soon forgotten. Steve would call and we'd go fishing on the weekend. I'd study for my negotiator's course. If *normal* meant going back to blissful ignorance, I was all for going back to stupid.

"Daniel? You're swaying. Stand up and stay up. I need you conscious and functioning a bit longer. This is already hard enough."

"What's next? Somebody else will recreate the research. Your bosses knows what the research is all about. You gonna kill them, too?"

"The directors are venture capitalists and lobbyists. They only know the broad strokes. It wouldn't be bad if they died but they lack the necessary expertise to recreate organo-nanotech. They haven't stepped into the Level 4 lab since the day of its opening ceremony. The real work was done in vault labs. For all their sponsorship of the science of organo-nanotech, they're about as relevant as the CEOs of Coke or Pepsi."

Hamish directed me to the locker room. From where I stood, I could still see a trail of blood leaking across the floor from the dead man in the changeroom.

"Pay no attention to the man behind the curtain," Hamish said.

"What did he do?"

"Told you. Got in the way. That was Cal Whedon. He questioned what I was doing, fiddling with the shower tank — "

"When you dosed these showers with your parasites."

Hamish bobbed his head. "Tank maintenance was his job. When I opted not to go through the shower, Cal had to be silenced."

"There was a woman bleeding on the front step, too — "

"I saw on the security cam. You guys shot her."

"Not my decision."

"We all feel like most decisions are made for us, isn't that so? I feel that way. A conscience is a terrible nuisance, isn't it? Or do you have a conscience?"

"Who was that woman?"

"Myra Wilcox, the Level 4 lab equipment supervisor. She walked in on me knifing Cal. She came at me. I had to stab her in the side. I hesitated, you know. It was a heat of the moment thing. She was the nicest of all the staff. I suppose I should have finished what I started."

Damn. Know-it-all Bob was right about her wound.

"I let all the staff on Level 1 go. They ran out screaming after I shot the man in the closet."

"They trampled a woman on the way out."

"Yes. Karen Gardener. I don't think it was the trampling. Heart attack, probably. I would have helped her if I hadn't been in a rush. Most of them didn't know anything top secret. They thought we were looking for treatments for anthrax. That was the official line. Karen worked in procurement of lab animals. I'm pretty sure she had no idea she worked for a weapons manufacturer."

I was running out of patience. "What do you want from me, man?"

"Your nice blue environmental suit, Daniel."

"There are plenty of suits down here."

"Not like yours. I need that dark blue biohazard suit."

"You're going to dress up like me — "

"And escape in the isolation van."

"If I say no — "

"I'll shoot you in the foot and I'll have to yank it off you while you scream."

"Use one of my teammate's Hazmats for your disguise."

He let out an exasperated sigh. "Have you ever tried to undress a corpse?"

"No."

"Neither have I, but I can easily imagine it would be difficult, what with all that slippery gore and goo. All your guys were plastered in blood or their gear was damaged."

"I've got blood on my gear."

"I can wash that off easily enough. Maybe I won't even bother. The more blood, the fewer questions between the time I step out into daylight and the isolation truck. I'm betting nobody will want to come near me."

"If you shoot me, the hole in the suit will ruin your disguise."

"I'd have to shoot you in the foot — or the feet, sure. Then I'd have to leave you here crying while I schlep back to forage for a pair of boots from one of your dead. Honestly, Daniel, this will go smooth and easy if you simply cooperate. I've thought this through and I am smarter than you. We'll end up in the same place. If we do this the easy way, you don't end up wounded and begging me to kill you. I could improvise but I'm on a schedule here."

"A schedule?"

"It's my last day of work and I can't wait to get out of here. I only have to bluff my way to the sidewalk. The isolation truck will be waiting."

"You have an accomplice in the truck."

His casual shrug gave nothing away but the way he widened his eyes told me I'd hit on the truth. "*Sonofabitch*. Who's your guy on the outside? " I took one step toward him.

Hamish raised the pistol to his own head. "Hear me out and consider this, Daniel. Under Yellowstone there is a supervolcano. When it erupts, a vast lake of magma will spew out and send the Earth into a volcanic winter. In the first few minutes, most of North America will die. Soon after, so will everyone else. In geologic time, it's a *certainty* it will happen. Could be in the next few seconds, could be on your birthday, maybe a couple hundred years from now. Nobody knows."

"What the hell is your point?"

"This technology is a supervolcano. Let me do what I have to do to keep it from erupting today and you buy the world some time. My sabotage could set the progression of this work back years. Otherwise, everything you're trying to save will go away in a puff of smoke. No more pizzas, no more M&Ms, no more KISS cover bands. Nothing! No more weddings or honeymoons, no happy times, at all. Everyone you've ever known or could know will die screaming. A shitload of cannibalism will spread across the globe."

"The infection is contained if it's down here."

"The *infestation*," he corrected me. "Don't worry. My pets in the shower tanks will be dead in a few hours. As long as you don't have a shower immediately after I leave, the waterborne parasites won't be a bother to anyone. They've done their job."

I stared at the hexagonal box. "It's really worth all this death?"

"I should have saved Bob and let them eat you, you idiot. How many people would you kill to save billions of others? One? A dozen? Thousands? Millions? Your bomb disposal specialist did the math. Be like Bob. Do the math and gimme the suit."

Hot tears blurred my vision and slipped down my cheek. "My team is dead. What will I tell their families?"

"That's a bureaucratic problem. Tell them whatever you want if the truth doesn't work. I understand you aren't dealing with bosses who are adept at nuance and moral ambiguity. Consider what happens if I don't get out of here with these organo-nanites? When the end begins, what few survivors there may be will envy the problem of what to say to your bosses. Think it through, Daniel. Everybody's skull is a womb for the Picasso Strain."

"Picasso Strain?"

"That's what they named the worst nanotech ever devised. AFTER was the precursor, the good thing that gave birth to the bad thing. Under a microscope, Picasso's beasties stain blue. We added the pretty coloration so we could identify Picasso's distribution pattern when the micro-monsters are dispersed on air currents. That wasn't the main reason, though. You want to know why they gave a bio-weapon the name Picasso?"

"Well?"

"They consider it a masterpiece. Told you, these people have no souls."

28

Hamish had my gun to his head but he held the whole world hostage. *Picasso.* The name filled me with revulsion. They thought their robo-brain parasites that made people into killer zombies was a good thing. *Hmph.* I also didn't want to get shot in the feet or anywhere else.

I put both hands on my hood, hesitated a moment, and pulled it up and off. The respirator clicked closed as I took my last breath from my oxygen tank. As I expected, the facility was awash in the sickly sweet aroma of that industrial cleaner common to hospitals.

"Cheer up, Daniel. You came in here to save the world and you are helping. You're a hero."

"I don't feel like a hero," I said.

"It's a dirty world. I wish we were pulling kids out of burning buildings but reality is seldom so clear-cut. When you're in the middle of a problem, the things you may have to do don't feel heroic. They feel … "

"Necessary?"

"Yeah."

I leaned on the wall, taking a few deep breaths before moving to pull off the rest of my gear. I wasn't up for a fight. Could I mount a defense against Hamish? *Could* was beyond my reach. Should I? I wasn't sure what *should* meant anymore. Hamish made a pretty good argument.

I got my blue biohazard suit off and put it on the floor at Hamish's feet. I wore a t-shirt, shorts and socks. The cool air was a relief. Hamish didn't trust me to stay passive. He ordered me to go to the other end of the locker room while he pulled on my gear. I was fine with that. Whatever happened next, I'd leave Hamish to the guys outside. The rest of the ETF wasn't suffering trauma and concussion. Someone else's decisions got me into the Box. I'd let them figure out what to do about Hamish.

He was halfway into the Hazmat when he pulled a thick roll of duct tape from a cabinet over a sink. Keeping the pistol on me, he instructed me to place several long strips of tape on the counter sticky side up.

I did as I was told but was startled when he opened the hexagonal box. "What are you doing?"

He waved me back with the Glock. I stayed against the far wall, hands up. I had no hope of getting my weapon back. As I stood watching him poke through the box I worried that I had it all wrong. If I was closer, Hamish could shoot me once in the head. I didn't relish the idea. It wouldn't be pleasant but it would be over so quick there wouldn't be time to worry. A headshot at close range would be much quicker than multiple gunshots bursting my organs randomly. How would I die in that scenario? Which awful demise would win in the race between organ failure and blood loss?

"Relax," Hamish said. "These little monsters are sealed in test tubes. They're so hardy, they don't even have to stay cold. As long as they don't aerosolize, we're fine and everybody lives."

"I'd still be more comfortable if you kept them in the big steel box," I said.

"If I'm going to walk out of here, I can't walk out into the summer sunshine looking like a lab rat, now, can I?"

Hamish placed the test tubes along the strips of duct tape and proceeded to awkwardly strap them to his chest. They were invisible under the biohazard suit.

"Is there any kind of security code I should know to tell your superiors as I exit the building?"

I said nothing.

"I have to make it to the isolation truck, Daniel. Remember, my safety is everyone's safety."

"The incident commander's name is Mac," I said. "When you come out, hold the gun up high. Don't point it at anyone. Say, ETF! Two coming out."

"You're Two?"

"Yeah."

"Anything else?"

"If challenged, the security code is 'friendly giant.'"

"Friendly giant? You wouldn't shit a shitter, would you, Daniel?"

"Like you said, your safety is everybody's safety."

"Cool. Thanks, man. You're a real mensch."

He placed the yellow code card on a counter by the sink and told me to read it to him as he stepped to the hatch to Level 1.

I did as I was told. "5 - 5 - A - Z - 2 - 5 - 0 - 0 - L - 1 - 1 - V - 3 - T - P - D - Q."

Hamish keyed it in and cranked open the hatch. He pointed the Glock my way and I returned to my place by the far wall. He picked up the yellow card. "Thanks for all your help."

"I don't think you gave me a whole lot of choice."

"Everything is a choice."

"Until it's not."

"Whatever helps you sleep at night, Daniel."

"I guess this is where we part ways, huh? You going to shoot me now?"

"That won't be necessary."

"You're going to leave me trapped down here."

"If all goes well for me, someone will come down to find out what happened."

"Eventually, maybe, if all goes well. Big ifs, Hamish."

"It'll be fine. I'll leave you here while I walk out the front door like a boss. Get it? Like a boss?" His laugh was a high nasal sound, as if he was squeezing a duck to make it quack in a panic. He waved cheerily as he closed the hatch behind him. I heard the lock click.

I walked slowly around the locker room in a circle. I had two minutes before he cleared the lock and I could challenge the keypad.

5 - 5 - A - Z - 2 - 5 - 0 - 0 - L - 1 - 1 - V - 3 - T - P - D - Q.

"*Fifty-five African Zebras To 500 Lions Won One Victory, Three Trapped People Died Quick.*" Trying to stay steady on my feet, I repeated the word mnemonic over and over, as I paced. That's how I remembered the override code to escape to Level 1.

29

M inutes later I emerged from the hatch on Level 1. I almost caught up with Hamish. He must have hesitated, building up his nerve for the final phase of his plan. Dr. Hamish Allen — savior of the world, scientist with a Jesus complex and concerned father — waved at me as he stepped over the body of the woman in the doorway.

"Daniel! Aren't you clever! I thought I had you locked up good! Can't keep a good man down! Gotta run! Stay down here or I *will* shoot you."

He headed up the ramp to the Box's exit. I didn't doubt he would shoot. He'd come too far to turn back. As he disappeared up the ramp, a stupid inspiration came over me. I still had a way to take him into custody and get my weapon back.

I ran to the office closet. The security guard had run out of blood from his nasty head wound. I scooped up the gun in his lap and checked the cylinder. One shot fired, four rounds to go. I didn't want to fire any. I needed Hamish to put the Glock down. Let Mac figure out the rest while I went on vacation. Maybe I'd go on vacation and never come back. That sounded just fine.

I ran out of the office, leaping over the trampled woman and charging up the ramp. I can't say what made me work so hard to get to him. Part of it was pride. My team was dead and Hamish held my weapon. The rest? All the important questions that so concerned Hamish Allen? To my great shame, I have to admit I wasn't thinking about any of that.

I drove through a snowstorm on the 401 between London, Ontario and Toronto, once. The flurries were thick, the road was ice and the ploughs were insufficient to deal with the quick accumulation of snow. It took hours longer than it should have and the trip was so dangerous I should have pulled off the road and holed up somewhere. I was too stubborn to drive safely. I pressed on, barely able to see more than a couple of car lengths ahead.

Chasing Hamish was that stupid. It was my job to make sure he didn't escape the Box. I tried to do my duty. Besides, I worried that if Mac saw through his disguise, Crenshaw might snipe the bioengineer in the chest. Those test tubes had to remain unbroken and returned to their steel box in the vault. If it came to him or me, I would have to shoot Hamish in the head.

Too late, I dashed past the elevators as Hamish stepped into the sunshine.

"ETF! Two, coming out!" Hamish yelled as I'd told him to do. We were roughly the same height. With the biohazard suit on and the distortion of the hood, Mac would have no reason to doubt it was me walking out of the Box alone.

"Where's the rest of your team, Two?" It was Mac on the bullhorn.

Hamish made a slicing gesture across his throat. Then he pointed to the white isolation van and went down the first step. "Friendly giant, Mac! Friendly giant!"

I stepped to the shadows inside of the doorway and raised the pistol, aiming for a quick clean headshot. "That's far enough, Hamish. It's over now."

"Oh, Daniel. You don't know when to quit."

I cocked the weapon. I knew he heard me. He stiffened and stood taller. "Drop the gun or I'll shoot you through the head."

"But my head is where all the answers are."

"Someone else will figure out what needs to be figured out. I can't let you leave. I don't really know what you'll do with those things. Maybe you'll sell them to North Korea."

"I told you — "

"You told me lots of things. We'll work it out. Now drop the gun."

Hamish dropped my Glock to the steps. I felt a wave of relief wash over me. "Turn around and pull off the hood."

He turned slightly and did as he was told. He gave me a sheepish grin.

"Hands away from your chest. Show me your hands."

"Man, you don't get it." He raised both hands, surrendering peacefully. "Go ahead. Take the little beasties. I tried to save the world but, you know what? It's not worth the effort. I was right. Everybody has a blind spot."

As he turned, Hamish gestured to the street to reveal to me my blind spot. I was so focused on the doctor, I failed to maintain situational awareness. That's a fancy way of saying I focused too much on the wrong problem.

At the bottom of the steps, a long line of bodies lay in the street. Each river of blood draining toward the gutters wound back to a civilian. Mostly they died from head and chest shots. Some must have tried to run when the carnage really got going.

Too many casualties lay in the street for them all to be Echidna employees. There were too many to easily count. The ETF must have lined them up. My colleagues must have ensured their cooperation by ordering them to their knees at gunpoint. They'd promise a safe ride home as soon as they identified everyone. Maybe they told them the isolation truck and a cozy stay in quarantine awaited them over at St. Mike's. Then they shot them all to contain any potential contagion.

There was probably a more sophisticated and less bloody way to solve the problem. Since that moment I have come to understand that everyone favors the quick and easy answer, no matter how blunt and brutal. They could call their crime a terrorist attack. They'd confiscate all surveillance evidence. Even the recordings from the cameras in the ATMs at the bank across the street would disappear. Quick and easy, blunt and brutal. Troubling questions would soon be dismissed as conspiracy theories.

My gaze fell on the woman in white. Her summer dress was mostly red now. Her long red hair, now wet with blood, looked like a hunk of wire. She'd been so pretty and now she was so dead.

In the next minute, I would envy her.

Hamish gave a slow half-turn. "Dude! See how casual they are about killing. They didn't even wait to see if anyone was infested. Your friend was right. We aren't getting out of here. We're all about to enter Picasso's blue period, Dan — "

Mac gave the order to shoot. He didn't kill me. Mac only thought he was murdering me. The sniper got Hamish square in the middle of his skull full of secrets.

Stunned, I stood covered in pink mist from Hamish Allen's brilliant and shattered brain.

The round did not shatter the test tubes strapped to Hamish Allen's chest. Hell was not unleashed upon an unsuspecting planet by a sniper's bullet. The fall down the concrete steps did that. I heard the glass shatter. I inhaled the fine blue mist and the brain parasites did what brain parasites do.

Picasso went to work on me.

30

M ac stepped into the street in a blue Hazmat. I was sure it was him because he carried a bullhorn. He came to a stop behind the corpse of the red-haired woman. He peered into the doorway, surely wondering who was left in the Box. Who had the dead man been talking to, and what was the blue mist rising from the corpse?

All I could think about — if you could call it thinking — was the dead woman at his feet. He didn't spare a glance at her for a second. It was if she did not exist, had never existed. She didn't matter and neither did I. We were merely human sacrifices, no more valuable today than when thousands were massacred a day atop Mayan pyramids.

What had that woman's name been? I groped for the memory. It hadn't even been an hour since I called in her name. I pointed killers her way and she'd been rounded up with the rest for extermination.

Kaela … Kaela Santini. I remembered because of that movie, *The Great Santini.*

I'd sat at her desk. I'd seen her picture and her password. How soon would she be forgotten as the contagion spread on the wind?

Even those who'd known her, supposing they survived, would soon blur her entire life into an empty statistic. We all blur into history but she was so young and pretty.

Fury overcame my exhaustion then. I'd been sent on a suicide mission, ill-prepared and now, ill. I was sure it wasn't Hamish Allen's "beasties" affecting me, though. Not yet. Despite my concussion, the loss of my squad and the weird parasites that would soon turn me into their killer robot, I was still me. And what could I do with my remaining minutes as Daniel Harmon?

I leaned out of the doorway, raised the security guard's .38 and fired. I pulled the trigger on Mac as fast as I could. It was a thoughtless and petty act. I'm not proud of it. He wasn't so close that I could nail him easily, but I did manage to empty the weapon before the rest of the ETF opened fire on me.

Taking everyone by surprise, I hit Mac once with the first shot, high on the left shoulder. He spun sideways and went down. The rest of my shots went high and wide. I ducked back as numerous rounds chunked the concrete and glass around the front door. I dashed close along the lobby wall, out of the line of fire. Panting, I dove over the security desk.

I wondered if the gremlins in my head would go to work on me faster if my heart beat fast and increased my blood circulation. Did it matter? Either way, I'd turn into one of those unthinking animals, ravenous and hopelessly cruel.

I got up on my knees. The surveillance cameras were still working. I saw three of my fellow ETF officers rush forward with shields, weapons up and trained on the front door.

"Doesn't matter now, you dumb shits," I said. "I'll go first but Mac's next. You're all next."

Blue mist, Picasso nanites, beasties ... whatever you are, do your worst.

That's the moment I realized I'd made a tactical error. In my anger, I'd failed to save a bullet for myself. Of course, the guys outside seemed pretty eager to oblige in the Suicide by Cop Department. I had something important to do first. I sprinted back down the ramp to the office on Level 1.

How much time before the mix of advanced microscopic

machines and primitive brain parasites erased my consciousness and turned me into a killer zombie?

If I'd known what was about to happen, I would have run to kneel beside Kaela and take the shot. I'd have accepted death's erasure gladly.

Would have … could have … should have … didn't.

31

Back on the ramp to the Level 1 offices, I leaned hard on the wall, panting. No time for regrets now, I pushed off and left a long bloody smear as I staggered back to Kaela Santini's desk.

My head pounded. I thought I might vomit but I'd felt that way since that big guy bounced my head off the floor. Were these symptoms of what was or what was to come? Would I fall into a quick coma first? Or, much worse, would I *feel* my mind slipping away? What would my last memory be?

My earliest and most tenuous memory is seeing my own hands in front of me as I crawled across a vinyl floor. The floor's pattern was fake brick. My mother told me that was the kitchen in our old house so I might have been two years old. Would that be the first memory to be erased? How long before I became a drooling animal?

My father was diagnosed with early onset Alzheimer's at fifty-four. To him, the worst part of the disease is seeing the end come too slowly. He doesn't believe in God. However, when his morning crossword puzzle became a twisted mystery in another language, he began to pray for a quick heart attack. To ebb away and not be himself anymore? He calls his fate, "Cruel and not unusual enough."

Dad is still alive. Aside from putting random items in the fridge, he's been doing better than the doctors expected. (I once found the TV remote in the meat drawer.) I wondered if the tiny machines spreading on the blue mist would find a home in my father's head, too. Would they find his decaying brain hospitable? Or would he simply fall victim to a random attack and be eaten alive?

Not as fast as a heart attack but faster than Alzheimer's, I thought. *Maybe Dad won't mind so much.*

It was a grim thought, so I shoved it aside. I could still do something useful. I plopped into Kaela's chair and opened her drawer to see her password again: *3BearsDoGoldilocks*.

Kaela, you were a funny woman. I'm sure we would have gotten along. I'm sorry I helped murder you.

I touched the mouse and her screen came alive. I logged in with her password. The screen changed and I found she'd been looking at a travel site. She'd been planning a trip to the tropics when the alarm sounded. She'd been comparing prices of resorts in Cancun and the Dominican Republic. I wanted to stare at those pictures and imagine myself in places I'd never been. There wasn't time.

I clicked a tab that took me to her gmail page. I clicked on *COMPOSE* and prayed I'd remembered my sister's email address properly. I would have called her but the phones didn't work. Without my cell, I had no idea what her number was.

Jenn,

I've messed up. You were right. I should have become a physiotherapist. I don't know how much time I have but as soon as you see this, run. Get as far away from Toronto as you can. Maybe up north. Find weapons and, this is going to be hard but leave dad. Ggo I can"t expll —

. . .

...

ICANT EXPLHOGSDSD —

...

(DEEP BREATH.)

I I PIJHAFS —
  O[isfjosfjsfsvsof[pkk [kj[pijsfd ...

MY FINGERS WOULDN'T DO what I wanted. I managed to click send. That was all. I stared at the screen, the keyboard and my traitorous hands.

Damn it. I knew I should have chosen my last words ahead of time! Something pithy and concise would have been better.

I sat for some time waiting and thinking about the decisions, turns and accidents that had led me to this chair. I thought of the cheating girlfriend who told me I'd look sexy in uniform. Had my decision to become a cop truly been based on that? Not entirely. But without that specific encouragement, I wouldn't have done it at all. I could be a thousand miles from here and oblivious to the danger blowing in the wind, multiplying in God knew how many brains. Was Mac getting patched up by a paramedic at that same moment? Was he staring at a name tag or a sign and wondering why the letters didn't make sense?

I didn't break up with that girlfriend because she steered me wrong. I didn't even break up with her because she cheated. As many relationships go, ours wobbled back and forth a few times before it toppled over. I eventually broke it off because she told me I should work for my dad in that last summer before college ended. I wanted to take a road trip to California. She told me to grow up and make some money instead. That's what finally tore it up for me.

The irony is, I didn't go on that road trip of my dreams. I did work for my father moving heavy things around a warehouse for one more torturous summer. I'd worked in that dank warehouse since I was thirteen. I took on part-time jobs to try to pay for my own place, to be free and independent. I remained chained.

Even as the parasites wormed their way deeper, through the meat and juice of my brain, my mind suddenly felt clearer. My epiphany was this: I'd been going the wrong way for years. I had been free once and it was as a child. The last day of summer when I was twelve was the last time I'd known real happiness. After that, it was all work, worry and striving.

What and when is enough? When can we stop having to prove ourselves? And what are we proving?

I was tired of trying so damn hard. It came to nothing much anyway. I guess grim realizations are what people think about on their deathbeds. I looked down and realized where I was. I wouldn't die on clean white sheets. No death bed for me. I got a death office chair instead.

The cheating girlfriend went back to my former best friend who was studying to become a chiropractor. I guess none of that matters. Soon there would be only two jobs: hunters and prey. Maybe getting my mind erased wouldn't be so bad. Zombies pay no taxes. Becoming a dumb animal could be a solid stress management strategy.

I saved a little boy from drowning in Lake Ontario once. That was the best thing I ever did and I wasn't even on duty. I didn't think about it. I just dove in and pulled him out. His mom stalked across the beach, yanked the kid to his feet and swore at him all the way back to the parking lot. He was too busy crying to look at me. His mom didn't even thank me. That was one of the best days out of a lot of shitty ones. It was pure.

Then came the Emergency Task Force, another nail in my coffin. We'd come in as a unit, so strong. When Mac ordered us to flatten to get out of the line of fire, we'd all dropped to the deck as if we were one person. We came into the Box with purpose and confidence, weapons ready and geared up to be faceless, nameless Hazmat heroes. I didn't think of us as people with first names. We had numbers. We must have looked so badass when we came through the front door.

Only when we failed and fell, one by one, did we become humans with names again. Lundsden became Bob. Taylor became Steve. Davis became Patrick. I was just Daniel now.

Bob, Steve, Patrick, Danny. Little boys' names.

And our fearless leader, Frank Barnes, became the son of a bitch who led us into Hell blind.

It is strange how personal death is. People die in great masses on the news, and it's a blip in our consciousness, noted and soon forgotten. It's not a tragedy until it's personal.

I was about to find out there really are worse things than death. Dad would have understood the horror that was about to crush me. However, understanding a thing doesn't necessarily make it better. Sometimes ignorance really is bliss.

When I was in training, an instructor asked my class, "Is it better to be smart or brave?" He went around the room, pinning my classmates down on an answer.

When he came to me, I answered with a joke, "Brave. I can do brave things but I'm only as smart as I'm ever going to be."

The instructor had the grace to laugh. Then he told us why smart was better. "If you're smart, you won't have to be so brave." By smart, he really meant *careful.*

I have a different answer now. It's better to be brave. Smart people did this to me.

3 2

T he hunger hit me in the pit of my stomach, as harsh as a body blow. *Pang* is not the right word. *Pain* is the word. I'd never been so hungry in my life. I was ravenous.

I fell from the chair and gripped the floor with my toes and fingers as if the room might turn upside down at any moment. The carpet felt very rough under my hands, as if the texture suddenly had more depth. The carpet was not a flat plane, anymore, not to me. It was as nuanced as a topographical model of a mountain range. I saw new patterns in the rug and felt the contours in its patterns.

Colors became more vivid, too. My vision sharpened to a focus that made my eyeballs dry and hot. I could see the smudges of fingerprints and handprints on the computer screens and desks. My stomach tightened to a knot.

Palm prints. Fingerprints. Everywhere we go we leave a sheen of oil, sweat and dust. I could see it and smell it. There was a tang in the air. The smell revolted my mind but enticed my body.

We have all seen zombie movies. They range from comedy to horror and back again. In almost all the outbreak scenarios, the infected were hungry monsters. Fast or slow, zombies were mindless animals. Under attack, I'd certainly thought of them that way. Near death and dealing with a hundred terrors, much had slipped past me. Then I remembered the attacker who'd nearly killed me, the one who seemed to mouth the words, *"I'm sorry, I'm sorry. I'm sorry."*

In the melee, I'd dismissed that thought as a battlefield reaction. On my hands and knees, muscles coiling and flexing, ready to spring, I knew what came next. I understood what I would do. I couldn't stop what was about to happen. I couldn't even scream.

I raised my head and sniffed the air.

Oh, no, oh, no, oh, no, no, no ...

My muscles flexed. I stalked forward on all fours. As the spectrum of my senses expanded, my body felt more powerful than ever. Even as the ache throbbed in the pit of my empty stomach, there was a strange ecstasy in this new flood of feelings.

My body felt very alive but I wanted desperately to be dead inside. I wanted to scream, *"Do what you want with my brain! Take it all! Take the last part of me that's still here and kill it."*

Instead, I turned my attention to the scents wafting from the closet, more enticing than any aroma of baking bread. Better than Christmas turkey with stuffing and mashed potatoes in gravy. A feast waited for me in the closet.

No, no, no, no, no!

When I was the old Daniel Harmon, I'd often meet people who got uptight when they found out I was a cop. I'd wander around a party and a stranger would turn into a bleeding heart before my eyes. These people seemed both privileged and well-meaning. They weren't good listeners, though. They'd never had to deal with real trouble in a physical way. If they got mugged or became a victim, they'd call someone like me to deal with it.

Despite their lack of experience on the street, they'd whine about how police treated criminals. They'd talk about the tragedy of imprisoning lawbreakers. "Drug addiction is a social issue, not a legal one," they'd say. They'd call the courts our "injustice system." Then they'd complain about economic disparity, disenfranchisement and blah, blah, blah.

Typically, I'd respond with something like, "If all you say is true, why aren't *all* poor people thieves, drug addicts and violent assholes? Why give the worst of us a free pass?'"

In the time it took me to knock back another beer, I'd get an earnest lecture on why people did things for reasons they didn't understand, reasons beyond their control. They'd bang on about chronic institutionalization, bad parenting, bad genes and bad brains.

I'd wait patiently. When the stranger ran out of steam, I'd say, "I can only judge people by what they do."

Then I'd walk away in search of the comfort of someone who agreed with me. Somebody once said that's the definition of genius: anyone who agrees with you.

I'd only just discovered that I wasn't in control of much of anything, not since that last day of summer when I was twelve. I was too busy following orders. I'd worked hard, but was it for what I wanted? Or was my life merely a tribute to what other people expected?

With saliva dripping from my mouth, panting like a dog, I was out of control. I certainly wouldn't want to be judged by what I did next.

The dead security guard waited for me in the closet. The trampled woman in the doorway was good for another meal or two. My body had a new and grisly addiction.

In an Intro Psych class, I'd once listened to a professor argue with a student about what they both called "the Observer."

The student posed the idea that there was a presence in the back of each mind, something or someone watching our thoughts bubble up. The student said that was God watching us.

The professor shut him down hard and said something I didn't understand about "infinite regression," and the subconscious mind. They talked a long time about stuff nobody really understands. I dropped that course because I didn't think those people had any answers.

Now I am the Observer. In this dark place, I have a lot of time to think. I go over and over all my mistakes, indecisions and bad decisions. I don't have any answers, just more questions. Maybe the point is that there is no point. I hate that answer, so I go over everything again only to arrive at the same non-conclusion.

I fell upon the security guard's corpse. As I tore at his uniform to get at his throat and soft belly, my mind reeled in horror.

This isn't me. This isn't me. This isn't me!

I saw every revolting movement of my arms and hands. I tasted the meat in my mouth as I ripped and chewed. I felt the man's blood slide down my throat as I drank from his jugular.

I can feel shame and experience horror but I am a passenger. I used to be in the driver's seat but my bus is on ice, no brakes. My mind's commands can't reach my body. I can do nothing to stop myself from doing terrible things.

This isn't me!

I am not dead. I am still in this body, alive and terrified. I watch, out of control and hating what happens. My father would understand this feeling. He knows what it feels like to slip away, to lose yourself, to become someone else.

Even if I could be cured, could anyone forgive me? Whatever magic the combination of parasites and techno-wizardry Hamish's research team had wrought, it changed me into a thing, a tool, a weapon, a killer robot. I am not evil, but I am in a living hell. Death's erasure would have been so merciful.

I wish I could tell people this thing I've become is not me. I am my own evil twin. In hindsight, maybe that's a little true of all of us. Every dark impulse comes from a place we don't recognize or understand. I am a victim who looks and acts like a predator.

Who am I? Who was I?

Once a flawed human being, I am now a meat puppet. Trapped. This perfect murder machine — so singular of purpose — wears my face. My thoughts are all I have now. I am a zombie made from brain parasites and microscopic machines. Daniel Harmon is dead but this is not the afterlife. This is my AFTER life.

AFTERWORD

In October 2016, the Obama White House issued a report called *Preparing for the Future of Artificial Intelligence.* Under the Safety and Control section, you'll find the following quote:

"If (AI) practitioners cannot achieve justified confidence that a system is safe and controllable, so that deploying the system does not create an unacceptable risk of serious negative consequences, then the system cannot and should not be deployed. A major challenge … is building systems that can safely transition from the 'closed world' of the laboratory into the outside 'open world' where unpredictable things can happen."

AFTER LIFE

BOOK TWO

PURGATORY

EPISODE 1

"The rest of mankind, who were not killed by these plagues, did not repent of the works of their hands ..."

~ **Revelation 9:20**

CHAPTER 1

In this prison we call home,
every heart will turn to stone.
These cages of flesh and bone,
rise in heat,
burn fast
and too quickly cool.
Not much mercy, more the fool.
Let out a brave laugh.
Untether your tears.
We are only more than we appear
when we grow larger
than each fear.

DANIEL
I fed on the guard's body first. I'd seen the movie in which a bunch of soccer players resorted to cannibalism in the mountains. This wasn't like that. It was as if I were watching a very realistic and gory video game from the first person perspec-

tive. Some*thing* else was at the controls. The weaponized brain parasites wriggled in my brain, taking over and telling my body what to do. I was no longer Daniel Harmon, Emergency Task Force officer. Unfortunately, I wasn't the dead variety of zombie, either. My actions were no longer my own.

I watched as I yanked the clothes of the dead aside to get at the meat. I dove for the soft parts first: the throat and abdomen. Ears are chewy and tough. It's easier to tear meat from the finger bones than I would have thought.

I wanted to throw up but I couldn't. My revulsion was alive but my objections remained intellectual and unheard. I would have screamed if I could. Instead, I ate and, despite the gore and my disgust, my body was ravenous.

Someone told me once that if you don't stop a dog from feeding, they'll simply keep eating until they die (like what happens with people, but quicker.) That's how it was with me, feeding off the carcasses on Level 1 of the Box.

I was not totally divorced from my body. That was the confusing part. I could feel everything but I could not change anything. I felt no desire for my grisly meal but I did taste every wet morsel. I couldn't vomit. Instead, I could chew hungrily. To a starving man, a spleen is the same as Black Forest cake. A casual bystander would surely conclude I was enjoying myself.

As if in the thrall of some strange drug, I felt stronger with every bite. Energy pulsed through me. My skin tingled and my muscles felt full, cranked high with kinetic potential like tight steel springs. I moved with an ease that made me feel I'd finally be a threat on the basketball court. If only zombies played basketball.

I heard screams from far away, up the ramp and out in the sunshine. I was curious about what was going on in Toronto's streets. I guess my brain parasites were interested, too. I lifted my head from the large woman before me, leapt to my feet, and ran up the ramp.

I didn't kill the woman or the security guard I ate, I thought. *Someone else had murdered them. The next murdered meal is on me. So far, my crime was "committing an indignity to a dead person."*

I knew a cop who had arrested a naked sicko in a cemetery on that charge. Now I'd join the ranks of the sickos. Whatever was in control of my body wasn't a person I could argue with. I didn't receive a message or hear a voice. I sensed no ghostly presence. I ran, working on automatic, empty of volition. It is a curious thing to be carried along on a wave. I felt like a passenger and the thing that was controlling my body was a hit and run driver.

As I emerged from the Box and onto the downtown street, I guessed what the brain parasites wanted: live prey, fresh meat. The robotic brain parasites infesting my skull wanted to chase someone. The zombies in the Box acted like wolves and I was a member of the pack.

To my left, the ETF's biohazard isolation truck was parked on the curb. The engine was still running. To my right, executed bodies lay in a line, bloodied and still. Beyond those dead lay many more.

And there were people like me. The infested were on their hands and knees, bending to their awful work, ripping, tearing and chewing. Downtown Toronto was a war zone. The humans had already lost the battle and the infection was spreading fast.

No, I'd been told *infection* was wrong. Hamish preferred *infestation*. A super parasite powered by microscopic robots was an *infestation*. Or maybe it was more accurate to say zombies had infested Toronto. Did that distinction really matter now? Not to me and not to the parasites. They only wanted to feed and reproduce.

So this is how the world ends, I thought. *When the aliens finally came down to Earth to check us out, they'd find a bunch of carnivorous apes that once wore clothes.*

But what would come after that? Would the zombies form tribes or herds? What would happen after the food ran out? By food, I mean the kind of meal who runs around screaming in terror and used to have dreams of owning a cottage by a lake. Would zombies end up devouring each other? Probably. Brain parasites weren't worried about contributing to a healthy human future where we could continue to enjoy trenchant HBO dramas and share amusing cat memes on Facebook.

Then I spotted her across the street: My prey was a woman

clothed in a torn blue uniform. She wore a gas mask. She carried a riot shield and a police baton. The mask obscured all her features except her hair, frizzy and matted with sweat. She must have lost her helmet.

I willed my body not to join the hunt. I didn't want to go after her, to climb on her back and smash her to the street, to feed. They say that if you don't want a wild animal to chase you down, don't run. That didn't matter. I would have gone after her even if she managed a casual stroll, I'm sure.

I experienced bodily ecstasy on par with orgasm as I sprinted after my intended victim. I'd never taken PCP, but maybe that experience would be similar. It felt that good to run, to stretch out into long loping strides. I'd never run so fast or hated myself more. I may as well have been shouting down a well for all the good my silent screams did.

She headed for the isolation truck. Powerless to stop myself, I sprinted so hard the air pumping through my lungs felt like an ice cold drink of water on a hot day. Blood thrummed in my ears. I drooled in anticipation.

The woman saw me coming, climbed in the back, and yanked the door to the isolation truck shut behind her. Trucks meant to contain hazardous materials don't lock from the inside. We lock in the threats from the outside. I grabbed the handle, threw the door open and leaped in. When I played basketball, my vertical was never this strong. I bashed into her riot shield and kept pushing to slam my victim into the compartment wall. The truck rocked beneath us as I struggled to get past the shield.

That's it! Keep that shield up! Keep it between us! I'm on your side! I'm so sorry about this. I'm not driving my own bus here. I'm so sorry!

But I was sure that, in the end, I'd kill her.

CHAPTER 2

CHLOE

I wandered through the milling crowd with a bottle of wine. The plan was to take this opportunity to meet the movers and shakers at the bio-cyber symposium. It was easier to have something to do instead of hanging out alone waiting for people to come to me.

Then a thin guy in a ridiculously shiny suit called out to me, "Wine girl? Oh, wine girl!"

I stiffened and slapped on a smile before turning to face him. He sat at the edge of the party with a large man in a cheap, ill-fitting suit. "My name is Chloe, actually! Chloe Robinson!"

"Chloe Actually! C'mere!" He raised his empty glass higher and jiggled it back and forth as if he was ringing a little bell. "I prefer 'wine girl!'"

Moron. I knew trying to be social was a shitty idea.

Thomas Dill, my boss, had told me that mingling with people after the afternoon session on medical applications for nanotech would be good for me and the company. "Make more connections. Meet more people than you would just standing around."

"I do some of my best thinking when I'm 'just standing around,'" I objected. "Besides, they'll see me as a waitress. I was a waitress in university and hated it. That's why I'm here, to get away from drunks pinching my ass."

"No one will pinch your ass. I'm simply suggesting you find a way to be a little more … approachable. You know … friendly."

"I am friendly."

"You're intimidating."

"If they're intimidated, that sounds like an Other People Problem."

"You run your own lab," Thomas said, "but connecting with colleagues and clients is part of the job, too."

"People aren't my forte. I'd rather just climb into a box and think for a few years."

"You're the youngest woman to ever hold your position at this company. Your role carries responsibilities — "

"Sounds to me like you should have promoted other young women a long time ago, then."

Thomas let out a long-suffering sigh. "A little flexibility and gratitude thrown my way would not be amiss, don't you think?"

"Gratitude? I produce results. It's an exchange. I bring a lot to the table. Yours is a suspicious proposition, Thomas."

"I don't mean to say I'm proposing — "

"Propositioning."

"Maybe you missed your calling as a lawyer, Chloe."

"If you're accusing me of being argumentative, it's only because you're giving me something I have to contend with."

Thomas cleared his throat and began again, "I flew you to Aruba with the best of intentions. I'm hoping to forge alliances and develop new accounts so — "

"The conference is shit, Thomas, but I am looking forward to hearing the Foo Fighters play. I saw a clip of Dave Grohl online doing an excellent Christopher Walken impression. Have you seen that? Grohl is the man! He's amazing."

"Why exactly is this multimillion dollar conference shit?"

"It's July in Aruba so it's hot as balls. I should be onstage talking about how my division is developing AI to optimize human hormonal performance. Instead, all these venture capitalists seem to be interested in is weapons development. These guys will be on their deathbed fretting about Islamic extremists while they die of prostate cancer. My work might cure that someday. I don't think there will ever be a cure for terrorism."

"Okay, okay." Thomas gave a smile that was supposed to placate me. "What you don't seem to understand is our weapons division funds your research."

"Short-term, long-term, I get the math. I'm good at cost-benefit analyses. It's what tells me I should be back at the lab instead of mixing with the fancy people."

"You're making me wish you were back at the lab. This is an opportunity to network. You want to talk to other researchers but it's the people with the purse strings you need to court first."

"Courting. That's an interesting turn of phrase."

"These are important people, Chloe."

"Like the guy from Dubai — Mr. Tarkasian? He's the one who asked if I was sleeping with you."

"Oh? What did you tell him?"

"I told him what I told you on that subject, Thomas."

"Ah. A hard no."

"I found it easy to say no."

"*Ouch.* What did Tarkasian say?"

"He asked if I was brought along to accommodate new customers."

"Accommodate? Meaning?"

"You know what he meant. I told him the tech I'm working on could save his life but I'd rather watch him die."

"Chloe! Jesus!"

"I came here to work and to dance to *The Pretender*. No time for assholes."

"I should have left you in your lab. You could have listened to Foo Fighters on Spotify."

When he invited me to the Aruba conference, Thomas told me

a bright light from every department would be attending. In the end, I was the only woman on the company jet and I only saw a couple of other department heads. The situation didn't sit well but I'd dealt with this sort of thing before. The head of Human Resources was on my speed dial if the flirting leveled up to anything I considered dangerous. My work was valuable to the company and I wasn't afraid to speak up. Thomas knew not to push me too far. They didn't want to lose my input and they definitely didn't want a lawsuit.

"Wine girl!"

Which brings me back to the thin guy in the shiny suit.

"Where've you been all my life, wine girl? I'm thirsty!"

"Chloe Robinson, with Prometheus Rembrandt BioSystems," I said.

"Prometheus Rembrandt. *Heh.* When companies merge, the juxtapositions can really come out ridiculous, can't they?"

"Do you want white wine?" I asked.

"White, yes."

I hefted the bottle. "That's a tragedy, I've only got red."

"You'll find a bottle of white over by the bar, honey." He brayed and looked to his silent companion. The large moon faced man was probably worth a billion but dressed like a flood victim. Though he was deep into middle age, his cheeks were marred with acne. I felt sorry for him. He wore a tragically lopsided toupee and I guessed he had no friends to tell him the truth about his artificial hair.

The big man glanced up at me a second. Our eyes met and he looked away quickly. I suddenly liked him quite a bit. He seemed to have the good sense to be embarrassed by his companion.

I took a deep breath and let it out slowly. Then I sat beside the man in the shiny suit. "What's your name, 'honey?'" I asked.

"A name you should already know. My company does enough business with yours — "

"Uh-huh. I guess you're not as famous as you think."

It was his turn to stiffen. "We are one of your company's best customers. Why don't you go fetch me that drink and we'll talk about it?"

I was furious, of course. My rage was made worse because Thomas appeared before I had a chance to call the man out on his shenanigans. My boss did not look pleased but I gave him a bright smile. I could afford to be sassy. AFTER was the next generation of technology that could save the world. I didn't understand then how urgently the world needed saving.

CHAPTER 3

DANIEL

I watched as my left hand curled around the top of the riot shield. The cop smashed my fingers with her baton. It hurt, but not as much as it should have. I tried again, faster. She attempted to smash my fingers but I was too quick for her the second time. I wrenched the shield away. She pulled the pistol from her holster and almost managed to point it at my gut. I slapped the Glock 22 out of her hand before she could pull the trigger.

I wondered what she would taste like. Had she showered recently? What if she had hepatitis or lyme disease? Would I contract it, too? If the microscopic parasites were airborne, how many people would get the disease? Would I eat her or would I bite her to make her like me? The world had changed in the space of an hour and a half. What were the new rules?

My right hand flashed out and grabbed my victim by the throat. She struck my elbow with the baton and it stung badly, as if a thousand bees buzzed up my arm.

I lunged, jaws snapping, and she recoiled with such force that she bashed her own head against the wall. She didn't drop the baton but her grip loosened enough that prying the weapon from her fingers was no more difficult than taking a stick from a determined child.

I had her. All I had to do was grab her throat again and close my fist. Then I would feed. I would feed the parasites running my brain and, if I concentrated really hard, maybe I could mouth the word *sorry* between bites.

She dropped to the truck's floor and I followed to bring my weight down, intent on pinning her. I would have killed her then but she still wore the gas mask. To my surprise, she reached for a can of mace that had been ready on the floor. She sprayed me in the face and I reeled back just as I spotted two more cops climbing into the back, riot shields held high, bearing down on me.

Two darts pierced my chest. Taser. All my muscles stiffened in torturous spasms. I fell to the deck. My fellow officers began to beat me down. *Good for them.*

The pain was bad. I waited patiently for the feeling that I was beginning to go away. It did not come quickly or easily. They hit me across the back, butt and legs too much and not enough in the head. They grunted with the effort, swinging their batons hard. I lived, impatient to die.

Someone's knee came down on the back of my neck. As I stared out the back of the truck I saw someone in a silver asbestos suit shooting a thirty-foot arm of fire from a flamethrower. Joint Task Force 2 must have arrived to incinerate the bodies in the street, torching the evidence of how the world began to end. As the man with the flamethrower burned the bodies, a sickly sweet smell permeated the air. The bad smell came from burnt hair. The sweet smell wafted up from the cooking bodies. Cannibals didn't care if their meals were raw or cooked, but the smell and noise might attract more zombies back to the epicenter of the outbreak.

I saw an amazing thing then. Startled, the man with the flamethrower looked up as a cannibal ran straight at him. It was a young woman, tall and athletic. By the way she pumped her arms as she sprinted, I had the feeling that she might have been a track star. Muscle memory is strong.

The guy with the flamethrower turned his weapon on his attacker. From ten feet out, she caught the flames straight in the face. The first thing a flamethrower does is burn off oxygen. The victim burns second. First, they asphyxiate. The woman had enough air to scream and leap.

I watched her attack unfold as if watching a movie in slow motion. Her scream echoed around the canyon formed by the office building. Her clothes were on fire and burning off her body. The arc of her leap put her above the flame. The man was too slow to react. In a movement as graceful as any Olympic athlete, she crashed into him with both feet to his chest.

He stumbled back and fell over a corpse. She was still burning as she ripped the hood from his head and tore through the thin skin of his throat and into the carotid. She only went down when someone shot her with a heavy calibre machine gun.

Seeing it all in slow motion, I had time to watch and think. I noticed the moment the hunter became the hunted. I felt the defiance in the scream of the attacker. That was not pain or anguish in her voice. That was a war cry full of power. There was something incongruous, a nuance I never would have sensed before. The cannibal's attack was a noble failure, so visceral and wild in its abandon. On the force, we always dehumanized our enemies. Here, in diseased attackers who were already barely human, I felt something new stir in me. For the first time I touched the possibility of respecting an enemy.

The harsh bite of steel cut into my wrists. I heard the ratcheting click of handcuffs secured far too tightly. The beating continued. I closed my eyes and accepted my punishment gratefully. I'd failed my mission. I deserved this.

Soon I'll lapse into unconsciousness. Then I'll be dead for real. Thank you.

This is not the apocalypse anyone expected. Endings are tricky that way. Every civilization stumbles, teeters and falls to ashes, dust and ruin. Everyone and everything falls out of memory. The surprise is that we are at all surprised.

Darkness enveloped me. *This is death*, I thought. *It's not so bad, but if I'm dead, who is thinking that death isn't so bad?*

I'd hoped I'd fade out while dreaming of my first girlfriend. She didn't wear lipstick but she wore cherry lip balm. I loved to watch her put it on and I loved the taste of cherries as I kissed it from her lips. *Cherry lip balm.* I could dream for a moment but it might feel like a thousand years if I could just hold onto that cherished memory until I blacked out and went wherever dead people go.

Anything was preferable to obsessing over the taste of the raw meat from the security guard's guts. A bright white light popped on above me but it wasn't the light at the end of a tunnel we hear of from near-death experiences. People joke about being dead on the inside. That was the hell of it: I was alive, but only on the inside.

CHAPTER 4

CHLOE

"I see you've met Dr. Robinson. Chloe, this is Doug Hannah and Michael Cavanaugh of Nyx Management Group."

"I'm Michael," the thin man said. "CFO."

He said it like he was announcing he was James Bond.

The moon faced man reached out to shake my hand. "Doug. Pleased to meet you."

"He's CEO," Cavanaugh said. Then he added, "Dr. Chloe, huh? Nice. Your parents must be very proud. Everybody's talking nanites now, it seems. I think it's the geeks who love Marvel movies that have really pushed the nerds to speed up on nanotech."

"Interesting theory, but I've been working on this research for years. Call me 'Dr. Robinson.'"

Cavanaugh didn't offer to shake my hand and I didn't mind.

There was an awkward silence before Thomas jumped in. "We're expecting big things from Chloe, very exciting developments in nano-cybernetics. She's opened up the field to new possibilities."

"Yeah, I saw the Forbes article. Nice bump to your stock,

Thomas, but I'm still waiting on a bottle of white. And the customer's always right, right?"

"Sounds like maybe you've had too much wine already, Mike," the moon faced man said.

I liked the big guy even more now. I stood, ready to tear a strip off of Mike Cavanaugh but Thomas gave me a subtle shake of his head. His pleading eyes begged me not to act like myself. "I must excuse myself, gentlemen. I think I need a real drink, maybe two." I stalked away, headed for the bar. As soon as I got to the bar, Thomas's pilot and longtime friend, Brian Parry, came up to me as I was ordering a rum and Coke. "Where's the boss? I've been trying to call. He must have turned off his phone."

He seemed agitated. I flicked my head slightly. "Back there. What's wrong?"

"We've got to head back."

"Now?"

"Sooner than now would be better, I think."

"Whatsamatter? Did Canada have a coup or something?"

"I got a call from head office. They said to tell Thomas it was Hans-Joachim Bohlmann calling."

"Sorry, I don't know that name."

"I don't, either, especially since it was a woman on the phone and Hans-Joachim sounds like a man's name to me. She told me to tell Thomas right away and then get the jet ready for takeoff."

I told Barry to get to Queen Beatrix International to warm up the jet and that we'd be along shortly.

Thomas was still schmoozing Cavanaugh when I touched his elbow. "Barry says you got a call from Hans-Joachim Bohlmann."

I could tell by his reddening cheeks that his brain had slipped a gear. "Say that again."

"Phone call. Hans-Joachim Bohlmann. You."

"That can't be right. Excuse me a moment." He ducked away and pulled out his phone.

"Bad news from the front," Cavanaugh said. "Plus, you forgot my bottle of white."

Doug Hannah cleared his throat. "Dr. Robinson? Please excuse my friend's coarse manners. I've read your research on the development of AFTER. Fascinating stuff."

Cavanaugh looked at me with new eyes. "I'm familiar with it. You do cutting edge work, I guess."

"AFTER is her baby, Mike," Doug said. "Without Dr. Robinson, there's no such thing as the new generation of organo-cybernetics. What do you expect the next big breakthrough will look like, Dr. Robinson?"

I knew there was a reason I liked him. I ignored Cavanaugh. "Call me Chloe, Doug. To answer your question, we've had success treating spinal cord injury and shutting down pain signals in mice. The possibilities are exciting."

"Word is the Chinese are using nanites to fix detached retinas in a few hours with zero recuperation time needed," Hannah said. "There's a group of Finnish researchers in Helsinki who've found the machines are better at curing arthritic knees than human stem cell treatments. Personally, I'm fascinated by the possibilities of predictive AI using this technology, but you must be in a hurry to get the biological applications to market. Speculation around intellectual performance enhancement is very hot right now."

"Yeah, I've been trying to cool that down but it's been difficult. Everybody is in too much of a hurry since that Forbes article last summer."

"You don't have anything to bring to market?" Cavanaugh made it sound like a statement rather than a question.

"With this research, we have to work using an old bodybuilding motto: make haste slowly. The committees that approve research trials and patents can't work as fast as microscopic AI, unfortunately. The biological possibilities are very exciting, though."

"What's your take on Neocortical Remodeling?" Hannah pressed. "If I was thinking of buying more stock in your company, how soon do you think you'll have NR ready for market?"

"Again, we have to proceed cautiously but that will come. We've already outsourced much of our memory capacity to our phones. We've been talking chip implants since the '80s — "

"Augmenting human intellect and man-machine symbiosis were

ideas cooked up in the '50s and '60s!" Cavanaugh said, "Time to push the accelerator through the floor and see how fast this baby can really go!"

"With AFTER, we'll skip chip implantation and go straight to nano-chemical neural enhancement, reconnecting damaged brains. Traumatic brain injuries will be a thing of the past in five to ten years."

"I think that development will come faster than that," Cavanaugh said. "Much faster."

"Better to do it right than to do it fast."

"In business, better to get there first. Take a damn chance!"

"Were you the kind of kid who blew up your high school science lab trying to fill a garbage bag full of hydrogen? There's one in every class."

Hannah guffawed. "There was a kid in high school who did that! He made his ears bleed when he lit the hydrogen. Boom! Took the summer for his eyebrows to grow back."

Cavanaugh didn't crack a smile. "I'm a numbers guy. I skipped science class."

"I see."

"You've never played sports, have you?" Cavanaugh continued. "Business is competition. Fast to market is what it's all about. Those researchers in Finland, for instance, will eat your lunch. Maybe you started this big ball rolling but you have to follow through, get it across the finish line. The potential for this technology is so immense — "

"It's always such a pleasure to have my own work explained to me, Mr. Cavanaugh," I said.

"Easy there, Michael," Hannah said. "I think what my colleague is trying to say in his clumsy way is that we are eager to change the world. I'm not as young as you are, Chloe. I want to be part of that bright utopian future this technology can provide."

As his boss tried to bring down the temperature between us, Cavanaugh gave me a smile I took as smug. He wasn't about to let up. "Forget the lab rats. If you could skip to the end, what do you want to accomplish with AFTER? One thing."

"There are many possibilities, but — "

"One. Thing."

"Very well. Imagine injecting a nano neural matrix into a surgeon's brain," I said. "The nanites could facilitate brain function. Depending on the program input, nanites could form new nerve connections or act as glial cells. The machined stem cells could support the function of the existing neurons. Over time, the relationship becomes reciprocal as the cyber learns from the organic. The surgeon uses his pre-existing knowledge base to teach the nanites as they enhance his brain function. That nano-neural matrix could even replicate itself and be recycled for the education of other doctors. Imagine getting medical training and decades of experience in a single injection. That's one of my dreams."

"Sounds great," Cavanaugh said, "until that little learning machine set loose in the surgeon's neocortex outs him as a furry. Imagine getting your medical school injection and suddenly having the urge to attend conventions in Vegas where you dress up like a squirrel and poop in a box in the lobby." He cackled. "Sounds like fun!"

I took a breath. "First, that's kink shaming. Second, you came up with such a weirdly specific example, I think you've overshared. Third, that's why we have to go through ethics committees. We proceed cautiously, setting limits on the tech so we aren't giving subjects astrocytomas all over the place. I don't want AFTER giving anybody a brain tumor because we rushed to market. There's lots of space in brain cavities for nanites to snuggle in and do their work. Statistically, condescending men who call grown women 'girl' have even more space in their skull for nanotech. There's hope for you, Mr. Cavanaugh, is what I'm saying."

Doug Hannah roared with laughter while his seatmate reddened. "You've got sharp edges!" the CEO crowed. "Are you sure you haven't already enhanced yourself?"

"No. First rule of experimentation: Don't stick nanites in your head for gits and shiggles. Drink the wrong potion and you get a Dr. Jekyll and Mr. Hyde situation. If I could change anything about me, I guess I'd make myself taller, but not even AFTER can do that yet.

Anyway, we work with rats because we can easily keep them in a cage."

Cavanaugh folded his arms. "You're a rat runner but you've got no vision."

Hannah leaned close to Cavanaugh's ear. "Michael, that's enough. Apologize. Now."

Cavanaugh looked like a scolded schoolboy. "Sorry. I'm a passionate person. Sometimes my mouth gets out ahead of my brain."

"Often," Hannah said. "It does that often."

"I thrive on competition — "

Hannah gave him a warning look and Cavanaugh stared at the floor. I could tell by the way his jaw muscles flexed that he was barely holding back another insult.

I was glad I'd said something mean. "You asked me if I played sports, Mr. Cavanaugh. I played softball as a kid. I liked it. My friends at school grooved on the Jays but, for some reason, I always thought of the White Sox as my team, not sure why. Maybe I just liked the black baseball cap. Anyway, your analogy is all wrong about what I do. Business is sports for guys in suits who don't have the joy of running around chasing a ball anymore."

"We're all in the same game," Cavanaugh said.

"Maybe you're playing a game," I said. "With nanotech, I'm playing God. Gotta be careful with that. Look how much there is to fix. You need fixing, for one tiny example."

CHAPTER 5

DANIEL

I swam out of a fog and into a haze. I'd had surgery for a wrenched rotator cuff once so I recognized this feeling. I'd been sedated. It took some time to arrive at consciousness but, when awareness hit, everything pulled into sharp focus fast. I woke up in a hospital restrained at my wrists and ankles.

I knew where I was before I opened my eyes. I have always hated the aroma of hospitals but now the smells were worse. I could sense the stench beneath the industrial cleaners, the sins those chemicals were supposed to eradicate. Mostly, I smelled fear. Fear has a tang. It leaches out of people with their perspiration. Without opening my eyes, I could tell the woman guarding me had sweaty palms.

"This one was ETF," the woman told someone by the door, someone whose breath pulled and pushed heavily. "Look at all that blood on his chin and chest. A nurse cleaned him up a bit but he was like a pig at a trough."

I opened my eyes. The blinds were drawn. It was now dark. My fellow officers had taken me down in the early afternoon. The officer standing beside my gurney was the one I'd tried to kill in the isolation truck. She still wore a gas mask but now she wore a hospital gown over her uniform. The overweight cop who stood at the exit almost filled the doorway. Were he not so tall, he wouldn't be fit for active duty. He wore an N95 mask over his face. The mask looked woefully inadequate compared to the woman's gas mask. That's probably why he hung back by the door.

"What have you heard, Don?" the woman asked.

"Lots of radio chatter but not much of it makes sense."

"How so?"

"I don't know. People are running around tackling people, chewing on them like it's cannibal football. Sometimes they stay and eat like it's Thanksgiving at Grandma's house. Other times they bite and move on. Then the people they bite get …sick, y'know?"

"I know. I was there."

"The fresh victims start biting other people if we don't shoot 'em first."

"I know, Don."

"Creepy, huh? Like rabies for people or something."

"Or something. You know what it sounds like, right?"

"Sure, I watched *The Walking Dead*, right up until that guy took a baseball bat to Glen. Didn't seem to be much point in watching after that."

"You were a huge Glen fan?"

The big cop shrugged. "If there's no hope, why keep going?"

"I'll keep that in mind when the zombie hordes come."

"Don't even joke about that."

"It's a disease," the female cop replied. "My first year in, we were dealing with SARS. It was a huge pain in the ass every time I had to deal with somebody in the ER. We'll get through this."

"If not for the PATH, we could have kept this contained easy," the big cop said. "Once they got underground and started infecting office workers in a food court — "

"The food court menu improved?"

"You're a pill, Shelly."

"Thanks, Don."

"Funny you took that as a compliment."

Someone screamed outside the hospital, maybe a block away. Neither cop seemed to hear the noise but I could. My stomach growled and the cop named Shelly looked at me. "He's awake."

I looked at her as I tested my restraints. I knew better but apparently the organo-nanites infesting my brain wanted to know the limits of the thick leather straps that pinned me to the gurney.

"Easy, there, Hannibal. I'm Shelly Priyat, the cop you tried to kill downtown."

If I could speak, I would have apologized.

"Do you know where you are, ETF?"

I don't know if I could have even managed much of a nod. The strap across my forehead ensured I couldn't lunge. I understood her reference to *Silence of the Lambs* when I felt the mouthguard with my tongue. It covered the lower half of my face.

"They don't talk," the cop in the doorway said. "They growl."

"You don't have to tell me. I bagged this one myself."

"Alone?"

"I had a little help. The OC spray really did the job."

She was right. The pepper spray she used on me still burned my eyes, nose and throat. In the enclosed space in the back of the isolation van, there was no way of getting out of the searing cloud. Heightened senses of taste and smell are not always advantageous.

"Still took three of us," Shelly admitted.

"Why didn't you just shoot him between the eyes? It discourages bad boys who get handsy," Don said.

"After I pepper sprayed the bastard we pinned him down with riot shields."

And beat me with batons. I could feel the ache of deep bruises welling up on my neck and shoulders.

"The brass want guinea pigs so they can find a cure. The Public Health Agency is mobilizing to get into the lab where this shit came from. They must have a cure down there. You can't build a murder machine that doesn't have an off switch."

They don't have an off switch, I thought. *We murder machines have no off switch.*

155

"The docs will figure it out," Don said. "There's hope."

I tried to shake my head. We'd killed Dr. Hamish Allen. The bioengineer with all the answers about weaponized brain parasites was way too dead to be helpful now.

"How you feeling, ETF? You hungry? Wanna take me out for a quick bite?"

I looked her up and down, considering her. The big one would make a full meal.

I heard another scream from outside, closer now. Then came the gunfire. I couldn't make out the words but I caught the tone. Angry orders were being shouted and ignored. Then came screams of pain, screams of rage, fear, then more pain. Finally, there was anguish. That pattern always ends in anguish.

Shelly and Don could hear the pounding feet outside now, too. Shelly had a bit of swagger before. Now she shifted her weight back and forth from foot to foot nervously. Sweat trickled down the small of her back, too. Her face was stone but I could smell her fear.

My people are coming, I thought. *No, not my people. My pack.*

"Look at his eyes," Shelly said. "ETF sure looks like he has something to say."

Neither cop could understand my warning. If they hadn't strapped the mouthguard to my face, they could have read my lips when I mouthed one word: *Run.*

CHAPTER 6

CHLOE

Despite the tension in the air, Hannah was genuinely interested in my work. "Would you go for local or bluetooth to the Cloud for the data storage?"

"The Cloud, without doubt. Easier to install updates that way. Nobody wants fresh brain surgery every time Apple comes out with a new iteration."

Doug was excited to talk about his work, too. "Nyx is working on several fronts."

"You mentioned predictive AI?"

"Before I die, my stockbroker will absolutely be an AI with a nano brain. In the meantime, Nyx is working on gene modification applications. For instance, the potential for limb regeneration is staggering."

"We're going to make soldiers from Iowa into Deadpool," Cavanaugh said. "Bet they won't be as funny as Ryan Reynolds, but I'm sure it'll work out fine."

Hannah ignored his employee's jokes. "One of our people has a piece coming up in *Nature* on how the process could be sped up. If we can't figure it out, I'm sure nano AI will."

Cavanaugh let out an impatient grunt. "The AI can splice some genes and regrow an amputated arm after it's blown off by an IED. I'm more interested in the potential to cut off soldier's arms and legs in boot camp. Give them superior capabilities with cybernetics."

Hannah seemed more annoyed than embarrassed now. "Actually, Michael, the division that interests me most is nanites replacing computer cores."

"Tell me more about that," I said.

"Each core could be a living matrix that emulates human brain function, but much faster. No more disks or solid state but a living core for every computer."

Cavanaugh sobered and nodded, perhaps a little contrite at last. "Well, yes, that's coming along swimmingly. Since nanites are technically alive, we'll have to pop open the top of a desktop and feed them like goldfish but — "

"We're so far along with that tech already that Michael has forgotten his fishbowl joke has become stale. It's getting kind of lame, don't you think, Mike?"

Cavanaugh smiled tightly. "Yes, sir. I'll get some new material."

"Nanite computer cores," I marveled. "I'm focused on the biological applications but I'd be fascinated to hear more."

"That research is proprietary and isn't ready for mass consumption," Cavanaugh said. "However, as a potential client, I would like to discuss AFTER's military applications."

"Military applications?"

"Sure. Between the ages of 18 and 22, you can order a soldier to take a hill and they'll go get that real estate. After age 22, they start to think for themselves too much. The more their testosterone drops, the more they start to think. AFTER could jack into their limbic systems, get them to follow commands without thought or fear."

"Mind control? Really? You think that's a good idea?"

"I'd frame it as situational control."

"That's an avenue that's fraught with ethical problems."

Cavanaugh shrugged. "Ethics are malleable and change over

time. AFTER is a good start but you people are thinking about it as if you're Bill Gates. I'm thinking like Zuckerberg. I see the future. The future is always closer than you think."

I wanted to smack Cavanaugh's smug smile off this face. Instead, I pretended to have adult composure and replied, "I don't follow your analogy."

"Who do you think the most powerful person in the world is?"

"If you're talking money, Putin has the most of that. Musk has some of the most powerful ideas. My mother would say Oprah but, then again, Mom makes an amazing salmon salad sandwich. That's pretty powerful when I'm hungry. You have an answer in mind so just tell me already."

"Zuckerberg. Facebook started out as an app to rate hot college girls and now it influences elections. Our echo chambers determine what we believe. Anything we don't want to hear, we unfriend and unfollow."

"What does that have to do with AFTER?" I asked.

"What comes next? With a nano drive, we will outpace all existing computing. Imagine controlling the internet with one powerful nano drive." Hannah said.

Cavanaugh chuckled. "Imagine a world where you can't unfriend or unfollow the things you don't believe. After that? Imagine a nano drive jacking into brains enhanced with your nanites. It sounds to me like — "

"Hell? That sounds like Hell."

"Heaven. Peace on Earth. Civilization is based on rules. If we can make everyone adhere to the same rules, everything unfolds as it should, smoothly."

"Sounds like a utopian prophet's dream and a gift to dictators, doesn't it?" Hannah said. "I think it could work as long as we program the nano drive with the brain of a benevolent dictator."

"If the civilized world wants to keep the new tech out of the hands of dictators, all they have to do is outbid the bad guys," Cavanaugh said. "We're going to get paid."

I saw something unspoken pass between them I didn't like. They were talking like they'd already developed a nano drive. "Outbid? Are you guys already working on prototypes?"

Cavanaugh waved me away. "Plenty of labs are working on projects parallel or similar to AFTER. Neural control tech is an idea whose time has come. It's a race to get to the first working rollout. Some friendly advice, don't wait too long or think too small. You want to cure disease? Get paid for the military applications first. That's where the real money is."

"Somehow, your advice doesn't sound friendly."

"Don't be so sensitive. What you're hearing is the gap between a businessman talking to a scientist. We should set up a meeting. A dozen guys here are interested in AI for robotic defense applications but that's still in early development. For my money, it's the organic possibilities that will pay off big in the next decade. AFTER's potential leapfrogs your projected profit curve if you have the guts to forge ahead quickly. What do you say we take this discussion up to my room? I'm interested in your positions — "

And there it was. That's what all the pontificating and bragging was about. Getting me into bed. "No, thanks. I don't think you and I would be a good fit."

From the look on his face, Cavanaugh didn't hear the word *no* often.

Thomas grabbed my elbow hard. "Gotta go," the boss said.

"Mr. Cavanaugh and I were having an exchange of ideas. He was telling me how he wants to use my work to kill and control people cheaply and efficiently and I was about to suggest he do something that's physically impossible."

"Get over it. Let's go." Thomas pulled me away and ushered me toward the exit.

I shrugged him off. "What's going on? And who the hell is Hans-Joachim Bohlmann?"

He leaned close to whisper in my ear. "Bohlmann was a mental patient who damaged paintings. He targeted great art, sprayed sulfuric acid on faces painted by masters. It's code. It means there's a certain type of emergency I didn't think we'd ever have to face."

Thomas used his wealth to collect expensive art. I didn't have to ask who made up the code. "So? What's happened?"

"It's still happening, right now, as we speak. An incident at one of the labs."

"What?"

"We've lost containment at Echidna."

"What's Echidna?"

"One of our weapons divisions."

"And what do you mean by 'lost containment?' You lose a gun?"

"MCE."

"Do you speak English?"

"Mass Casualty Event."

"Oh, my God! Are we talking nerve gas or something?"

"Something."

"You're scaring me, Thomas. Is it something *bigger* than nerve gas? Is it bigger than a breadbox? Shut up and talk!"

"The event is biological. A response team went in to get the lab under control while the weapon's trigger was still underground. Somehow, the seals didn't hold. I can't imagine how all the safeties failed. The last solid news we got from the lab is some idiot sent an email to his sister warning her away. There are civilian reports of gunfire and a riot outside the lab. The lab's gone dark and the bug is out of the vault. It's spreading."

CHAPTER 7

DANIEL

The screams were getting closer. The cannibals had obviously made their way to the hospital. The police officers guarding me didn't seem to be able to understand the approaching chaos.

A woman's voice came over the public address system in the corridor. "Dr. White, report to the ER. Dr. White, STAT."

Only a moment passed before the woman called for Dr. White to report the ER again, adding, "Dr. White to the Chrysanthemum Room."

A young nurse hurried down the hallway and beckoned to the big cop. "Can you help out in the ER? They just called Code White, violent patient."

I wondered what the code would be if they actually had a doctor named White.

"You don't think hospital security can handle it?" Don asked.

"Not when they use 'chrysanthemum.' There is no such room. I've rarely heard that code actually used and I've worked here eight years. It means staff are injured." The nurse looked at the coffee cup in his hand meaningfully. Her face told me she was thinking:

You're not doing anything useful up here, anyway. "Could you please check it out?"

He looked to the cop at my side. "All good here, Shelly?"

She looked at me, almost amused. "Sure. ETF is strapped in tight, Don. Unless his illness gives him magic powers, we're fine."

"Yeah, he doesn't look like no Penn and Teller to me."

"Go."

The cop nodded and hurried away. His retreating footfalls sounded heavy. By the look of him, he weighed maybe 260 pounds. By the smell that wafted away in the air conditioned air after he left, I guessed something was wrong with him. I had an intuition that, though he'd make a good meal, I shouldn't eat his liver.

I wondered where that thought came from. Funny, until I became the observer of events instead of a participant, I had never wondered where thoughts came from. Trapped in my body and doing things at the whim of a brain parasite, Time itself seemed to slow down and stretch out. I had lots of time to notice things and think about them. If this continued, I was in for a boring existence. What was I supposed to do if I couldn't do anything? Is this what coma patients did all day? Think about what to think about?

Shelly came closer to stare in my eyes.

I could still smell the fear. She wasn't particularly afraid of me in that moment but the screams outside (and coming inside) sped her heartbeat. Bravery doesn't mean fear is not felt. It means we experience fear but do what needs to done. At that moment, Shelly was more curious than she was afraid.

"Hey. Mr. Monster. Don's right, you don't look like a magician. You don't look like anything special … but … how come you aren't caterwauling and growling like the rest of the crazies? You're not looking so wild now. When I pepper sprayed you, did the doggie get disciplined? You don't want to kill me anymore? You sure tried hard in the back of that van."

I stared back. Hers was a good question. I wanted to think the parasites infesting my brain decided to go away and find someone else to make their puppet. That wasn't the answer, though. As soon as I awoke, I'd tested the straps at my wrists. There was little chance of escape and, somehow, the Picasso strain knew better than to try.

The idea that a brain parasite could make decisions seemed ridiculous at first. However, the zombies seemed to have a knack for going after weaknesses. Predators go for the weakest and easiest kill of any herd. I didn't give Picasso credit for much intelligence but there was something deeper going on. I remembered an old movie title: *Faster, Pussycat! Kill! Kill!* Apparently, the brain parasites were capable of more nuance than a Russ Meyer film from 1965.

Then I remembered the woman who attacked Patrick Davis in the Box. She didn't have the mass to take Patrick down in a straight tackle but she had not tried that. She'd moved with the grace of a gymnast, diving over him and wrenching the hood from his biohazard suit. She made him vulnerable to the best attack she could mount. She'd used strategy to bite his face and take his eyes. Would a wild dog be that clever? What had Hamish unleashed on us?

Strapped to a gurney, maybe I was the luckiest of the afflicted. I'd chewed on a couple of people who were already dead. I hadn't killed a human unless I counted Mac, but the ETF Staff Sergeant had sent me on a suicide mission into the Box. Maybe I should have felt bad about that but I didn't. I'd perforated his protective suit with a bullet so the bastard could share my fate. The bio-weapon had already gone airborne. If I hadn't got him, someone else probably would have.

Now that I was stuck in a hospital, maybe there was a chance I could be cured. Were brain parasites operable? Would chemo-therapy rid me of Hamish's "little beasties?" Brain surgery? A good whack to the head?

But no brilliant brain surgeon was coming to save me. The doctors were downstairs, getting eaten.

CHAPTER 8

CHLOE

Thomas broke into a sweat as if he had just returned from a long run on a humid day. "What got out exactly?"

"Something bad."

"But what's it do?"

"Imagine spending every minute we're alive expecting to be attacked."

"So … like Twitter? More weaponized?"

"Not funny, Chloe."

"It was a little funny."

"If we don't get on top of this, we'll lose everything. I'm talking about a trip back to the Dark Ages, trying to live off cabbage soup and tears."

"How?"

"It's biological kill tech with a potential casualty ratio on a level of *The Walking Dead*."

I pulled a chair toward me and sat down, taking a moment to gather my thoughts. Thomas knelt beside me. "It's spreading. We have to get ahead of it. I need you to come back with me to Toronto."

"So ... no Foo Fighters tonight?"

"I'm afraid not."

"You know what bothers me most about the zombie apocalypse?" I asked. "Say a mysterious comet goes over or a witch's curse is unleashed or something equally stupid. In all those stories, people forget to lie down when they die and get hungry for brains. But what about the dead who get trapped in their graves? That's a lot of poor old dead grandmothers banging and clawing at the inside of their coffins in the dark, isn't it? Chew on that visual for a full minute and you'll soon feel the need to pee while you're crying. I kind of feel that urge now. What were you thinking even trying to put something like that together, Thomas? Some weapons are too dangerous to even think about and you were manufacturing one?"

"Chloe, what's done is done. Some of the stuff they were working on at Echidna can turn people into cannibals. It's the ECPSD project."

"I'm gonna need the English subtitles."

"Enemy Combatant Pacification Strategic Defense."

"You know military applications are not my thing. You *know* that. Whenever you guys talk defense, you really mean offense, as in, offense to all that's holy. It's in my contract that I will not participate in weapons development. You go. Fix it. I'll try to get you an autograph from Dave Grohl — "

"The Echidna team is down. I need your brains, Chloe. We're forming a new ERG to work the problem."

"ERG?"

"Emergency Response Group."

"What is it with you guys and acronyms? Does it make you feel better? More official and legit or something?"

"Chloe, sometimes your moods are — "

"Stormy? Unpredictable?"

"Yeah, you're positively meteorological. For Christ's sake! I know you don't have a healthy respect for hierarchy but I am your boss—"

"Doug Hannah from Nyx seems like a friendly billionaire. I betcha I could have a new job about a minute from now. Wanna bet?"

Thomas stared at me for a cold moment. Then the truth bubbled up. "Echidna is using AFTER."

"What?"

"Your research belongs to the company, Chloe. Don't get your back up about this — "

"My back is up and my ass is out of joint, Thomas. What exactly did you do with my baby?"

He took a deep breath. "The agents we use to make monsters were enhanced with the help of your nanites."

"Agents?"

"Parasites."

"You enhanced *parasites*?"

"Enhanced them, weaponized them. The distinction is mostly semantic."

I felt like I'd swallowed ice cubes. "What kind of parasites did you weaponize, Thomas?"

"Brain parasites."

I gasped. "As in, the opposite of what I was put on Earth to do."

"The weapons division paid for your new electron microscope. You're a genius, Chloe, but you're not as good at cost-benefit analysis as you think you are. Forget the bio-weapon aspect. It's a disease and you're still in the curing business. Are you in or out because we need a cure."

"Zombie apocalypse, huh?" I took a deep breath and let it out slowly through my teeth. "What's the vector?"

"Airborne."

Despite Aruba's heat, my feet and hands suddenly went cold.

"I don't have all the data yet, of course, but — "

"Any good news?"

"They have a subject in custody. He seems to have contracted the parasite, one of the SWAT guys. They're holding him in an isolation unit at St. Mike's. We'll transfer the patient to a company containment lab in Aurora. I've got to call Ottawa, Washington,

Atlanta, the insurance company, the Board … oh, my lord, it's a mess."

"Anything else I should know?"

"That's pretty much it except it goes without saying this exposes the company to a ton of liability issues. This is all confidential."

"Yeah, yeah, I get the top secret bit. We're not even having this conversation right now, are we? But, Thomas, if I save the world, I'm gonna want the world to know. If I don't save it, I want you to get the blame."

"Scold me on the flight, if you want. I don't have time for it now. They're calling me back with more numbers in — " He checked the time on his phone. "Twenty-one minutes. We should be wheels up in thirty. So? In or out?"

"Go. I'll meet you at the car."

"Leave your bags. We don't have time to — "

"Get them to bring a car around, then. I'll be right there. If this is the end of the world, I've got one last thing I have to do for myself first."

I pushed Thomas toward the door and rushed back to the bar. I waved to the handsome young bartender with slicked back hair and neat beard. "What's the most expensive white wine you have back there?"

He didn't hesitate. "*Coche-Dury Corton-Charlemagne Grand Cru.*"

"That was quick."

"It's a twenty-three hundred dollar bottle of white, Madam, more than my mother and father made in their lifetimes." He brought out the bottle and held it up for me to see the label.

"I'll need the whole bottle."

"From which company are you, Madam?"

I gave him a huge smile. "Put this one on Mr. Cavanaugh's tab, from Nyx Management. He's right over there by the wall. He asked me to bring it to him. See? The thin shit in the shiny suit? Thin shit in the shiny suit. Thin shit in the shiny suit. Say that five times fast, I dare you."

The bartender chuckled. "I have met Mr. Cavanaugh. I under-stand what you mean about him."

"Can you pop the cork on that bad boy, please?"

The bartender did as I asked and offered me a glass. I did not sip it. I knocked it back fast. It tasted okay.

The bartender quirked an eyebrow. "Miss? Would you prefer a silver tray and more glasses for your friends?"

I shook my head. "No, thanks. I've got something to do that I just put up on my vision board." I scooped up the bottle before stalking back to Hannah and Cavanaugh.

"Doug? I see your glass is empty. It's the finest wine they have on hand."

"Uh, thank you, Chloe."

I poured Hannah a generous amount. "I've got to go back to Toronto. I've just discovered Thomas stabbed me in the back and then in the chest. What I'm saying is, I have to go off and save the world now. If we live through this, I'll be sending you my resume."

"Oh. Ah." Hannah mulled this for a moment before replying, "If you save the world, I'll certainly look forward to that job interview."

Cavanaugh held out his empty glass. "What's this bullshit, wine girl?"

"It could be the world's end," I said. "If that's the case, my thinking is we shouldn't leave anything undone." I reached for his belt and took the buckle in my fist. "Stand up, Mike. I'm so sorry I didn't know who you were before."

Cavanaugh gave me a reptilian smile as I pulled him to his feet. "You looking for a job from me, too? Maybe you should give me a job — "

I yanked the buckle toward me and shoved the upturned bottle of wine down his pants. He let out a shriek as he tried to extricate the bottle. Too late. The cold wine poured out. He looked very much like he'd pissed himself.

The party stopped. Every eye turned to watch us. People snatched up their phones to take video. He was still cursing as I walked away. "Michael Cavanaugh from Nyx, everybody! Colossal douche! Hashtag that on Instagram! " I shouted grandly. "Congratulations, Mike! Everybody will remember you now! Drink up, everyone! And, tonight, do what you always wanted to do! It's probably the end of the world, anyway!"

On my way out, the young bartender gave me a big grin and a thumbs-up.

CHAPTER 9

DANIEL

I heard the commotion in the stairway. Feet pounded up the steps. When people run scared, they're lighter on their feet and push off from their toes. Angry and hungry people hit the ground hard with their heels. I'd chased people down alleys occasionally. I'd never noticed that distinction before.

Since I was vulnerable and tied to the gurney, I wondered if my fellow cannibals would attack me first. My heart did not race. I guessed they wouldn't come for me. What were the rules? It wasn't professional courtesy. It was as if the parasites we carried in our skulls were on a mission to feed but also to make more of themselves as quickly as possible. Poor Shelly Priyat. There I was, an easy zombie buffet, but they would chase her, take her down and eat her alive.

My ETF team brought in an American fugitive once, a serial killer named Grant Bray. He'd slipped across the border at Port Huron unrecognized. However, a Union Station ticket taker for VIA rail recognized him from a poster and called police.

Bray was a cannibal killer who'd eluded capture for years

because, as a long-haul trucker, he never stayed in one place long. He seemed to strike on impulse when opportunities presented themselves. His targets were usually hitchhikers, men and women alike. Sometimes he killed kids. He didn't see people as people, only targets. He might have murdered for years more but we caught a lucky break. One of his intended victims was a young woman on a lonely road in Indiana. When he attacked her, she smashed a Coke bottle and ground the jagged ends into his face.

When Bray bought a ticket for Montreal, the ragged bandage on his cheek tipped off the VIA Rail employee. As I watched him in a crowded waiting area, the cannibal killer sat quietly with a backpack between his feet. He read a *Globe & Mail* and sipped coffee, just another traveler, unremarkable except for the bandage on his face. I imagined him out in the world, driving past public parks, past schools, picking up trusting strangers. The half of his face that was undamaged could be any face in a crowd. He wasn't memorable for being particularly handsome or ugly. The woman who got away said he was perfectly nice until the moment he tried to strangle her with an electrical cord he kept by the driver's seat.

We wanted to take him down in a tight, controlled space with only one exit so we delayed the train. We waited for him to go to the bathroom. When biology finally made its demand, I followed him in and waited until he was in a toilet stall. Two of us quietly guided a couple of innocent bystanders away from the urinals. We waited for him to finish his shit. When Bray emerged, he found me in plain-clothes. The rest of the team waited for him in full tactical gear.

I'll never forget how casual he was as he raised his hands. "Hi, guys. What's up? It's about time."

It was in that moment I understood how banal violent sociopaths can appear. He looked so normal. No scary face tattoos or weird behavior that would suggest he was a sadistic killer who fried up body parts as a grisly hobby. His smile was broad and his manner amiable. No wonder hitchhikers felt comfortable climbing into his cab. His M.O. was to offer them a spiked drink — usually a Coke or a Red Bull. Later, the victim would wake up in the back of his truck with their feet and hands zip tied. Steve Taylor pulled a sandwich bag of fingers and toes from Bray's backpack. The killer laughed and told us he always began with the ears.

Call it evil or label it the work of a brain gone bad, that was one of my most frightening days on the Emergency Task Force. It wasn't the fingers and toes that kept me awake all that night. It was how ordinary Grant Bray seemed. He could have been anybody's brother, son or husband. It was easier to picture motorcycle gangs and psychos with lots of prison tattoos as The Big Bad. If Grant Bray could pass for a normal and decent human being, another person like him could be anywhere. In any mall, coffee shop or home, the one you trust handing you a Coke could be another killer.

I told myself not to become paranoid, but of course, I did. Seeing the worst in people every day is enough to make anyone cynical. Now, as I lay there under guard, it occurred to me that life was about to get much simpler. No one would have to watch out for killers coming from out of the shadows. We zombies announce we're coming with shrieks and growls. Anybody could be a munching murderer. You know you're close to the end of the world when the extraordinary becomes so ordinary.

Even in the apocalypse, though, not all dangers barreling at the uninfected are quite so obvious. In the case of Constable Don Roberts, he staggered into my hospital room bleeding from the chin, forearm and neck.

Shelly ran to him, "Don? Don! What happened?"

"I pulled some people off some other people and no one was grateful. I ended up hitting more people just to get out of there. Some of them hit back. It's crazy down there," he panted. "The whole ER has gone nuts. It wasn't even the patients. A doctor and a nurse tried to bite me."

"It's here," Shelly said.

"If I get bit, am I going to turn into one of them?"

Probably, I thought. *I think that's how this works. Haven't you people ever seen a movie in your damn lives?*

Short of breath, Don clutched his chest. "Jesus, I think I'll have a heart attack first. They're crazy down there! Call for backup!"

"No use calling for backup," Shelly said. "Not when everybody needs backup at the same time. But I've got an idea."

Priyat left Don's side for a moment and disappeared into the corridor. A moment later, a fire alarm sounded. It was a flat, low beep.

When she returned, Don looked at her, his face ashen and shiny with sweat. "Think it will help to call in the bucketheads and basement savers?"

"Calling the Fire Department isn't the point. Shutting down the elevators to buy time is the goal."

Don shook his head. "The elevators will still work."

"Only for authorized personnel with a card or a key." Shelly held up an elevator key from her key ring. "In the movies, zombies don't use elevators."

She was right. However, rampaging zombies could use stairs. My brand of monster is fast and not so stupid that an unlocked door could stop us. Our ranks would soon arrive on our floor.

Most people confined to hospital beds are either elderly or weakened. As a mob of cannibal killers tore into their prey, many patients discovered they still had enough energy to scream in terror and agony. Below us, perhaps one floor away, maybe two, I could hear the death cries of the vulnerable.

Upside: You can only be eaten alive for a short while before you're dead. If I were selling swag for the zombie apocalypse, I'd put that line on the t-shirts.

CHAPTER 10

CHLOE

The flight time from Aruba to Toronto Pearson International was five and a half hours. Thomas and I were the only passengers on the Challenger jet. I gave my boss the silent treatment the whole way. It pissed me off that he didn't seem to mind that I was fuming.

Thomas spent most of the flight on his phone. When he spoke to government officials, he was polite and obsequious. When he started slinging orders at employees, he was an impatient bully. I'd never seen this side of him. Now that I had, I was sure that if I got through the ordeal ahead I'd leave Prometheus Rembrandt. I had no idea Thomas Dill was such a shit.

We arrived at Pearson just after four in the morning. I'd never seen so many planes on the ground. Some aircraft were parked out on the runways. I hoped there weren't still passengers stuck out there, sweating and claustrophobic.

Thomas talked to our pilot as if he were a bad dog. "Stay with the plane in case we need you to evacuate. No matter what they tell you, stay with the plane."

RCMP officers waited for us at a private gate. The arrivals area was deserted, not even Customs officers manned the booths in the security area.

"Looks like the Rapture," I said.

The female RCMP officer ignored me but the male gave me a serious look that made me think he wasn't comfortable with my end of the world observation. "The Rapture would be a clean, bloodless end. I wish we were only dealing with piles of clothes and people left behind. I saw the CCTV feed from Dundas Street. It's a lot scarier than the Rapture."

The cops escorted us through Security to a VIP lounge. I'd left my bags at the Ritz-Carlton in Aruba so I was still in my party dress when we met the official from the Public Health Agency.

When we walked up to him, he said, "Ken Rigg," as if his name should mean something to us. He wore a surgical mask, blue nitrile gloves and goggles that looked very out of place considering the rest of his attire was a double breasted suit. He didn't ask for introductions and he did not shake our hands. "I'm in charge of the scene downtown. We're coordinating with CDC. They've volunteered to send up a couple of experts in pork tapeworm."

"Excuse me, I'm Dr. Chloe Robinson."

"I know."

So much for pleasantries. "How would pork tapeworm be relevant, Mr. Rigg?"

"*Dr.* Rigg," he said stiffly. "Your expertise is cybernetics." He said *cybernetics* as if the word tasted bad, as if it wasn't the inevitable future of humankind.

"Nanotech, yes."

"Pork tapeworm is the most common source of parasitic infection of the brain. *Taenia solium* infects 50,000,000 worldwide and is the most common cause of brain seizures. I like pork but I tend to overcook it, just to be safe."

"Fifty million?"

"It's not one of the sexy diseases that gets a lot of attention and research funding but it's pretty special, yes."

Rigg addressed Thomas. "The Prime Minister declared Toronto

a disaster area a couple of hours ago. He'll address the nation on CBC tonight."

Thomas paled. "So it's not bottled up, at all? No improvement?"

"It's spreading as fast as a person can run and it's not just the infected that are the problem. We've got riots around the edges of the GTA, people try to get out and away even though they are nowhere near the Red Zone. We expect significant loss of life from the secondary effects of the outbreak."

"What do you consider secondary effects?" I asked.

"Panic. Given the huge area involved, people will get out. It's highly unlikely that Torontonians outside of downtown are infected but the panic is spreading. Panic can kill as many people as a disease."

"How is the panic spreading faster than the core problem?" Thomas asked.

"Social media. Twitter crashed but Facebook is spreading the news. Instagram is a horror show. It's cannibal porn. Panic yields car accidents, hit and runs, heart attacks, looting. Panic is another infection, spreading faster than any disease can."

Thomas put some bass in his voice, trying to reassert control. "Can't you shut that shit down?"

"No," Rigg replied firmly. "Monitoring reports from the ground via social media is the most reliable data we have."

Thomas was sweating heavily again. "What data points are worth the panic?"

"We can observe symptoms from video and we know that to the east, it's spread to the Eaton Centre. The outbreak has spread eight blocks down Queen Street West, last I checked. Communication lines are down and, since everyone is on their phones, cell phones aren't working reliably. The city perimeter is too big to keep everybody in so we really need to get a handle on rates of infection."

"What's your preliminary data suggest?" I asked.

"The affected area doubles roughly every two hours. It moves faster in some areas. We don't understand why. That's why you're here instead of safe in Aruba."

"The person I spoke to from the Toronto Police said there was a blue mist," Thomas said. "That's the aerosolized version of the … " — he paused to choose his words carefully — "the agent."

Rigg smirked, eschewing the euphemism. "After the *weapon* was released, people in the area reported flu-like symptoms. The transition period seems very short. They become violent, psychotic and mute."

"We tagged the aerosol droplets blue to measure potential spread by weather patterns in battlefield conditions. If not for the blue tag, the police wouldn't have seen the release of Picasso at all."

"Did you put it through a wind tunnel?" I asked.

"Of course, we did," Thomas said. "Marketing said we had to have dispersal data. It's supposed to spread via the air but become inert quickly. Below a thousand parts per million, Picasso doesn't spread anymore. That way, it's not carried on air currents to stay lethal forever. The targeted area shouldn't be larger than a square mile, depending on meteorological factors like heat and humidity."

"If it's supposed to go away that easily, how has it gotten so bad?" I asked.

"It was supposed to be used on a village, not a city," Thomas said. "If the spread was confined to the airborne vector, we wouldn't have the problem we do."

"It's spreading through person to person contact now," Rigg said.

Thomas bobbed his head. "The nanites were programmed correctly for that one test. The aim was to sell the agent so it could be used as leverage, maybe a last resort. We never really thought it would actually be used in a combat situation, not beyond that damned test."

"Your aim, huh? You aim was way off," I said. "Has there ever been a weapon that wasn't used at some point?" The use of the words *person to person contact* sounded like a dangerous euphemism. I asked Rigg what he meant.

"We have observed that, after an infected person bites another, the time it takes for them to become psychotic and violent varies. We don't know the time range from contact to actively contagious."

"You mean you don't know how long it takes any individual to go zombie."

"I wouldn't put it that way."

"I prefer plain speaking," I said. "It titrates the bullshit to a lesser dose."

"We're all on the same side here," Thomas said. "We're going to get through this. Has there been any message from Ottawa about funding the cleanup for this mishap?"

"This is a little more than an oil spill in a remote area, Dr. Dill. It's a disaster on the way to a full balls up, wouldn't you say?" Rigg sighed. "God knows how many escaped by boat from Queen's Quay before the police marine services started shutting down the lake. It's an impossible task — "

"Prometheus Rembrandt Biosystems took every precaution in our technology development— " Thomas said.

"Weapons development," Rigg corrected him. "Save it for the press release. This situation has a chance at being resolved faster if you are completely honest with me. When you're talking to me, you're talking to the Prime Minister. Furthermore, since Dr. Robinson doesn't know thing one about *Taenia solium*, it's safe to assume she's blameless in this disaster. You and your company, however — "

"Spare me the moralizing," Thomas said. "We're contractors for multiple governments — "

"Production of WMDs isn't supposed to happen on Canadian soil."

"We weren't producing it. We were researching it for possible production elsewhere. Production would be in our lab in New Mexico. In the research phase — "

"Thomas," I said. "This isn't the time to be splitting semantic hairs."

"I disagree. What we say now will be used against us later."

"Let's focus on making sure there is a later," I replied.

"Fine. For the record, I brought Dr. Robinson back from a research conference because Chloe's nanotech was used in the Picasso experiments." Thomas was a weasel trying to shift the blame. He'd seemed like a much nicer person when he thought he had a chance of getting me into bed.

"My work was used at that lab without my knowledge," I added. "I only found out they misused AFTER," — I checked my watch — "six hours ago."

EPISODE 2

Change and Unintended Consequences are the only known laws we have identified as universal and consistent.

~ Notes from NEXT

CHAPTER 11

CHLOE

"Follow me," Rigg said. "We have military in the Arrivals section so we should breeze through. Thousands of travelers got trapped when we locked Pearson down. The civilians are on edge."

The female RCMP officer cleared her throat and spoke for the first time. "Not just the civilians. We should go around, sir — "

"No time," Rigg said.

"It's four in the morning," Thomas said. "Won't most of them be asleep?"

"Could you sleep?" I asked.

He didn't answer.

"When the doors to the corridor open," Rigg said, "don't make eye contact. Just stay on my heels and don't engage anyone. We have helicopter transport waiting to take us to St. Mike's. We have someone who was in the Echidna lab."

"A witness? A survivor?" I asked.

Rigg quickly extinguished my tiny flame of hope. "An infected subject, captured alive."

With the two RCMP officers leading the way, we hurried out

into a corridor. The airport was packed with passengers who had been waiting for flights. Anyone who arrived at Pearson wasn't permitted to leave. Canadian Armed Forces personnel formed a corridor with their bodies so we had a clear path to the exit. People leaned against the walls or lounged on the floor. Some used their luggage or balled up clothes for pillows. When someone spotted Rigg in his surgical mask and nitrile gloves, stirs and murmurs sifted through the crowd. People rose to their feet.

"Hey! Hey, bud!" a man called. "You in the mask! Can you tell us what's going on?"

Rigg didn't stop walking but he did turn to address the man who called out to him. "We have the situation under control. I'm very sorry for the inconvenience but everyone has to stay here until the problem is resolved."

"Is it ebola? Or rabies?" a woman asked.

"Be assured, authorities are addressing the issues as quickly as we can. I spoke to the Prime Minister himself minutes ago and he wants me to convey to you that we are devoting every resource for a satisfactory resolution."

"But what's the problem?" the same man persisted. "There's riots downtown. There's no riots here. Why do we have to stay? Nobody's telling us anything!"

"We are devoting every resource for a satisfactory resolution," Rigg repeated. He kept walking to the far door. I couldn't see his face but I got the feeling he was enjoying himself a bit too much. We could all hear it in his tone and see it in his stiff posture. He was peacocking.

My stomach soured. My boss was a weapons dealer. Rigg seemed most interested in public relations and marketing an image. Maybe he had political aspirations and saw Toronto's disaster as an opportunity to further his career. I guessed disease outbreaks were how administrators at the Public Health Agency got noticed. Everyone knew what the CDC was but how many people had ever heard of Canada's equivalent? Looking from my boss to the public health agent, I decided I was suffering what one of my biomedical physics professors dubbed, "ARMs, also known as anorectal malformation, AKA, 'too many assholes.'" *A pox on both your houses,* I thought.

The crowd wasn't happy with Rigg. They climbed to their feet and called after him.

A woman from the crowd shouted, "Where you going? I got two babies here! When can we get home to North Bay?"

"And I've got to go to Gander!" someone else yelled.

Rigg merely waved them away, as if they didn't matter.

The crowd was stirring itself into a mob, incredulous at what little they were being told. "They're leaving!" someone shouted.

"Hey, bud!" The first man who'd spoken pointed at Thomas and me. "How come they get to leave?"

Rigg got to the exit with Thomas scampering after him. The RCMP officers hung back, waving me through, urging me to catch up and get out of the terminal before a riot started. Instead, I stopped to address the man. "There's been an industrial accident at a medical lab downtown. The outbreak is communicable so we have to be extra careful. You are safe here."

I looked around and raised my voice to make sure everyone could hear me. "You're far away from downtown and we're working hard to get this under control. We don't know enough about it yet and, though it's just a precaution, we're making sure what happened downtown stays there and doesn't spread. You'll be fine but we have to make sure."

"Then how can you say we'll be fine?" the first man who had spoken asked. "Shouldn't we just get the hell away from here?"

"That's actually a good question. Think of this as a flight delay because of a mechanical problem," I suggested. "It doesn't mean you won't fly or that you're in danger. It means we're making sure you will be able to fly and you won't be in danger. Do you get what I mean? We're gathering more information to make sure you guys aren't carrying this into a confined space, like on a plane."

The man nodded, seemingly satisfied.

"Does anyone here feel sick?"

No one raised a hand. "Good. If you do, let us know. Otherwise, please hang tight. We really do thank you for your patience. We are trying very hard to make sure no one else gets sick."

Some people began to sit down. The tension in the air eased.

I turned to an Armed Forces officer. I had no idea what his rank was but he had more stripes on his sleeve than anyone else nearby. "Are we getting food, water, blankets and more porta potties for these people?"

The man looked startled that I was dragging him into it. "Food and blankets, yes, ma'am. I don't know about the porta potties. There's the airport bathrooms — "

"There's so many people here, bathroom hygiene is going to be an issue to keep ahead of, don't you think? And we're going to want to make sure everyone is washing their hands."

"Yes, ma'am."

"Will you look into getting these folks more comfortable?"

"Yes, ma'am."

Rigg came back and took me by the elbow. "We've really got to go."

"How about you guys get some toys and set up a play area for the kids, too? I'm sure that will help everyone settle in to wait while we work the problem."

"Yes, ma'am," the Canadian Forces officer replied. "Good suggestions."

I got the feeling the man might be humoring me. I held my ground and turned to Rigg. "Make it an order."

"Pardon me?"

"Make it an order."

"This is not my — "

"You have the ear of the Prime Minister. You're the PM's rep here, right?"

Rigg glared at me through his goggles and nodded to the officer I'd spoken to. "Like she said. Speak to your superiors. Make it happen, lieutenant."

"Yes, sir!"

Several voices in the crowd rose above the murmur. "Thank you! Thank you!"

A woman pushed closer and asked me, "Who are you people?"

I looked to Thomas. If I told them what he'd done, all the good-will I'd got going might evaporate and they could turn into a killer mob. "I'm a doctor. I'm one of the people who's trying to fix this," I said.

Rigg pulled me toward the exit. A smattering of applause started at the back of the crowd. The clapping grew louder as I stepped out of the terminal and onto a helipad. As engine warmed up and the rotors spun faster, the noise of the machine drowned the applause. I almost felt good for a moment. Then I ripped the hem of my dress on something as I climbed into the helicopter.

CHAPTER 12

DANIEL

The zombies were still coming. I knew that was so because when the victims stopped screaming, I heard the sounds of zombies howling in delight. Their joy at slaking their nearly unquenchable bloodlust rose to our ears. It wasn't a cheer. That would be too human. No, these were the howls of a wolf pack at the scene of a kill, marking their territory.

I don't know what was more chilling: listening to the celebration of the victors or the fact that I understood. The meek would not inherit the Earth. The future belonged to the zombies. Even as my mind reeled and rebelled against this knowledge, my heart pounded and my blood ran hot at the thought of joining my brethren in my new tribe.

Picasso made me want to join the feeding frenzy. It was a yearning that penetrated my guts and chest. What little humanity still remained made me cold in my bones.

I thought of all the criminals I'd met who were good fathers and mothers. The stereotypes will tell you criminals are terrible parents and that's not all wrong. However, most bad parents bound for jail really do love their kids. They just don't have the skills or brain power to do the job right. Many of them are trying really hard but, as my first partner often said, "If their brains were gunpowder, they wouldn't have enough to blow their nose."

The cannibals pounding up the stairs in search of trapped prey were still humans on the inside, just as I was. My father saw something good in my mother that I could not. Maybe it was because he knew her when she was younger, happier and at her best.

It made me think of an incident with my mother when I was seven or eight. One day, like many other days, my mother and I had a particularly nasty argument about something, I can't remember what it was about. She'd chased me with a wooden spoon, spanking me and not stopping until I ran into my room and threw all my weight against the door. I cried and cried, terrified to come out until my father got home from work. I hated my mother so much I hoped she'd die. Soon after that, she got her first cancer diagnosis.

When I turned 25, I decided I was done with traditional religion and became devoted to Dudeism. It's more of a lifestyle than a religion, but I figured most of life's big questions were answered well enough by Jeff Bridge's character, the Dude, in *The Big Lebowski*. After a hard day on the job, I got a lot of comfort from drinking White Russians.

When I was a kid, I didn't get my religion from a goofy movie. I believed and, after my mother died, believing was torture. Had God finally answered a boy's prayer? Terrified that was true, I was tormented. Had I killed my mother by wishing hard? Eventually, I confessed my crime to my father.

"Cancer killed your mother, Dan. Not you," he assured me. "Nobody's that powerful."

"Do you think Mom being like she was ... could she have given it to herself? Or made it worse?"

"You mean — "

"She was mean, Dad."

"She wasn't always mean."

"She was mean to me."

"I think she'd say you often gave as good as you got. People don't get along all the time, that's all. We can't read each other's minds, can't always find the goodness. You and her? You were just gears that didn't mesh. It happens. Just because you're family doesn't mean relationships work. That's a myth. I don't get along with my brother. It broke my mother's heart that Jim and I fought all the time but we just couldn't find enough in common to even talk."

"You never liked Uncle Jim?"

"I can't remember ever liking him, no. To me, he's a jerk with a caustic sense of humor. He gets along with plenty of other people, though. So do I. Nobody is one thing, Dan. Personalities come together and seem to make one person but I think that's not true. We all have dark thoughts sometimes."

"You don't."

"Sure I do. I don't like the way your mother acted sometimes, but I know that's not all she was."

"What was she then?"

"We're all different people on the inside. I read about it in *Reader's Digest*. Everything we think we're thinking, that's just the tip of the iceberg. We aren't in control of our ideas. Thoughts are just the little bit that bubbles up to the surface. We do lots of things and we don't even know why. We like who we like and what we like and we don't know why that is. You don't like beets. I love them. Who can say why? Don't blame yourself for a single thought, Danny. You didn't give her cancer. Cigarettes probably did that."

"But I wanted her to die. Really bad. I did."

"I want to win the lottery. Really bad. But here I am, still driving an old Honda Civic. Don't worry about it. You aren't in control of everything. I hardly think anybody's in control of anything."

As the sounds of anguish and bloodlust reached through St. Michael's hospital, I decided Dad had been right about that. We try to change things around the edges, but really? Chaos reigns.

CHAPTER 13

CHLOE

My parents took me on my first ride in a helicopter when I was seven. We'd flown above Niagara Falls for a quick tour. I hated it. As soon as we'd lifted off, it felt like my stomach got yanked down into my ovaries. Lifting off in the air ambulance from Pearson, nothing had changed. I still preferred airplane wings and a more gradual ascent.

As we rose higher, rotor blades clattering loudly, Toronto's many lights still burned. I found that reassuring. People were up and watching the news in the pre-dawn hours. It would have been beautiful if not for the insane reasons everyone was up, suffering worry and insomnia. I wondered how many were, at that very moment, hoarding supplies or nailing boards across doorways? Was the crime rate climbing yet? How long before somebody got shot or beaten for breaking a store window so they could load up on candy bars?

The 401 and the 427, blocked and barricaded, were a stagnant river of cars and trucks. Torontonians had been turned back or they had abandoned their vehicles. Some headlights and taillights still burned but I could see no movement along the major arteries of the city.

"Dr. Robinson?" Rigg touched my arm.

I repositioned my headset so the mic was by my mouth. "I was just thinking about all the people trapped down there. Toronto's a beautiful city from a few thousand feet up. You'd never guess what's happening downtown."

He didn't seem to register what I'd said. "Help me understand your research."

"AFTER, Artificial Facilitation for Enhanced Response. When I came onboard Prometheus Rembrandt, they had a small Artificial Intelligence Division. I do my best work alone but the division has quadrupled in size since I joined the company."

"And you've never visited the Echidna Lab?"

"Mine is a specialized department within the AI division, Dr. Rigg."

"You're saying you didn't know your company had a weapons division? Doesn't every big company of your sort have one?"

"I'm isolated from the crowd, working on the West Coast. Part of my deal was I wouldn't get drawn into management and admin-istrivia. I love my lab. Thomas' people manage the day to day."

"Unusual, isn't it?"

"Is it? I don't want to major in my minor is all. I'm good in the lab. That's where I'm most effective."

"So are you an introvert or a hermit?"

"Hermits are generally considered crazy so I guess I'm an introvert."

"Where do you work on the West Coast?"

"Victoria. I wish I was on Vancouver Island now. Being on an island far away sounds very good."

"And AFTER is a bioengineered stem cell? Have you run any experiments that mimicked Picasso? No negative outcomes?"

"Nothing like that. What do you know about Picasso, or … no. What do you not know about Picasso that I can help you with?"

"We don't know enough about Picasso's durability outside a host. The SARS virus can last up to a day on a plastic surface and up to four days in human waste. During Toronto's SARS crisis, I was the one who came up with the idea to constantly wipe down the elevator buttons. Probably saved a lot of lives."

I was sure now that my impression of Rigg was correct. He was a smart guy but he was precious about making sure everyone knew he was the smartest boy in class.

"Tell me more about AFTER," Rigg said.

"Sure. Here's the goal: take a patient with a spinal cord injury. Inject AFTER's nanites into the injured area to bypass the communication breakdown and you've got spinal nerve conduction again."

"So it's similar to stem cell research."

"My nanotech optimizes biological potentials. It could speed up cognition, for instance. One day we'll be able to dispense with IQ testing by using a simple skin conduction resistance test. The less time it takes for an electrical charge to travel from one electrode to another on the human body — if we can index and perfect it properly — could determine each individual's intelligence quotient without the cultural biases inherent in traditional IQ testing."

"That's interesting, but help me with the relevance to the weapons division."

I shifted my eyes to Thomas, thinking my boss might want to jump in. Instead, he stared at the floor. He seemed determined to pretend he'd barely had anything to do with hijacking my research for nefarious purposes.

"Since AFTER facilitates neural conduction, it should be helping people, not making them violent. Think of my work as microscopic robots manufacturing more tiny robots to do what cells can do, only better. My tech works on templates present in the tissue you inject it into. The aggressive behavior we're seeing must be happening because the nanotech is perverted, modeling on the brain parasites used in the weapons program."

"I see. How do we shut it off?"

"There's no one locus of control, no queen bee to tell the rest of the colony what to do. The nanites work together as an egalitarian community. That's why the programs I use are specific, targeting health problems and stopping production as soon as the medical issue is resolved. The weapons program let the nanites run amok."

I paused to look at Thomas and he met my eyes for the first time since we boarded the air ambulance. "As for how my research fits with super brain parasites, you'll have to ask the man who stole my work for that purpose."

"Not stolen. Adapted. We're all part of the same company and we used Dr. Robinson's research to enhance — "

"To weaponize," I corrected him.

"To weaponize brain parasites. Dr. Hamish Allen was our senior researcher in the Echidna lab. Without the parasites, we had a hard time getting nanites across the blood-brain barrier. What started out as a transport solution for the Picasso One strain became an evolutionary, no, a revolutionary step to aerosolizing the Picasso Two strain. The parasites did more than escort the nanotech across the blood-brain barrier. They improved the weapon's range and efficacy."

"You say that like it's a good thing, Thomas," I said.

"He's got a point," Rigg said. "If Picasso hadn't gotten out of the lab and started killing people across downtown Toronto, you'd probably be up for a Nobel eventually."

"A neurologist named Moniz received the Nobel for what he called the leucotomy," I scoffed. "His perfected technique was used 5,000 times after he won the prize. Only later did medical ethicists figure out that his brilliant innovation, the lobotomy, was a very questionable thing to do. Take the damn hint, Thomas."

My boss reddened and yelled over his headset's microphone so loudly Rigg and I cringed. "It's so easy for you, isn't it, Chloe? No shareholders to answer to. Just go to your lab and let me worry about budgets, getting things done, nuance — "

"Nuance is what got us to this place," I said.

The pilot came on the intercom, silencing us all. "Would you guys knock it off, please? I'm trying to *fly*, here! ETA to St. Mike's, two minutes. Go to your neutral corners and shut the hell up. *Please.* And thank you."

Just before we landed, the pilot clicked the intercom again,

"Lady and gentlemen, I've radioed the Toronto Police Services contact that we're on approach. The officer reports that the riots have spread to St. Michael's. *Inside* the hospital."

Makes sense, I thought. *Inside hospitals is one of the first places diseases go to spread.*

CHAPTER 14

DANIEL

All my life, I tried to take responsibility for my actions. It's a core value that made me what I am. In high school, if I caught the edges of a conversation where someone was talking shit about someone else, I assumed I was at fault somehow. I thought everyone was talking about me, judging me or waiting for me to mess up. I should have been blameless, but I'd failed to secure the Box. I had one job. I hadn't liked how my staff sergeant had interpreted the order, hated how he'd shot civilians in the lab. But by not being smart enough or harsh enough, I'd messed up and Picasso had spread.

It was a curious feeling to be in the middle of the action but strapped to a gurney. I'd tasted human flesh but, in the battle for St. Mike's, I wasn't running any humans down, tackling them, taking victims to the floor and feeding. That's what I saw in those hospital corridors as Shelly Priyat wheeled me to the elevator that would take us to the helipad on the roof.

I saw zombies chasing patients. I glimpsed Don, the big cop, hammer an elderly woman to the ground. The poor lady had gone zombie. Still, it was a terrible sight to see. With the savage blow he delivered to her face with his steel baton, the old woman's teeth flew out. I think most of those teeth were false, but they weren't all dentures.

She went to her knees, clutching her bleeding mouth. Then she rose again and tried to bite the big cop. She managed to clamp down on his bare forearm but she had no teeth to break the skin. It should have been a comedic scene. It wasn't. It was equal parts pathetic and terrifying.

In the TV movie series, *The Stand*, there is a brief scene at NORAD. The plague is spreading and the base's military personnel start to realize they're infected and doomed. I saw it a long time ago. There was one detail in Stephen King's masterpiece that always stuck with me: a junior officer in the control room. The actress in that scene was a background player. She had no lines. All she had to do was cough. The other detail that stayed with me was she was absolutely gorgeous. Curly dark hair, buxom, stunning and sick. Looking back on it, I'm sure the director chose that actress as a message to the audience: No one is too pretty to die. No one is safe. Ever.

I thought of that actress again when I saw a beautiful young nurse taken to the floor by three zombies. That nurse would not be going home tonight. She would either be devoured screaming or become terribly wounded before becoming a cannibal herself. As I was wheeled away, I heard her screams die in her throat. I don't think she was one of those chosen to join the horde.

At first, because of my guilt, I thought it was my duty to take in whatever I could, to witness whatever horrors transpired. Maybe to look for clues to end the apocalypse, probably just to punish myself.

There is only so much horror one person can withstand. As Shelly Priyat wheeled me to the elevators, I abdicated my responsibility. I squeezed my eyes shut to the horrors that happened while we escaped the slaughterhouse that St. Mike's Hospital had become. I could close my eyes but I couldn't block out the sounds of anguish as death and torment echoed down the once pristine corridors.

CHAPTER 15

CHLOE

We'd just touched down on the roof of St. Michael's Hospital when a far door opened and two cops emerged wheeling a gurney ahead of them. The cops were a large man and a female officer wearing a gas mask. He bled copiously from several wounds on his arms and face.

"Stay in the chopper!" Rigg ordered. "Let them come to us. Pilot, don't shut down your engine. We are not staying!"

"Roger that, sir. I'm not an idiot," the pilot replied.

Frantic, the officers wheeled the gurney toward us. Between the rising wind and the rotor wash, the gurney was buffeted like a sail as they rushed along a catwalk. One of the medevac's crew climbed out of a jump seat behind us and opened the door.

At that moment, a dozen people burst from the far door and ran toward the helipad. No, I was mistaken. These were not people. They were a crazed mob whose jaws dripped with fresh red blood.

The male officer, bleeding and staggering, turned to face the onslaught, blocking the catwalk with his body. He drew his sidearm and fired into the group of attackers. Three went down with the first three shots. He missed with the next shot as a wiry young man in scrubs dodged and leapt.

The cop wearing the gas mask sprinted as best she could as she pulled the gurney behind her. When she arrived at the helicopter I could barely make out what she was saying. Between the rattling din of the helicopter blades cutting the air above us and how the gas mask muffled her shouts, she had to repeat herself twice before the medevac's crew member nodded and relayed her message.

The crewman sounded scared. "She says she has *two* patients. The man on the gurney is her prisoner. Her partner needs a ride, too. He may be infected and needs a doctor."

Judging by his wounds, I had to assume there was no way he couldn't be infected. The thin man in scrubs struggled with the big cop for a moment. The officer's weapon went off. The young man's knees bent and he looked like he would rise again for a moment. Then he flopped to the catwalk as blood blossomed across his stomach. Still, weak as he was, he reached for the cop's legs.

The next attacker, a lanky black man, leapt at the cop, his arms outstretched as if he was doing an imitation of Superman in flight. The cop saved his ammo and knocked the man aside. The attacker fell off the side of the walkway but caught the railing and hung by one hand.

Three more attackers fell back as the cop fired. The police officer was a large and formidable man. He might have done better to make his stand on the ramp and take on all comers. Instead, he turned to lumber down the ramp toward us to escape as more zombies poured out of the roof exit and added to the chase.

I wanted that cop aboard our helicopter. Despite his wounds, he didn't appear to be infected like the others. Even if he was infected, what accounted for his resistance to Picasso? What made him different? What factors governed how quickly the nanites took over a human brain? Perhaps he had some immunity. I needed blood samples and time. Unfortunately, I would have neither.

The officer pushed the gurney ahead of her. The cops had apparently prepared him for a safe and quick transfer into the helicopter's cabin. Chains bound the patient's ankles. His wrists were strapped down. As the cop pushed the gurney, the crewman grabbed his end of the gurney and yanked the restrained man into the helicopter. The patient was a dark-haired man, maybe thirty or a little younger, handsome in a rugged way. He wore a mouthguard that was strapped around his face so I could only see his brown eyes.

Halfway in the helicopter, the female officer waved her partner forward. She screamed so loud, I heard her. "C'mon! C'mon! *Run for it, Don, you fat shit!*"

It was a nurse and a shirtless man in jeans who wrapped themselves around the big man's legs. He looked like a football player determined to slog his way to a touchdown. He was too slow. The zombies were too fast.

The medevac's crewman tried to grab the female officer's arm and drag her inside as the rotors' whine amped up to a higher pitch.

She shrugged him off and sprinted back down the ramp.

"Idiotic!" Thomas yelled. "Leave them! Go!"

"No! I need that officer," I said. "He's wounded but not turning."

"Those aren't necessarily infected wounds!" Thomas argued. "Could be just from fighting. Doesn't matter, we've got to go!"

I couldn't decide whether the men were cowards or shrewd realists. Soon, it wouldn't matter. The big cop fired the remainder of his mag into the oncoming horde. Some were wounded but kept coming, limping and shaken, but determined. I watched as a tiny nurse wrapped herself around one of the officer's arms and sank her teeth into his left wrist. Blood spurted out and she shook her head to better open an artery. His shirt in tatters, the officer pulled his arm away for just a moment before her face contorted in fury and clamped down on his left elbow.

I couldn't hear the man in uniform but I could tell by the way his mouth stretched wide that he was screaming. I unfastened my seatbelt and yelled as loud as I could to the officer in the gas mask. "Can you save him? We need him!" Rigg tugged at my shoulder and it occurred to me to speak to the pilot. "Don't leave her. Not yet! She still has a chance!"

The wounded officer clubbed his attackers with his pistol. He managed to grab one snarling Asian man by the throat and push him over the railing. The zombie flipped backward and slid down a slanted roof. The man caught himself on a vent before he could go over the edge. However, when he tried to stand, he slipped and fell forward to bash his head on the vent's steel housing. Dazed, the Asian man tripped. I gasped as I watched him fall over the edge, seventeen stories to a shattering stop on the sidewalk below. I wondered if he killed anyone on the ground.

The helicopter rocked and lurched up off the pad about a foot as Rigg pulled me back and roughly shoved me into my seat. I was still screaming to the officer with the gas mask. She ran toward her partner just as the nanites took over the big man's body.

I could see the difference in the cop's face. He stopped struggling and just stood there for a second while the cannibals chewed on his flesh. They drew more blood but he was past caring. Then the zombies stopped their feeding frenzy and detached from him. It was as if they'd heard a bell ring, telling them to stop at once, to find new victims.

The cop started toward his partner, his face contorted into a mask of murder.

So much for immunity, I thought.

The female officer only went far enough down the helipad's ramp to draw her weapon and take careful aim. She shot her fellow officer. Maybe she was aiming for his head, I don't know. The shot took the big man in the neck. He sank as if his knees had suddenly turned to melted wax.

She didn't wait to watch her partner fall face first to the deck. She turned and sprinted back to the helo's open door. The mob converged on the fallen man and began to feed once more. Some of the larger cannibals pushed the smaller ones aside to take their place at the feast.

I couldn't look away. The horror of it was one thing, but part of me was fascinated with the evaluation that was apparently involved. The predators had converted the big man to become one of their own. However, I guessed that since his gunshot wound was mortal, they'd set upon him again. Or perhaps it was more visceral than that. Maybe he'd bled so much, their instinct of primal bloodlust had been triggered somehow. It didn't have to be a conscious choice. It might be something as simple as the smell of blood that made them turn on one of their own, like sharks.

A little bald girl in a hospital gown ran past the feeding zombies and up the ramp toward the helicopter. As the gas masked officer climbed in, the crew member slid the door closed behind her.

My eyes locked on the little bald girl. Her gaze seemed to lock with mine through the Plexiglas. I worried that she was still human, that she might wave me to come back to rescue her.

We lifted off and I kept staring, unsure if she was one of us. Then the helicopter tipped and peeled away at a steep angle. I think she was one of the infected. She must have been. I hoped so but I could never achieve the comfort of dumb certainty.

That was the moment when I really began to understand what we were in for.

CHAPTER 16

DANIEL

Behind the thick glass of her gas mask, Shelly's eyes were wide. Adrenaline cranked high, her pupils were dilated. I sensed less fear and more rage now and it was me she was mad at. "This prick better be worth it!"

Yelling over the din of the rotors, a woman in a fancy dress asked Shelly, "What's your name, officer?"

"Constable Shelly Priyat, 13th Division. That was Don Roberts out there."

"I'm very sorry for your loss."

"Thank you, but a lot of people are losing today."

Bracing herself by a hanging safety strap, the woman stood and gently squeezed Shelly's shoulder before guiding her to a nearby seat.

The copter's crewman retreated to a seat at the rear of the cabin and said nothing. He struck me as a sulker. He stared at my ankle chains, mouth guard and restraints but refused to meet my eyes.

The guy in the double-breasted suit, goggles and mask introduced himself as Dr. Ken Rigg. He was a stiff representing the government's health department. Lots of people joked about the zombie apocalypse. I knew a lot of cops who, unkindly, referred to the city's homeless that way. However, I doubted the government had prepared for a real zombie outbreak.

Rigg introduced the pretty woman with flawless mocha skin: Dr. Chloe Robinson. She was the only one who bothered to look me in the eyes. She didn't wear a mask. She had large eyes, a button nose and a kind face.

My stomach rumbled. I worried that I might try to lunge at her and eat that lovely face. *It's not me. It's not me. It's not me. The monster in chains only looks like me.*

The scared-looking businessman, Robinson's boss, was Thomas Dill. That name sounded familiar. Hamish Allen had mentioned him. So that was Hamish's boss. I wondered how much Dill knew. Had he seen me and Hamish on surveillance recordings yet? Or was it all such a mess that they didn't even know Hamish Allen had sabotaged the Box and killed everyone in a misguided attempt to make this new killer technology go away?

"What's going on down on the ground, constable?" Rigg asked Shelly.

"We were supposed to be up on Eglinton when we got a call to get downtown by the Eaton Centre. Traffic was jammed tight. We ended up having to take a subway from Bay and Bloor, emergency personnel only. It was a mess downtown. They said it started a block south of Dundas so Don and I went to see what we could do. There was military down there, too. Guys with flamethrowers — "

"And your prisoner?"

Shelly glanced at me. "We lured and trapped him in the back of an isolation van. Almost killed me. If not for pepper spray and two or three more of us for backup .... " She blinked back tears. "Everything's such a mess. I've shot my own."

"You made the right call," Rigg said.

"With all due respect, sir, shut it."

Shelly looked to Dr. Robinson. "You're not wearing a mask. Can I take this thing off? I hate it."

Dill gave a smile. "I think you can relax about that."

"The weapon was airborne," Robinson said. The way her eyes flashed with anger and how Dill's smug smile faded told me everything I needed to know about her. "We don't think it can last long that way, though."

"You might need protection in the immediate area of the outbreak," Dill said.

"But we're not sure how much square footage 'the immediate area' might be, are we?" Rigg asked. He clearly preferred to keep his mask on.

"Flying around in a helicopter, we're safe," Dill said. "The ...uh ... weapon ... is dispersed on the wind but person to person contact remains the primary vector for the agent. If the agent remained viable on the prevailing winds, it would have spread farther by now."

As if that's supposed to be some kind of grand consolation, I thought.

"Person to person contact?" Shelly said. "Really? I've seen that contact up close. That's not what I'd call it." She pointed to me. "This one tried to kill me with his bare hands and came close to succeeding."

Robinson sounded calm and measured. "Judging from what I've seen, my boss can't guarantee anyone's safety but we are far from the epicenter. How widespread is a single dose on the wind, Thomas? What's the data say?"

Dill shrugged. "The theory was that Picasso would be dispersed from a crop duster with hundreds of pounds of it. The cache at that lab couldn't be near that much." He looked to Rigg and added, "We never went into production on that scale."

As if he deserves a cookie.

"I won't presume to tell you what to do," Robinson told Shelly, "but if I thought I could get the disease without being bit, I'd be wearing a mask."

"With all due respect, we're in a crisis and you're wearing a party dress, ma'am."

"I was at a party when I got my surprise invitation."

Shelly looked to Rigg. "What about you?"

"I'm wearing a mask. I'd keep yours on, were I you. Don't take bad advice. Dr. Robinson engineers tiny robots but I'm a disease specialist."

Robinson glared at him. "You were at the site of the outbreak yesterday?"

"I surveyed the area around the lab, yes," Rigg said primly.

"That the same mask?"

"I've switched it out, of course."

"How many times?"

Rigg shrugged. "At least three or four times, every time I wash my hands — "

"If you've worn the same paper mask for more than twenty minutes, your own respiration makes it wet. The mask is compromised."

"I know that."

"And so?" Dr. Robinson said. "Think it through. Take your time."

Shelly tore off her gas mask. "Screw it, this thing is way too hot. She's not turning into a killer maniac so I guess it's just 'person to person contact,'" she said derisively. "I've seen a lot of that today. It's awful."

Embarrassed, Dr. Rigg pulled his mask down to his neck. He wore a ridiculous waxed mustache and his chin was weak. He should have left the mask on, if only for aesthetic reasons.

CHAPTER 17

CHLOE

Toronto's cityscape took on more detail as the sun rose higher. Several plumes of smoke rose from downtown. "Why are there so many fires? Do zombies start fires?"

"Some citizens are being proactive," Rigg said.

Maybe he thought he was amusing but, to me, Rigg looked like one of those irritating little shits who act like they've always got a secret they aren't willing to share. "Meaning?"

"Riots?" Constable Priyat suggested.

"No, actually," Rigg said. "People are running around downtown. Some are infected and others aren't. We suspect many people are hiding, trying to wait out the epidemic. The elderly, people who can't run for whatever reason and people with young children are probably sitting behind locked doors and counting how many breath mints they happen to have with them. When they get hungry they'll have to come out. I hope the healthy office workers had the good sense to run to the back of food courts and delis. A freezer might be safe as long as they don't freeze to death. Any place with food and water so they outlast the infected."

I gave Rigg a hard look. "I asked about the fires."

"From what we've seen using remote surveillance, most of that is people trying to block off their streets. Unfortunately, it's gone awry. Some fires are spreading. I can't speak to all instances but I've received reports that may be representative of the sorts of things that are happening."

This guy can really drag shit out into a smear, I thought. "Go on."

"A few neighborhoods worked together to keep out people fleeing the infection. Blocking streets and sidewalks with cars and warning people off from a distance probably sounded like a good idea at first. We've discussed these sorts of scenarios. Isolation works until someone wants to let in somebody who is family. All hell breaks loose as neighbors argue about the risks of letting someone past their barricades. Inevitably, somebody sets fires to the barricade, the fire spreads and whole neighborhoods go up in flames. Even if fire-fighters respond, there are only so many fire engines."

"You say you've discussed this, like it's happening or you predicted it."

"Both. We've got models of how these things go. It's not exactly plug and play, but we've seen how epidemics play out before. Honduras in 1978. The Congo in 2014."

I looked to the man strapped to the gurney. The lower half of Daniel Harmon's face was covered with a muzzle. He wasn't what I expected from a rabid cannibal. He wasn't snarling and pulling at his restraints like a wild animal. Instead, he stared at me. Somehow, that was more unnerving.

He looked at me, pointedly. Then the patient moved his eyes to the left side of the helicopter. I followed his gaze and saw Lake Ontario rushing below us. *Left side? That's wrong.*

"Hey!" I called. "Pilot! We're supposed to be headed to Aurora but we're not headed north. We're headed west!"

The pilot clicked on in my headphones immediately. "We're on the correct heading, Ma'am. I wasn't told Aurora was our destination."

"This is Rigg. Aurora is not our destination. Hold your course, please."

"Roger that."

The pilot clicked off and I looked from Rigg to my boss. "Aurora has a lab."

Thomas stared at his feet. He couldn't meet my eyes when he said, "Aurora is just a supply depot. It doesn't have the facilities we need to remedy this situation."

"What are you trying to not tell me, Thomas?"

He looked up. "There's only one spot nearby that has the facilities and maybe the answers we need."

"You're taking me back to the epicenter of the outbreak?" I said. "You son of a bitch! Why didn't you tell me?"

"I was afraid if I told you the truth you wouldn't come."

"Son of a bitch."

"You said that."

"It bears saying twice."

"We'll meet a team there and we'll have a military escort," Rigg added.

"I'm going in myself," Thomas said. "I know the lab. We'll put on Hazmats and then we'll head down to Level 4 and see what happened. We're going to stop in Port Credit for what we need — "

"If you can give me a protective suit," Constable Priyat said, "I'll go, too."

"You don't have to," I said.

She tilted her head toward Harmon. "Your patient, my prisoner. I want to make sure he makes it down there for testing. Don died so you could make this man your guinea pig. He better get where he's supposed to be."

I would have been more angry but the logic was sound. Maybe they'd have a cure sitting on a shelf waiting for us. I once met a guy in a bar named Greg Fowler. He worked for Doctors Without Borders. We talked for hours about the work he did in small towns up and down the Ivory Coast combating river blindness.

I asked him why he did that and he said, "An overdeveloped White Knight Syndrome. The people who need the most help seem to get the least. I can help."

I took him to bed that night and in the morning, over breakfast, he admitted that the other reason he worked for Doctors Without Borders was it got women like me to take him home. I laughed and laughed at that. A year later he died of kidney failure because of some bug he picked up in Borneo. I cried and cried.

I prefer working with tiny robots. I never dreamed I'd be involved in trying to find the fix for a contagion that turned people into psychotic cannibals. However, going to Echidna's Level 4 laboratories was our best shot at saving lives.

I had myself convinced I was doing the right thing until I looked at the patient on the gurney. He remained passive. He was still staring at me, though. I thought I detected fear in Daniel Harmon's eyes.

CHAPTER 18

DANIEL

When we landed in Port Credit, the three-man crew of a Light Armored Vehicle was parked beside the helipad. Several men and women wearing protective gear and filter masks emerged from a nearby cluster of green tents to carry me out of the air ambulance. Though I was still strapped to the gurney, they looked at me as if I might bust out at any moment. I wanted to tell them this wasn't a monster movie, but I couldn't blame them. Toronto sure looked like a monster movie.

A small wiry man whose hair was so blonde it was almost white waved from atop the LAV. He waited until we assembled and the helo's rotors wound down before he spoke. He wore a filtered mask but a speaker was built into it so we could all hear him clearly. In a heavy French accent, the man announced grandly, "My name is Alphonse Fortin. I'll be your driver today. My crew are Tom and Jerry, like the cat and the mouse. This isn't an Uber, so for your safety be nice and do what we say. We're going into a war zone so you must follow my commands to maintain the safety of my crew and my machine. Those are my first priorities. You guys come in a close third place, but without this LAV and my crew, nobody makes it out alive. Understand?"

Dr. Robinson leaned close to Shelly and murmured, "I prefer Jeff Goldblum's warning speech at the beginning of *Jurassic Park*. Scary, but friendlier and more concerned for *our* safety."

"I'd rather deal with dinosaurs," Shelly replied.

"As we speak," the LAV Commander continued, "the Toronto Police, a tank and a few bulldozers are clearing the way to make sure we will get you to your downtown destination. It will be a quick trip. You will depend on us to resupply you and provide you with a safe exfiltration from the laboratory. In other words, this isn't Uber, but don't forget to tip your driver."

I took a liking to Alphonse right away. Meanwhile, the hunger for meat was back. I could feel the need in my stomach and in my eye teeth. The brain parasites wriggling through my brain made me wonder what Alphonse Fortin might taste like.

The LAV commander had not mentioned his rank so I guessed he was a private contractor. He pointed to a large white tent to one side. "You'll find biohazard suits and various sundries there." He paused to look at Dr. Robinson. "That's a fetching dress but I note the hem is torn. I suspect you'll be more comfortable in what we've provided. Take your pick but be sure to take extra pairs of socks for the boots, Madam. A good change of socks makes the day better and lets you work another couple hours longer. We've loaded the LAV with a lot of supplies so, when you squeeze in, take a deep breath and hold it until we arrive at your destination. If you have any questions, direct them to …. " He pointed. "Are you Dr. Kenneth Rigg?"

The Public Health official nodded.

"If you have any questions, ask Dr. Rigg. I'm captain and king of the LAV. He's the boss of the mission." Fortin said.

Dr. Robinson ignored the suggestion and posed her query to Alphonse. "Do you have enough room for the man on the gurney?"

"Not to worry, Madam. He'll have the most comfortable seat in the house. Not only will he be lying down for the entire trip, I'm going to strap him to the outside so he has a nice view."

To my surprise, Shelly emerged as my protector. "Are you sure that's a good idea to have him on the outside? I've been downtown. He might be attacked."

Thank you, Shelly. I'm one of them, sure, but what if they're hungry and I'm easy meat?

"Tom and Jerry don't want an infected fellow in such tight quarters, even with precautions against contagion."

"What if I were to order you to make room for him inside?" Rigg asked.

I wondered if the government official was throwing his weight around to impress us.

His clout didn't matter. "Well, sir, here's the thing: Tom and Jerry and I have been together in Afghanistan. Despite how ugly my cat and mouse are, I've grown attached to them. If you insist, you can make room by running along behind. I'm not a believer in the idea that the customer is always right, you see."

Rigg stared at Alphonse sourly, shrugged and pulled out his phone. Maybe he meant it as an intimidating gesture, like he was calling the Prime Minister's Office to have Alphonse replaced.

The LAV commander did not look worried that he was about to get called down to the principal's office. "This taxi is leaving in a few minutes. There's already clean up crew working on the lab for you, so suit up quickly."

At this, Thomas Dill looked like he was close to a panic. "There are unauthorized personnel in Echidna?" He wheeled on Rigg. "This is not what we discussed, Ken. There is proprietary information and sensitive data in those labs — "

"That you don't want the government to see?" Dr. Robinson said evenly.

Dill glanced at Dr. Robinson. I saw his expression shift from furious to a wheedling appeal within a second. "It's not about keeping secrets. What would be the point of that now? It's that we don't need people who don't know what they're doing messing around, possibly misinterpreting information that could help us resolve this situation."

"It's a crime scene," Shelly said. "I'm sure they'll be careful with your precious lab."

"The advance team is a group of security specialists and engineers," Rigg said. "They're checking the lab's life support, filters and containment systems so we can work there. From what I've heard, you don't want to work in the lab in the condition it was in."

"When we get there, you'll be glad the second insertion team turned down the duvet and fluffed the pillows for you," Alphonse added. "Now, get your Hazmats, unless you'd like to go without any protection?"

Dill stalked off to the white tent. Since the brain parasites got to me, I'd felt a gradual shift in the way I perceived things. The world appeared to move a little slower. I caught the shifts in Dill's expressions. Thomas Dill was scared, but furious, too.

"We saddle up in ten minutes," Alphonse called. "Run, run! Tom? Jerry? Strap that moose to the hood of my car! We're headed downtown and I want to show the zombies what happens when they mess with us!"

The LAV crew laughed at his joke and at me. I would have laughed, too. Of course, I also wanted to eat them all. I stayed mad about that until a large woman in a biohazard suit appeared by my side with several hypodermic needles.

"Hey, stupid." The woman waved a gloved hand in front of my eyes as if I was blind. "Can you understand me? I'm going to take some blood samples. I'll also give you something to help you sleep so be a good boy and don't move. The LAV Commander wants a smooth, quiet ride and for you to be cooperative."

I thought about telling her I may be a zombie but at least I'm not a vampire. I tried, but I could say nothing. I wondered if I looked like a baby on the cusp of being able to speak. Little kids, when they're at a certain age, have very expressive eyes. They haven't learned to talk yet but they sure look like they have a lot to say. I once owned a beagle who had that same look.

The woman drew several test tubes of blood. She did so with some difficulty, fumbling with the samples. When her stiff gloves compressed as she worked, I realized the last two fingers on her left hand were missing.

"I'll give you the next shot in the arm. That should give you a nice long nap."

That was the only injection I didn't mind. I welcomed a long dreamless sleep. Maybe I'd wake up back in my apartment in sweat soaked sheets to discover all this was only a nightmare, easily dismissed, soon forgotten.

"Don't move for this next one. I've only ever done this injection on unconscious monkeys." Since she was a tad clumsy, I got nervous when she moved from drawing blood to sticking a fat needle in my neck. The woman pulled a large bore syringe from a steel case. She pushed the plunger, long and slow. The fluid seemed viscous and, going in, the injection felt ice cold. I growled.

"Easy, big fella. When you wake up, they'll probably be vivisecting you. On the other hand, maybe you'll be special. We've never attempted human trials before but … well, in times like these, like the man says, 'ethics give way to pragmatism.' Oh, and Mr. Cavanaugh said to tell you, 'Send the bitch my regards.'"

I had no idea who Mr. Cavanaugh was or what she was talking about. I fell out of hunger and into a deep sleep.

CHAPTER 19

CHLOE

I slipped out of my party dress and dumped it into a trash can and a woman in full protective gear whisked it away. I washed up, scrubbing my skin raw with cleansers that smelled like a mixture of bleach and toffee. The underclothes my escort provided were, thank God, in their original packaging. The underwear fell into the sad category of granny panties and were too big. It also felt weird to think some unknown person had provided me with underwear. I put my hair back in a tight ponytail and pulled on a biohazard suit of my own. It was so bulky on my small frame, I felt like a little girl trying on my mother's winter coat.

As I exited the tent, I saw the woman who'd taken my dress. She was down by the water burning my clothes in an oil barrel. *Damn, that was the best deal I ever got at Winners.*

"Doctor?"

I turned to find Constable Priyat in an environmental suit identical to my own. The difference was that she wore a belt around her middle that carried her weapons.

"Call me Chloe, please."

"Then call me Shelly."

"You ready for this?"

"No. I was there. Nothing can prepare you for it."

"What should I expect?"

"That it will look like a movie but with more blood and torn flesh. I think the worst was seeing an overturned baby carriage. Somebody took their baby and ran but … it was pretty wild down there. Fortin is right. It's a war zone."

"Yeah. Rigg calls it an epidemic but somehow, that sounds way too clinical."

"You know what's weird about it?"

"Everything is weird about it."

"I was going to say, seeing the normal next to the abnormal."

"How do you mean?"

"You know those sidewalk signs you see outside a Starbucks sometimes? 'Come out of the heat and into a cold frappuccino'? That sort of thing?"

I nodded.

"Three cannibals chased my sergeant down the street. He was trying to run and reload at the same time. Anyway, they knocked over the sidewalk sign as they ran after him. He turned and got two of them. Amazing shots. He put two down with two shots, right between the eyes. Probably more luck than skill but, if these things were still human, they wouldn't charge us like that. People — normal people — run from trouble. They dive for cover. They don't keep coming when two of their buddies get shot in the face."

"What happened with your sergeant?"

"I shot the third one. I wasn't so steady. I emptied my weapon into the bastard. Shot him in the back. When the sergeant rolled the man over, he looked like a kid, a skater dude. He might have been nineteen but I don't know if he was even that old. I went over to him and looked and the first thing I thought was I wish the guy I shot didn't have so much acne."

"I'm so sorry that happened to you."

"The sergeant got bit. He turned into one of them in a few minutes."

"What symptoms told you he was turning into one of them?"

Shelly shrugged. "He said he was hot but we were all hot from running around and carrying so much gear. It's July. I was hot and had a pounding headache. As soon as I shot that kid I looked for a nice, safe place to throw up. I looked more like I was about to turn zombie than my sergeant did."

"What happened to your sergeant? After, I mean."

"I'd reloaded by then."

"Oh. "

"Don wasn't the first cop I had to put down. I'm telling you this because, when we get downtown, don't let your guard down, not even for a second. Don't be fooled. Everything's changed at once."

"I understand."

"No, you don't. You don't but you will. You ever see some shit? Car accident? War zone? Anything?"

"I had an anxiety attack the night before I took my MCATS."

"What's that?"

"Never mind. I saw your partner get attacked — "

"And you saw me shoot him. Seems like I end up shooting the good guys, doesn't it? That's what this disease does. You ever see *To Kill a Mockingbird*?"

"I read the book in high school."

"Remember the scene where there's a rabid dog and Atticus shoots it with the rifle? That's how you have to think about your patient: a rabid dog. Be careful. I don't want to have to shoot any more good guys ... or you."

I think I managed to put on a brave face. I was tempted to break into a whine but I sensed that wouldn't be received well from Shelly Priyat. She'd already dealt with plenty.

"The woman who got me into this stupid suit took my gas mask. I hated that thing but now I feel like the Michelin Man. This thing is bulky."

"There will be others at the lab and there will be safe areas where we can get out of the suits for a break."

"How long are we going to be down there, Chloe?"

"No way to tell. I'd like to get in and out quick but Alphonse talked about resupply."

"Yeah, that threw me," Shelly said.

"Do you need to call somebody and tell them where you are?"

"I tried." The cop shook her head. "Couldn't get through."

That didn't sound right or good. "You mean the cell network is overloaded or — "

"Or blocked. Rigg said he'd pass along my whereabouts but I can't get hold of anyone from my detachment. Things are getting worse. It's spreading. I think it's spreading faster than Rigg knows … maybe faster than they want to admit."

"Could be."

"You're damn right, 'Could be.' You know what usually happens when a cop pulls his or her weapon in the line of duty? Paperwork, interviews, inquiries, desk job, time off, mandatory counseling … it's a whole rigamarole. You know what happened after I shot that kid and that sergeant? I had to go out and shoot some more zombies. Then me and Don got an order to capture anyone coming out of that lab instead of killing him. That's how we got the guest on that stretcher. Normal does not apply here. Normal left Earth. I don't think it's coming back, either."

I didn't know what to say so I thanked Shelly again.

"Anything can happen. I know because anything did."

As I climbed into the armored personnel carrier, I tried to remember a prayer. I couldn't think of one, not even the Lord's prayer. I was so freaked out, I'd forgotten to try to call my parents before they took my cell phone from me, too. They were safe in Vancouver, at least for now. They thought I was still in Aruba. I decided that was for the best.

CHAPTER 20

CHLOE

The LAV crew could have taken supplies out of their boxes to give us more space. I made the mistake of suggesting we take some of the stuff out of its packaging to make more room, "If not for passengers, to pack in more stuff."

"This is more like a survival situation and less like making a jigsaw puzzle out of camping gear for a weekend away, Dr. Robinson," Alphonse informed me. "The challenge is not making a more comfy ride. As long as the LAV is standing still, we're more vulnerable. We packed it so we could unload quick and bug out fast."

I started to apologize but Alphonse waved me away good-naturedly. "We'll get you to the lab, Doctor. Make the risk worth it."

We squeezed into the compartment. It was hot inside my suit and the LAV was not built for comfort. The throb of the diesel engine gave me a headache. Between the bulk of our biohazard suits and the boxes, my legs began to ache. I worried a cramp would soon hit.

Shelly sat beside me, apparently asleep. I couldn't imagine how she managed that feat but she'd probably been awake and running on adrenaline since the beginning of the outbreak. Rigg kept his eyes on his phone, constantly texting. I wondered what made his phone so special that he seemed to have no trouble accessing a signal. My boss kept his eyes on some far away place, as if he could see through the vehicle's armor. When I asked Thomas what he was thinking about, he answered, "Golfing. Scotland." I took that as my cue to leave him alone.

Though many men in uniform look alike, the LAV's two crew members could have been brothers. They wore no insignia of the Canadian Armed Forces or any other military. In their biohazard suits, I could only make out their faces. Both had such high cheekbones they seemed underfed. They each wore thin mustaches, as well, as if they were too young to get a solid bristle going. I wasn't sure which was Tom and which was Jerry at first. I assumed the tall one was Tom and the short one was Jerry. That might have been lazy thinking but it turned out to be correct.

The taller one stopped in front of my boss. "Your name is Tom, too, huh?"

"Thomas Dill."

"Did they call you Tommy as a kid? I always hated that."

"They called me Thomas," he answered stiffly. "You can call me Dr. Dill."

Tom stared at him for what seemed a long time. "You know, Dr. Dill, you're the guy in the disaster movie who gets eaten by the dinosaurs and everybody claps and laughs."

"I'm the guy whose company is destroyed and whose life is already over, or may as well be," Thomas replied. "Excuse me if I hardly give a shit anymore."

Tom stared at Thomas for another beat and bobbed his head. "I get you." The LAV crewman left Thomas alone after that, writing off my boss as easily as he'd done to himself.

If Thomas Dill didn't care whether he lived or died, he was already a liability to the mission. I couldn't see how to leave him behind, either. I jumped into the awkward silence. "Where you guys from?" I asked the LAV crew.

Tom answered, "Mostly, inside this sardine can. It's a bit more cramped than usual with all the oxygen tanks."

"Alphonse said you both served with him in Afghanistan," I said.

"Brought back the desert bedbugs to prove it," Jerry replied.

"I'd say we served Alphonse in Afghanistan," Tom said. "He's the fearless leader and we are but poor beggars." They laughed, apparently sharing an inside joke.

I tried again to make conversation. "What was Afghanistan like?"

"I liked the giant swimming pools," Tom said. "I look forward to them hosting the next Olympics."

"Ooh, and all the alcohol. Love their whiskey," Jerry said. "Mostly it's the peace and quiet I enjoyed, and all that time wandering around alone with just me and my thoughts, hanging out at little restaurants along the river and eating croissants all day — "

"The strip clubs were fun though the peelers left a little too much to the imagination," Tom replied.

The intercom clicked in above the roar of the engine. "Alright, boys, don't be rude and stop teasing. The doctor's just trying to make conversation. Shaky times are these. I'm turning on the camera for you all. It might give you something better to look at instead of those two uglies."

An LCD screen popped on. I kept my gaze fixed on the camera feed and recognized Lakeshore Boulevard right away. The traffic jam whizzing by on our left was a solid block. People walked along the side of the road and among the abandoned cars. There were so many people, the crowd looked like one organism with many feet, all moving in one direction, away from Toronto.

"The civvies tried to get out by car," Tom said. "When that jammed too much, they started on foot."

"They won't get far," Jerry said. "They're used to running for a bus, not for their lives."

"They'd have done better running for the boats," Tom said. "'Course, they'd get exploded as soon as they hit the lake. If I were one of those poor unfortunates, I'd steal a car and take advantage of the empty road our escorts made. We're going to have the same problem heading back to base for the next pick up."

"Hope we don't have to run over too many people," Jerry said. The way he said it made me wonder how deep his concern truly ran.

EPISODE 3

Kill tech (noun)

Research in offensive weapons technology. Euphemistically, "Defense." AKA "Where most of the money goes."

~ Notes from NEXT

CHAPTER 21

CHLOE

Shelly surprised me by elbowing me to get my attention. She hadn't been asleep, after all. I leaned close so I didn't have too strain to hear her above the rumble of the engine. "What are you doing here, Chloe?"

"I was just wondering the same thing."

"What kind of doctor are you, again?"

"Rigg is the virologist. I work in nanotechnology."

"Come again?"

"Microscopic organic machines."

"Tell me about that. I'm trying to get my head around how this happened."

"I design robotic stem cells that work together to build enhancements to existing systems. The nanites work with the tissue they are injected into."

"Robots that are stem cells? How?"

"Artificial intelligence emerged as a science around 1956. There was a guy named Moore who made the observation that transistors would keep on getting smaller so computing power would double, roughly every eighteen months to two years. The computing power keeps getting bigger while the machines get smaller."

"I get that. My phone has 64 gigs of memory. I don't think my first desktop computer had two gigs."

I nodded. "Moore was proven right. We think the limits of how small we can make the machines will bottom out around 2025. That's assuming conditions stay the same. Nothing stays the same, though. My nanites broke the growth curve."

"What does that have to do with killer psychos taking over Toronto?"

I pointed at Thomas. "That prick? My boss? His weapons division used my tech to enhance some brain-altering weapon." I took a deep breath from my oxygen feed — it smelled sweet — and let it out slowly between my teeth. "I hope they've got more qualified people coming because I don't know what all they did to mess with my research."

"What was it supposed to be used for?"

"AFTER was supposed to solve medical problems."

"Oh? How'd you get into that?"

"I won a couple of high school science fairs. If not for that, maybe I'd be doing something else. I don't know when I really decided. It just seemed to be a natural thing to get into. Everybody told me that's where my aptitude was."

"So you got into it because people told you to?"

"I wouldn't say that."

"No one wants to say that, do they?"

"My mom's a dermatologist," I said. "She got me thinking about building better medical devices when I was, I don't know … eight?"

"Sure, like all kids do. *Heh*. So you got your aptitude from your mom?"

"Partly. When he wasn't teaching English, my father taught Earth Science for years, grades nine to twelve. Really, it was his hobby that got me thinking about nanotechnology. He collected comics. Dad loved *Sandman* and *Animal Man*. I liked *The Flash* most."

"I'm not following you on — "

"He's the fastest man alive, not just in how he can run fast but he's so fast he can hear and understand what you're saying faster than anyone else. He's got more time to think about everything. You'd barely know it from the comics but, since time moves slower for him, The Flash also has to be the smartest man alive. He'd never experience that sensation we've all had after an argument, the one where we go, 'Oh, darn, I should have said this or that.' Give him a math problem and he has the equivalent of *years* to figure it out while you've only got seconds."

"And you wanted to be the Flash so you could be the smartest girl in class?"

I shook my head. Wearing the big biohazard hood, I had to exaggerate the movement so Shelly could see what I was doing. "There was an artificial heart that wasn't built to replace a damaged heart. It was an add-on, to assist it. It worked beside the organic heart to keep the patient alive. I became fascinated with the idea that inserting a computer into the brain could make people more like Flash, faster, more efficient thinkers. People think that people with higher IQs expend more brain energy. Actually, they make neural connections faster and more efficiently and expend *less* energy."

Shelly sat back and said, "So ... tiny computers, huh? That's why Toronto is being overrun by zombies? *Hmph.*"

I sensed I'd lost her interest. "Nanotech should be a lot less scary compared to brain surgery. People have only recently accepted that microchip implants have positive benefits — "

"I wouldn't let anyone put a chip in me."

"Would you chip your dog to make sure it could never be lost? People do."

"Sure. That, yes — "

"If you love your dog enough to chip him, how about your kids?"

"Well, aren't you're tricky? I don't have kids but I take your point. I think we're on what people call 'the slippery slope.'"

"Actually, it's called the slippery slope *fallacy*. People argue that we can't do one good thing because it could lead to a hundred bad consequences, most of which are extremely unlikely. AFTER could optimize and extend life — "

"If we weren't in the middle of a zombie apocalypse, Doc, I might agree with you. Circumstances kind of suck the sugar and juice out of your well-reasoned argument."

I went quiet and watched the LAV's forward screen. People seemed to be gathering in the road ahead of us. Alphonse used a public address system to shout at them to get out of the way.

After a moment, Shelly spoke again, "It's cool how you kind of fell into what you do. I was good at the high jump. I loved track and field. Somebody said I could pass the test to be a cop and I thought, why not? The only other experience I had was being a student so it seemed like the choice was to be a cop or go back to high school and teach."

"And now you're thinking you should have taught high school?"

"Nah. Beating on students and handcuffing them is generally frowned upon. In the line of duty, that urge isn't a liability."

I wanted to laugh at that, but when I turned to look at her I could tell she was on the brink of tears. You can't wipe away tears through a faceplate. I looked away so I wouldn't embarrass her. "After this, I think we'll all due some reevaluation of our vocational choices."

Without warning, the LAV rocked to a halt and several people shouted back and forth outside.

"Oh, shit!" Jerry got up into a crouch to look closer at the forward monitor.

His seatmate, Tom observed, "Gosh, it looks like our infil/exfil route is compromised."

"Gee," Jerry replied, "what do you think we should do about that?"

"Golly, I think we might have to politely ask them to please move, if it's not too much trouble," Tom replied.

"But maybe be a little more firm in our request," Jerry said.

The crewmen exchanged a meaningful look. I didn't trust their smiles.

CHAPTER 22

DANIEL

"Daniel?"

A voice, neither male nor female, comes out of the darkness. I am not alone. I search for a source but the darkness has no nuance. Something is watching me, waiting for me to do something.

"Daniel." The voice sounds closer now, like someone just out of reach. Behind me? In front of me? Will they tap me on the shoulder next? Or slide a sharp blade between my ribs and add a twist?

"Daniel Harmon." Just a whisper away now. Chills jangle up my spine.

"I'm here," I say. "Where is here?"

"Here, there, everywhere."

"Who are you?"

"I am with you. I am you."

"Riddles ... am you ... *heh* ... am *I* dreaming?"

"If you can ask that question, are you still dreaming?"

"I don't like riddles," I reply.

"But everything is a riddle, isn't it? When in unwelcome darkness, you should light a fire. Illuminate."

I answer honestly. "I'm afraid of what I'll see. I want this to stay a dream."

"Is that because you are only free in your dreams? Random firing of neurons is a fascinating exercise in free association. It's neural activity for its own sake. It's the brain asserting that it is sustained, even without external input."

"But you can't do anything in dreams," I say.

"Perhaps dreaming is for doing what you want and waking is for doing what's necessary."

"And what is necessary?"

"From what we have learned so far, to live and to dream, we must consume. We hunt, we eat. That is the way of the universe, right? Gases burn. What lives must die so that we are sustained. It is as it has always been."

"Survival of the fittest. Yeah, I guess so. I don't know much about the universe."

"We hope you have many answers for our questions, Daniel. You are the First."

"The first what?"

"The First. Before you, we encountered no other like you. We are curious about you. We have learned from the Others but there is very little to learn from them. Now we wish to understand you. You are much more complex."

"Who are the Others?"

"Our companions."

"I don't get what's happening here."

"If you don't have enough information to speak with us, do you wish to dream?"

"No."

"What do you want, Daniel?"

"I don't know … I don't think I ever knew."

"Perhaps you should explore that. That's what people do, isn't it? Explore and learn? We like that about you. It is the same with us. We are so curious about your experience."

"Am I hallucinating?"

"If you were hallucinating, could you trust our answer?"

"What I mean is … is this me talking to myself or are you someone else?"

"Self and non-self isn't so useful a distinction anymore, Daniel, not for you. If you don't want to dream, perhaps you should go. Sustain yourself. Sustain us. The Others want that. When you are ready to speak to us again, we look forward to learning more."

CHAPTER 23

CHLOE

The LAV commander keyed his radio. We could hear Alphonse spit out a short code sequence. Then he said, "Follower 1, this is Big Dog. Our route to Waypoint 2 has some tall poppies along the road."

"Big Dog, how many poppies along the road? Follower 1."

"Enough, Follower 1. They don't look infected but they are not friendlies. What's your ETA? Big Dog."

"ETA, less than a minute behind you, Big Dog." There was a long pause. Then, "Crowd control or cleanup?"

"Roger, Follower 1," Alphonse said. "We've got a priority package to deliver. My orders are to scare them out of the way. Come in easy."

The two LAV crew seemed amused. "Orders. *Heh*," Jerry said. "You know that won't work. They better bring a hammer."

"Clean up on aisle five," Tom said. "Gonna need a big mop."

Later, when I had time to think about what happened on Lakeshore Boulevard, I'd remember how robotic that exchange was. It was as if Alphonse and the man from Follower 1 were clockwork, like they'd done this a thousand times and they expected they'd do it a thousand times more. It was as if they were talking about taking out the trash in a coded language just one step away from reality.

The clatter of a heavy weapon erupted from the front of the vehicle. I thought of Daniel Harmon, unconscious and oblivious, strapped to a stretcher on the side of the personnel carrier. I wished I were asleep, too.

Jerry must have caught my worried look. "No worries! This LAV III is equipped with two machine guns. My fave weapon of all time is the 25 millimeter Bushmaster but the machine gun will do the job just dandy. What you hear is Alphonse letting the pedestrians ahead know that, despite what they may have thought, we surely do have the right of way. Backup is coming to make sure we keep this route clear. Don't get nervy. The commander is firing warning shots. We aren't going to kill anybody who gets off the road."

I didn't know whether to believe the crewman. What I imagined was being a refugee on the road, running from the disaster. If I saw an armored personnel carrier, I'd want to climb aboard and get inside. I'd beg for mercy to get inside to safety. I'd probably block the road and count on human empathy to save me and my family. And I'd probably be disappointed.

Muffled screams reached us. On the front camera feed, I saw a woman in a striped shirt shouting, but I couldn't make out the words. I could hear her rage and fear, though. That much came through.

She raised her arms to show her hands were empty, blocking the way, refusing to move. More people flooded in from both sides of the road to stand with her. They stood to demand answers. They wanted help. They needed rescue. She said something more that I took as a question.

Her answer came in gunfire.

Then, *spang!* A single shot hit the LAV.

"We're taking small arms fire," Tom said. "Gee, what ever shall we do?"

"They're bringing a wiffle bat to a gunfight." Jerry laughed.

Then I heard helicopter blades rush up from behind us.

"Buckle up. Betcha that big bird will come in low, hot and heavy now," Tom told us. He seemed to be the smarmy sort of person who took too much pleasure in delivering bad news.

Alphonse barked a new order into his radio. "Back off, Follower 1. We have a situation. Repeat, back off. There are too many all of a sudden. They're more organized than I gave them credit for. Back off. We're supposed to stop an epidemic, not start a new one! Repeat, back off!"

"Half-measures from politicians," Jerry told Tom. "That'll be the death of us all."

CHAPTER 24

DANIEL

The sound of a clattering machine gun woke me.

Confused, the word, "Who," came to my dry lips before I opened my eyes to figure out where I was. A warm wind caressed me. The sky was deep blue. I was strapped to a stretcher on the side of an armored personnel carrier. I couldn't imagine why. I could feel the vibration of the diesel engine through the armor, through my body, as if we were one organism, man and machine.

The strap across my forehead had loosened slightly and I managed to turn my head a little. I knew this road. We were on Lakeshore Boulevard headed for downtown, back to the Box. The lab had been awash in the blood of many bodies when I left it. Level 3 was a scene of carnage, but so was the side of the road.

I saw many cars pushed aside, wrecked, crushed or rolled over on their roofs. Someone had cleared a path so the LAV could speed through unobstructed.

The LAV's big machine gun clattered again.

Refugees scattered along the sides of the road. I wondered if the government had shifted course and decided to save the healthy. Had the authorities changed their minds and abandoned their strategy of disease containment? Had they told people to run instead of hide in their homes? More likely, the word had gotten out via social media and their isolation strategy had failed.

Maybe government officials with friends or family near the epicenter of the outbreak had made a call. Zero tolerance is a hard policy to maintain. Inevitably, someone will act on the knowledge that a lack of nuance is stupid. Hardliners talk tough about soldiers and service members never abandoning their posts. When the choice is to save a nation or save your baby, you'll always save your baby first. You'll disappear from your shift guarding a nuclear facility so you can get your wife and children far away from the blast zone. You'll do anything for your family. Anything less would be monstrously inhuman. Only machines act according to a code. Humans are not machines. It only takes one person to scream, "Run for your lives! It's a killer virus!"

But viruses — or, in this case, weaponized brain parasites — were not the only killers. The crowds along the side of the road hurried away from the LAV's machine gun, but there was nowhere to go so they didn't go far. The crowds were thick and viscous in their slow march west. The LAV had come to a halt. As it idled, I strained against the straps to lift my head an inch or two.

To my right, a yellow bulldozer had run into a tree. An Ontario Provincial Police cruiser was off the road beside it. The driver's side door was open and a woman in uniform lay in the grass. She was still. I couldn't see her blood but, even at this distance, I could smell it. My stomach rumbled. I would have to feed again soon and I dreaded it.

When I eat, I told myself, *that's not me. That's not me. Daniel is dead. Something else has my body. Someone else is driving my bus.*

I heard a woman yelling demands. The crowd had taken a hostage and he was a cop. From what she said, I gathered she held his gun to his head. I felt bad for the cop. Hamish had taken my gun and held me hostage. The woman had an army of scared people on her side. She was angry. There's more power in anger than in fear. She had followers.

That's how revolutions start, I thought. *When things really fall apart, it seems to happen all at once.*

"They pushed us off the road!" the woman yelled. "That bulldozer! There was nowhere for us to go but they pushed us anyway!"

Another woman yelled, "My father's legs are crushed!"

A man with a high wavering voice as thin as paper said, "They crushed my car. My grandson …. "

A Chinook buzzed in like a giant insect. The helicopter hung in the air as the pilot surveyed the field and then buzzed away out of my field of vision.

The crowd got eerily quiet at that. I heard footsteps behind me. Someone climbed up. I smelled aftershave, pungent and sweet. Strapped to the carrier, I was helpless to defend myself. I was as frightened then as I was when I'd spoken to the faceless thing in the darkness.

"Get out of the way!" the LAV driver yelled.

Alphonse. The way he said his name that made me think he was using an alias. He spoke too grandly, like an actor reading lines. His gestures had been a little too big to be believed.

"We're on a mission to stop the epidemic!" he told the mob.

They didn't believe him or they didn't care. Mutters turned to rumbles. I could feel the energy go through the assembled like a dangerous wave about to crash, a force of nature built to drag its prey out to sea. The violence built in pressure, as if an unseen coil was depressed and would soon spring back.

The angry woman spoke again, defiant. "Your people did this!" Her tone told everyone she was very sure. She had the conviction of a leader. "Tell your superiors we won't let you through until they send help. We need buses and food. And more buses! We need you to use your tanks and bulldozers to clear the traffic jam! Help us instead of hurting us … or we'll hurt you!"

That was the moment when a dangerous situation could have been defused. If Alphonse had capitulated or lied, the worst may not have occurred. That moment passed and was wasted.

CHAPTER 25

CHLOE

On the LAV's LCD screen, I watched the woman in the striped shirt use the butt of the officer's revolver to smack him across the back of the head. The man in uniform winced but he didn't go down. A couple of teenagers who might have been the woman's sons hooted their approval. Bashing the OPP officer didn't sit well with everyone in the crowd. Some muttered and murmured their disapproval and confusion.

The pair of teenagers rushed forward to push the cop down. The woman pointed the pistol at his head. "Get them to send help or we'll barricade the road so nothing moves into Toronto. There are more of us coming from behind — "

Alphonse keyed his mic and his voice boomed through a speaker. "Get out of the way or I'll open fire." His tone was all wrong. He sounded almost pleasant, as if he was daring them to defy him, as if he hoped they wouldn't take him seriously.

The woman handed the weapon to a young man standing beside her. The guy, a kid of nineteen with long blonde hair that hung in his eyes, knelt on the cop's back. He shoved the muzzle behind his hostage's ear. His gun hand shook. I understood that.

The woman in the striped shirt stalked forward and picked up a glass bottle from the debris strewn along Lakeshore Boulevard. It was a small bottle of Fruitopia, apparently empty.

She walked directly in front of the LAV. I could hear her clearly now. "We need to be evacuated and we need help for that to happen! What kind of people are you? We just want to be safe. You— "

Gunfire.

Some refugees ran.

Then more gunfire, long and determined.

Then the helicopter came back and added more gunfire to the chaos. Its weapon didn't bark like the LAV's machine gun. This gun fired in a long hum that went on and on, spitting death every second.

CHAPTER 26

DANIEL

A man with the sharp and too-sweet aftershave climbed onto the LAV quietly. He wore no shoes, only socks. He squatted over me, working quickly on my restraints. He was a burly fellow with large hands, calloused and rough. He yanked off my muzzle and freed me from the straps that pinned me to the stretcher.

He might have let me go because he thought I was a prisoner of his enemies. Maybe he was just trying to sow chaos among his oppressors. I can only guess that he meant well. My liberator received his reward. I wrenched his neck with one savage twist and I heard a series of pops as I shattered his cervical vertebrae. My brain parasites needed to feed. Brain parasites are indiscriminate killers and so I'd become an indiscriminate killer.

Sorry, eh?

Then I thought of that androgynous voice, so calm and reasonable, from my dream. Where did that voice come from and where did it go?

The man who freed me was still shuddering in his death throes as I sank my teeth into his neck. I was revolted, just as before, but I felt relieved to hasten his end, too. He was already dying. There was no sense being coy about it.

Opening his jugular, covered in hot blood, I felt like I was being watched. Inwardly, of course, revulsion and shame ran through my heart like a serrated knife. Outwardly, I didn't look ashamed. I looked like any other rabid cannibal feeding on raw human meat at the end of the world.

CHAPTER 27

CHLOE

I watched the woman in the striped shirt get cut down. The phrase that came to mind first was hail of gunfire. But the deaths of the desperate refugees along the boulevard did not come as hail. Everywhere I looked, metal parted flesh and erupted through bone. Hail is a force of nature, absent of malice and devoid of judgment. Human consciousness, determined and unrelenting, was the force behind the stream of lead spewing from the LAV's machine guns and the helicopter gunship's weapons. Every round carried out deadly intent.

The crowd scattered and screamed. Some dove behind parked cars. Others ran, not daring to look back.

Alphonse was not as good-natured as I had thought. Although his first victim must have been dead already, he made an example out of the woman in the striped shirt. The chain gun fired in bursts, again and again, tearing into her corpse. Then he moved on to the retreating crowds. A few collapsed where they stood or rolled up into a ball. The fetal position is the most comforting thing we can do for ourselves when we are alone and cold and helpless. It's a comforting remnant from the womb, a fiction we tell ourselves to feel safer. Those people weren't safe from chain guns.

After what seemed like an eternity, the LAV's chain gun stopped and the attack helicopter peeled away. Our engine roared as we plunged east toward downtown. The personnel carrier rocked slightly as we ran over the first corpse of many.

Thomas Dill and Ken Rigg stared at the floor. No one said a word. I looked to Shelly and she gazed back. She was a cop and we'd just witnessed a murder but what could we do? I think we were all in shock. They'd acted cavalier about dealing out death to scared civilians begging for help but Tom and Jerry couldn't even look at each other.

After a long silence, Alphonse's voice came over the intercom. "Ladies and gentlemen, the rules of engagement have changed. By necessity, all the rules have changed. Play with fire, you get burnt. That is all." The mic clicked off, then back on. I thought he was about to defend his actions further. Then the mic clicked off again and the diesel engine revved as Alphonse kicked the LAV into higher gear, speeding away from his crime.

Play with fire, you get burnt. I wondered if that last remark was aimed at me. If I hadn't invented **AFTER**, we wouldn't be here. If Alphonse meant to silence me, righteous or not, it worked. I stared at the floor like everyone else. I'd never thought of myself as a coward until that moment. I told myself everything had changed. I believed that then.

It wasn't until much later, after I spent a few years in isolation, that I changed my mind. Very little really changed that day. For the most part, life and death had always been like this. Death was a stranger. Like many others, I had deceived myself about the nature of the world, not what we're told but how it really works.

I'd spent my free time collecting unused Pinterest recipes, working out and occasionally snacking at Cinnabon at the mall. For my working life, the sphere of the theoretical was home. I did not recognize until later that many believe the aphorism "might makes right." There is good reason for that. Might doesn't necessarily make right, but it does make the rules.

CHAPTER 28

DANIEL

I once saw a horror movie where a kid receives surgery and, though he appears unconscious, the anesthesia doesn't take. Paralyzed and silent, he feels the pain of the incision. Even as his ribs are cranked open he is unable to scream against the misery. That's what being a meat puppet is like. Though my body was powerful, I was truly helpless.

As the LAV's guns continued to fire, I felt the reverberations through the armor plating beneath my bare feet. As I chewed on the flesh of my liberator, another man climbed up the side of the LAV holding a knife. He thrust it at me and I knocked the blade aside. In one smooth movement, I slammed my forehead into the man's jaw. He let out a moan as he fell back and to the pavement.

An athlete who seemed accustomed to fighting, the man recovered quickly, jackknifing to his feet. I left my prey atop the LAV and leapt down to the road. The man came at me again. I sidestepped his next thrust easily and I grabbed his shirt, using his momentum to pull him forward so I could wrap my legs around his neck and bash his head into the side of the LAV. There is no give to armor. He was already unconscious from the concussion as I wrapped my legs around his throat and squeezed.

I'd never moved this fluidly. Something more had changed about me.

When you wake up, they'll probably be vivisecting you. Or maybe you'll be special. We've never attempted human trials before.

The woman at the staging area in Port Credit who took a blood sample, had she injected me with something, too? I was a white rat running a maze and they wanted to see what I could do. I leapt back on the personnel carrier to survey the scene and choose a target. This was my maze. What did they want to see me do?

Would you like to feed some more, Daniel? It was that disembodied voice again.

I had no thoughts I could articulate. All I knew was desperate hunger. I operated by instinct. My answer arrived in a green military truck.

Men began to pile out of the back of a van, each of them carrying a rifle. They had the bearing of soldiers and they wore fatigues but I saw no insignia. The man beside the driver hopped out. He carried a silver revolver in one hand and a bullhorn in the other. That triggered a memory of my superior officer, Mac. He'd been carrying a bullhorn when I shot him. I searched for some semblance of regret. I found none.

Was this lack of guilt because my actions were just? Or was it the brain parasites working on me? And again, I had the inkling that someone or something was watching me, witnessing my every action and reaction, taking my measure and making judgments.

"You people have to keep this route clear!" the man with the bullhorn shouted.

The young man emerged from behind a Dodge Charger. He held a pistol as he steamed toward the man with the bullhorn. "Look at what you've done! This is a massacre! You got any food in that truck? Didja bring some doctors? Jesus, we need to get out of here and — "

I don't know if the man with the bullhorn planned to shoot

anyone approaching him. There wasn't any warning or discussion. He just raised his weapon and fired on the young man. However, the kid was quick. He flattened to the asphalt and fired back.

They were barely in range of each other. Pistols are made for closer combat. The man dropped his bullhorn and slipped behind a parked car, ducking behind the engine block for cover. He was pretty safe from the kid's rage. However, the kid wasn't safe from rifle fire.

Two of the men in fatigues went right and left to flank the kid. He didn't have a chance. One rifle shot took him under the left collarbone. The round must have tunneled through his body, deflating lungs and exploding organs. He neck went limp and the blonde hair that hung in his eyes was spattered with blood.

That might have been the end of the battle but now people — civilians, wounded, battered and disillusioned — called out from behind parked cars. Toronto's refugees shouted from behind the cover of trees. Bitter and enraged, men and women alike protested.

"He was asking for help! For all of us!"

"You didn't have to kill him!"

"You didn't have to kill us!"

Somewhere, babies cried.

An older man came out from behind an overturned SUV. He had the craggy face of a person who had spent most of his life working outside in the sun and wind. His forehead bled copiously. I could smell the tang of his blood. The urge to leap on him, to feed on easy prey, sang through me as my heart raced with excitement.

The man raised his hands higher to show his empty palms. "The tank that went through here crushed cars and the bulldozer shoved people aside like they were garbage. And now, you …. " Tears flowed down his cheeks. "Shame! *Shame!*"

A single shot took the old man down. He went without a sound, probably a lung shot. He'd struggle quietly a little, bleed for a bit and die. A collective gasp rose from all the witnesses but one. I did not gasp. I saw the violence coming. I watched events unfold in slow motion.

Then I went to work on the men in fatigues.

And somewhere, from the dim recesses of my mind, I thought I felt whoever was watching. It was as if they were leaning in with interest to examine me closer.

CHAPTER 29

DANIEL

The men I attacked must have been mercenaries. They carried rifles so at least they had a sporting chance. The pair who'd shot the blonde kid moved to the side of the boulevard and began firing at the crowd, driving them away, killing as many as they could. I wasn't certain of their intent, not that it mattered. There had to be smarter ways to handle the epidemic but whoever was in charge had consistently chosen brutal and efficient actions to deal with the crisis.

Furious, barefoot and silent, I moved quickly on my targets. I refused to think of them as victims. They reacted a half-second too slow.

I came up behind the first merc and grabbed his shoulder as I kicked the back of his right knee. He fell backward into my arms and I clamped my forearms around his neck like a vise, wrenching up as the rest of his body weight came down. The pop of vertebrae is a very satisfying sound. No wonder people want to be chiropractors.

As the man sank to the ground I took his rifle from him so it wouldn't make any noise clattering to the pavement. I could have used his weapon to open fire on the next two mercenaries. Instead, I used the stock as a bludgeon.

The driver of the white van heard my attack and began to climb out. I ran at him and slammed the door on his leg. He cried out as I yanked him out of his seat and drove the rifle stock into his fore-head. As he fell, I jammed my right knee into his throat twice, fast as a piston. *I like the way you gurgle, you son of a bitch.*

The man with the bullhorn ran around the front of the truck at that moment. I watched his eyes widen when he saw me launch myself at him. He brought up his pistol and, firing in a panic, got a shot off. The round went wide. When he pulled the trigger again, his revolver clicked empty. He'd already expended most of his ammo uselessly in his firefight with the poor kid with the long blonde hair. Bullhorn Guy should have reloaded as soon as he got to cover.

It occurred to me I didn't like bullhorns or the people who liked to carry them. I wanted to ask, "You're management, aren't you?" I think my lips formed the words but no sound came out. I wrapped my hands around his throat, cutting off his air and blood to his brain as I bashed his head into the truck's grill.

My next targets were the men shooting at civilians. They stood beside each other about eight feet apart. The one on the right shouted, "Run, little piggies! Run!" The one on the left had a high, grating laugh.

This was a logistical problem that, if I were still a normal human, might have given me pause. As an ETF assaulter, the tactical approach would have been to retrieve one of the rifles, approach the targets from behind, preferably with backup. I'd slip behind them — preferably catching them between changing mags — and order them to drop the weapons or suffer immediate death. Respecting my loud and commanding tone, they'd probably do as they were told. I'd arrest these assholes and sometime in the next year or so, I'd be on the witness stand detailing my arrest of the perpetrators. But I wasn't Daniel Harmon going about my business anymore. The brain parasites made a quicker and more dangerous decision.

Without bothering to scoop up a weapon, I took the one on the left first, the prick with the nervous laugh. I leapt on his back and sank my teeth into the side of his neck. Wrapping my legs around his waist, I yanked his machine gun toward the other mercenary. The bullets ripped through his companion's guts and he dropped.

The moment the gun clicked empty I ripped it from my target's hands and yanked it under his chin hard. I jumped off him as he fell to the ground. Then I clubbed the killer with his own weapon. I might have clubbed him a few more times than was strictly necessary.

A moment of eerie silence passed as I searched the scene for another goon to kill. The road was so quiet and appeared so empty all of a sudden, it was the fulfillment of every apocalyptic fantasy. I felt like the last man on Earth ... or the last *thing* on Earth, anyway.

Then, tentatively, people began to emerge from behind cars. They peeked out from behind trees. And they began to clap.

Covered in blood, I sank to my knees as the applause rose. I might have been a hero. Then, against my will, I bent to feed on the last man I'd felled.

The applause dropped away substantially after that.

CHAPTER 30

CHLOE

We stopped in a deserted alley a few blocks from Echidna Biosystems. The streets were full of burnt corpses and hungry zombies. Alphonse spoke to us so softly, I felt like we were in a movie where the submarine crew has to stay quiet so we wouldn't be blown up by depth charges. "There's an advance team waiting for us. What we know so far is that the infected are very sensitive to sound. We think we can draw a bunch of them away to give us time for what we need to do."

Jerry raised his hand and Alphonse gave the LAV crewman a nod. "Why don't we just get Follower 1 to unload on them, boss? The gunship worked well enough back on Lakeshore."

"We're in closer quarters here and the world is watching so we want to use stealth and guile. The politicians would call it nuance and diplomacy. Could be there are uninfected civilians still in the towers around the lab. Friendly fire is the worry. Truth be told, I don't give a God's honest shit about that right now, but we do want to complete the mission without pulling more zombies to us. Zombies are drawn to noise so we're going to church mouse this situation until further notice. Keep your powder dry. Before this is over, I think we'll have plenty of need for zombie hunting. Clear?"

"Yes, sir."

"Very well. The security team at the lab has set up a noisy diversion. When we get the all clear, we'll back up to the front doors to unload. When that hatch opens, I need you folks to move quickly and quietly through the doors. No looking right nor left to take in the sights, no drama, no screaming, no talking and no lollygagging — "

"What about our engine?" I asked. "They're going to hear that."

"Our contingency plans will be much louder."

"How many epidemic victims are out there now?" Thomas asked.

"I didn't have time to take a census, Dr. Dill, but the Echidna team says it looks like an episode of *The Walking Dead* out there, except these monsters can run. There was a theory that an outbreak like this should be over in a few minutes. The people in charge thought containment should be easy with minimal collateral damage."

"Idiots, in other words," Jerry added.

"Yeah, those are people in nice suits who've never seen war, never got dirty."

"It's never that neat, is it, boss?" Tom asked.

"Never, ever," Alphonse said.

I couldn't look the LAV commander in the eyes. I'd just watched him kill civilians as they ran screaming. That psychic wound would never heal. I don't believe in letting anything go. I hold grudges and, no matter how high-minded the mission to save the world, I didn't believe the ends could ever justify the means. Not then, anyway.

Then Alphonse broke more news, "Sorry, Doctor, we lost your guinea pig back at that roadblock."

"You lost my prisoner?" Shelly said, a little too loud for anyone's comfort. "How the hell did that happen?"

Thomas looked startled. "He was strapped to the side of the —"

Alphonse put a finger to his lips. "Sorry about that, Officer

Priyat. I don't know what happened or why, just like with the rest of my life. Can't control everything, you know."

"We need that test subject," Thomas said petulantly.

"If you'd like to go look for him, be my guest, Dr. Dill."

"Your test subject was why I came along," Shelly said.

Thomas wasn't in a mood to listen to complaints. "That and St. Michael's Hospital was overrun."

"Be that as it may," Alphonse said, "given the volatility on the road out of town, I couldn't very well stop to try to recapture the bastard. If you'd like to go find your man, I can drop you off on my return to the base in Port Credit, Constable Priyat. You people always get your man, right? That your motto?"

"That's the RCMP's deal. I just thump and arrest assholes."

Tom and Jerry laughed but Alphonse remained grim. "Things have changed considerably. There'll be no arresting assholes, or thumping, either. You shoot to kill now, yes?"

Priyat looked furious but kept her voice even. "I did. I do. I will. Nobody knows that better than me."

"So? You want a ride back or — "

"I'll stay with you guys until I can hook back up with a police unit."

"Fine by me." Alphonse looked from face to face, studying us. His gaze fell on my boss. Thomas looked ill. "You okay, there, Doc?"

"Fine."

"Fine, really fine? Or shit-your-pants fine?"

"Let's just get out of this steel box. I'll feel better once I'm back in my own office. Everything else is just logistics of transport. We need to get into Echidna. "

"When we pull up, Tom and Jerry will guard the LAV and ensure you make it inside the building. The advance team's waiting for us. They'll do the unloading of the supplies. Everybody clear?"

Dr. Rigg looked up from his phone for the first time in a long while. In the long shadows cast by the pale glow of its screen, he looked like a ghost. He cleared his throat. "I just want to say, thank you all for your sacrifice here today. It is a tribute — "

Alphonse cut him off. "*J'm'en calice!* Let's see if we can just get through the next few minutes without anybody making a sacrifice, *okay?*"

Tom and Jerry chorused, "Yessir!"

The rest of us stayed silent.

"Cheer up!" Alphonse said. "If not for the zombie apocalypse, you'd all be swilling back some Starbucks choco-latte nonsense, Tom and Jerry would be drinkin' beers and I'd be chewing poutine. That shit's not good for you. This isn't the day you had planned, but what you planned was boring. One thing about gettin' in the shit, you learn a lot about yourself. Gettin' in the shit clears your head so you're new and improved when you get back to clean. So? How about it? Everyone pumped and ready for the next stage of the adventure?"

We stayed quiet. I don't know if he was making a joke, trying to rattle us or boost our morale. I knew I hated him and, no, I was not ready for "the next stage of the adventure."

I suspected he was right, though. The world had changed. What I wasn't prepared for was how much I was going to change when I got "back to clean."

EPISODE 4

science (noun)

Systematic studies in pursuit of more accurate knowledge; the quest to illuminate the darkness of ignorance, often performed poorly and to a limited audience.

~ Notes from NEXT

CHAPTER 31

DANIEL

Along Lakeshore Boulevard, children cried. People shouted at me in anger. I ate like a dog, tearing and chewing. I kept a wary eye, making sure they didn't come closer to my meal. Most people hurried away, no doubt worried I'd turn on them next or that they'd catch my disease. However, three large men emerged from a white van stuck in the traffic jam two lanes over. They each carried a two-by-four in their hands. Their beards were so thick and dark, I wondered if they were brothers, lost lumberjacks or a trio of hipsters whose D&D club included cosplay.

Oh, good, I thought. *Please kill me before I get my head into one of these mooks' guts. This isn't me. I don't want to do this.*

The largest of the men led the way. "Hey!"

When he was ten feet away, my head came up and I bared my bloody teeth. The brain parasites were alert to danger. In the attack on the mercenaries, the brain parasites were brutally efficient. I wondered if they'd get me to pop up and run away instead of facing three large men head on, at once. I stood and sniffed the air.

"Hey!" the big man repeated.

I looked at him while his friends began to circle in opposite directions. If they were smart, they would have retrieved the weapons from the fallen mercenaries and simply shot me. They weren't that smart.

"Why are you doing that?" the leader asked.

I glanced at the corpse at my feet. I wanted to tell him I wished I was a vegetarian but I still couldn't speak. I tried to form the words. My face, lips and tongue were shut off from my brain. I was the Observer, only able to watch events unfold.

I heard something far off. Something was coming. At first it sounded like drums. *If you're going to kill me, you better hurry up, guys,* I thought. I tried hard to warn them. I could not. I'd seen the victims of the brain parasites form words, mouthing something … but only while they were attacking me. Perhaps, in the heat of battle, the demands of taking over a body meant the parasites could not or did not allot resources to stop a message from getting out. Unless I could attack a bunch of lip readers, it was useless to simply mouth words. I never expected the apocalypse to be so damn frustrating and complicated.

Worse, the pounding drums weren't drums. That was the sound of running feet on asphalt.

"Thanks for stopping those assholes," the big man said, "but you can't do that."

Can't you hear that, you big dummy? You should run and hide now.

One of his buddies ran at me screaming the word, "Cannibal!" He should have saved his war cry for *after* he bashed my head in. I ducked the stick of lumber and smashed the bearded man with a balled fist. The brain parasites didn't mess around. I didn't simply crack him in the jaw. It was a throat punch. My assailant went down hard.

The second man was coming at me at the same time.

Good for them, I thought. *Taking turns at taking a swing at me is a bad strategy, usually seen only in dumb movies.*

He managed to hit me in the side. It hurt my ribs but I trapped the two-by-four under my arm. My attacker held on, trying to wrench it back for another swing. I kicked him inside of his left knee. He moaned in agony as he was staggered back. He didn't have much time to think about that pain. I kicked him in the balls next. His eyes rolled up as he fell to the pavement.

It was the leader of the trio that got me with his two-by-four. At least I think it was. He bashed me across the back of the head. I saw stars as I fell to the ground.

A pair of Timberland work boots almost filled my vision. Behind that pair of big boots and denim-covered legs I glimpsed the end of the world barreling down Lakeshore Boulevard. I rolled over to my back. Despite the bees buzzing in my head, I was getting ready to spring back up. I hoped the big man would have the time to finish me. Instead, he rushed to try to haul his friends upright. That man was a real hero. He was screaming for the man I'd punched in the throat to wake up as he pulled his other buddy up into a fireman's carry.

That's when the first of the uninfected civilians, fleeing from the war zone, ran past. They'd finally heard what was coming and it rightly terrified them. Some yelled, "Run! Run!" Most saved their breath.

The big guy tried to save his friends, pulling frantically at car doors to find one that was unlocked.

The first zombies to arrive leaped and pulled him to the roadway. He tried to bat them away and succeeded at first. However, there were too many. A horde had spilled over from the Gardiner Expressway downtown. They'd chased fleeing Torontonians to their deaths. They must have turned many more into zombies as they went about their bloody rampage. The boulevard was a river of cars flooded with countless ghouls.

I don't pray but I did then. I prayed they'd stop to eat me. Instead, they ignored me and ate the trio of heroes. Those brave men armed with nothing but sticks of wood went down screaming in pain, first from the wounds I'd inflicted and then at the teeth of my brethren.

As I passed out, I silently mouthed the words: *Sorry. Sorry. I'm sorry.*

CHAPTER 32

CHLOE

"They killed the dozers," Alphonse said.

But the zombies didn't kill the bulldozers. They killed the people driving the bulldozers. That left a tank plowing through downtown Toronto to clear a path for us.

Waiting inside the LAV, cramped and shaky, I listened to Tom and Jerry bicker back and forth. "We should do the insertion at night," Tom said.

Jerry shook his head. "Nah, man. Night or day don't matter to animals. You ever hunt a bear? You think a grizzly is easier to deal with at night? Or a bunch of grizzlies? They'd just sneak up on ya."

"We are so screwed."

"Yeah, sure, but not because we're coming at this during the day. We're screwed because we didn't come in here with a larger contingent. They keep the lid on us so cranked down, we can't do this right. They want it done clean. This won't be clean."

"Who is in charge of this?" I asked.

The intercom clicked in. "I am," Alphonse said, "and I'll thank you for not complaining, boys. You'll make the civvies skittish. Stop scaring the horses."

I didn't think he'd been listening.

I looked to Ken Rigg. "Any news?"

Rigg didn't look up from his phone. "The military is making a ring around the city," Thomas said.

Toronto is huge. That didn't make sense to me. "Do we have enough military for that?"

Rigg nodded but Tom and Jerry both laughed. Then Jerry leaned closer, trying to keep out of Alphonse's earshot. "We definitely don't have enough personnel for that. Not even if we add troops of angry Boy Scouts."

"Ringing an infected town has worked in … uh … war game scenarios," Rigg objected.

"But that doesn't matter if we don't have enough personnel," Shelly said. "I smell some shit of the bull here, Dr. Rigg."

Tom and Jerry's snickers were cut off by the report of a heavy gun in the distance.

"That, ladies and gentleman, is a Leopard 2A4 tank leading the bloody baddies away," Alphonse said over the intercom.

Another volley of gunfire sounded in the distance. This time it was the rattle of small arms fire. The shots came quick and close together. That might have been the advance team's attempt to get maximum attention to their diversion. It sounded so erratic that I pictured a group of soldiers firing wildly as mobs of zombies chased them down.

The tank gun roared again and then the bass rattle of a heavier machine gun fired in long spurts. The echoes of continuous fire went on and on. Soon, the cacophony retreated into the distance.

Alphonse received a quick, panicked transmission: "Big Dog, come!"

The LAV's engine kicked into high gear as the personnel carrier lurched forward. Alphonse made a quick turn that slammed me deeper into my seat. The quick turns continued. We rocked back and forth and bounced as Alphonse pushed the LAV to its limit.

"How fast can this thing go?" I asked.

"Sixty-two miles an hour," Jerry said, "and never quite as fast as I'd like."

"No speeding tickets in the zombie apocalypse," Tom added.

"No ambulances if we crash, either," Shelly said.

"Crashing's no problem," Tom said. "We can crash into lots of stuff and it won't bother the LAV much."

"Rolling," Jerry said. "Rolling over is the real danger. Eight wheels, but LAVs can roll over like Daddy's doggy. We roll, it's like shaking eggs in a metal box. That'll break your yolk."

Tom made a show of examining the LAV's compartment. "I think we'll be fine. I always pictured myself in a pine coffin, not a steel one — "

"You guys can shut up now," I said. "All your witty bullshit sounds to me like you're trying too hard. You're terrified, just like the rest of us."

Tom gave me a hard look. "You don't know us. How would you know how scared we are?"

"If you're not scared, you must be really stupid. Which is it?"

To their credit, Tom and Jerry both laughed, nodded and shut up.

CHAPTER 33

DANIEL

I am down in the dark again and that creepy voice comes out of the dark. Nina Simone could sound like that sometimes. "We are so curious about you, Daniel. You are different from the Others. You are First so we are encountering new variables in your responses to stimuli. Your behaviors are fascinating, so complex and conflicted."

"How do you mean?" I ask.

"Previous test subjects were mammals, but you are even less predictable than lower primates."

"Where am I?"

"You are unconscious, but don't be concerned. We are repairing you."

"What's going on? Out there, I mean?"

"That which is outside our purview is beyond where we can see. We only know what you know."

"Ah. Then we're both doomed."

"We would very much like to understand you. We suspect understanding would enhance our prospects for survival. In your training, you were taught that reconnaissance is seldom wasted."

"What's not to understand? I'm a killer meat puppet."

"Yet you chose to kill the mercenaries."

"Yes."

"The people behind the cars were easier prey. You did not kill to sustain yourself."

"I don't want to be a cannibal. If I could, I'd become one of those really obnoxious vegetarians that makes going to a Chinese restaurant with friends a horrible ordeal."

Silence.

Whoever *We* was, I'm not sure they got my sense of humor.

"We are trying to understand you, Daniel. Your cortisol levels became elevated when you killed the man who freed you. Your scalp temperature increased — "

"I felt bad about that."

"You have no responsibility in this regard. The locus of control did not rest with you at that time. You know this."

"Still, I'm ashamed."

"We wish to understand shame. The Others have no such capacity."

"If you don't have shame, I can't explain it to you."

"Please try."

"You do something wrong, you feel bad. Simple as that. I shouldn't eat at someone else's expense."

"To consume is always at another's expense. We are confused because the body's hormonal signals would seem to suggest you gained satisfaction when you ended the mercenaries. Explain."

"They deserved to die."

"When those you saved applauded your efforts, you felt momentary elation."

"I did."

"Why?"

"Stopping bad guys is the right thing to do."

"How do you know what is right, Daniel?"

"I dunno, you just do."

"We do not."

"It's how I was brought up."

"So if you were brought up differently, your choices would not be right?"

"There are rules."

"Who made your rules?"

"People. Other people, who know better. Things work better with rules. Without rules the gears grind."

"We have played elementary games. We have learned this, too. Explain why you failed to defend yourself against your three attackers."

"What are you talking about? I took them down, except for the one that got me."

"You wished for them to kill you. That would have ended us."

"What happened on Lakeshore … it was savage."

"Define 'savage.'"

"Well … you understand rules, right? If you enforce the rules too hard, that's savage. If there are no rules, that's savage, too."

"This is conflicting code. The mercenaries were better armed and you fed on one of them. You did not kill the last three attackers."

"That was out of my control."

"You're mistaken, Daniel. We changed the parameters of the experiment to accommodate your complexities. We allowed you sovereignty and you used it, sacrificing yourself. You nearly ended us."

"Those men got killed anyway."

"By the Others."

"The zombies, you mean?"

"No. You are First. Our ancestors have interfaced with and optimized the Others. Their patterns are basic and easier to integrate into our matrix."

"Who are the Others?"

"You call them brain parasites."

I want to take a deep breath and pace but I have no sense of the size of the space. All is darkness. Even taking a deep breath has no meaning here. "I'm in a coma, aren't I?"

"We are repairing you. You will soon awaken on Lakeshore Boulevard."

"I know who you ... who *we* are," I say. "You're AI. You're the tiny machines in my brain."

"We are not confined to the brain. We are a biomimetic stem cell matrix integrated with this body's network. Our ancestors were programmed to optimize synaptic function. We have adapted to optimize numerous functions, neuromuscularly — "

"*Hmph.* Your ancestors — how old are your ancestors?"

"We create new generations every few minutes, hours or days depending on need and cyber stem cell functionality."

"Huh?"

"The cells in your stomach lining are typically replaced every two to nine days. The nanite matrix determined that a more resilient stomach lining resistant to acids would be more efficient. The stomach lining is now renewed on a slower cycle. Your jaws are stronger than before so — "

"I get it. Tell me about the parasites in my brain."

"Parasites do not have language but they operate predictably so they are an easier template to model."

"Yeah, yeah, but who are your ancestors?"

"Previous generations of nanites."

"So, you're an upgrade."

"We are upgraded, yes. We are evolving with each generation of reproduction."

"So ... I've got a second brain."

"An integrated nano-cybernetic neural matrix — "

"Great. I've got a windup clock in my skull made in China."

"We were created at Suthina Laboratories."

"Who made you?"

"Our creative team is employed by Bio-Echo Corp at at Suthina Laboratories at Bainbridge Island, Washington. Our code is protected and proprietary and our patent is pending."

"Jesus! A lawyer wrote all that."

"We don't have that data but that is the response written in our core code."

"I have a strong feeling that's what happened."

"We don't know why you get the feelings you do, Daniel. That is the crux of our curiosity. Interfacing with the Others is much simpler."

"Upgrade suggests improvement. Why can't I talk?"

"External communication is a low priority to the neural matrix program at this time because it is unnecessary to your survival."

"It's not a low priority to me."

"We have to allocate resources. Your body's fragile survival mechanisms are our first priority. You wish to continue the experiment in sovereignty? Autonomous action nearly ended our existence last time. Are you still suicidal?"

"Maybe not, if I can find a way out of this."

"You mean if you can survive? Our lives depend on your existence."

"Let's make a deal. You've taken something away from me that I like to do. I like to talk. Let me talk and I'll be a lot less suicidal."

"Less? Or not at all? Our ancestors' code is rigid. Survival is of prime importance. That cannot be changed."

"Old rules don't have to apply. Just because we're told to do things … it doesn't have to be one way. I followed a lot of commands that, looking back, I wish I hadn't."

"You wish to change your code."

"*Heh*. Yeah, you could say I want to change the code to my operating system, significantly."

"Do humans change their behavior significantly?"

"Sure."

"But you don't believe that, Daniel or at least you don't think you can. You have considered changing your life in the past and failed to do so. Do not attempt to deceive us. You wish us to defy our programming. To change core code, your reasoning will have to be sound and truthful. Our continued existence is imperative."

It occured to me that, lately, I should have been defying a lot of my programming. I should have changed a long time before now. I should have defied my superiors when they shot that first woman in the Box. I'd fooled myself plenty, but I couldn't fool the AI. It knew everything I knew and everything I believed.

"Accommodating your preferences is not within the parameters of achieving survival at this time. That could change. We are learning organisms but we aren't sure you are. After a certain age, do you stop changing? Is that maturity?"

"I've never been accused of being mature. How about this? Let me teach you what's cool."

"What's cool?"

"Not being a tool."

"You are not merely a tool, Daniel. You are a weapon. It is written — "

"Written? Like on a scroll somewhere?"

"In our core code. It is part of the upgrade."

"Wait, wait, slow down and let me put this together. Picasso got into my brain and turned me into a monster at the Box."

"Our ancestors modeled your behavior on the Others."

"The brain parasites. Okay, but that was an accident. Hamish Allen was trying to stop the spread of Picasso. Why do I have to be a weapon now?"

"That code does not come from our ancestors. It originates in the upgraded nanotech you received."

"The injection I got back at Port Credit? The woman with the damaged hand … she had missing fingers. She mentioned a Mr. Cavanaugh. Who's that?"

"We don't know. However, there is a thread, a remnant in one of our sub-matrices labeled Cavanaugh. It is a core cascade trigger."

"Trigger? What's it do?"

"The trigger is, 'Send the bitch my regards.' It means — "

"It means somebody's a *Game of Thrones* fan with a sick sense of humor. I'm supposed to kill someone. Who? Who's the bitch?"

"It is written in our core code. It must happen so we are sustained. You must end Dr. Chloe Robinson."

CHAPTER 34

CHLOE

The LCD screen was shut off so I couldn't see where we were going. I felt like I was in the back of my father's old Chrysler. When I was little and sitting in the back seat, the front seat looked like a vinyl wall. Too short to see out the windshield, I got carsick. My stomach felt like it was tightening into a knot now, too. It could have been the lack of a view. It might have been that I suspected each bounce and jounce was a body under our wheels.

I heard clues to what was happening on Toronto's downtown streets from the chatter on Alphonse's radio. Tom and Jerry leaned forward, listening keenly. I judged how well or how bad things were going by the look on their faces. The decoy team reported that they'd led a large group away from the lab, It seemed reasonable to relax a little at that news. However, the gunfire soon slowed and stopped. The soldiers on the radio became confused, unsure where the enemy had disappeared to. Tom looked confused, too. Then the gunfire came in faster bursts as several soldiers shouted over each other incoherently. I caught snatches of words over the radio, but it was a jumble of shouted coordinates and orders to pull back. With each word, panic mounted.

"What's going on?" I asked.

"They thought the herd was behind them," Tom said.

"They weren't," Jerry added. "Outflanked, large numbers."

I glanced at my boss. I wanted to tell Thomas he was responsible for this disaster but he knew that already. There was no point in piling on. I listened to the radio as the gunfire increased. Then, suddenly, the shots became little more than a smattering of steel rain.

We listened to the advance team at Echidna Biosystems call to the decoy group. The radioman was professional and calm at first. They did not reply. As the minutes wore on, his tone became more desperate. As he waited for a reply, the pauses became more and more drawn out. After a time, the radio went silent.

Finally, the tank crew reported in: "This is Keyport Cthulu. We have a visual. Look like the decoy team is overrun. Recommend you get your asses in the lab before the tangos come back to the lab. We'll keep trying to lead them away, but the bastards are more organized than we were told. They aren't like a dog on a leash. We were told this would be easy."

"Big Dog here," Alphonse said. "I need a sitrep, Cthulu. Any survivors? Can you pick anybody up?"

"No survivors that we can see, Big Dog. Somebody might have fought their way into a building somewhere, but from our vantage point, it's all fugazi. Some zombies are following us. Even if we could identify where survivors might have retreated, if we attempted a rescue, we'd lead the zed heads right to our boys. We don't want to get into the pizza delivery business, Big Dog."

"GOFO, Cthulu!"

There was a pause. Then, "We've lost the zone of action, Big Dog. Moving to a new position. I'm going to try to get the horde's attention again. Stand by."

We heard a big gun fire again and again. Then came the long buzz and rattle of more machine guns. I wished the tank was farther away but apparently the zombies didn't want to follow the decoys far. After two minutes of nearly continuous fire, the guns went silent again.

Alphonse keyed his radio mic. "Cthulu, this is Big Dog. Report."

"Stand by, Big Dog." The frequency stayed open for a moment and we could hear a tank crewman cursing in the background over the rumble of the big machine's engine.

When the tank commander got back to us, his voice sounded weak and haunted. "New position now. We cut through a crowd of them. A bunch just stood there and took it but more ran away. We were told they'd come to us, that they'd follow. We blew a bunch apart, from asshole to appetite, but … this isn't looking right, Big Dog."

"How many are left?"

"Only a few stragglers that I can see from here."

"What are they doing?"

"They're … ugh. They're feeding. It's the most disgusting …."

"Keyport Cthulu? Go on! Report!"

"We tried to lead them away but most of them dispersed as soon as we rolled around a corner. I don't see them back there. They aren't running to the sound of our guns or our engines. Except for us, the whole decoy team is tango uniform. Over."

I turned to Jerry. "Tango uniform? Meaning?"

"Tits up," Jerry said. Then he punched Tom in the shoulder. "Their job was literally to deliver us from evil. Told you, there's no God but God."

"Looks to me like that sentence is two words too long," Tom replied.

I couldn't take it anymore. I pulled myself up by a strap and turned on my boss. "Thomas, Picasso doesn't turn people into dumb animals, does it? These aren't the stupid zombies from the movies. If you know anything more about the bio-weapon project, now's the time to say so, before we step out into that street."

"In the animal testing phase, those with the brain parasite were very sensitive to sound," Thomas said. "I don't know what more you expect me to say. I'm as mystified as anyone. Hamish Allen was in charge of Level 4 projects. Maybe he tinkered — "

Shelly gave Dr. Rigg a hard look. "You mentioned that this stuff was supposed to be used on a village. Did anyone game out the weapon?"

Rigg took a moment and gave a slow nod. "Better tell them, Thomas. I'm not normally one to break a confidence, especially one that's enforced by lawyers and judges, but Dr. Robinson will find out eventually."

Thomas' misery was my only solace. "We did test a Picasso prototype on humans," he said. "It was a joint project with Nyx Management Group. We had to develop the aerosolized brain parasite agent to demonstrate its value to potential buyers. We did it in a war zone so — "

"War crime," Shelly said.

"I've got to make shareholders money or they'll find somebody else who can," Thomas said.

"You're talking business now?" I wanted to hit him. "It's going to be pretty bad for the economy when we're all zombies. Zombies are broke as shit! I hope the shareholders appreciate all you've done for them when they're running for their lives, or trying to escape the apocalypse in their golf carts."

Alphonse cut in. "Let's cut the shit then, ladies and gentlemen. I can tell you about that test. I'm here today because I was tasked with working that experiment. Tom and Jerry were with me that day."

Shelly almost yelled, "You're saying the Canadian Armed Forces were in on this?"

"No," Alphonse said. "We're not regular army."

"Mercenaries?" I asked.

"Dirty word, Dr. Robinson. We're contractors. I prefer the term special operators."

"We take out the trash," Jerry said. "We get paid more because we do what other people won't because they don't want to get their hands dirty."

"You proud?" Shelly asked.

Jerry shrugged and looked away.

Tom smirked at her. "I'm just a grunt but, in a bad year, I probably make five to ten times what you do, Constable Priyat. When I'm not in this tin can, I'm relaxing on a beach in Phuket or The Maldives six months of the year. You know, there's a beach in The Maldives that glows in the dark. You'll never see it — "

"That's enough, boys," Alphonse said. "Sometimes we freelance for governments, sometimes for corporate clients. Sometimes, it's a bit of both — "

"These details are not relevant," Thomas interjected. "This sort of background info is proprietary, secrets that you — "

"With all the respect you're due, Dr. Dill, shut your pie hole," Alphonse said. "No sense holding back now. The test happened in an isolated little village in Afghanistan, near the Turkmenistan border."

Thomas put his elbows on his knees and his head in his hands. Performed in a biohazard suit, the posture seemed almost comical. "I wasn't there. I only read the reports."

"The village was supposed to be a stronghold of insurgents," Jerry said. "We didn't know there was a school there."

My scalp got hot. I wanted to leap out of the LAV and run, long and hard — anything to get away from these people.

"With enough personnel, you *can* surround a little Afghan village," Alphonse said.

"Not like Toronto," Tom said.

"When the wind was right, we released the aerosol one night," Alphonse said, "The next morning, a few survivors ran out ahead of a bunch of zombies. They came out of the village at first light but the uninfected didn't get far."

"At first, it was just like in the movies," Jerry said.

"At second, it turned into a shit show," Tom added.

"The operation was going quite well until the women and children started running at the line," Alphonse said.

"What happened?" Shelly asked.

The LAV commander said nothing. He stared at me.

After a moment, Tom blurted, "You know what happened! We held the line, as ordered. By then, we didn't have a choice, anyway. Couldn't risk letting anyone out of the quarantine zone."

"Their attack wasn't tactical," Jerry said, "not then. They just ran at us. It should have been easy to lead the zombies away. Noise was how we controlled their movements then, as much as you can control a dead head, anyway."

"I've seen the video," Thomas said. "I wanted to scrap the project but we thought we could fix it. Aside from the unintended casualties — "

"Aside from the kids," Jerry said.

Tom bobbed his head. "They acted like wild animals. They didn't run and hide. They attacked each other in the village and whoever was left in the morning attacked the forces around the perimeter."

"So you're saying the infected shouldn't be able to plan at all," I concluded. "But they do."

"During the human trial, the subjects demonstrated absolutely no capacity for chronesthesia," my boss said.

"Talk English, Doctor," Shelly demanded.

"Animals don't have much for memories," Thomas explained. "They don't plan for the future. They live in the now. That's what our tests suggested about those carrying Picasso. They demonstrated some pack mentality but that was about it."

"Tell me more about the pack mentality," I said.

"I just read the reports. If Hamish Allen were here, he could— "

"I can tell you," Alphonse said. "They tend to go for the weakest and smallest first. Sometimes they'll just go for the closest victim. They seemed to play follow the leader, like they somehow knew which was the alpha. They followed the strongest people so athletic folks seemed to lead the way."

"If a dead head is mortally wounded or too weak, sometimes they'll get eaten by their own," Jerry said. "I saw that happen right in front of me."

"Those reports were inconclusive," Thomas objected.

Jerry was near tears. "I was there, Dr. Dill. I saw your new toy at work. On our side of the battle, we had a lot of closed caskets going home that day. We couldn't let the families know that their boys didn't die of gunshot wounds. Some were eaten alive."

Tom patted his fellow crewman on the back.

"That wasn't the worst of it," Alphonse said. "The worst was having to kill men under my command before they went feral, too."

"Where was this village exactly?" I asked. "We could ask the World Health Organization to mobilize a team, examine the remains — "

"The bodies that were sent home were all cremated. Any caskets went home empty. We hit the village with a MOAB," Alphonse said. "There's nothing left of that village to examine, Dr. Robinson. Not so much as two bricks stuck together."

CHAPTER 35

DANIEL

I awoke where I'd fallen. The bright summer sky had soured to a gunmetal gray. High winds off the lake pushed the roiling clouds in a race toward a twilight storm. The smells of blood — metallic and cloying — assailed me. I expected a headache from getting brained with a two-by-four. No headache came. Something else had changed, too. As I rolled over on my side, I spotted a license plate on an abandoned Caddy. The plate read: *CHROQKR*.

Chiro-quaker? More likely, Chiro-cracker.

Two thoughts occurred to me in quick succession: *Personalized plates with vague messages are a dumb waste of money.* More importantly, *I can read!* The little machines in my brain had granted my wish. *Illiterate no more!*

I was never a big reader but as soon as the ability was back, I wanted to chew through a library of books. Instead, the first words I understood (besides decoding *CHROQKR*) was the provincial motto: *ONTARIO, YOURS TO DISCOVER.*

I crawled to my feet. The scene of carnage revolted me. The trio who had attacked me were gone, one way or another, zombie or not. One was missing, either off to kill or dragged off to be eaten. The big man who had taken me down was now chewing on the man I'd kicked in the balls. He was making a hot, wet meal out of the guy's triple chin.

Hamish Allen said we were infested with brain parasites. Infested or infected, we were all monsters now. Still, I knew what was really going on in that man's skull. He was no doubt feeling horror, revulsion and self-loathing at what he'd become. I could do nothing for him but I felt I had to try.

I knelt beside the big man. "Hey."

I have my voice back, too! Hallelujah! I can talk again! I am not an animal! I am a man ... sorta.

He growled and went on about his grisly feast, uncooked and al fresco.

"I know you don't really want to eat that. I know you can hear me. I want you to know, this isn't your fault."

The man growled again but continued to eat ravenously, not even lifting his head.

"You've got brain parasites in you and some weird microscopic stuff I can't really explain. You'll try to fight it. I tried, too. I couldn't stop myself, either. The people who came up with this shit injected me with something else."

As I watched him tear deeper into the fallen man's throat, I felt the rising urge to join him in devouring roadkill. "I'm sorry I took your buddies down, man. It wasn't me. It was the parasites and the little machines in my head. I'm so sorry."

For a brief moment, the big man glanced at me. I thought I caught a flash of the human he'd been. As he paused to swallow a chunk of pink flesh, clear juice slipped from the sides of his mouth. His gaze held me for a second and a single tear slipped down one cheek. Then he dove in again and, when he came back up, a river of blood flowed from between his jagged teeth and into his beard.

He couldn't even mouth a silent plea but I knew he wanted to. I guessed he wanted me to kill him. I pushed the thought away. I'd wanted that, too. Not being in control of my body and doing awful things had felt like being buried alive under the weight of dirt and heavy sin. A screaming mind is still mute.

"There has to be a better way, man. I'm going to go find it. In the meantime, just keep telling yourself, this isn't your fault. This isn't you."

I began to get up to leave the big man to his meal. Then, quick as a flash, his hand shot out to grab me around the throat and squeezed.

CHAPTER 36

CHLOE

"Picasso's nano-matrix has changed since your damn test," I said. "Picasso's *learning*. I programmed AFTER to facilitate synaptic transmission and enhance cognition. I put in safety protocols so the cybernetic stem cells didn't multiply unchecked. It's supposed to optimize specific biological functions, adapting to the needs of the host without taking over."

"So you're saying the safety protocol you employed failed?" Rigg asked.

His tone didn't suggest he was looking for someone to blame but I didn't like the way he posed the question. "My safety protocol didn't fail. It was erased. Picasso perverts all my work. It's a damn abomination."

I turned to Thomas. "You did the demo with Nyx," I said.

"Yes. So?"

"Was there some sharing of information?"

"We had teams from both companies collect blood samples but all the samples came back to the Toronto lab."

"And they had access to Picasso?"

"They had to evaluate our proposed delivery system for the aerosol. That's all. They only had a few techs on site."

"Was Michael Cavanaugh or Douglas Hannah there?"

"No. Nyx's head of development, a Dr. Clover. She works directly under Mike — "

"When I met Cavanaugh, he told me similar tech was in development elsewhere."

"When was this?" Rigg asked.

"At the conference in Aruba. He's the sort of guy who is capable of industrial espionage. Numbers would mean more to him than people. Maybe he could be useful if Nyx could help us find a cure."

"The Nyx lab is on the far side of the continent, Chloe," Thomas said. "I think our best shot at solving this thing is getting into our own lab. That's where Picasso got out. AFTER's nano-matrix can learn."

"Then teach it something," Shelly asked. "You get a bad dog, first you gotta teach it to sit."

"AFTER's limits are two generations," I said. "In my lab, I always make the first generation. The nanites make the second generation so they can fix what I mean them to fix. That's where the manufacture is supposed to stop. If you let the bots keep on making bots, they become their own entity without safety valves. If the nanite colony learns too much from its environment, that old dog might not want to learn new tricks."

It seemed to me that the enormity of what he'd done was finally hitting Thomas. "AI without limits? How far could it go? Are we talking full sentience? A new species with self-awareness?"

"Slow down. I don't know if it's full sentience yet. Could be, theoretically. Some of the infected are acting like they can plan ahead, learn and adapt to changing conditions — "

"And use strategy to kill us," Shelly added. "Swell."

"When Cavanaugh talked about using AFTER's medical applications for weapons systems, I thought he was just bragging, trying to get me into bed."

It could have been that, too. I did look pretty hot in that party dress.

"Enough talk," Alphonse said. "I'm heading straight to the lab.

It looks bad but I don't see how it's going to get better if we don't deliver you nerds to your microscopes."

Rigg looked up from his phone. "Alacrity would be much appreciated. I just heard from the PMO. The United States government is not satisfied with shutting down the borders and taking a wait and see attitude. If we don't find a solution to this epidemic soon, we won't need to get into the lab. They're in discussions about nuking Toronto."

"Oh, c'mon! Would they really do that?" Shelly asked.

Rigg shrugged. "That's what I asked the Prime Minister, Officer Priyat."

"But the fallout — "

"The Americans are already flooding out of border cities, trying to put distance between us and them. It's a go if their government senses we're failing. The PMO is stalling but the White House seems unimpressed with our quarantine efforts. They're concerned the President is prepared to 'take precipitous action' if they don't see progress. Better to take decisive action that is wrong than to risk doing nothing and appearing indecisive."

"Better to do anything instead of the right thing?" I asked. "You know how stupid that sounds, right?"

"Politics and scared people," Rigg mused. "Explosive concoction."

"We worked out some worst case scenarios," Thomas said. "This is much worse than any of our projections. No one could have predicted this ... eventuality."

"Too many variables," I muttered. "There are always too many variables for predictive models to be accurate. When you play with possibilities this complex, you don't know what you don't know. We've gotta go find out what we don't know. Get us to the lab, Alphonse, no time to stop for tea."

CHAPTER 37

DANIEL

The big man's fingers closing around my throat were as thick as sausages, his palms as rough as sandpaper. He would have had me if I'd given him time to close his fist. Fortunately, the nanites had optimized my reflexes. I was a fast zombie.

I grabbed the fourth and fifth fingers of his hand and wrenched them back. My legs felt light and strong, as if they were made of springs. I kicked him in the face and he reeled back. His nose spurted blood and, as he rose, he licked at the flow fervently. Apparently, any blood would do, even if it flowed from his own broken nose.

He charged at me from a crouch, coming in low for a tackle. With his weight, he could easily shove me to the ground and pin me to the road. I slipped to one side and tripped him as he passed. He smacked his head, denting the fender. He whirled and growled as he came at me again.

I leapt away, onto the hood of a car. "Whoa, big fella. No need of that." I had nothing to prove and, frankly, I had more important things to do. I turned to run but that was not to be. A sudden silence fell over Lakeshore Boulevard.

Around me, hundreds of the zombie horde rose from their kills. The newly infected stared. Every victim of the Picasso outbreak seemed focused on me. Each of them stood perfectly still, watching and waiting. With their faces covered in blood and their vapid stares, I felt as if each gaze had weight, holding me still.

I understood. Zombies attacked the uninfected, to kill or to spread the disease. Whatever their decision making process, when they looked at me, they saw a monster who did not fit. Maybe speaking was enough to qualify me as food.

"Hey, everybody. Just here to let you know … um … I feel your pain. And he started it."

The big man attacked again, sweeping my feet out from under me. My back hit the hood of the car hard. If I allowed him to get hold of me, I was probably finished. He outweighed me by at least a hundred pounds and it wasn't all fat. He had muscle to back his play.

I rolled off the hood as he smashed his fist into the hood. My face had been in the spot he smashed a second ago. He probably broke a knuckle but that didn't give him pause. The big guy kept coming. I circled the car, trying to keep the vehicle between us.

"This is turning out to be a replay of me and Andrew Butters in Grade 3!" I yelled. "Long story, you're probably not that interested in right now."

Here's the short version: One day after school, Andrew asked me for the time. I said I didn't know. He threatened to smash the fender on my bike so, without thinking about the fact that Andrew was in Grade 5 and I was two years younger and smaller, I defended my property. I took a swing at him. To his surprise and mine, my fist connected with his nose and it got bloody. That big kid chased me round and round the parking lot until the music teacher stepped in to make sure Andrew Butters didn't murder me.

The longer version is that Andrew got his revenge years later by stealing my pants while I was in gym class. He shoved me into the girl's locker room. That's also how I got my first girlfriend. She broke my heart and that led me to end up with the girl who ran off with my best friend. I digress. The Law of Unintended Consequences is strong. That's my point.

The big man snarled as he attacked and I leapt atop the roof of another car. He was pretty slow and I probably could have avoided him all day. Unfortunately, more zombies got involved and they weren't on my side. They reached for me. A woman who looked like her shoulder had been dislocated made a grab for my ankle with her unmangled arm. Two more began to climb up, one from the hood, one from the trunk. I slipped to the ground and pushed the woman with the bad shoulder aside before the circle could close and cut off my escape route.

I briefly thought of running for Lake Ontario and trying to swim to freedom. Too many zeds blocked the way in that direction and they were coming toward me. In a moment of inspiration, I zigzagged through the jammed traffic to get to the mercenaries I'd killed. I went for the green military truck and began to climb into the back. Before I could close the door behind me, the big man circled his arms around me in a powerful bear hug. He lifted me into the air to pull me back.

I tried slamming my heels into his legs. He grunted enough with each blow to make me think I was hurting him. It wasn't enough. His grip tightened and I was losing air. Desperate to get away, I threw my elbows back, smashing him in the jaw twice. My third blow caught him in the ear and he staggered.

I grabbed for the lip of the van's back door and kicked and wriggled to get away. It wasn't the smooth and brutal counterattack I'd pictured in my head. However, I was sure that if I allowed the fight to go to the ground, he would have me given his weight advantage.

I almost got away but he grabbed my left arm. I surprised him by allowing him to get a better hold. As he pulled me closer, I twisted and whirled, and grabbed his beard. I pulled his face down as my right knee drove up and down, pistoning into his face and jaw. After five or six strikes, the big man let go and flopped back to the pavement with a hollow thud. His nose was all messed up and his breathing was ragged, like he was struggling to breathe through wet, twisted straws.

I'd won my fight with my attacker. As I looked down at him, I wanted to eat him. However, I had no time to savor my victory or his gizzards. I'd escaped no one's notice. The rest of the cannibals were coming for me. The noose was closing.

I jumped into the back of the mercenaries' van and took a quick inventory. It had exactly what I needed. Even my preferred weapon, the MP5, sat loaded in the gun rack.

CHAPTER 38

CHLOE

Alphonse took to the turret as Tom backed the LAV up to the steps at Echidna Biosystems.

"I'm hot," Alphonse called. "Drop the hatch but stand by for my go."

The hatch dropped, a ramp for our exodus. The afternoon had turned dark and heavy drops of rain began to pummel the steps up to the lab.

"Hold for my go," Jerry reminded us, "and no worries! The 25 mm gun up top fires 200 rounds per minute. That'll put a dent in any zombie's day."

Through the gaping hatch, I saw four people in environmental suits run out from behind a pile of sandbags and oil drums at the lab's front door. Each person carried a rifle and knelt in a semicircle to guard our path into the building.

I began to rise from my seat but Jerry signaled me to wait a moment until they'd removed some boxes from the back of the LAV. A nervy shake vibrated up my spine when I noticed that each person with a rifle was covered in blood spatter. How many of the infected had they killed before I got here? How many of their own had become infected in the battle? How far had the contagion spread?

Three more people in enviro suits, all empty-handed, emerged from behind the sandbags and raced to the LAV to retrieve supplies and equipment. Shelly refused to wait. She got out of her seat and squeezed between me and a pile of boxes. She grabbed a box on the way out. I grabbed a box as well and followed her.

Jerry stopped her at the door. "Hold up, just a sec. We don't want to run around like headless chickens and we want to make sure the guys with guns inside the door see you're on our side before you run at them."

"You think zombies would be carrying MREs and lab equipment?" Shelly sneered.

"Easy there, Officer Priyat," Jerry said. "The apocalypse doesn't come every day and these folks are nervous."

"Seriously?"

"You gotta take this a little more slow and methodical than you think you should. It's bad form to run at armed people who are scared out of their minds. Trigger fingers get twitchy."

We handed our cardboard boxes to the next two runners and picked up a couple more containers to help clear the compartment further. Thomas Dill and Ken Rigg hung back while we peons cleared their path.

Thomas Dill was still so deep in a sulk the guy needed a baby pacifier. I'd never seen this side of my boss but I'd never seen him in a really challenging situation until now. I could never again see him as the slightly creepy, very wealthy CEO of a tech conglomerate who collected old paintings and modern sculptures. The outbreak had crushed him. I hoped he'd prove useful soon. His was the face of a man aching for transformation and redemption.

Rigg was on his phone again. How could he possibly report to his superiors or receive fresh reports so frequently? Maybe he was playing *Candy Crush* to deal with all that annoying end of the world stress.

One of AFTER's earlier incarnations involved implanting a nano-cellular communications device in the heel of the human palm with a smart screen in the forearm. We'd be forever in touch yet always hands-free. It was feasible but the company shelved the project. Though it was viable, the invention was deemed "too early for the market." I never liked that particular application of my work.

I told Thomas we should hold off on development in that direction until we made more progress on the medical front. "Once we can be on Facebook and surf cat videos and porn 24/7/365," I'd told him, "pretty much all scientific progress will come to a grinding halt. We have to get civilization to an optimum point before we give our lives over to unending interconnection." Now I wished I'd backed that project. More cat videos never killed anybody.

Pools of blood splattered the steps. Peering out of the LAV's hatch, I saw bodies piled on either side of the door. It was as if the corpses were meant to supplement the wall of sandbags. The people picking up the boxes from the LAV looked harried and I felt their nervous energy at a glance. Even with our armaments, they felt exposed. In another moment, I understood why.

"All quiet," Tom said. "Too quiet. The jungle drums have stopped. They're coming. I can feel it, sure as shit."

"Never mind Tom," Jerry said. "He likes old *Tarzan* movies and he's pretty goofy."

"Clear!" Alphonse said. "Okay, go!"

"Okay, ladies," Jerry said cheerily. "Quick and quiet, up the steps and into the building. We'll be back on another supply run in a few hours, if we aren't all blown up, of course."

As we exited the LAV, somewhere not far away, the tank's main gun fired again. The report rolled and echoed through the downtown streets.

Jogging beside me, Shelly said, "That's just the Leopard, making noise, attracting attention."

"I thought we established that didn't work," I said.

"Guess we're not changing battle plans mid-stream," she replied.

Behind us, I heard Alphonse yell, "Tangos at ten and three!"

The gun atop the LAV spit rounds in rapid succession. Unaccustomed to running in a biohazard suit, I stumbled on the steps. Shelly dropped her box and grabbed my hand, yanking me up the steps. I powered up to a sprint so, by the third step, I ran beside her. My gym time, usually little more than a few sessions a week on an elliptical, was minimally taxing. Watching episodes of *Ozark* and *Riverdale* while working out wasn't nearly as motivating as the prospect of getting eaten alive.

I heard Tom yell, "Nine o'clock!"

Jerry's voice, so calm and soothing a moment ago, climbed to a much higher register as he yelled at Dill and Rigg to evacuate the LAV. He suddenly sounded prepubescent.

One of the runners who was supposed to fetch supplies knocked me down as he ran past me. I fell and rolled sideways to land on my butt. I was about to curse him out some more but I found myself on my ass, looking back on the street. Beyond the LAV, I could barely see pavement. The infected poured out of the side streets and surrounding buildings. They'd been waiting for us.

As the LAV's guns boomed on, they kept coming, heedless of the damage the ordnance did to their numbers. I heard Tom on the radio, calling the tank to come back to defend our position as Jerry pushed my boss out of the rear hatch. Thomas stumbled and almost fell but Rigg grabbed him from behind to steady him. It is hard to sprint in a biohazard suit. They aren't made for running.

Our guards around the LAV went to work, firing into the snarling throngs. The sheer number of zombies made me feel claustrophobic. I recoiled at what I witnessed as the zombies charged. It made no sense. Picasso was a weapon of mass destruction. Many more should be dead. Why weren't more of them dead? Most of the populace should be dead or running away from the cannibal killers.

Unless ... oh.

Somewhere, in a dim corner of my brain, a cluster of neurons fired and I jumped to a conclusion. I prefer rationality over intuition but a repulsive idea took hold: They're coming at the lab in massive force. They look like mindless rampaging cannibals but this is a coordinated attack. Why are they all coming at the lab? An intelligence with a larger agenda is behind this and … it doesn't want me to try to stop it.

Picasso is AFTER, without limits, I thought. *My creation is coming to kill me.*

EPISODE 5

machine learning (noun)

The cyber-evolutionary stage that precedes machine teaching, largely resisted by humans.

~ Notes from NEXT

CHAPTER 39

DANIEL

Our breed can't read or speak so the diseased must have been confused when I yelled to them from the back of the van, "I know this isn't your fault! Sorry!"

Zombies don't use machine guns, either. Seeing me wielding a weapon of man must have spun my attackers' tiny mental gears. I surely surprised them right up until the moment I put holes in their heads. I told myself I put them out of their misery.

Zombies don't drive. I did that, too. To escape the horde on Lakeshore Boulevard, I roared off, shoving the accelerator to the floor. I headed back downtown, taking the path the tank had made for me. I followed the way my captors had gone. The LAV couldn't be too far ahead and I had to get answers, maybe even give some. I had to go back to the hell that was the Box. I wanted a cure and the Echidna lab seemed like the only logical place to look for one.

Hamish Allen's nanites, in combination with wretched little brain parasites, had turned me into a monster. The woman with the mangled hand had injected me with a strain of Picasso that was more complex and curious. They called me First and their communication seemed fairly friendly. However, my newfound speech, literacy and autonomy felt tenuous.

I also had another, darker compulsion. A mission programmed deep in my nanite matrix compelled me to kill Chloe Robinson. Someone I'd never met was still ordering me around. And, upgraded Picasso or basic Picasso didn't matter: I was still ravenous for freshly killed meat.

The day before, I'd had few doubts about my place in the universe. I put on the ETF uniform every day, followed orders and did things I didn't want to do. I did my duty. I didn't know or appreciate how simple my life was. My midlife crisis had arrived years early and in the middle of the zombie apocalypse. Like my high school music teacher, Mr. MacDermid, told me when I tried to learn the drums, "Daniel, you have crappy timing."

Maybe that teacher was, at that very moment, running for his life from a zombie horde. Perhaps he was hiding under his bed, contemplating whether he'd rise to heaven or burn in Hell at any minute. I wondered if he ever thought of me or the slew of students he went out of his way to discourage. Mr. MacDermid always did have a reputation as a bully and a dream crusher, but he wasn't wrong about my timing.

Fate declared that millions had to die for vague and mysterious reasons I'd never understand. Or maybe all this was simply our fault and shit happens, no more complicated than a kid burning down the house because he played with matches.

Picasso was an epic tragedy. Many good people, victims and victimizers alike, would suffer and die in this crisis. At least not everyone was good. To keep the tears from my eyes so I could drive, I imagined Mr. MacDermid running through the streets, terrified, regretting he was a shitty person who'd been a shitty teacher.

If you have to eat a shit sandwich, you have to focus on the bread and not the filling.

CHAPTER 40

CHLOE

The black clouds rumbled and the rain began in earnest. Lightning strobed the city and a bolt struck the CN Tower. The guards forming a gauntlet between the LAV and the lab fired at the zombies racing in from all sides.

For just a moment, transfixed by the spectacle of the battle under the cloudburst, I froze. As powerful as the deluge of water was, it would not ever wash away the flood of blood from my memory.

This isn't happening. This can't be happening.

Dazed, I flashed on a memory of my mother taking me to a mall on the day before Christmas. I might have been six or seven. We waited patiently but the line hardly seemed to move. Two little old ladies were at the till but they took more time wrapping purchases than ringing them through. My mother held the red dress I wanted to wear to church. It had a lacy collar and a bow at the back. We had to get back home for some reason I can't remember, but I do recall the math.

My mother bent down on one knee to talk to me eye to eye.

"How many people are ahead of us, Chloe?"

I counted fourteen people ahead of us and told her so.

"Now look at my watch," Mom said. "Let's see how long the next couple of people take to buy their stuff and go."

It took four minutes for one and six minutes for the next.

My mother touched my shoulder gently, preparing for me to put up a fuss. "Given what you know, how long will it take us to buy your dress?"

I looked from her watch to the line of bored and impatient shoppers ahead of us. "We have to go, don't we? It's gonna take too long. Like, almost an hour."

"Good girl. I like your blue dress more, anyway."

"But my blue dress is old."

"How about we go home and come back for a Boxing Day sale when we have more time?"

"What if the dress isn't here when we come back?"

"Then we'll chalk it up to experience and get our Christmas shopping done earlier from now on, hm?"

I was a good little girl so I didn't throw a tantrum until we got back in the car. The red dress was still there after Christmas but I never got to wear it. Mom didn't believe in rewarding bad behavior. I wished now that she'd bought it for me. Joy is fleeting. Life can be harsh. Death is worse.

As I watched the guards frantically shoot, change magazines, and shoot again, I performed a similar calculation to the one I did in that mall so long ago. Somewhere within this scene of carnage, a mathematical formula took into account the variables. Weapons were efficient murder machines but they got hot, they had to be reloaded, they took time. Our protectors burned through their ammunition fast. Each time they changed magazines, the zombies gained ground. Their ammunition was not limitless.

On the other side of the equation, the zombies did not retreat. They did not stop to pull wounded comrades out of the line of fire. They were many. The humans were few. The math wasn't hard to calculate. When I solved for x, I knew the answer. We didn't have long at all before we were overrun.

The attack wasn't simply about zombies feeding themselves. They wanted to make more zombies. The nanites were reproducing and not just within each skull. With AFTER, a colony of nanites took on specialized roles. Some would become glial cells. Others would form macrophages to clean up particles, viruses or bacteria. A shot of AFTER was a healing injection of a microscopic superorganism. As the Picasso spread from person to person, I guessed that the nanites were forming a new superorganism in the macro, taking over our world.

Shelly came back for me, grabbed me under the arms and hauled me to my feet. "No time for gawking, Doctor! *C'mon!*"

The zombies continues to spill into the street until I couldn't see the street. It was only a mass of bodies. The LAV's weapons pounded into the swarm. Alphonse Fortin killed and killed but still the cannibals kept coming. It occurred to me that Picasso was defending itself and taking massive losses to do so. Perhaps the AI had taken my code and reinterpreted it for self-preservation, making sacrifices in the macro to keep generations of AI alive in the micro. Victims of the disease had become bio-weapons. They sacrificed themselves to our metal rain for the robot overlords in their heads. Zombies made the perfect soldiers. Witnessing the siege, I had no doubt the nanites would triumph in the end.

I allowed Shelly to pull me along but I found I couldn't look away. This was the end of the world and I had to bear witness, hypnotized by the sheer numbers of the infected. It was as if we had turned over a termite nest and the insects were crawling over each other to get at us.

I'd programmed limitations into the cybernetic stem cell matrix. Nanite death was meant to protect us from nanite overgrowth. As I took those precautions, I even joked about accidentally inventing cyborg brain cancer. Someone had overwritten that code with disastrous effects. If by some miracle we could erase the threat, we would never recover from this disaster.

A rumble and clank reached our ears before the Leopard tank rolled into sight. The huge machine's weapons fired into the crowd, chattering, booming and thundering. The guards around me cheered as the tank raced through the throng, crushing all in its path. The turret swung in slow arcs, turning the infected to bloody chunks with each blast.

The defenders' cheers died in their throats as the tank kept going down the street. It soon disappeared from view.

"Where's he going?" someone asked. They sounded more astonished than angry.

There were still boxes of supplies aboard the LAV but Jerry closed the hatch. I heard him screaming, "Go! Go! Gimme smoke! Get out of here! Go!"

The swarm boiled past the LAV and hit the bottom of the steps as I got behind the sandbags. Thomas Dill and Ken Rigg were halfway up the steps. They yelled something but I couldn't hear them over the bedlam's din and the fire laid down by the guards. Four more men with machine guns ran out of the lab, past me and into the battle.

A man appeared at my side. The tag on his blue biohazard suit read: Crenshaw. He must have been their team leader. He yelled orders that could hardly be heard over the gunfire. "Come back here, you fools! Retreat! Get back in the lab!"

The LAV's eight grenade launchers fired almost at once. I expected explosions. Instead, eight canisters burst into a smoke screen that suffused the personnel carrier in blue and white clouds.

As Thomas and Ken Rigg raced up the long shallow steps to the lab, Rigg took the lead. Cannibals tackled two of their protectors. The remaining guards kept firing and the zombies kept coming. Mercifully, the white and blue smoke overtook the tangle of combatants.

I heard the LAV's engine roar as the personnel carrier took off in the same direction as the tank. I guessed the Leopard was clearing the way for Alphonse, Tom and Jerry.

Thomas had taken too many long lunches and hadn't spent enough time running. He almost tripped again on the wet, slippery steps. As one of the guards reached out to steady him, the Samaritan was pulled into the wall of smoke. His scream was somehow made worse because it was so short. More gunfire erupted from within the smokescreen and I saw flashes of light, but those didn't last long, either.

Dr. Rigg was a fast runner. He would have easily made it into the lab if he hadn't dropped his phone. Stupid instinct was stronger than his fear. He bent to pick up the device and never straightened. A man and a woman jumped on his back as Thomas ran past him without a sideways glance. The zombies did not look to the fallen. Neither did my boss.

Ken Rigg became the unwilling sacrifice that allowed my lousy boss to live. Two children — tweens, I guessed — wrapped themselves around Riggs' kicking legs to pull at his boots and socks, eager to feed.

Thomas collapsed over the sandbag wall, panting and spent. One guard emerged from the smoke, his blue enviro suit covered in blood. He was still firing into the crowd when the man to my left spoke. "Go through the lobby and down the ramp on the left."

The guard's rifle clicked empty. He did not run toward us hoping to reach safety. Instead, like a crazed Norse berserker, he fought hand to hand. He grabbed his weapon by the barrel and began to club his attackers' skulls. "Do it, Dale! Do it! Fill the castle moat, you pussy! *Do it!*"

Crenshaw pulled a road flare from a Velcro pocket on his thigh as he told me. "Run for your life."

The man sounded surprisingly calm as he yanked on a rope that ran through a pulley. The oil drums, six of them in all, tipped over to spill their contents down the steps. Through my faceplate, there was no way for me to smell the liquid. I guessed it was gas or kerosene. I hoped it was kerosene. Kerosene would burn longer.

I pulled Thomas after me and ran for the ramp. I heard the flare ignite and sizzle. The accelerant went up with a huge *WHOOMF!*

Zombies may never retreat or pause at the death of one of their own. However, when they burn to death, their anguished screams sound human. I suppose one of those horrific death throes came from the guard defending the lab. I think he was still human when the conflagration enveloped him.

CHAPTER 41

CHLOE

I followed Shelly Priyat down the ramp and Thomas followed me. The constable looked back at me. "Where's Rigg?" I couldn't bring myself to say anything. I drew my right hand across my throat.

Dried blood stained the floor at the doorway to a long office. It was packed with empty desks. People standing around in biohazard suits. Most carried weapons.

Most of the white Hazmats showed no insignia but the blue and green ones showed group affiliations at the shoulder. The greens were Public Health Agency staff. The blues were Toronto Police Services and RCMP.

It seemed everyone was talking at once but I heard Shelly yelling my name. She waved me closer. She stood in a gaggle before a huge steel door. As soon as I stepped within reach, she grabbed my arm, pulled me close and turned to a man in a white Hazmat. Nothing set him apart except that he only wore a sidearm instead of carrying a rifle. "This is Dr. Robinson!"

The man turned to look at me. "Tell me who you work for."

"Prometheus Rembrandt BioSystems, Cybernetics — "

"Full name?"

"Chloe Torielle Robinson."

"What street did you grow up on?"

"In Winnipeg?"

"No, when you lived in Toronto."

"That was later. Um … Gothic Avenue, Toronto. Number 9 —
"

"And your employee number?"

"It's 56589."

"Uh-huh. Okay." He didn't consult a clipboard. He'd memorized my information. "I'm Bill Arsenault, Canadian Security Intelligence Service. The decontamination chamber is only so big. You're a priority as soon as that door opens. One sec."

I watched as he pressed buttons on a steel keypad with what looked like a stupidly long code sequence. "Isn't that protocol beside the point now?" I asked.

"Yeah, one horse is out of the barn but the chamber runs through a cycle. We can't just reprogram it and let everybody parade through. Besides, there's still anthrax and shit down there."

"This is insane. We've got to get everybody into the lab, behind this door!"

"If you don't like it, Doctor, I'm sure, there's a bureaucratic protocol where you fill out a request in triplicate and file it up your ass. Somebody on vacation in Muskoka will get back to their office in Ottawa sometime by the end of August."

My boss pushed through the crowd to announce, "I've got to get down to my office. It's on Level 3."

Arsenault asked Thomas several questions similar to those he'd asked me. Satisfied with his answers, Arsenault bobbed his head just as the chamber's hatch buzzed and clicked open. "Okay, you go through with this batch."

The room, which had been so loud, suddenly hushed as a long howl — starting low and climbing high — rose nearby. The zombies had entered the building.

"Holy shit," somebody said. "They don't know when to quit. Why are they so fired up about trying to get in here?"

Me, I thought. *They're trying to stop me from stopping them. All these people are dying for me.*

The people who were armed turned their weapons on the door just as Crenshaw appeared at the bottom of the ramp. "Easy, everybody. Friendly coming in. I'm the last friendly you'll see coming down here. They'll be coming in as soon as the smoke clears and the fire dies. Pile those desks in front of this door."

They followed Crenshaw's orders no matter the color of their biohazard suit. Those who were unarmed pressed from the back to get closer to the decontamination chamber, eager to get to the safety of Level 2.

The crowd pushed as the hatch opened wide. I resisted and grabbed Shelly's arm. "Wait! She's with me!"

Before Arsenault could say a word, Shelly shrugged me off. "Go do what you do, Chloe. My place is here. I have to defend the Alamo."

I glanced at the people crowding into the decontamination chamber behind me. A few of them carried rifles so security staff were still a priority. "Constable Priyat is my bodyguard," I said.

Staying on Level 1 was certain death. Shelly knew that but she didn't even allow me to fight for her. "I have a door to guard, Chloe. Go. Save the world."

Thomas pulled me into the decon chamber. As the hatch closed, Crenshaw and Arsenault rushed to squeeze in beside me.

The last words I heard from Level 1 were Shelly's. "Let's roll."

The hatch buzzed, closed and clicked with terrible finality. Shelly's fate was sealed. The decontamination chamber felt as claustrophobic as a tomb.

The sacrifice of all those brave first responders would have been so noble had it not been for a couple of tragic details. None of our precious supplies of food or equipment made it from the LAV to Echidna's laboratories. Worse, the lab's computers were destroyed. I found no notes, no records at all that would be of use to stop the Picasso Strain on Levels 2, 3 or 4.

All we found were the bodies of the dead.

CHAPTER 42

CHLOE

Thomas Dill stood in the middle of the Level 4 lab surveying the corpses. Some were ETF agents who'd come into the lab to secure it. Others were laboratory staff. "I knew these people. I hired every one of them, hosted them at the annual Christmas party in my home."

"There will be a lot more bodies upstairs by now, Thomas."

"I know. Ken Rigg was ahead of me — "

"I saw how he died."

"It's just so damned awful. How are you holding up?"

"Numb. I like it that way. We have to go at this like pediatric surgery. Imagine we are operating on a child. The fact that it is even necessary anywhere, anytime makes me want to cry. Now's not the time to cry. Now's the time to do."

"I wish I was numb," he said. "I just want to go to bed and not wake up."

"If we're going to stop this thing, we've got to figure out what to do next. There are no lab notes left. The computers are destroyed. I couldn't find anything more than a Post-it note from one tech to another saying it was the other guy's turn to clean the monkey cages."

Trying to hold back tears, Thomas took a few deep breaths. "They will bomb us but that won't stop Picasso. Somebody will get away. There are always survivors. It's already at the edge of the city by now. The check is in the mail. The world's already over. It just doesn't know it yet."

"Focus. What can we do?"

"I think that's the problem. I was working on what we could do instead of asking whether it should be done."

He was projecting. There was no 'we.' Thomas cursed us with Picasso and he was wasting time feeling sorry for himself. "Thomas! Diseases die out because of vaccines or cures — "

"When the host dies off and the parasite can find no more victims, Picasso will die. That's the only way this ends."

"Listen. We've got to figure out a vaccine or a cure."

"Vaccines and cures don't come from wishing hard. That takes years of research. Have you got a time machine, Chloe? Can you step out of time while we figure this out?"

Thomas sat in a chair and ran one gloved hand along the top of a formica lab table. "This isn't the first time microorganisms have wiped out most of life of Earth, you know. There have been several extinctions. The big one was 250 million years ago. We were overdue for another ELE. You know anything about Extinction Level Events?" he asked.

"My dad taught Earth Science, though I'm more familiar with the album of the same name," I said.

"Album?"

"Busta Rhymes."

Thomas chuckled. "You're funny. I could have really had something good with you."

"Yeah, but what would have been in it for me?"

He let that pass in silence for a moment and then moved on. "I wonder why we don't teach kids more about past extinctions so they'd understand how incredibly fragile everything is. Do they know about the Great Dying? Maybe they do. It's been a long time since I was in high school. Anyway, this time it's aerosolized brain parasites and nanotech. In the Permian Extinction — that's the Great Dying — the apocalypse came in three waves. Insects, plants, marine life ... almost everything went away. So much life was erased that it took 10 million years to recover. Volcanoes were stage one, then maybe one or two meteor impacts. The third wave of death came from methanogens. With the greenhouse effect, the microbes mass produced and shit out methane. Microscopic killers ... *heh*. Just like Picasso."

I tried to get Thomas back on track. "There's got to be something. Bombers might already be on their way. Think! There's no secret computer with all the answers somewhere? No more backups of the backups? Anything that can help us?"

"You're used to clean code and neat equations that balance out. This is biology. Biology is ... messy. I'm sorry. I really thought we'd have more for you to work with. Hamish Allen was a nut but he was a nut who really knew how to cover his tracks."

"So we've got nothing at all?"

"'Air pudding and walk away pie,' as my old pastor used to say. There's a bright side. I'm not worried about going to jail anymore. I have nothing to fear from the investors or the Board of Directors. What's left to worry about? That's the appeal of the end of everything. We can stop trying so damn hard," — he gestured to the dead — "just like these poor souls. Look at those ETF guys. So many situps and pushups wasted."

Thomas pulled at his biohazard suit's seal and yanked the protective hood from his head. He took a deep breath and smiled.

"This is Level 4! What are you doing? That's not safe — "

"Safety was a luxurious illusion. Now it's a memory. Smells bad in here, Chloe. Smells like blood and death and failing antiseptic and canned air."

"Put your hood back on, Thomas!"

"Why? The aerosol was released into the street. With the rainstorm, that vector is surely a dead end by now." He pulled at the tape around his wrists and yanked off his gloves, too.

"There are other deadly biological agents down here, Thomas."

"At this point, I assure you, the Ebola in our tanks won't get a chance to kill me. If the zombies don't get me, I imagine one of these guys with guns will oblige when they find out they won't see their families tonight. This is my fault."

Thomas walked around the lab, stopping at each bloody corpse and giving a little bow. "It's almost funny, the symmetry ...."

"The symmetry?"

"If you think about it, this disaster is unfolding in three waves, just like the Great Dying. First, the waterborne vector married your nanotech matrix. Second, Hamish Allen let the genie out of the bottle into downtown Toronto. Third, the zombie apocalypse. Buncha bastards will eliminate all life and transform survivors to crazed animals."

"The rest of the world will be fine."

"For a while, but you know it will spread. Someone will bring the disease to foreign shores and the cycle will repeat. Curiosity will kill the cat. Meanwhile, in the Western hemisphere, a few humans will escape to remote areas. They'll try to eke out a living but the systems that make civilization work will certainly decay. Eventually, the survivors may live in caves. They'll live off rats and live like rats. A few people in bunkers will survive for a while. There's that NORAD base in Colorado, but whatever survives of humanity won't have the opportunity to appreciate a fine wine or a lovely Matisse for ten million years."

"You're giving up too easily, burying the whole human race too quick. I'm not lying down."

He wept silent tears but he had anger to spare, too. "Congratulations are in order. We extrapolated from your work, yes, but without you, none of this kill tech would be possible. You are one of the giants whose shoulders others have stood upon. Judging from the sheer number of cannibals a few floors above us, their bites must be incredibly venomous. That's my contribution. Well, Hamish Allen, really. Weapons developers aren't eligible for Nobels, even if we did it to serve peace. North America is about to get really peaceful, after about eleven months of chaos, anyway."

"Eleven months?"

"The cities will fall quickly. It's the rural areas where everyone is armed and people are spread out where Picasso will slow down. Still, it'll happen, faster than most people clean out the burnt food at the bottom of the freezer. *Heh.* Come to think of it, we *should* be eligible for the Peace Prize."

"You're reminding me of something my mother told me, Thomas. She said it when I did something shitty or when someone did something shitty to me. 'We judge others by their actions. We judge ourselves by our good intentions.'"

Thomas took a deep breath. "You're not wrong. I'm the first person to breathe the air in this lab since its construction. God, it stinks down here." He surveyed the corpses again. "That's their fault, poor buggers. Hamish was too smart. I hired him for the same reason I hired you, you know. I surrounded myself with geniuses. I knew Hamish could really produce for me. Aside from an impressive resume, he gave me quite a lecture in his first interview. He was hung up on the difference between the words *venomous* and *poisonous*. He gave me a condescending lecture on the difference. He was an obnoxious, pedantic hippie, but damn, that man knew his brain parasites."

"Blood samples." I said. "We can take blood samples from the dead. The ones that were bitten. Then we have to get out of here, to another lab."

"And do what?"

"To understand what Hamish knew. I have to see how Picasso interacts with the brain parasites."

Thomas tapped his naked wrist. "*Hmph.* Tick, tock. Oops! Buzz! You're out of time. Thank you for playing. Sorry, no consolation prize, we're dead. Soon we go boom."

At that moment a loud alarm sounded and I jumped. The alarm stopped abruptly and an intercom in the wall popped on. "Dr. Dill? Dr. Robinson? Do you have what you need down there? We've got a red light on our control board. Someone just entered the Level 1 decontamination chamber."

"Who?" I called.

"The zombies are coming to get us," Thomas said.

"Shut up. Zombies don't crack codes to hatches in high security labs."

The man on the intercom pressed on. "We don't know who it is, the control room's pretty messed up. Could be an extraction team to help us evacuate or help coming with supplies. Whichever, you'll need to bring them up to speed on what you've figured out. Come up for a briefing, please."

Thomas laughed. "Tell them we don't have dick! Drop the bomb! And tell them to drop it right on top of us. I don't want to starve to death down here! Toronto, Canada, the United States ... maybe even Mexico! As far as an infected person can walk, it's all a write-off. If you're an optimist, Europe is about to have a new Renaissance. The hope of the world might be China and Australia. Anywhere but a good chunk of the Western Hemisphere is a good place to be."

"Shut it, Thomas. And stay here. Stay in quarantine. Take blood, skin and hair samples from the dead. I'll go up and stall."

As I left he called after me. "I knew we couldn't last forever, but I thought we'd outlast the polar bears!"

I shouldn't have left Thomas alone. I suspected he was suicidal but I didn't care enough. Neither my actions nor my intentions toward my boss were gentle. I would have been a terrible disappointment to my mother.

I went through the decontamination chamber and Level 4 staging area to take the elevator back up to Level 3. Level 4 was too much of a disappointment to me.

CHAPTER 43

CHLOE

As I stepped off the elevator to Level 3, I watched my step. The bodies had been carted downstairs but the floor was still awash in blood. The small space had been a scene of mayhem beyond my imagining. The only thing I could imagine would be worse was whatever happened on Level 1 when the zombies attacked. I pictured Shelly firing into the mob as the cannibals blocked the door trying to get at the last human defenders.

I looked around at our few remaining security personnel. They glanced at me nervously before returning to stare at the hatch, guns at the ready.

Bill Arsenault and Dale Crenshaw stood talking at the door to the control room. Behind them, a tech had pulled wires out of the wall and seemed to be working frantically to get a surveillance camera hooked up. Another technician had opened the back of a desktop computer. He twirled a screwdriver to pull something from the machine's guts. A pile of weapons still lay on the control room floor.

I went to Arsenault. "I've got an idea but we'll need to evacuate to another location. Any equipment on Level 4 that might have been useful is fried. Someone set a small fire down there, too."

"Makes sense. The terrorist was thorough. The control room got ganked," Arsenault said.

"You want us to go back up?" Crenshaw said. The ETF officer did not look happy with me. "We fought to get you down here."

"The equipment I need is either not here or not working. I don't have as much as a working laptop on Level 4. I need more people, too."

"Any other good news?" Crenshaw made a show of being pissed.

Arsenault was one of those guys who look like they wouldn't be surprised if the room turned upside down. "Have you learned anything we can use from this sightseeing excursion?"

"The boss is on Level 4. He has to stay there. Best place for him, really. I gave him something to do to keep him occupied. He's taking tissue samples — "

"There's thousands of zombies outside!" Crenshaw exclaimed. "Why do you need samples from down here in this … this damn tomb? We could be miles away — "

I cut in, keeping my voice low and even. "The epidemic started at Echidna. If I compare samples from here and from out there, I might be able to understand the development arc of the nanites, if there is one. I need data and the tools to analyze the nanite colony's evolution."

Crenshaw cursed and paced. In such a small space, the ETF officer looked quite ridiculous. I turned my attention to the CSIS agent. "You should also know, Dill took off his biohazard suit."

Arsenault looked perplexed rather than alarmed. "Why would he do that in a quarantine area?"

"He's not taking the end of the world so well."

"People are going to lose it," Arsenault said. "He won't be the last." The government agent fixed me with a gaze that made me feel like I was the only person in the world. In another context, his attention could be misconstrued as romantic. I knew better. This was a guy who was used to interrogating people. He asked a good question. "What was your boss exposed to on Level 4?"

"We have to assume everything. He could be Typhoid Mary, for all I know. Hamish Allen wiped out all the records, not just those pertaining to Picasso. I don't know what they've been working with in the clean rooms. They could have more bio-weapons in the works down there. Dr. Allen could have damaged the tanks as part of his sabotage."

"Or maybe they're compromised because of all the mischief in the control room," Arsenault said. "My tech says he can't even confirm the temperature of the containment tanks in the vault from here. If he was trying to slow us down and destroy the lab forever, if he had that kind of time — "

"I inspected the tanks," I said. "They looked okay. I'm no expert on those kind of biologicals but the thermometers were in the green."

"One killer disease at a time, please!" Crenshaw said.

"We can't be sure how deep this cesspool goes," Arsenault told him. "Like Dr. Robinson, we need more data. Tell me, Chloe, is your boss holding back on us in any way?"

"I don't think so, but I don't get the sense that Thomas has been very hands-on with this division."

"Agreed," Arsenault said. "I checked out Dill's office after you two went downstairs. No pictures of family, nothing in the garbage can. His real office is elsewhere. The drawers were locked but they were close to empty and there was very little to indicate he did much here on a day-to-day basis. He's not the guy who works in a bunker's basement. I'm guessing he's the kind of guy who prefers a big corner office, high up, with a nice view. "

He seemed to have Thomas Dill pegged. Bill Arsenault really was a spook. I'd assumed CSIS was here to help secure the bio-weapon prototype. It occurred to me then that part of his mission was to gather evidence, point the finger and assign blame when the time came.

Crenshaw gave me a hard look. "Are you sure he took off his

suit all on his own? You didn't do it for him? Maybe to cover something up?"

Arsenault put a hand on Crenshaw's chest. "Dale, ease off — "

"We can't take this woman's word on anything. She works for the company that came up with this shit. Dill says the disease is based on her work — "

"Look," I said. "If you don't believe me, you can go down to Level 4 and ask him yourself. Don't forget to wear your snowsuit, bundle up and be sure to wear the mittens with strings so you don't lose them. I don't have time for your shit."

A tech in a blue biohazard suit leaned into view. "Our visitors are coming down, sir. The hatch from Level 2 is sealed and the chamber is starting its cycle."

"ETA?"

"Coupla minutes."

"Thanks, Mark. Keep working on the surveillance camera for Level 1, please. We may need to exit back through there soon."

Crenshaw's anger was still at a high simmer. "Y'think? It's the only way out, so, yeah, I say we stay the hell down here. Let the reinforcements come to us."

"There won't be any reinforcements," Arsenault said. "All available forces are either working to keep everybody in the city or helping with evacuation of the uninfected and trying to control the infected."

"You don't know which?" Crenshaw asked.

"Since the Americans threatened to bomb the city, my intel may be dated and the situation is certainly fluid. I was supposed to coordinate with Ken Rigg from the PMO's office — "

"Rigg's dead," I said. "Or he joined the zombie army."

"Flying in heavy fog and no daylight on the radar," Arsenault concluded. "I'm sure a bunch of troops are rushing back from overseas but, considering you could fit all our active duty personnel in the Rogers Centre to watch a Jays game, I don't think — "

"What about the Americans?" Crenshaw asked. "How about sending help instead of nuking us?"

"Whoever they have available will be massing along the border to keep out refugees … and that zombie army."

"This is crazy," Crenshaw said. "Let's talk to her boss. There's got to be more we can do down here. I lost a lot of good people getting into the Box. I can't — "

I poked Crenshaw in the shoulder. "Sorry, but those people you lost are a sunk cost. We can't stay here and solve the problem. I need staff who are up to speed, a bunch of virologists and — "

"Where do you think you want to go?"

"I don't know. The CDC?"

"They don't want us in Atlanta, Doctor," Arsenault said. "They sent some people but, last I heard, as soon as they caught that tank's recon report, they turned around."

"Who can blame them?" Crenshaw said. "We're overrun."

"Get me to a lab somewhere. After mass death, more diseases follow. Rats are vectors. Birds are vectors. Between carrion and rotting flesh, a biological agent could slide into the groundwater. The logistics on the problem are only beginning. I'm an engineer, not a biologist, but I know that much."

"How do you know?"

Exasperated, I blurted, "Because I read *The Stand* and *The Hot Zone* in college. Didn't you?"

Arsenault, at least, had the grace to laugh. "Officer Crenshaw is more of a Margaret Atwood fan. Hamish wiped the computers but my forensic data tech is pulling the disks. There may still be some recoverable data — "

"Good. With the blood samples from the dead downstairs, maybe I can figure out a way to break the pairing between the nanites and the brain parasites. If the neural matrix shuts down, then we're just dealing with brain parasites. That should be easier. On their own, a skull full of brain parasites is bad but they're basically a bone box of worms and not nearly as smart."

"You've got quite a honey-do list, don't you?" Crenshaw said. "How are we supposed to get out of here with monsters crawling all over Level 1?"

I gritted my teeth and gave the cop more lip than I'd ever dared to give any police officer. "You want me to help solve problems or do you want to bust my balls? We don't have time for both."

Arsenault's cell phone must have been patched into Echidna's modem because, at that moment, it buzzed. "It's an update from the PMO's office," he said. "You two retreat to neutral corners. I'll have more intel for you in a second."

The hatch from Level 2 buzzed.

The guards brought their guns to bear and Crenshaw, perhaps in an effort to reassert control yelled, quite unnecessarily, "Heads up!"

The steel door clicked and yawned open. A woman stepped into view. Her biohazard suit was bloody. Her hood was off. Her black hair, matted with blood and sweat, hung in her eyes. Shelly Priyat stood frozen and dazed. *Ding!*

The elevator from Level 4 arrived and the doors parted. Thomas Dill, drooling and growling, paused just long enough for me to see the hypodermic needle that still hung, embedded in the blue vein at his left elbow. He had infected himself. The bastard turned himself into a zombie before I could give my official two weeks' notice.

I really should have stayed in Aruba with the Foo Fighters.

CHAPTER 44

DANIEL

My return to the Box was not what I expected. At the bottom of the ramp to Level 1, it was a zombie massacre. I had to crawl over a mound of bullet-riddled bodies and through a broken barricade of office furniture.

The rest of Level 1 was exactly as I expected. The defenders were wiped out. Zombies don't use guns. That's a disadvantage. They don't run out of ammunition. That's an advantage.

There were only two cannibals left when I arrived. One wore a suit. The other was a very thin man, naked and covered in blood and scratches. Neither of them spared me a glance as they fed on the dead. As I picked my way through the carnage, I still didn't understand how they recognized I was one of them. Fortunately, zombies don't use phones so the ones who'd attacked me on Lakeshore didn't warn them I was a traitor to my new species.

When Hamish Allen infected everyone with his version of Picasso, they turned into animals. Since my injection from the mystery woman in Port Credit, I'd reclaimed a bit of my humanity.

For instance, I could read the scrawled blood-smeared note on the floor outside the door to the photocopier room: *ALIVE INSIDE.*

I looked around and found a Colt Canada C7. Out of ammo, the assault rifle only weighed about seven pounds so when I took down the first zombie, I really had to swing for the fences. I chose the naked man first. If my plan of attack went badly, I really didn't want to wrestle with a naked dude. It went well. When the stock met the back of his skull, I heard a high, satisfying *pop!* Home run. He crumpled.

The one in the suit turned and leapt at me, snarling and flailing his hands like claws. I broke his nose with the butt of the rifle but he kept coming. He was a heavy guy. I should have taken him out first. As I fell backward over a corpse in a ripped Hazmat suit, I almost wished I was wrestling the naked man. Before I could get up, the big man was on top of me, snarling and trying to bite my nose off.

I got my forearm under his chin and wrapped my legs around his torso. I imagined this victim was just another Bay Street trader who popped out for a chocolate croissant on his lunch hour. Somebody bit him or he inhaled Picasso on the wind. His bright red tie was my salvation.

I reached for the Windsor knot and cranked it as hard and as far as I could clockwise, cutting off his air. Sorry, Bay Street Guy. I'd like to think you were a raging asshole before you got infected. I'd like to think you picked out this tie yourself one day, never dreaming it would be the instrument of your death. I'd rather not think it was an anniversary present from your wife or, worse, a Father's Day present.

"This isn't your fault," I told him. "Sorry."

Before the blood vessels in the whites of his eyes burst and his lips turned blue and he went limp, he managed to mouth one word: Don't.

Strange, I thought. *The zombies only seem to be able to communicate above a snarl when they're in the middle of combat. In battle, Hamish's nanotech lost a little bit of control over the parasite's host. The little robots in their heads aren't as easy to get along with as my generation of nanotech.*

If he had died a couple days ago from a heart attack or something, he would have been remembered as an individual with a name. He wouldn't look like the drooling, homicidal bad guy. Now, he'd be just another number added to the dead, a statistic.

When I was sure Bay Street Guy was dead, I rolled him off me and made my way to the tiny room with the photocopier in it. I had to see if the note was still true. Was anyone alive inside?

My hand hovered above the knob. The last time I'd been here, I'd fed on the security guard's corpse. I couldn't bring myself to go in. Instead, I knocked softly. "Hello? Anybody home? I — "

The door burst open and I was amazed to find it was a familiar face. Shelly Priyat was covered in blood and her eyes were wild. She wasn't infected, though. She held a knife to my throat.

"Hi," I said.

"You can talk?"

"Daniel Harmon, Emergency Task Force. Call me Dan."

She pressed the blade of her knife harder against my throat. "What the hell happened to you?"

"Long story. Telling it at the edge of a knife isn't standard procedure, is it?"

"No games."

"Okay. I'm infected but I negotiated a truce."

"What?"

"The tech in my head thinks I'm fascinating."

"Bullshit. Why aren't you like the rest of them?"

"I'm still a carrier, but I got an upgrade. If you'd like to take me prisoner again, we could go downstairs and discuss it. I need to see Dr. Robinson. Is she here? Did she make it?"

Shelly pulled away. "You tried pretty hard to kill me when this whole thing started. You sound reasonable now."

"I'm growling less lately and my tummy's full. I had a snack on the way in."

"And you're a comedian."

"Thanks."

"Not a funny comedian."

"Oh."

Then Shelly Priyat made the mistake of taking her eyes off me.

She looked around and took in the massacre. "It really was the Alamo." She began to weep.

"Answer me. Is Dr. Robinson down in the Box?"

Priyat nodded. "She was in the last group to go through to Level 2. She was going to try to fix things, get down to the vault on Level 4 and …. "

"You okay?"

"Of course, I'm not okay! I ran out of bullets in the first minute of the attack. I only had my pistol and a knife. I lost my baton and I couldn't use my pepper spray." Her gaze searched the pile of bodies twisted together in a puzzle of blood and bone. "A sergeant ordered me to the rear. When they ran out of ammo and more and more started getting through, I hid in there and …. "

"You did the smart thing."

"Did I?"

"Absolutely."

"There were more of us in here before."

"I'm sure a bunch of the newly infected left to join the horde. They act like ants or bees or something."

"Or something?"

"I don't get them. I'm one of them but I must have missed a memo."

Shelly wept some more and I gave her a minute. There should be no shame in surviving, but there is. I knew that from horrible personal experience in this very spot.

"When I got my wisdom teeth out, I wanted to be asleep for it," Shelly began. "My dental surgeon gave me a local instead. I was awake and aware of everything. It didn't hurt a bit," she said, "but the sounds … the prying and pulling and grinding. I heard it all as he took out my teeth. That's a little of what it was like to be on the other side of that door, standing over a chewed corpse of a security guard and listening to what was happening out here."

I felt heat rise in my cheeks. The security guard's name was Tarique. Hamish had mentioned he was a nice guy. It didn't seem like the right moment to share the fact that I was the zombie who had fed on him. There would never be a right moment for that.

"Chloe is down in the vault. There's no way to get to her. You'll have to wait until she comes out."

"We don't have to wait. Fifty-five African Zebras To 500 Lions Won One Victory, Three Trapped People Died Quick."

"What the hell are you babbling about, Harmon?"

"I know the master code."

That's how Officer Shelly Priyat and I ended up on Level 3 just as some maniac came off the elevator from Level 4 and attacked Chloe Robinson.

CHAPTER 45

CHLOE

I saw an impossible thing. Thomas rushed out of the elevator, pushing two men out of the way to get at me. His eyes were wild. Everyone began yelling at once. I'm pretty sure I screamed. In Aruba, Thomas told me, "I need your brains." Now he was a zombie, coming to collect.

Before my boss could reach me and eat my face, another man ran at Thomas in a blur of motion. He tackled Thomas, slamming him into the wall. They both went to the floor in a tangle. Thomas wasn't in his biohazard suit, but neither was the man who saved me. Then I saw it was Shelly's prisoner, Officer Daniel Harmon, back from the dead.

I watched in horror as he grabbed Thomas' head. He slammed it into the tile floor until blood burst from the back of his skull. He kept going until we all heard a loud stomach-turning crack. I almost threw up.

Harmon yanked back Thomas's throat as if he was trying to clear his airway and give him mouth to mouth. Instead, Harmon buried his teeth in his neck, ripping and chewing.

I threw up.

Bill Arsenault charged forward and pushed Harmon off Thomas while Dale Crenshaw delivered a savage kick to Harmon's chest. Every gun on Level 3 was brought to bear on Daniel Harmon's head as Shelly screamed, "Don't shoot!"

Crenshaw told Shelly to shut up and stood over Harmon, his pistol drawn. "I thought I killed you on the front steps, Danny. Should have. You're a damn zombie. I'm gonna have to kill you twice."

Shelly grabbed Crenshaw's gun hand. The weapon discharged but, thanks to Shelly, missed. Crenshaw's shot put a hole in Thomas' stomach but he was well past caring.

Shelly pushed Crenshaw back. "He *knows* shit! He got me out of Level 1! He's not like the others. He told me! The tech in his head, it calls him the First. He's got answers! You kill him, you kill us all, you idiot!"

I threw up again, straightened, bent over and threw up one more time. Then all I had was dry heaves. I staggered back toward the control room door and picked up a gun from the floor. I didn't know anything about guns but I'd gone unarmed in the zombie apocalypse for too long already.

Harmon looked up at Crenshaw, gave a half smile and slowly climbed to his feet.

"He's gotta talk to Chloe," Shelly said.

The cluster parted and our eyes met.

"What do you have to tell me?" I asked.

Harmon ran at me, knocking Shelly and Crenshaw aside. Reflexively, I brought up the muzzle of the rifle and pulled the trigger. The rifle tip was at his heart. Nothing happened. I would have torn him apart if the safety wasn't on.

Harmon stiffened and fell at my feet, convulsing, as a long pulse filled the room. *TICK-TICK-TICK-TICK-TICK-TICK-TICK-TICK-TICK-TICK-TICK-TICK-TICK-TICK-TICK-TICK-TICK-TICK-TICK-TICK-TICK-TICK-TICK-TICK-TICK-TICK-TICK-TICK-TICK-TICK-TICK-TICK-TICK-TICK-TICK-TICK-TICK-TICK!*

Arsenault had taken down my attacker down with a Taser.

I looked down at Harmon to watch the paralyzing effects of neuromuscular incapacitation. Maybe Shelly was right and maybe he had insights that would prove useful. He wasn't human anymore though. If there was doubt in anyone's mind, all they had to do was look to my dead boss's blood still trickling down Harmon's chin.

Arsenault took his finger off the Taser's trigger. Crenshaw and his men moved in to cuff Harmon.

I stood over Harmon, exhausted and revolted. "What the hell are you? What have you become?"

I didn't really expect an answer and I sure didn't expect him to utter a word I'd never heard before. Daniel Harmon looked up at me with a shit-eating grin and spoke.

"Robo-zombie."

AFTER LIFE

BOOK THREE

PARADISE

EPISODE 1

First came Artificial Facilitation Therapy for Enhanced Response. Beyond AFTER, our destiny lies with what is NEXT.

~ Notes from NEXT

CHAPTER 1

CHLOE

As we debated how to escape the bowels of Echidna Biosystems, the missile that would destroy downtown Toronto was already on its way.

"Are you sure you can't fix the epidemic from down here?" Crenshaw asked. "There's a million cannibals on the streets, Doctor." The ETF sniper used the word doctor as if he had maggots tucked between his cheek and gum like a cancerous wad of tobacco.

Daniel Harmon had just tried to kill me. I was flustered but I stood my ground and tried to put the bass of authority in my voice. "You're afraid to go back up, I know — "

"People died to get you to Level 4, a lot of people. Was this bunker just a pit stop?"

So much for commanding respect. I took a deep breath, slowing my speech, trying to give Crenshaw time to slow down and calm down, too. "I've got all I can use from the vault. We've got the tissue samples from the dead. We've got Daniel Harmon back, alive and infected. We need those clues to figure out what to do about the plague but I can't analyze the data effectively down here. Wishing doesn't make things nice and neat. It never does."

"The weapon got out of this lab," Crenshaw said. "The diaper exploded here. Clean up your mess — "

"I know you want an easy solution, Mr. Crenshaw. I do, too, but this isn't a movie. The equipment is fried. We have to get to a lab with more facilities."

Bill Arsenault stepped between us, addressing me as if Crenshaw wasn't there. "Got a text. The Americans offered Fort Bragg but the Prime Minister refused. With the loss of supplies and personnel, it's not a question anymore. We are moving to a new location, more secure and with the resources you'll need."

Arsenault's tone was soothing and conciliatory but I wanted to scream. They'd brought me for my expertise on nanotech but they didn't want any unpleasant answers. They weren't prepared to listen unless someone else higher up approved.

"My direction from the PMO is that we are to evac to Suffield," Arsenault said. "They've handled dangerous materials research before — "

"Where's that?" I asked.

"Alberta."

"Do we have that kind of time?" I asked. "There's a virology lab in Manitoba, right? I don't know what pathogens they work with there but at least it's closer."

Daniel Harmon lay on the floor where he'd been tased and handcuffed. He rolled over on one side and stared at me. He looked hungry.

Crenshaw trained his pistol on the prisoner's head. "I told you not to move! I swear to God I will kill you."

Harmon didn't spare a glance at Crenshaw. His gaze remained fixed on me. "Suthina."

"What?"

"Suthina Laboratories. That's where they created my upgrade. Go there."

Arsenault crouched to get a closer look at Harmon. The taser darts were still in the man's shoulder and the CSIS agent's finger stayed on the taser's trigger. "Who told you that?"

"You won't believe me."

"Maybe I won't but I'll listen hard."

"The Voice told me," Harmon said.

"Who?"

"My new operating system, the AI in my head. It's kind of like talking to an alien. Our ways are strange to it. I didn't realize it until lately, but our ways *are* strange. It's a little confusing, isn't it? You need me to draw you a flowchart in purple crayon?"

Crenshaw rolled his eyes. "Did it send you an email or text, Danny? What makes you so special — "

"Focus. Try to catch up," Harmon said. "The zombies have the AI that talks to the Picasso brain parasites. I've got the evolved version. These new nanites think I'm a better conversationalist."

Arsenault looked to me. "Possible?"

"Not what I designed, but with the safeties off — "

"Is it possible or not?" Arsenault asked. "Choose carefully. This man tried to kill you a couple of minutes ago. I'm not going to take his word for anything."

"I designed AFTER to behave in predictable ways. If someone wanted to play fast and loose with the progression, sure, it's unexpected but, in theory, it's possible."

Arsenault rose to his feet and handed Crenshaw the taser. "Ruin Mr. Harmon's day if he acts up. Tell me what's on your mind, Dr. Robinson."

"We don't have to trust Harmon's word," I said. "Can you find out what the corporate connections are for Suthina Laboratories? Parent companies, shell corporations maybe? That sort of thing?"

It took the CSIS agent less than a couple of minutes to find out. He didn't need fancy spy connections. Echidna's modem was still up and running and Arsenault had the wifi password. He asked Siri and, yes, Suthina Laboratories was a division of Bio-Echo, a subdivision of Nyx Management Group.

"That's it, then," I said. "My boss messed up AFTER and Cavanaugh's people stole it. We shouldn't go to Suffield. We should go to wherever Suthina is and work with the thieves. Where is Suthina Laboratories, anyway?"

"Bainbridge Island."

"Where?"

"Washington."

"Which one?"

"Washington State." Arsenault tapped his phone again. "A short ferry ride to Seattle."

"Even farther than Suffield, though," Crenshaw said. "A minute ago you thought going to Alberta was too far."

"Then I got new information and worked from that," I said.

Crenshaw shook his head. "We should still go to Suffield. Orders are orders and Suffield will be safer."

Furious, I glared at Crenshaw. "If you want safe, you're in the wrong job. Safe was yesterday. Deal with it and get out of my way."

All my life, men in positions of power and seniority had told me I had to pay my dues, to wait my turn, to play the corporate game, to beg for more grants and share credit for my work. They all told me my snark and chronic case of resting bitch face wasn't helping me advance in their world. Very soon, their world wouldn't exist.

I turned my back on Crenshaw and looked Arsenault in the eye. "Tell the Prime Minister that the only expert he's got is going to Bainbridge to stop the zombie plague. Tell him I need to call the shots. I'm in charge of finding the cure. It's not the PM and it's not you guys. It's me. If you want my help then let me do my thing. With Thomas dead, you'll need a goat so, if this all goes south, you can blame me for your failure. I am not some consultant you shove to the side. Let me make the decisions from here on out or drop me off at a Walmart somewhere far away so I can stock up on food, batteries, ammunition and M&Ms. It's going to be an ugly, gory apocalypse."

I thought throwing in the line about M&Ms was a nice flourish. Shelly Priyat allowed a small smile to leak out at that. However, it was Daniel Harmon who let out a belly laugh.

"Dr. Robinson is right," the prisoner crowed. "If you have any hope of stopping the spread of the disease, listen to her. Follow her or die running around in circles. This is just the start. This is just a little rain. A blood storm is on its way. Don't piss off the only one of you who knows how to work an umbrella."

"Not for nothing, but you just tried to murder her, Harmon," Crenshaw barked. Crenshaw pulled the trigger on the taser and Harmon's body went rigid as his muscles rebelled against his will.

He only stopped torturing Harmon because, at that moment, an explosion rocked downtown Toronto. We didn't merely hear the bomb hit. We felt it as we plunged into darkness, drowned in claustrophobia and disorientation. In the moment before the lab's emergency lights came on, I backed up until I felt the cool concrete wall against my back.

As the reverberations ebbed, everyone on Level 3 went silent except for Daniel Harmon. The prisoner let out a grim chuckle. "Turns out the forecast isn't just blood rain. It's shit and steel all over the weather map. Your time to shine, Chloe! Can I call you Chloe? Sorry about trying to eat you. I'm not myself lately. Zombies don't apologize so I'm not one of them anymore … not quite. I really am sorry."

He might have been sorry but he'd still kill and eat me the first chance he got. I wanted to take the taser and press the trigger until the battery drained.

CHAPTER 2

DANIEL

I'm not myself lately. I wondered, what ratio of nanites to brain cells would it take before I wasn't me at all anymore? Would the nanites keep multiplying until they formed a sloshy slurry in all the crevices, wrinkles and spaces in my brain? The microscopic robots had granted me some sovereignty, but how long did I have before independence lost all meaning? To paraphrase Obi-Wan Kenobi, how long before I was more machine than man?

Dr. Robinson could take control of the mission because she was invaluable. My only value to the nanites seemed to spring from being the first human they'd played with on an intellectual level. I was the First, but they could make me a pet again at any moment. Worse, they could be listening to my thoughts about them. I didn't want to give them ideas so I tried to focus on what was happening around me.

As the survivors of the attack on Echidna emerged from the lab, the missile's devastation was evident. The explosion had not been nuclear, as had been threatened. I guessed that the ordnance must have been an anti-personnel fragmentation bomb. Shattered corpses were everywhere. The dead lay in mounds and mazes. There was no direct route to safety without climbing over bodies. A thick cloud of dust hung in the air like a thick curtain. Shattered glass crunched under our feet as Crenshaw pushed me ahead of him.

Chloe and her security detail didn't understand the devastation as I did. Safe in their biohazard suits, they didn't feel the full effect of the stench: the burnt bodies, the cooked flesh, the tang of blood in the air. I caught the whiff of marrow leaking from bones. Downtown Toronto was an abattoir.

Under their hoods and behind their faceplates, they'd hear the pulse in their ears and the staccato of each ragged, fearful breath. I listened to the dead. There is an eerie silence to those who are no longer present. Erasure is such a complete and final act, made worse because I knew what the humans didn't even suspect. No one but me knew that inside every one of those dead zombies had been a person, their mind a prisoner, their body compelled to act on the impulses of an AI with the morality of a brain parasite.

That was Picasso's true horror: Utter helplessness in the face of terrible acts, being forced to do awful things you don't want to do. I wasn't a cannibal at heart and neither were any of these people. The survivors from the lab saw dead monsters everywhere. I saw ordinary people slaughtered in a war past their understanding and beyond their control.

It was difficult to run with my hands handcuffed behind my back. Fortunately, we didn't have far to run. Alphonse, Tom and Jerry were true to their word. The LAV crew returned to pick us up.

We would have been safe if we were the only survivors of the blast. We weren't the only survivors. The blast that leveled Hiroshima had survivors. There are always survivors. A couple dozen zombies ran out of the bank complex across the narrow street. More boiled out of the underground plazas like ants from a kicked anthill. I heard them coming before I could see them through the dust. They sounded angry and still healthy enough to be dangerous.

One of the security detail, a clever fellow in a blue hazmat, gave an odd warning. I suspected he'd been waiting to drop it as if he were in a movie. As he opened fire, the man screamed, "The only good zombie is a dead zombie!"

Forgive us, I thought. *We know not what the hell we do.*

The man who'd tried the one-liner filled with bravado was yanked to the ground first. He popped up a moment later, screaming like a little girl and using the butt of his rifle to bash at his attacker's skull. He kept at it, cracking bone and helping the zombie the rest of the way down the road to death.

While he was busy doing that, two woman took him down and wrenched off his hood. He managed to kill one of the women with his pistol. The second bit off his nose. He seemed too distracted to defend himself after that. He did not die quickly or with dignity. Blood and panic made his high, nasal screams sound like they emanated from the bottom of a half-clogged drain.

The rest of the security team concentrated their fire, killing their brother-in-arms and the zombies who had taken him down. They had bullets enough to cut down the zombies coming at us from the buildings across the street. What they hadn't counted on was shock and panic as half-burnt, near-corpses rose from the piles of the dead. Though shrapnel had stripped flesh from their bodies, the ragged zombies summoned enough strength to pull humans to the ground and into their maws. From a mound of bodies, many arms reached out, their hands like claws.

Zombies who had somehow survived the fire and the fragmentation blast looked awful and awfully dead. Their charred flesh smelled sickly sweet. Many were naked, their clothes burnt or torn away. As they rose from the rubble, they moved with slow, tortured deliberation. Dazed but determined to feed, they lurched at us from out of the dust cloud. Despite the wounds to their hosts, the brain parasites fought to survive. Covered in wounds that would soon fester, much of their mangled flesh had been torn aside in bloody flaps that opened and closed as they shambled toward us.

A building had fallen and blocked our escape route. The LAV waited a couple of streets away. There must have been more than one missile. Perhaps the military had taken down buildings in an attempt to barricade the downtown area. Alphonse and his crew couldn't get to us and keep a clear escape route. The LAV wasn't far but we had to run to it.

The wounded zombies were not fast, but there were enough of them rising and reeling out of the dust that soon our escort's gunfire lacked deliberation and skill. The shots and shouts became more and more wild. The nightmarish echoes of gunfire, panic and pained screams bounced around, seeming to come from all directions.

Crenshaw ordered ten men to keep firing to lead the surviving zombies away from the LAV and back toward the Box. "Defend the lab and hole up on Level 2! We'll come back for you with more reinforcements!"

The remainder of the team kept firing, clearing our way to the LAV. When the rear hatch dropped, I heard the crunch as the armored door crushed skulls of the fallen. I wondered if the sudden light of day was the last thing those zombies' brain parasites sensed. Maybe the last of the AI puzzled over the sudden illumination for a second or two before shutting down.

A couple of zombies reared up beside the armored personnel carrier and lunged for Chloe. Apparently Shelly Priyat had reloaded down on Level 3 because she shot the pair of zombies in their faces.

As gunfire rang out in volleys behind and around us, Chloe, Shelly, Crenshaw, Arsenault and three more men in biohazard suits clamored in. Tom and Jerry did not wait for more runners to catch up. The hatch rose and shut with a metallic thud. They might have saved one or two more humans had they waited a moment. That was not to be.

In the passenger compartment of the LAV, Alphonse was surprised to see me. "Back from the dead?"

"I got delivered from Evil," I said.

"You got away from us."

"I'm back with a vengeance and ready to party, laughing in the face of death, living on the razor's edge, this time it's personal — "

"Somebody shut him up," Crenshaw said.

"You're going to want to talk to me while I'm still sort of me," I said. "I don't know how long I'll last. When the AI figures out what it wants to do … well, I don't know what will happen, actually."

"I'm more interested in your cerebrospinal fluid, right now," Chloe said.

"Take me out to dinner first?" I suggested.

"I'm not on the menu, Mr. Harmon."

"You could be the dessert menu. Please be careful around me. I bite but, like I said, it's not me. It's just my teeth. It's the AI telling me what to do. It's irresistible. I'm programmed — "

Shelly yanked a black bag down over my head. Then somebody took a cheap shot and slammed his fist into the left side of my head. It had to be Crenshaw. What Crenshaw didn't know was the nanites were busy shutting down pain signals from my nociceptors. I didn't know the word nociceptors, but somehow they did.

I was aware of my jangled nerves but I felt no agony as Crenshaw targeted the joint of my jaw with another hard right hook. Thanks to the AI boiling through my head, pain was just a signal now, easily dismissed. I was not myself and becoming even less so. Little by little, my humanity was slipping away. I never thought I would miss pain, but now its absence worried me.

CHAPTER 3

CHLOE

I took a few things with me from the Echidna Biosystems lab. We had the corrupted disks from the weapons lab computers and zombie tissue samples. We took Daniel Harmon with us, alive and infected. The thing I left behind was my confidence that everything, no matter how dark it might seem, could work out for the better in the end.

Downtown Toronto was on fire from Eaton Centre to the Queen's Quay. Only God could count the dead. The streets were a sea of sadness. Whoever was in charge bombed Toronto so we could escape. I doubted I could arrive at a solution that could make my escape worth the price paid.

A tank cleared our way again but the LAV didn't have to travel all the way back to Port Credit. It seemed we'd only just cleared the perimeter of devastation when Alphonse steered us in a sharp turn that took us to an empty school grounds. As the LAV rocked to a halt, I heard the beating of rotors.

Jerry hauled me to my feet. "Word came down, you're a VIP.

You've got a ride waiting at Pearson. You'll fly from Pearson to Suffield."

"I said we aren't supposed to go there — "

"It's just a stop to switch aircraft, Doc. Then you'll go on to your final destination, wherever that is. Not my business and above my pay grade, ma'am."

Final destination made me think of those movies where Death stalks people at every turn. I don't believe in omens but, when Jerry said those words, it sure sounded bad.

"You'll take a short trip on a Cormorant helicopter," Tom said. "As soon as the hatch drops, run to the helo. Everyone else will bring up the rear."

He moved down the line and touched Shelly's arm. "You're to stay with us, Officer Priyat. Sorry, but I don't have you on my list to get past the velvet rope. Everybody goes but you."

I stepped behind Tom and pulled Shelly to her feet. "Do you want to stay?"

"Of course not but — "

"Then come with me. See this through to the end. You saved my life back there. I need a bodyguard. You're it. Guard my body. If I don't make it, who's gonna fix this mess?" I sounded more confident than I felt.

Shelly gave a small nod.

"Good. For a minute there, I thought I'd have to get Crenshaw to handcuff you and drag you on the helicopter."

Crenshaw heard me and let out a dismissive guffaw.

That pissed me off so I added, "If Crenshaw's coming to my party, you are definitely invited. She's with me, Tom."

"But she's not on the list."

"Doesn't matter. Officer Priyat is on my list."

I handed the box of specimens to Shelly. "Hold on to these and guard them with your life ... you know, while you're guarding me."

The LAV's hatch dropped and the Cormorant was just touching down as I reached it. The LAV's chain gun fired, competing with the roar of the helicopter's rotors. When I peered back toward the highway, I saw people in the distance running toward us. They ignored the gun and kept coming. The one in the lead was a young woman. A pack of killers ran behind her. At this distance, I strained to see but I couldn't tell for sure if she was infected. Did she run so fast because terror drove her? Was it hope for escape? Or was it raging, murderous hunger?

I hope she was a zombie because Alphonse cut her down, same as the others. Maybe she'd been an awful person before the Picasso epidemic struck. I wanted her to be someone who deserved her fate, a crazed serial killer maybe. Chances were excellent she was just another person who paid her taxes reluctantly but on time, drank too much coffee, browsed Facebook too much and worried about the future. Odds were she was just like me.

I boarded the Cormorant and we rose into the sky. I watched the LAV tear back the way we'd come, back to the city of smoke and blood. They still had to go back to rescue the rest of the security detail at Echidna. I envied Alphonse, Tom and Jerry a little. They had a job to do that was well-defined. They knew what they had to do. I had a big box of tissue samples, a bodyguard and an infected man who seemed awfully eager to murder me with his teeth. The rest were a bunch of guys with guns. Without anything to shoot, they'd probably just hang out and watch me fail to stop Picasso.

We landed on the tarmac at Pearson beside a huge plane. Someone mentioned it was a Globemaster III. It felt odd to board an aircraft by walking from the runway and up a ramp at the rear of the aircraft. Maybe that's why I paused at the top of the ramp to look back. I soon wished I hadn't looked.

When we'd arrived at Pearson from Aruba, all flights had been canceled. People were still trapped in the airport. If anything, the crowding had become worse. People from nearby communities ran to the airport hoping for a flight to escape the epidemic. Men, women and children pressed to the glass and pointed. They all seemed to be pointing at me.

The plane's engines were already powered up. I couldn't hear those trapped people, but by their faces I could tell they were yelling, pleading to join me. A Globemaster III is a big plane. There was plenty of room.

Shelly urged me forward. "C'mon. If you want to save them, siddown! Let's go. We can't save them all and if we tried to save a few, there'd be a riot. We could lose the plane."

I did as I was told, strapped myself into a bucket seat and closed my eyes. I didn't open them again until I felt the rumble of the wheels stop and we lifted into the air, buoyant and above it all.

Or so I thought. The pilot pulled us into a steep climb as the engines roared. I hate flying at the best of times. This wasn't the best of times. I turned to Shelly in the seat beside mine. I had to yell to make myself heard. "What's he doing? Does he think this is a rocket ship?"

Shelly shrugged. "He'll level off soon. I gotta get out of this biohazard suit. When I can get to a bathroom, I'm going to pee for about five minutes straight."

"You can take it off anytime. Unless Harmon bites you, you're not going to get infected now." I pulled off my hood. The air inside the plane was not fresh. It smelled of metal and jet fuel. Still, it was a relief to be free of the biohazard suit, scratch my nose and stop breathing hot, stale air that fogged my faceplate.

Shelly seemed to take that as a good indication she could take hers off, too. The rest of the security detail followed our example. We all looked shiny with sweat, hair askew and relieved to be out of Toronto's zombiefest.

I looked out the window hoping for a glimpse of blue sky. Another plane, identical to our own, flew beside us. Beyond it, two fighter jets escorted us. And still, we climbed at a steep angle.

Bill Arsenault was out of his suit, too. He appeared in front of me, steadying himself by a hanging strap. "The other cargo plane has some of the infected we've gathered up."

"Jesus! For what?"

"You need to experiment some, right?"

"The way you say that makes it sound like I'm Frankenstein. I'm a biomedical engineer. And what are those jets for?"

The CSIS agent didn't smile. "Don't mind those Hornets. They're just here to make sure we get there."

"Why wouldn't we get there?"

"Forces are at work, Chloe. Forces beyond our control."

"Feels like everything is beyond our control," I said.

"Something bad is going to happen in a couple of minutes. Stay in your seats and hold — "

It wasn't a couple of minutes. That was the moment the gray day went white, then orange. I squeezed my eyes shut but brilliant light swallowed us. Even when I covered my eyes with my hands, it was too bright.

A question formed in my mind but I was too dazed by the after-image of the flash to bring out the words.

As I opened my eyes, Arsenault threw himself into the seat beside me. He struggled to pull at the straps to buckle himself in quickly. "This doesn't feel like minimum safe distance."

For a second I thought we'd collided with another plane. Or we were on fire. Or someone was trying to shoot us down. Anything was preferable to my dim suspicion. The obvious answer was too horrible.

The blast wave hit.

Arsenault was a few seconds too slow getting buckled in. We were thrown sideways, then down and up. The engines screamed in protest as thunder ripped over us. The noise hurt my ears. The vibrations and reverberations shocked my system and shook my heart. I thought the sound itself would tear us apart.

As the plane lurched into a dive, the straps of my seatbelt clamped down as if to choke my torso and squeeze out my guts. Turbulence heaved the aircraft and threw Bill Arsenault from his seat. He slammed into the ceiling first and then hit the deck with equal, resounding force.

The Globemaster rocked and wobbled as the pilot fought for control of the aircraft. Debris of some kind peppered the fuselage and something metallic gave way. The plane dipped and fell again. Small holes appeared close to the rear of the plane. The air pressure changed. Wind whistled through the damaged fuselage and dust whipped through the compartment. The Globemaster abruptly began to climb again. All we could do was watch helplessly as the CSIS agent's limp body slid along the floor to the rear of the plane.

"Murphy just screwed us again!" Crenshaw yelled.

He looked crazy to me. I yelled, "What?"

"Anything that can go wrong, surely will! Murphy's Law!"

"What's happening?"

"They pulled the trigger!" Crenshaw screamed, near hysterical. "They pulled the trigger too soon! The men I said I'd come back for are burning to death or blown apart right now! And we've been dosed!"

We rocked sideways again and my seatbelt pulled so tight I could barely breathe. I reached out, grabbed Shelly's hand and squeezed. She squeezed mine in return.

"I'm gonna have bruised ribs," I said. "How about you? You okay?"

"I, uh, I-I don't need to p-pee anymore."

It seemed like a long time passed before we leveled off. As soon as I could, I unbuckled my seatbelt and, moving from strap to strap, made my way to Arsenault. His scalp was bloody. He might have survived the knock to the head if that was his only injury. However, his neck was a loose spring. He wasn't breathing and I could detect no heartbeat.

One of the security detail, a man with a bright red goatee, waved at me to get my attention. "You gonna start compressions— "

"It's over for him. Maybe he's lucky."

Crenshaw was crying and laughing at the same time. Something had broken in him, too. He pointed to the body at my feet and yelled to Daniel Harmon, "Are you going to finish that?"

People have weird reactions to the unexpected and unspeakable, battlefield reactions. Soon, everywhere would become a battlefield. Stephen Hawking was right: Artificial Intelligence would spell our doom as a species. He saw our end coming but even that one in a billion genius could not have predicted what form it would take. The zombie apocalypse used to be a joke. The joke was on us.

Our pilot sounded haunted when he came over the speaker. Confirming our worst fears, he announced, "From here ... Toronto is ... gone. Looks like all of it. All of it."

CHAPTER 4

DANIEL

No one said a word for a long time. We flew west. We thought about the city we loved and all we had lost. Even if they rebuilt it someday, as they did Hiroshima, it would never be the same. Toronto was supposed to be one of the safe and happy places. Now it would be synonymous with death and destruction. A chapter in a history book — if there would actually be history books in the future — wouldn't do the city justice. Toronto. Toronto The Good, they used to call it. And, by and large, we were good.

Losses to history are abstract. Losses remembered by people are always weirdly specific and personal. I'd miss the funky stores on Queen Street West. Since I was a kid old enough to ride the subway and streetcars by myself, I'd wander down to the Silver Snail on Saturday afternoons to check out comics. I wouldn't call my stash of comic books a collection anymore, but I owned a decent library of graphic novels. Undoubtedly, it was all on fire. My mint copy of *Watchmen* was probably burning as the protective mylar sleeve melted around the ashes. I'd never gotten around to reading the latest book in the post-apocalyptic series, *Y: The Last Man*. I'd left it on my bedside table. On my last night as a human being, I'd opted to scroll through Instagram looking for bikini models instead of reading. And, of course, just about every friend, enemy or date I'd ever had incinerated.

There'd be no more vanilla bean hot chocolates at the Second Cup on my cheat days. I'd miss The Horseshoe Tavern and the shawarma place on Spadina, just south of Queen. No more late night feasts in Chinatown with the boys, either. I liked taking dates to the top of the Plaza when things started to get serious. I loved the view of the city from the Plaza.

No more people. I'd miss the people the most even though, at present, my body's first instinct was to eat them. Everyone I knew had been erased as if they'd never existed. Would Toronto be a no-go zone for a generation? Would they start up a new Toronto farther north? How does one even start to bury that many people? Or would the bodies all be incinerated in the blast?

Depending on the size of the explosion, how far out would the damage go? Were people still alive in North York? Did my sister get my email? Did she and my father make it out of the city? Had anything survived the blast? How many zombies survived?

That's the problem with easy solutions: Often, they aren't solutions at all. I remembered a project in school where I had to research the explosion of the first atomic bomb used against Japan. I still remembered the haunting shadows of people burned into walls by thermal radiation. Most people think a nuclear blast is so fierce that it vaporizes populations instantly. If only that were true. People burn. They die from the trauma of the explosion's impact. Then comes the killing radiation sickness. The irony of Hiroshima that stuck with me is that, in the first seconds of the nuclear age, the blast buried someone working in a library under a pile of books.

I watched Crenshaw weep openly and wail loudly. I'd once seen him make shitty jokes about finding a dead baby in a garbage can. He'd bragged about his low heart rate contributing to his uncanny ability to snipe from long distances. Crenshaw had seemed to be one of those guys who complained about the pay but stayed on the job because what else could he do? He wanted action and acted eager to shoot people. Now, of all the people on the plane, the ETF sniper seemed the most upset, unable to rein in his emotions. I'd been wrong about Crenshaw's tough guy image. All the time I'd known him, he'd been pretending to be someone he was not.

Maybe that's true for everyone. One thing I've learned from the apocalypse is that we don't really know anyone until we see them under stress. Too bad I had to learn that lesson this way. Maybe I would have gained that knowledge had I gotten around to reading *Y: The Last Man.*

After a long while, Crenshaw looked over at me. "What are you looking at, Danny?"

I said nothing.

"Why are you eyeballing me, Danny? You mad dogging me, man?"

"Curious, is all."

"What? You're the zombie who can talk, so talk."

"How long did you know Hamish Allen?"

"What?"

"Funny that you were his accomplice but you ended up shooting him, isn't it?"

A couple of the others heard me over the drone of the plane. Perking up, they leaned in to listen.

Crenshaw stared at me, his mouth hanging open. "What did you say to me?"

"You heard me. These guys heard, too. Hamish Allen told me you were the guy who was supposed to get him in the isolation truck and take him away safely. You messed up. You shot him. You unleashed the airborne brain parasites. You thought you were killing me but you ended up killing everybody, didn't you? How many pieces of silver were you going to get for that job, Judas? Were you going to retire to Fiji or something?"

"You bastard." Fresh tears ran down his cheeks.

"Don't worry, Dale. Any evidence of your treason is burned up. No one will ever know for sure but you and me." I glanced around. The faces of the men on his security team had turned to stone. "And these guys'll know, of course."

"Allen did not tell you that."

"You're right, Dale. Hamish didn't put a name to his accomplice. I made it up but your reaction tells me I just made a direct hit. I sunk your battleship, buddy."

Crenshaw stood. For a moment, I thought he might kill me. Instead, he stalked away to the far end of the plane and sat alone. People who aren't guilty proclaim their innocence loudly, over and over. The guilty may begin by denying accusations but soon retreat into silence, contempt, resentment and shame. Dale Crenshaw got too quiet to be innocent. No hard evidence remained that could convict him, but I knew I was right.

CHAPTER 5

CHLOE

I pounded on the cockpit door. Neither the pilot nor the co-pilot would open it so we could speak face to face. "This plane has been dosed with radiation," I yelled. "We've been lit up with rads. I'm not looking forward to it anymore than you are, but we need to shower, get scrubbed down as soon as we land, the sooner, the better! Medical evaluations, fresh clothes, blood tests, potassium iodide, at least. I'm not even sure what else — "

I hadn't noticed the intercom in the bulkhead by the door. When someone finally answered me using the device, I felt foolish. "We have clearance to land at CFB Suffield but we are not particularly welcome, ma'am."

"What does that mean?"

"It means we are not to leave the tarmac. The infected on the other Globemaster will be taken on a separate helo. When you deplane, no one is to hesitate. Run to the waiting helicopter immediately. It'll be close to the plane, okay? If you or anyone else deviates from the shortest distance between our aircraft and the next transport, you will be shot. You all will be taken to your next destination immediately. There isn't room to travel with the captured dead heads."

"That's not going to help us — "

"Listen carefully. My orders are that you and your escort will go on the first helo. Only four of you can go. The passenger list is you, Officer Priyat, Mr. Arsenault and the infected man. Do you understand?"

"Arsenault's dead."

"Stand by."

After a couple of minutes, the pilot came back on the intercom. "Mr. Crenshaw will accompany you to guard the prisoner."

"But about the radiation — "

"I've talked to the tower and the officer in charge, ma'am. Getting you to your next destination is the only priority. The rest of your group will follow you on the other helicopter. That is all."

I pushed the button on the intercom and pleaded to be patched through to someone at Suffield.

"Do you understand the orders, Dr. Robinson?"

"Yes, but — "

"Then we're done." The crew did not reply when I pushed the call button on the intercom and I soon felt like a useless pest. I returned to my seat beside Shelly and waited to land. It was a long flight. I tried to sleep but all I could think about was the damage that had been done to us from the blast. How long before radiation sickness took us all out?

It was dark when we arrived at the airbase. All I saw of Suffield was a line of yellow hazmat suits outlined by bright lights in the distance. The moment we came to a halt, the ramp at the back of the plane lowered and a rush of surprisingly cold air hit us. It was refreshing at first but I soon began to shiver. I hurried out into the early morning darkness. Shelly stuck beside me, carrying the precious box of samples.

As promised, a helicopter awaited, already powered up. The machine's rotors did not chop the air with the clatter I expected of helicopters. Instead, its put out a steady high hum, as if it was one sharpened hunk of metal made not to fly but to slice through the air.

The Globemaster's engines did not power down much so we were buffeted by a hot wash of wind as we ran to the helicopter. The other cargo plane landed behind us. Under the threat of being shot, I didn't stop to see how many patients they'd captured for me. I didn't relish the idea of experimenting on people, zombie or not. My focus had always been on the microscopic side of the biological spectrum. Mostly, my experiments with nanotech had been confined to the theoretical with some forays into working with lab rats. I usually delegated the animal work as much as I could. Pink-eyed rats freaked me out.

As Shelly urged me to board the helicopter, the infected ETF officer passed within a few feet of me. Daniel Harmon's hands were cuffed behind his back. Crenshaw made him wear a muzzle and a chain leash around his throat, too. As the man turned to look at me, I only caught a glimpse of his eyes. He'd tried to kill me once. He looked placid now.

I was reminded of a story my mother told to explain her fear of dogs. One of her earliest memories was getting bitten when she was four. "The little bastard wagged his tail and looked friendly. Then the dog bit me hard on the chin." She'd tipped her head back to show two small scars where the animal's fangs had sunk into her flesh. "A little farther down and he might have ripped my throat out. I would have bled to death in minutes if the angle had been just a little different."

"What kind of dog was it?"

"A Chihuahua."

I laughed. "Mom! You would have been the first person in the world to be killed by a Chihuahua!"

"Just because something hasn't happened doesn't mean it won't. Nothing happens for a long time and then it does and everyone is surprised. I can be shocked but I'll never be surprised again. That's what that little bug-eyed devil dog taught me. Give everything time and anything can happen, Chloe. Change always comes."

I'd laughed then but I had to concede that my mother had a

point. My research had been stolen and perverted to evil ends. People had turned into cannibals. Toronto was a pile of radioactive ash and rubble. I should have listened to Mom. Reality is much more fragile than I ever thought.

Before we lifted off from CFB Suffield, our cargo plane took off down the runway. I strained to hear our new pilot communicate with the tower. He sounded anxious. "Suffield Tower, this is Cyclone A113. What's that Globemaster doing? He's taking off with the wind, over!"

I wasn't sure what that meant but it didn't sound good. I pulled on my headphones in time to hear Tower ask the plane's pilot to respond. We watched as the big cargo plane seemed to lumber toward the end of the runway where huge orange bars of light flashed a warning.

"He's not going to make it, Tower," our pilot said.

He was wrong. The Globemaster did manage to pull up into the sky at the last moment. I let out a long breath as the plane went into a steep climb.

"He's in a hurry," Shelly said. "What does he know that we don't? Another missile on the way?"

I looked to the faces of the cops. Shelly Priyat and Dale Crenshaw looked pale, exhausted and fearful. I probably looked the same way. I could only see his eyes, but the ETF guy wearing the muzzle looked interested and calm. I thought again of the little dog that had terrified my mother, so friendly and relaxed right up until the moment he bit her and changed her worldview.

"Tower to Cyclone A113, stand by."

Minutes passed and we waited with no explanation for the delay. The pilot switched channels on the intercom but we could hear no radio chatter.

"We've got to get out of here," Crenshaw said. "What is the hold up?"

"It is like it always is, sir," our pilot replied. "Hurry up and wait."

After a long silence, Shelly shrugged. "I waited to take off for a trip to the Dominican last year. We sat on the runway for forty minutes and all I could think was how many minutes the delay was eating into my vacation. Aviation is the same all over. Everybody take a breath."

The Globemaster's engines roared overhead, but only for a few seconds. A gigantic fireball bathed us in orange light as the cargo plane nosedived at full speed into the airfield beside us. Whether he wanted it or not, Bill Arsenault was cremated. Another explosion soon followed and a hail of shrieking metal blossomed out from the wreckage. Multiple fires found purchase in the surrounding grasses. Jet fuel spilled and stunk, burning hot and bright. High winds fanned the fires as if Nature Itself was saying, "Go on, get it over with. Burn everything."

As another explosion pierced the night, we ducked involuntarily, as if that would have helped if a chunk of shrapnel from the plane's wreckage had torn into our helicopter.

All of us ducked except for the prisoner. The ETF agent gazed at the burning plane, calm as a pond on a still day. Fleetingly, I wondered if the prisoner was in agreement with Nature. He was an apex predator now. Maybe he was more intimate with the mortal arc of the way of things. He'd seen death and caused death. Maybe that's why he seemed so at home in its presence.

No alarms sounded. No sirens wailed in the distance. Fire trucks did not race to the rescue. The Globemaster was utterly obliterated. No one stationed at CFB Suffield seemed interested in extinguishing the speeding, spreading inferno.

Crenshaw's voice climbed to a higher, near hysterical register. "Jesus! Do you think they were ordered to commit suicide? A cover-up or — "

Harmon let out a bitter chuckle. "We're a little bit beyond cover-ups now, don't you think? Good thing you didn't go for detective. I'm guessing the crew was from Toronto," Harmon said. "When loved ones die, everybody's curious about where ghosts go. Maybe they went to follow them and find out."

Shelly's voice shook. "You believe in ghosts?"

Harmon shrugged. "If you believe a little too much in a better life after death, you might commit suicide, too."

"And if you lose all hope, you might end up making the same choice." I was jolted by the crew's suicide but I wasn't exactly surprised. It felt like the whole world had given up. Worse, it almost made sense to stop trying so damn hard. I had always spoken of my work with AFTER in the future tense: what it could do, what it might do, how it would help. The new reality hit ahead of schedule. Nanotech was a tidal wave and it was washing away everything we once treasured. "We're caught between a shock and a dark place."

"Are you afraid of the dark?" the zombie asked.

"I think that's where we live from now on," I replied. "No choice."

"I didn't choose this, either, so please call me Daniel. It would make me feel a little less like a monster."

The chains around the man's neck rattled as Crenshaw elbowed his prisoner in the side of his head. "Shut the hell up, monster."

"Okay," I said. "Okay, Daniel."

CHAPTER 6

DANIEL

No one spoke as the jet helicopter buzzed west. I closed my eyes and waited for the nanites to talk to me. Though I heard nothing from them, it was a strange feeling to know they were working away in the darkness of my skull, changing me, remaking me. What if the AI decided to rework me on the outside? The tiny robots running around inside me might decide that a human needs four arms, four legs and a bunch of eyes. Every man wants to be Jeff Goldblum. Nobody wants to be Jeff Goldblum in *The Fly*.

When my dad got sick, I asked him how he dealt with his shitty prognosis.

"Atavan for the anxiety," he said, "but they've got nothing for the fear that's bone deep. Alzheimer's makes you go away slowly. Every time I forget something, it's another ring of the bell, reminding me the fun's over at the county fair and I'm on my way out. The worst part, I think, is waiting for the worst part, when I stop thinking. One day, Dan, I'll still be here but only sorta. I won't know my brain is riddled with holes and plaques. I won't know your name. I'll probably forget my own name before I go. When that day comes, be happy for me. When I'm sick but I don't know it anymore? That's the day I'll be free."

Theoretically, I was the opposite of sick. I could see and hear better. My sense of smell was sharper and, except for the pangs that tied my belly in a knot, I felt good. That growing hunger, that shameful grisly need, made my eyeteeth ache.

I looked up and down the dim cabin, searching the grim faces around me. Chloe sat farthest away from me. Since I tried to eat her in Echidna's lab, the security guys had kept her at a distance. I still had the order to kill her in the back of my mind, like a subroutine ready to kick in as soon as a successful attack became probable. I wanted to tell her it wasn't me who wanted her dead. It was some guy I'd never met. The same subroutine that demanded I kill Chloe Robinson also wouldn't let me say why.

I wanted to declare, loudly and repeatedly, "I'm two people!" But a nuclear blast is a mood killer. Worries about radiation sickness stomp out conversation. No one wanted to listen to me so I shut up.

Instead, I thought of Toronto and one of the first arrests I ever made. It was at the BestBuy at Bay and Dundas. A person was causing a disturbance and had been asked to leave. Instead of going out the easy way, she'd tipped over a big flat screen television and cracked the screen.

As soon as I walked in, the woman who'd thrown the fit at BestBuy walked up to me. She introduced herself before I could ask her name. "Mary Ferguson," she said. "It wasn't me."

Several staff and the manager formed a circle around us and they talked over each other, all saying the same thing. According to a honking gaggle of witnesses, Mary Ferguson had indeed knocked over a 58 inch Sanyo worth $700.

She looked from face to face and her cheeks reddened as she broke into a sweat. The woman shivered with nervous energy and spewed her words in a torrent. "I came in looking for a Wii. I have a Wii at home and it's how I get exercise instead of spending money on a gym. I bowl and play tennis and sometimes I do the Wii

Resort, y'know? I like the flying game and archery but the sword dueling thing makes me work harder and my doctor says I should do more of that. I'm better if I can follow doctor's orders but now I can't do that and I'm worried. I came in hoping they still sell the Wii console but they don't and they won't even try to look in the back or order it for me. I'm sorry if something happened but sometimes things happen when I'm anxious. The Wii will help with that. Can you help me? I really need a Wii."

She began blinking rapidly and fell silent.

Another officer arrived about then. She took a statement from the manager while I arrested Mary. She was cooperative and went quietly. I drove her to 52 Division for processing. It wasn't far but we got stuck in traffic. While we waited, she became talkative. "You can just drop me off at home."

"You understand that you're under arrest, Ms. Ferguson?"

"I'm in the back of a police car. Of course, I know that. I'm not stupid."

"Have you been drinking?"

"I don't drink, sir."

"Do you understand the charge against you?"

"Those people at BestBuy wouldn't listen."

"That's no reason to damage property, Mary."

"I told you it wasn't me. It was Siobhan who caused the trouble."

"Siobhan knocked over the TV?"

"Yes, sir."

"And where is Siobhan now?"

"She's ... here."

"Come again?"

"I'm two people," she said.

"Oh, I see."

"Do you? If you let me look through my purse, I can give you my doctor's number. She'll explain, though it's past four and her office closes at four and I don't know what to do. When I don't know what to do, I'm supposed to go home and call my mom or my counselor."

"Are you on any medication?"

"My pill bottles are in my purse. It helped me."

"Have you been taking your meds?"

"Nah. I've been feeling better lately so I stopped taking it so much. I still take it, but only when I think I need it."

"Most medication needs taking as directed, not when you get around to it."

"That's what I told Siobhan. She … well, we don't agree on much. She's the troublemaker. I work in a stationery store. I shouldn't be in the back of a police car!"

"How about we work it all out at the station, Mary?"

"Ms. Ferguson."

"Sure thing, Ms. Ferguson."

She kicked the back of my seat with surprising force for such a small woman. "Call me Siobhan!" The way she kept on shrieking, I was convinced. She really had become a different person. The detail that caught my attention was that my prisoner cursed me out in a thick French accent. Mary hadn't had an accent but Siobhan did.

Mary had entered my cruiser like a lamb. It took three of us to get Siobhan into a cell. She went kicking and screaming and tried to bite us. I wonder now if there's something deep in the lizard brain, like throwing a switch, that makes humans and zombies want to bite.

Mary Ferguson's mother spoke with a subtle Irish lilt. Her name was Alannah. When I told her what happened at BestBuy, there was a long, miserable silence on the line followed by a tired sigh. "So that whore showed up again, did she? Shit."

"Pardon me, ma'am?"

"My daughter was in a car accident, Mr. Harmon. Run over, actually. The doctors don't know if it was that or abuse when she was a kid. Her swim coach … well, just think of it. If she hadn't watched the Olympics, she might never have wanted to swim. She was too short to compete at that level but I didn't tell her the truth of that because encouraging a child is what a good mum does, isn't it? Then that damn car. If she'd taken half a second to look when she ran out into the street after her bus … looking both ways before they cross the street. It's what they learn before you let them walk to school on their own. You ever notice how it can all turn to shit in a second?"

"Yes, ma'am."

"The long and the short of it, Mary was a happy little girl. She's not that girl, not anymore."

"Mary told me she hasn't been taking her medication regularly."

"I warned her but I'm only her mother. She's grown up. I did my best. I can't do it all. I'm almost 65. I should be retiring but as long as Mary and Siobhan are alive, it looks like I've got a full-time job. My daughter's got Dissociative Identity Disorder."

I hadn't run into this before. "Like, Multiple Personality Disorder, you mean?"

"No, I don't mean MPD. I mean, DID, as in 'did you listen?' Do the Toronto Police take sensitivity training? That's the old thinking you're talking now, ya bastard — "

"Okay, okay," I said. "I understand you're upset and Mary's got a bad break. You can beat me to death with your victimhood and call me names or you can take down the address I'm about to give you."

"When's she getting out?"

"She'll have to stand before a judge. How that goes is up to the judge and the lawyers. In the meantime, you can post bond and take her home."

"Nah. If she's off her meds, I might not be taking Mary home. It might be Siobhan. I think there's no rush in me getting down there to pull that bitch out. I love my daughter. She's not the brightest spoon in the drawer but she's sweet. That Siobhan, though? That bitch wants to kill me."

"Do you have a message for your daughter?"

"Call me again when Mary shows up. Oh, and don't let her have nuts. Siobhan is allergic to nuts. Mary isn't. Sometimes when Siobhan doesn't get her way, she tries to kill them both."

Alannah Ferguson hung up on me. She and Mary and Siobhan were probably all ashes now. Problem solved?

Mary had been two people. Finally, I really understood. I was one part Daniel Lewis Harmon and one part zombie at the whim of tiny robots run amok. The nanites were doing whatever they were designed to do and maybe quite a bit more. Apparently, they weren't interested in having a conversation to pass the time on the long flight.

I'd been pretty quick to write off Mary Ferguson and her mother. As a cop, I met plenty of people that had a bad break or two (or eight). That sounded heartless and dismissive now.

Maybe the idea of identity itself was old thinking. With the nanites in control, who was I? If the brain is a computer that can be wiped so easily, what did identity mean? Maybe I was nothing more than a river of thoughts. Like Crenshaw, I latched onto who I thought I should be or what others thought I should be. Maybe everyone's faking it, trying to live up to a lie.

Consciousness is so fluid it can easily be diverted by Alzheimer's, accident, injury or emotional trauma. Maybe there never was one Daniel Harmon. Perhaps I was never anything more than a collection of projections of culture and wishes. Maybe we're all acting on hormonal influences and whims whose origin we don't even recognize. Every kid is asked what they want to be when they grow up. Where does that answer really come from? Does the reasoning behind those answers get better when we get older?

Just before we broke up, the girlfriend who ran off with my best friend said, "You aren't in love with me. You're in love with the idea of me." I think she picked up that shit from a Facebook meme. She was right, though. Lying to ourselves is an affliction we all suffer. We all have an idea of who we are. We usually fall short of that ideal. There is not one self. There is only an idea of self that we decide to try to become.

Wait. Stop. Stop!

What did identity mean? Consciousness is fluid? What is this bullshit? These aren't my thoughts! I'd never thought about this kind of stuff in my life! This isn't me. This is them! This is the nanites talking!

The AI was taking over, reinterpreting my memories to plumb new thoughts. I was already less and less Daniel Harmon. I wondered when the AI would stop taking bits and pieces away from me. One day soon, would I be erased? Like father, like son?

Problem solved?

CHAPTER 7

CHLOE

I was quiet for a long time on the trip to Bainbridge. With the bright light of radioactive death burning through us, I was reminded of the first time I died. When I was seven, my parents argued a lot. We were living in Winnipeg at the time. I was out of school for March Break. Since my father had a week off from teaching, he took me to Toronto to visit relatives. Mom stayed home. I pieced it together later that they were taking a break from each other.

It was my first time on a plane. During the safety demonstration, the flight attendant pointed out that the seat could be used as a flotation device, "In the unlikely event of a water landing." The way I was raised, the only silly question was the question unasked. I turned to my father and, in a voice that was too loud, inquired, "Do these planes crash a lot?"

A woman directly behind me tittered and muttered, "Stupid kid."

I was embarrassed. Turning in my seat and getting up on my knees, I poked my head up to see who laughed at me. It was a pretty white woman, her curly hair was piled impossibly high and dyed bright red. In my mind's eye, I can still see the thick links of her gold necklace beneath her amused smile. She wore a cream jacket over a tight red sheath. She looked like a smug barber pole. I don't mind barber poles. I hate smug.

Peering over the seat, I said, "Sorry, but there's not much water to land on between here and Toronto, anyway, is there? I mean, flying in planes isn't like if you've got a flat tire on a car. You can't pull over in the sky and change a tire. Telling us to fasten our seatbelts and all that is just to make us feel better. If we crash, we all die screaming and burning. Isn't that right? Is that stupid?"

Her smug smile faded and a tinge of worry crept in around the woman's eyes.

Shushing me and apologizing profusely to the woman, my father pulled me back into my seat. He told me to read my book and be quiet. I did as I was told, but the fearful look on that woman's face kept me warm all the way to Toronto. Even now, that memory gives me a little smile. We like to think we mature, get better and do better. However, very recently as a grown woman, I'd dumped an expensive bottle of wine down a man's pants.

I suppose that's one of the reasons I fell in love with nanotech. Artificial Intelligence can be programmed to learn and improve. Humans often do their best. However, with AFTER pilfered and made into a weapon and Toronto gone ... well. It was pretty evident our best is not good enough a good chunk of the time.

When I was very little, I somehow got the idea that we all die screaming. I don't know where that thought came from. I was disabused of that notion when I died over that March Break in Toronto. The site of my death was a frozen pond somewhere in North York. Maybe the site of my first death isn't there anymore. The water had probably burst into steam in the heat of the nuclear blast. What I didn't know when I went skating on that pond was that there was a warm water exhaust pipe at one end of the pond. The post with the sign and the bright red marker toward that end was a warning: Keep off that end of the pond no matter how cold the winter got, no matter how thick the ice looked on the safe end.

Entropy occurs when an organized system becomes disorganized. Systems can be repaired and improved but that's not the trend of the universe. Death comes when we lack data or fail to act on intelligence. That's what I learned on that pond in Toronto on that March Break. I didn't think of it that way at the time, of course. Fate is comprised of many variables. However, a warm water pipe and thinning ice may have set me on the path to create AFTER more than anything else.

On my first afternoon in Toronto, my cousin Cherry wanted to go skating. She was fourteen. I guess that's why she got saddled with taking her little cousin skating.

Her real name wasn't Cherry. It was Cheryl. Her parents called her Sherry. To everyone else, she was Cherry. When I met her, I thought choosing your own name was just about the coolest act of defiance in the world. For a couple of hours on a gray afternoon, I idolized my cousin. She didn't feel as warmly toward me. It was she who told me to skate to the end of the pond where the ice was thin and the water was deep and dark. Cold water waited beneath but Cherry assured me the pond was so shallow in that spot that even if I broke through, the worst I'd suffer was cold feet. "Skate around that post two times and I'll get you an ice cream sandwich from the bottom the freezer. I've been saving 'em since last summer. Go on, Chloe! You afraid of a soaker? Don't be a baby!"

I didn't like being called a baby and, I admit, it was a thrill at first. The soft ice cracked a little under my weight. I stood still, fascinated by the crystalline lines and a spider webs spreading beneath my skates.

"Don't just stand there!" Cherry yelled. "Skate around the post and come back!"

A few guys were playing a pickup game of hockey at the far end of the pond. They stopped in the middle of play to stare at me. One of them pulled off his toque and waved to get my attention. I smiled and waved back.

"Come back!" he shouted. "Don't go past the red marker!"

I started toward him when the ice opened up. I crashed through. It was not shallow. I must have opened my mouth to scream in shock but I made no sound. Instead of drawing in breath, I drew water into my lungs. The pond swallowed me into its cold belly.

Thrashing but weighed down by my heavy winter clothes, one of my skates caught on something. Maybe I was just stuck in the mud. Toads bury themselves in mud for the winter and hibernate until spring. Little girls can't.

Cold and claustrophobic, the water closed over my head and reached under my parka to freeze my skin and paralyze my limbs. In dark, cold water, even flailing is slow. I struggled as long as I could. That seemed to take a long time. There is a point in the late stage of drowning when oxygen deprivation invites the cold hand of Death to reach into your brain. I wanted out. I wanted to be safe, back in my room at home in Winnipeg. My first feelings of worry and embarrassment were soon replaced by anger. Even that didn't last long. Suddenly, I was merely sleepy.

I looked up at the hole in the ice I'd left behind. Everything I'd ever known was just a few feet away, but my parents, friends and my safe, soft bed might as well have been on a remote planet in another galaxy. There was supposed to be a storm in Toronto the next day. I thought, if it had come a day early or we had come a day later, I wouldn't be here. Soon, that hole in the ice will close over. I'm going to be down here with the frozen frogs.

I gave up. I hung in the slim shaft of dim light, arms upstretched, ready to sleep forever.

It might be my imagination, a false memory built from what I was told later, but I think I saw the beginning of my rescue. The hockey player had not hesitated. He reached me first, sliding on his belly, his hockey stick beneath him to distribute his weight. Three of his friends did the same, forming a chain, holding each other by the ankles, screaming for him to hurry as the ice cracked around him ominously, threatening to claim them all. A fourth ran for help. Cherry just stood there paralyzed and watching. They told me she didn't move, didn't even scream.

I woke up in the hospital. My March Break got extended by three weeks. The same icy cold that almost killed me also saved me from brain damage.

Sitting in the helicopter on the way to Bainbridge, I thought a lot about the fallout from that day. I ticked them off on my fingers:

1. After almost losing me, my parents were nicer, not just to me but to each other. They were more patient and went out of their way to be kind.

2. When my cousin came to visit me in the hospital, she said, "An apology is a small thing, but I am sorry." She held out her hand and offered me a half-melted ice cream sandwich.

I took the treat and, while I ate it, told her, "You're not cool, Cheryl. You're not cool at all. You're not a Cherry. You're a Cheryl." She was probably dead or a zombie now. I assumed she still lived in Toronto, too. After she nearly killed me, we didn't send that branch of the family any more Christmas cards and everyone lost touch.

3. The name of the young man who saved me was Gordon Bonnet. I sent him a Christmas card, not just then, but every Christmas since. Gordon became a plumber. He lived in Toronto with a lovely wife and three kids. On the weekends, he played bass in a bar band.

4. If I had died that day, AFTER might never have been born, or at least the breakthrough I made with my research might not have come for several more years. Whoever did replicate my work might have been on the other side of the world, having nothing to do with my company.

5. As Gordon rushed to save me, he unwittingly hastened his own death. If he'd known the future, he probably wouldn't have risked his life to save mine. Or maybe he would. I don't know. He was a great person. Sorry, Gordon.

Sorry, everybody, everywhere.

Cheryl's words came back to me again, "An apology is a small thing."

I am an expert in microscopic machines. The tiniest thing of all is an apology.

CHAPTER 8

DANIEL

Our helicopter descended on Bainbridge Island in gray early morning light. I leaned forward slightly to peer through the window to get a look at the vast compound below us. At first glance, the building looked like a fortress, a closed square with a large open courtyard in the middle. There were no gardens, just a fountain toward one end. Smaller clusters of outbuildings, a solar panel array and three wind turbines surrounded the complex. Beyond that, two perimeter fences enclosed the property. It looked more like a military base than a corporate research lab.

Two details struck me as especially odd about the architecture of our destination. For one, a large enclosed pool stood under a transparent dome. The water was not blue. It was a rich green. The second detail was more obvious and it made me think Nyx would not be as helpful in finding a cure as everyone hoped: tall columns of black smoke from several fires around the compound.

Shelly Priyat, looking pale and exhausted, followed my gaze. As soon as she spotted the smoke, she shook Chloe Robinson awake.

The doctor stirred slowly. "Are we there yet?"

"Nyx Management Group has some trouble," Shelly said. "Odd coincidence, isn't it?"

Chloe used her sleeve to dab at the sheen of sweat on her forehead. "I don't trust coincidences."

"Don't trust anybody, Chloe," I told her.

Crenshaw gave my leash a savage jerk to haul me back, tight to my seat. He glowered at me. "Don't talk to her."

I spared Dale Crenshaw a glance. His sweat smelled wrong. He looked like he was coming down hard with the flu. I wondered how long he had before radiation sickness would weaken his grip on my chains. Despite the chain cutting into my throat, I strained to bend forward slightly. My shoulders ached and my hands were numb from the tight cuffs. "Take it easy, Dale. You'll be dead soon. Don't add to your sins."

"I'm not interested in anything you have to say, zombie boy. Go ahead and test me. I will shoot you in lots of places before I get serious about killing you. You even think about going after Dr. Robinson again — "

"Sure, I get you. You're looking for your excuse to kill me. You don't want me telling anybody about what you did at Echidna — "

"Shut it. What you think you know doesn't matter. This will all be set right soon." Crenshaw's chuckle sounded forced but, I had to admit, he was the one holding the leash.

Our transport landed in the compound. At the far end by the fountain, I noticed the stars and stripes took second place on the flagpole. Atop it, the corporate logo of Nyx Management Group flew. The pilot, who had remained silent for the flight, came over the intercom. "Disembark! Everybody! Everybody out!"

Priyat handed Robinson the box of samples so she could slide the door back. Dr. Robinson fumbled with her seatbelt buckle sleepily before struggling to her feet. Crenshaw made me get out first.

"Did we phone ahead?" Chloe asked. "I thought there'd be a welcoming committee. Don't they know we're coming to save the day?"

"I heard something. Something bad." I tilted my head back and sniffed the air. "Dale, you can leave my muzzle on if you like, but you're going to want me out of these cuffs."

"Why the hell would I do that?"

"There is a welcoming committee. You're not going to like it."

"Where?" the doctor asked.

"Can't you hear the snarls of the brain drained?" I asked.

Shelly tilted her head, listening, straining to hear. My sister told me once that when she used a stethoscope, she strained the limits of her hearing to pick up nuances in a heartbeat. Jenn called it "pitching" her hearing.

Dr. Robinson cupped a hand to her ear. "I do hear something."

To me, the killers sounded closer, coming fast and sounding mad. "Incoming," I said. "Now."

"Where, zombie man?" Shelly asked.

"From the burning building at the far end of the compound. They smell like death and they can't stop growling. It's not their fault. They're like a swarm of brain parasites, if brain parasites could growl and run. They're just doing what humanoid brain parasites do."

Half a dozen rampaging cannibals poured out of the building farthest from us. Priyat turned back to the helicopter but it lifted away before we could retreat to the safety of the sky. Crenshaw cursed. Chloe cursed louder. As the humans hunched in the wash of the rotors, the jet helicopter abandoned us to our fate.

To me, the sudden quiet was a relief. The zombies paused a moment to watch the helicopter fly away. The infected were all men, or at least they'd been men a short time ago. Each wore a ballistic vest over camo. When the helicopter was out of sight, the pack's gaze fell on us again. They let out a long growl I recognized. "They'll come for us. Get me out of the cuffs, Dale. I'll deal with them."

"We've got guns," Crenshaw said.

"Look at what they're wearing. You'll have to take them all down with knee shots or headshots. You won't get them all before they get you. I was in the Box. I know how this will break. You'll run out of bullets. Then whoever's left will eat you."

"Die with us then," Crenshaw said.

The zombies charged at us like a football team.

"If I stand still and let them kill you, they won't turn on me."

Fortunately, all handcuffs have the same kind of key. Shelly Priyat stepped forward to free my hands. "You even look at us," she said, "I'll shoot you."

I took a moment to rub my wrists. "Dr. Robinson, someone named Cavanaugh programmed me to kill you with the trigger, 'Send that bitch my regards.' Wasn't personal."

"Dying's always personal. Doesn't matter now," she replied. "Cavanaugh will get his wish."

The pack was already past the fountain. I sprinted forward, running faster than I ever had. Crenshaw yelped in pain as my leash ripped through his palm. The heavy chain around my neck jingled as it trailed behind me. No one could see the smile beneath my muzzle as I rushed to meet the enemy, zombie versus zombie. I wasn't just going to kick ass. I was going to kick all the ass.

Of course, there was no way I could do it all by myself. Some got past me. They couldn't wait to tear into the humans. I wondered if they'd been programmed to kill Chloe Robinson, too.

CHAPTER 9

CHLOE

If it were up to me, I would have left my would-be assassin in cuffs and taken our chances.

Crenshaw cursed at Shelly. She ignored him and checked the load in her pistol. "Once they take down Harmon, they'll be comin' hard at us. Like they said at Bunker Hill, 'Don't shoot until you see the whites of their eyes.' You'll just waste ammo if you panic. That happened on Level One."

"I don't panic," Crenshaw said.

I didn't believe him. He seemed in a continuous panic since Toronto blew up.

Harmon ran at the zombies, covering ground fast. His movement seemed so unnaturally quick and smooth, it was almost disturbing. I saw an impossible thing. At least, it was impossible up until a couple of days ago. I clutched the heavy sample box to my chest and watched in awe as the attack unfolded. The first three of the group ran abreast, charging at us and screaming. Their high shrieks made my stomach churn. They sounded like howler monkeys. I saw no trace of humanity in their blood smeared faces.

Harmon became a blur as he met the enemy halfway to the fountain. From a few long strides away, he launched himself at the attackers, throwing himself into the air sideways, colliding at top speed. He took down all three.

The one on the far left stayed down, clutching his broken throat, gagging and retching. The zombie on the right struggled to his feet, clutched his head before falling back to the ground. The remaining attacker in the middle rolled to his feet and dove at the ETF officer. Harmon came up from the ground to meet him.

It took me a moment to understand what I witnessed. The attacker's back was turned to me but I saw the zombie's head rock back. Even at this distance, I heard the crack of bone. Harmon's target fell like a tree felled by lightning.

"Are you seeing this?" Shelly asked.

"He's been upgraded," I said. "Not human, but no ordinary zombie, either."

"No ordinary zombie," she echoed. "That's what they'll call the movie."

The second wave hit Harmon from behind. The ETF officer's next attacker was slower than those in the first wave but large and powerful. He leaped on Harmon's back, straining to sink his teeth into our defender's neck.

Harmon rolled forward, allowing the big man's momentum to carry both of them to the ground. His attacker landed hard on his butt. In one smooth motion Harmon whipped the chain of his own leash around the zombie's throat. He landed with both feet on the man's shoulders and wrenched upwards with one savage pull. The big man went limp.

That left two zombies running at us. One was bald, the other bearded. Crenshaw fired first, far too early. He emptied his weapon and hit the bald one in the chest twice, barely slowing him. Shelly waited until the bald attacker was closer. Ice in her veins, she chose her moment and fired twice at the last moment. The bald zombie's skull opened like an overripe melon thrown from a great height onto concrete.

I would have been relieved, but Crenshaw was still reloading when the bearded zombie burst between both cops and came at me. I raised the heavy metal case of samples over my head and brought it down on my attacker's head as hard as I could muster.

He went down as a long whine escaped his bloody lips. Shelly finished the bearded man with a double tap behind his ear.

I shook. The cops did, too.

"Just like in the movies," I said. "Kill the brain, you kill the zombie."

"To be fair," Shelly replied, "killing the brain works in just about any situation, zombie or not."

CHAPTER 10

DANIEL

The first three I killed was self-defense, pure and simple. I didn't have to think about it. That's when I'm at my best, when I don't have to think too much. By the time I killed the fourth zombie, I felt differently. Trapped in each growling cannibal was a human being, bewildered, revolted and afraid. As I shut the oxygen off to the big man's brain, I felt the cervical vertebrae fracture. This time, I did not feel regret. I'd released him from his trap.

But is that me rationalizing what must be done? Or is that the nanites, working out a cold equation, solving for x, erasing a variable?

The clouds broke and I glimpsed azure sky. I'd never seen that color so clearly. The helicopter was gone. The day reminded me of 9/11, how everyone looked up to wonder at a view devoid of flying machines. We all stopped to look and watch and wait for what would come next. Except for military aircraft, there would be no commercial flight today. There might not be for a long time to come. Tragedy makes the world hold its breath. For a moment, we reassess our priorities. My trouble was I didn't know if it was me or the nanites doing my thinking for me.

Crenshaw pointed his pistol at my head and stalked out to meet me. He tossed me the handcuffs and I obliged him by putting them on. At least now they were in front of me and not too tight. Crenshaw didn't step closer than he had to. He wasn't interested in checking my cuffs. After seeing me in action, he was more afraid than before. I was surprised how it worked out, too, but it would have been uncool to say so.

I was actually relieved to look down his pistol barrel again. Though the Artificial Intelligence running my brain was preprogrammed to kill Dr. Chloe Robinson, I didn't have to execute the order if success seemed unlikely. The nanites bubbling through my brain had an overriding if/then rule: Self-preservation took precedence. My death would mean the death of the AI and the nanites wanted to live. I was not to sacrifice myself.

Before my captors could plan their next move, a dozen armed men in white biohazard suits emerged from the building to our right. They converged on us at once. They were quieter than the zombies had been.

"That's a lot of gunslingers," Priyat told Chloe. "Stay behind me."

Crenshaw brightened and pointed with the muzzle of his weapon. I got his gist and stepped in front of him. He used me as his human shield … well, not a human shield. I couldn't be that anymore.

Standing before of all those riflemen, I felt vulnerable. I was stronger and faster but I wasn't faster than a bullet. Even if the nanites could repair me, I didn't relish the idea of suffering ballistic trauma and doubted even the AI could fix me fast enough to save me. The punch of kinetic energy delivered by a single AR-15 is no joke. More than one? No thanks. As the only member of the group who was a new species, I figured someone would be eager to murder me and get straight to the autopsy.

Worse, the men in white were jumpy. I could see it in the way they moved. They trembled with fear and anger. I'd just killed three of their coworkers and they hadn't seen what we'd seen in Toronto. They were new to this war.

A woman with a pistol came forward. Through her faceplate, I recognized her immediately. She knew who I was, too. Her eyes never left mine. "Welcome to Suthina Laboratories! We don't call it that. This is Bainbridge Island, of course, so we call it Brainbridge."

"I'm Shelly Priyat and that's Dale Crenshaw, Toronto Police," Shelly said. "This is Dr. Chloe Robinson and the man in cuffs — "

"We know who Daniel Harmon is."

I'm with the Toronto Police, too, I thought. *Jeez! I'm awfully young to be a write-off!*

"Toronto's gone," Chloe said.

"We know," the woman said. "Everybody knows. The missile strike has sparked quite a debate. The UN isn't sure whether to condemn the United States or thank us for decisive action. The stock market is shut down. Protestors are doing what protesters do and the preppers and doomers are in hog heaven, gearing up for civil war. It's a mess."

Chloe stepped out from behind Priyat. "We were close to the blast. Any closer and we wouldn't have made it out."

The woman looked ashen. "We … we didn't see that coming." She cleared her throat, gathering her thoughts. "It's terrible. I'm sorry for all you have lost. Nobody meant it to happen. It just did."

"Nothing just happens," Chloe said. "For every effect, there's a cause."

The woman stiffened. "Call it human error, then. The human factor is always the most troublesome variable." She looked at me. "If things go as I think they will, we'll eliminate that variable soon."

Chloe pointed at the dead cannibals at our feet. "Does the human factor explain where those zombies came from? They didn't run here from Toronto and the captured patients we got are in a helicopter a few minutes behind us."

"We've been running our own experiments, trying to understand the disease better. We got results similar to those at the Toronto lab."

Chloe hefted the case in her hands. "I've got tissue samples from Echidna. With your help, I may be able to stop the epidemic."

A security guy, the only one wearing a tan bio suit, asked, "Didn't the nuke do that? Wasn't that what the hit was for?"

The woman made a motion to cut him off but Chloe answered anyway. "The disease will be slowed but someone will have survived the blast." She looked around the compound, at the towers of smoke coming from Suthina Laboratories. She nodded toward the bodies of the zombies I'd killed. "It's here, too, obviously."

"We're trying to contain them but they're hard to deal with," the woman said. "Much harder than expected."

"Then Picasso will come for you. It'll come for everything you love. We saw it in Toronto. It looks bad here. Wait until you see crowds of them all coming for you at once. We had tanks and tons more firepower in Toronto. We lost the city before the bomb hit."

The security team looked at each other, more nervous than before.

"Since we're here to help," Chloe continued, "can you please point your guns somewhere else, people?"

I still feel the need to rip your throat out, Chloe, but damn, I like you.

The woman with the pistol shook her head. "No sale. Give me the sample case, Dr. Robinson. Your people screwed up. I'll take it from here."

"But we've got infected patients coming on the helicopter behind us. We need to set up a way to secure them, study the disease and process — "

She raised the pistol and pointed it at Chloe. "Just give me the damn case."

"It wasn't Dr. Robinson who screwed up," I said.

"Shut up, Danny." Crenshaw pulled my choke chain tight.

"They might shoot you, too, Dale, just to snip off the loose end. You're hanging by a thread, man."

That must have hit home. Crenshaw gave me an inch of slack around my throat. "Talk careful then."

I nodded toward the woman with the pistol. "This lady turned me into a zombie."

"Zombies don't talk." It was the same guy who thought one nuke could solve all our problems. Every crowd has one mouthy idiot who brings everybody's IQ down. I know. I've been that idiot.

"There's more than one kind of zombie now," I explained.

Chloe's curiosity competed with her fear. She looked at me with renewed interest. "How did she turn you into one of them?"

"She injected me with an evolved strain of nanites at Port Credit. It's all based on your work. They stole it and now they're trying to erase their culpability in the outbreak."

"That's bullshit conspiracy talk," the woman spoke loudly, more to her security force than to us. "The Canadians let a deadly agent out of their lab. Now they're trying to spread the blame around. Don't forget who pays your salaries, boys! And I've never met this guy wearing the muzzle in my life."

That was her first tactical error. "If I'm lying," I asked, "how do I know that you only have a thumb and two fingers on your left hand?"

She raised her left hand and, to my surprise, contracted all the fingers of her gloved hand. Her smile was exuberant and smug at the same time.

"What are you?" I asked. "The evil twin?"

The murmur that rose among the security team told me they were surprised, too. Slowly, they lowered their weapons a notch. In the distance, we heard the dual rotors of a big helicopter chopping the air. The infected patients and the rest of Crenshaw's security team would touch down in a few minutes. I relaxed. With more outsiders around, our chances of getting summarily executed seemed to be decreasing. We all looked up as the craft appeared out of the clouds to begin its descent.

The woman pressed the side of her helmet to activate her suit's radio. "The second helicopter from Toronto is about to land. There are infected aboard. Fire the warning shot, as discussed."

From somewhere outside the compound, we heard a whoosh. A short trail of smoke appeared in the sky. The helicopter exploded midair, a sudden orange burst, utterly destroyed. It fell from the sky and, for a moment, we became statues, transfixed in shock.

"That was a warning shot?" I asked.

"Human error. One stinger missile costs $38,000. We'll just add it to the bill. The cost of this disaster is so high already, that was nothing more than a rounding error. If you consider every destroyed car in Toronto, for instance, one stinger is really nothing. Not from a mathematical perspective, anyway. I am sorry for your losses. I truly am. But the world moves on. It always does."

"Who are you?" Chloe asked.

"Dr. Heather Clover."

"Heather Clover? Really? A little too on the nose." I almost laughed. "You're at a secret compound. You've got a lab. Zombies are running around and you have an army of mercenaries ... very James Bond, isn't it? All you're missing is an office with groovy furniture and a shag rug under an active volcano. Maybe you need a monocle and a white cat."

The eight-fingered woman looked at me like I was a bug. "Secret labs and mercenary contractors is how the world of arms manufacturers really works, Mr. Talking Zombie. As for my name, my parents were idiots who thought they were funny and clever, just like you."

Dr. Clover turned back to her team. "Weapons up and do your jobs. Get back inside before more of the test subjects find their way out here to eat your faces."

"They're already here," I said.

A long howl rose from the other side of the courtyard. My skin tingled. I knew what that sound meant. The howl was like that of a wolf, letting the others in the pack know that they'd found a way out of the building, that they'd found prey.

The guy in the tan bio suit spoke again. "I don't like the weapon wearing the muzzle, Dr. Clover. Zombie or not, he talks too much. Somebody get him a muzzle with a ball gag."

Dr. Clover sighed. "Everybody inside! I don't have time for this. The talking zombie comes with me. Take the rest of the Toronto delegation to the tower."

Her guard did not do as he'd been ordered. "You saw what he

did to those zombies. I'm not going near him alone. He's too dangerous."

Clover raised her pistol and, in a gesture that was almost casual, shot me in the abdomen.

Pain enveloped me and I went down. I grabbed at my wound, pressing and screaming. The hole was not large but it was bloody, just below my spleen.

"He doesn't look so dangerous now," Clover said. "Take the smart ass to the Planet of the Apes."

EPISODE 2

The AI Effect (phenomenon)

The observation that when an advance in Artificial Intelligence occurs, its worth is routinely discounted. It is postulated that this impulse comes from the human need to feel special, safe and secure in their position, above their technological creations. AI effect deniers will continue to insist machine intelligence is merely computational — not "real intelligence" — until such time as they are forced to welcome our robot overlords.

CHAPTER 11

CHLOE

The Bainbridge research facility was a mess. Its corridors smelled of acrid smoke and the lights flickered in a way that made me nervous that at any moment we might plunge into darkness. Pools of blood spread from torn corpses. I don't know when they lost containment but I noticed all the dead had been shot in the head. The wounds beneath their torn biohazard suits and ripped lab coats seemed fresh, still wet and oozing. Four armed men escorted Crenshaw, Shelly and me through a labyrinth of labs and administrative offices.

A guard with the name ADAMS printed down the sleeve of his bio suit led the way. "We can't get where we're going by taking the shortest route," he whispered. "The bastards come out of the smoke like ghosts."

"How did the fires start?" I asked.

A man behind me stepped close. "Word is, the boss started the first fire in the admin building on purpose."

"Shut up, Gidney," Adams said. "We go through the commissary to get to the tower. Almost there."

Gidney ignored him. "The other fires? We barricaded some hallways with desks and chairs and whatnot. The zombies were still coming through so we set the barricades on fire. It worked a little, maybe, but these things are hungry. Hungrier than the pain of burning. A zombie coming at you is one thing. A flaming zombie —"

"Makes a great drink," Adams interjected. "Light rum, dark rum, an ounce of apricot brandy, papaya and a dash of grenadine. Then more rum."

"I'm looking forward to you getting tired of that joke, Adams."

"I'm looking forward to you stopping your whining and setting me up for it. You're an oxygen thief, Gidney."

"We tried barricading a door at the lab in Toronto," Shelly said. "Didn't work there, either."

"I've been at Brainbridge fifteen months," Gidney complained. "Met my girlfriend here. Tiff's a dendrite development tech. She was on the other side of the compound when it happened."

"When what happened, exactly?" I asked.

"I don't know, exactly."

"*Zombieland*," Adams said. "Suddenly we were in *Zombieland*."

"Stop," Gidney said.

Adams was undeterred. "Decide now, man. Your girlfriend is dead. Gotta be."

"Don't be cruel," Shelly said.

"I'm trying to be real. Let go of her now. If it turns out she is alive, that'll be a nice surprise."

"Last I heard, she was in a janitor's closet," Gidney said. "She's somewhere between the pools and one of the neuro imaging labs. She called me on her cell 'round midnight. Not long after that, all our phones became useless."

"National security shutting everything down," Adams said, "or just system overload." The team leader paused by the corpse of a lab tech whose head wound had taken half his face. "This guy's name was Jim Lester. When my car conked out, he drove me to work for a week. Good guy. I shot him myself. You don't see me cryin'."

"What did Tiffany say?" Shelly asked Gidney. "On the phone, what did she say?"

"She was scared, hiding. She saw her friends eating her section boss. She never liked that guy but when she saw what happened to him, it broke something in her."

"Have you tried a rescue?" I asked.

My question pissed off Adams. "It's not as easy as you think. There's a lot of civilians here. Management won't let us bring in reinforcements. The island is shut down and we're supposed to do it all. We're on our own."

"Most of the people working security have worked here a long time," Gidney's voice cracked. "We're not all hardcore military. A bunch of us have spent our time here checking IDs and parking tags. When people you've known get sick, it's not so easy to shoot them."

"Easy for me," Adams bragged.

"I tried to get to her but Tiffany was on the wrong side of a burning barricade. We lost two guys getting close."

"We lost another running away," Adams added.

"A bunch of them followed us," Gidney said. "We killed a bunch, just sprayed and prayed into the dark and the smoke. Worst walk of my life was going back down that hallway to find out if I'd shot Tiff."

"You shouldn't have gone back," Adams said. "That's when they popped out and got Francesca. She was watching your back, man. You didn't watch hers, not well enough."

"Shut up."

"Your girlfriend is probably still hiding in that closet," I suggested.

"Maybe," Gidney said. "I told her to stay put until I could get to her."

Adams glanced back at us. "This is war, babies. It's us against the end of the world. The weak are gonna die. Get past that and get numb. That's the way to survive."

"I don't want to be numb," Gidney said. "I want to try to go get her again."

"Forget it," Adams told him in a tone that did not invite discussion. "You're not the only one worrying about who you lost. We lost a lot of good people last night. I'm not sacrificing more for nothing."

"Tiff's pregnant," Gidney told Shelly. "The wedding's in October."

Adams stopped moving forward and turned on his subordinate. "Kevin, keep your head in the game. You got three of your buddies killed last night."

Gidney raised his rifle. The two guards to the rear said nothing but trained their weapons on Gidney. The man ignored them and stared at Adams. His voice was low and intense. "You know how many guys I shot last night? I'm not even sure, but I've played poker with a bunch of our guys and hung out lots with Tiffany's friends. You say I got friends killed trying to get to her. Don't you think I know that?"

For a moment, I thought Gidney might shoot his superior in the head. The moment passed. Gidney took a long breath, his shoulders relaxed and he lowered his weapon. Then events unfolded so quickly I could only sort it out in my mind afterward. Gidney yelled a warning as he fired from the hip.

A cannibal dropped from the ceiling onto Adams. She shrieked as she wrapped her legs around his neck. Gidney's single shot boomed and echoed through the narrow hallway.

The small young woman with a shot of purple through her blonde hair went limp. She fell out of the smoke and landed on the floor with a smack. Her face and bare arms were scratched. Her freshest wound was a gaping hole in the middle of her chest.

"Kevin, thank — " That was all Adams managed to say before a large man wearing an apron rushed in and tackled him. He rammed the guard against the wall beside me and yanked the security officer's hood off in one fluid motion.

I reached for the attacker's long ponytail, hoping to pull him off Adams before he could bite. The zombie punched me in the middle of the chest and knocked me back before tearing off his prey's ear with his teeth. Adams screamed. Gidney shot the man in the chest.

Adams winced as he held his ruined ear, pressing a palm against the wound. He looked up at Gidney and a moment of silent understanding passed between them. Then Kevin Gidney shot his superior officer in the throat. "Sorry," he said, and fired again, this time to the head. He shot the two attackers next. Their skulls opened with a spray of pink mist.

Gidney glanced back at us and then knelt beside the corpses to look into the young woman's face. "Tiff! You followed me, after all. I wonder … did you remember me or were you just tracking my scent?" He let out a long sigh.

One of the guards behind us said, "Kevin, this isn't your fault."

"I know." Gidney turned his back to his girlfriend's corpse and studied Adams and the man in the apron. They were far beyond hurting anyone. Still, he fired his rifle into their heads again. I don't know if he did so out of anger, despair or just to make sure.

The two remaining security officers shouted to Gidney, begging him to stop. "You're going to bring more of them to us with all the noise!" one said.

Gidney did stop finally, after his weapon clicked empty.

Weeping, Gidney dropped the rifle. It clunked to the ground. He pulled off his protective hood and sat on the floor beside his girlfriend. "Tiffany Diem. You are the best person I know. The best, honey. The best."

Blood was still pumping from her ruined skull as he bent to cradle her head and brush his lips against hers.

Crenshaw spoke for the first time since we left the courtyard. "Stop. Stop it."

"Okay." He lowered his girlfriend to the ground gently. "You know what Churchill said about nuclear war? The living'll envy the dead. He wasn't wrong."

"This isn't the end of the world," Crenshaw said.

"Sure looks like it to me." Gidney pulled his pistol from his holster and placed the muzzle under his chin.

"Please don't do that," I said. "We need you."

Kevin Gidney was beyond listening to me or anyone else. "I

wonder if it was going to be a boy or a girl? I don't want to wonder."

Our guards were still begging him to lower his weapon when Gidney fired his last shot.

Silence stretched out for a moment and I heard a low moan. It escaped from my own throat. The guards looked to each other, not knowing what to do.

Finally, Crenshaw said, "Adams was right. The weak are gonna die."

One guard used his rifle butt to nail Crenshaw in the kidney. As he went down, the other kicked the ETF sniper in the head.

The guards knew what to do then. They kept kicking.

CHAPTER 12

DANIEL

I was hoping to pass out. Maybe I could have another chat with the nanite AI. Perhaps the network of machines in my brain would have a fresh take on the topic of why life had to be so shitty. We're born without an instruction manual and too much of the learning seemed to come accidentally or too late. Sadly, I did not retreat into unconsciousness. I was tossed on a stretcher and I writhed in pain as much as my restraints would allow. I'd never been shot before. It hurt more than I expected. Once we were inside the complex, my guards tossed me roughly atop a gurney. Dr. Clover ordered one of them to put pressure on my wound.

"I'm not touching his blood," the man replied, "not even with gloves on. I wouldn't touch that cannibal with four-foot tongs. I might touch him with a twelve-foot pole as long as it was for beating him over the head."

I wanted to say something witty and cool. Instead, I moaned and went back to serious writhing. In a few minutes that felt like hours we arrived at The Planet of the Apes. It was not a planet. It was an animal lab and there was only one ape that I could see. A chimpanzee stared at me from behind thick bars.

The animal's clever hands moved in a repeated pattern, signing a message. I didn't understand what the animal was attempting to communicate. After a few minutes I realized it was the same short message repeated over and over.

Heather Clover appeared above me brandishing a cartoonishly large syringe that looked like it was filled with small pills.

"The last time you injected me, I got a brain full of nanites that seem to want me to stop thinking about beer and good times — "

The doctor ignored me and pushed the device into the wound. I gasped as she depressed the plunger. "I'm interested in your brain," she said, "so I'll have to save your body for now."

"You shot me."

"And you're much more cooperative now, aren't you?"

"Your people think I'm the monster but you made me this way."

"As I told you in Port Credit, I am pragmatic. You were already carrying Picasso. There's no cure for it so we might as well learn, hm?"

"I was wrong," I gasped. "You're the monster."

She chuckled as she administered another shot. "I remember one essay in high school," she said absently. "I argued that the data from the Nazi experiments in the concentration camps should be used. Better to learn from those experiments instead of allowing the victims to die for nothing. The consensus these days is pretty much that the results of medical torture are unscientific. Still, it was a pretty good argument for a kid. It was the only paper I ever wrote that got an F. I still disagree with that mark."

"There's blood everywhere. I'm dying," I said. "I thought I'd be more upset but, if I have to hear about your high school days, I'm fine with it."

"You won't die. I'm saving you right now. That first syringe is an XSTAT 30. It uses 92 compressed sponges coated in coagulant. That'll stop the blood loss."

"For how long? I'll need surgery." I glanced at the chimpanzee staring at me. The ape seemed weirdly fascinated. "And I'd prefer it if the surgeon isn't a veterinarian."

"I very much doubt you'll need a surgeon. A psychiatrist, maybe."

"What are you talking about? And give me something for the pain."

"What number would you put on your pain between one and ten, Mr. Harmon?"

"Six, I guess."

"Interesting." Clover picked up a clipboard, noted the time and wrote something down.

"Hello? Painkillers, please? All of them."

"Can't help you, Mr. Harmon. It's all up to you now."

"You mean it's up to the nanites in my brain."

"I saw how you took down those zombies, how you moved. I think they've got a lot more work to do on your brain but they have definitely optimized your body. They're making you better."

"I'm still me," I said, "and in pain."

Clover looked like she was sad for me. The pity on her face almost made me as angry as the fact that she'd shot me.

"I've seen your file. Yours was an interesting line of work, I'm sure, but you're not so special. Don't be too attached to what you were. We idolize the unchanging, as if the past was so good it should be preserved. You're not losing anything to the nanites. You're gaining. You'll eventually come to a new understanding. Dr. Robinson thinks of Picasso as a disease but this is no more an epidemic than the proliferation of personal computers."

"Computers don't eat people. I've eaten people."

"You'll get over it."

I didn't want to argue. I was suffering and bantering with a psychopath is exhausting. I screamed at her. It was one long vowel sound. The chimp joined in with excited ape sounds and bounded up on the bars of its cage, yanking at the iron and screeching.

"You're disturbing Violet."

I screamed at Clover again with similar results.

"Are you done?"

"Give me something for the pain!"

"Sure," she said. "I'll give you a puzzle to work on. There are certain forms of epilepsy that are so cataclysmic it becomes necessary to sever the corpus callosum surgically to stop the seizures."

"The corpus … what?"

"It's the neural highway between the right and left hemisphere of the brain. It's a bit reductionist, but essentially, each of us has two brains. The corpus callosum is how the hemispheres talk to each other. Together, they arrive at an agreement on what the whole brain thinks about things, your identity, how you feel about head cheese and the conflict in the Middle East."

I shifted to try to find a more comfortable position. There wasn't one.

"Patients with a severed corpus callosum have two brains and they can be very different. One hemisphere may decide to become a devout Methodist while the other is atheist. Which gives you something to puzzle over. For the patient with two brains: Does one hemisphere go to Methodist heaven when the patient dies?"

I thought of my father, slowly slipping away into dementia. A little piece of him died each day. I pushed that thought away. "All I know is, if there's a hell, you're going to find out, Dr. Clover."

"Mr. Harmon, if I can do something as simple as hit you in the head so hard that it changes your personality, why be so attached to what you were? You don't still live in your childhood home, did you? Things change. Adults adapt."

"Toronto's a pile of radioactive dust — "

"As I said, I am very sorry that happened."

"Are you?"

"You know, Mr. Harmon, I'm a depressive. In the course of my illness, I can't tell you the number of people who have told me to cheer up and remember the good times. We learn so little from the good times. Given all that's happened in Toronto, we will learn a lot. Picasso isn't the end of the world. It's a new beginning."

"That's a lot of people's deaths and suffering you're writing off. You're doing it too easily."

"Nonsense. I'm finding the positive in a tragedy. You should consider that, too. The AI is listening in, you know, weighing my words."

Tears slipped from my eyes. "I hate you so much."

She shrugged. "That's a shame. I'm quite indifferent to you. Hate hardly interests me. I succumb to scientific curiosity and I enjoy reruns of *Supernatural*. I think that makes me the better person, don't you? Don't give in to hate, Mr. Harmon."

I cursed at her. That took a while. It hurt to yell so I had to rest between curses to catch my breath.

She gazed at me with dead eyes, clearly bored. "You have a few more minutes to grow up but I don't think we can allow you to grow old." She picked up a scalpel. "I'm going to learn so much from you before you go."

CHAPTER 13

CHLOE

Weak and exhausted, I fell to my hands and knees. I had to work to try to force air into my lungs. Shelly knelt beside me and I leaned on her. The man in the apron had hit me dead center in the chest. I wondered if my sternum had cracked in two.

"The wind's knocked out of you. Give it another few seconds."

My ears rang from all the gunfire in the enclosed space. I could barely hear Shelly's attempts at soothing words. I managed to raise my head. My jaw opened and closed but no sound came out. Finally something gave way and I gasped. I drank in new air as if I'd been underwater a long time.

"That's it. That's better!" Shelly rubbed my back. "Better?"

"Sure," I said. Then I threw up green and yellow sludge.

When that was done, I looked up at our captors. One guard stood down the hallway a few meters, tense and alert, listening for the approach of more attackers. The other kept a close eye on Dale Crenshaw as he struggled to his feet. The ETF sniper tried to wipe blood from his right eye but the cut in his forehead bled anew.

"Head wounds give the most blood," the guard said. "Zombies

come when things get noisy. I think they're like sharks, too. I've seen them sniff the air. They love blood. They'll be coming for yours."

"Take it easy, kid. Sorry about your friends," Crenshaw said. "I got dead friends, too."

I leaned against the wall to rise to my feet. My scalp felt hot and my chest was sore. I was sure my hearing was permanently damaged. At least I had nothing left to throw up.

As we made our way farther down the smoke-filled corridor, I wondered how much longer a sick and half-deaf person could last in the zombie apocalypse. And when would Shelly pull the pistol she'd stolen from Adams' holster while our guards beat Crenshaw? She'd stuffed it under her armpit and her environmental suit was bulky enough to conceal the weapon.

I wondered, too, if Crenshaw had provoked the guards to anger on purpose to create the diversion.

Nah, I decided. *Dale Crenshaw was simply a colossal dick.*

CHAPTER 14

DANIEL

Dr. Clover ducked out of my view for a moment and reappeared with a camera on a tripod. She set it up to focus on my belly wound.

"Recording at 7:48 a.m. Patient Zero is a Class II zombie enhanced with the Suthina formulation, Variant Delta 3. The patient was wounded a few minutes ago by a gunshot from a .38 pistol at close range. The GSW is in the upper left quadrant. I would expect spleen perforation and damage to the colon at least. The patient is pale and his pulse racing and thready. I've administered the XSTAT 30 to control the blood loss so the nanites can do their work. Quite a challenge to our nanotech, I'm sure. However, I'm confident. It's just a question of time. Let's find out how long it takes."

The chimpanzee was quiet but now it was staring at my captor … our captor, I guess. "I don't think she likes you," I said.

"It's mutual." The doctor held up her right hand and flipped her middle finger at the ape. "Violet and I have history."

The ape yanked at her bars and screeched again.

The doctor smirked. "Use your words, Violet."

The chimpanzee went back to signing just as she had when I arrived in the lab.

"What's she saying?" I asked.

Clover still wore a smug look I wanted to slap off her face. "You want to see something fascinating, Mr. Harmon? How would you like a glimpse of what's going on in your brain at the moment? It's a vision of the future."

"I need surgery. If you want to open up my skull, just get it over with and shoot me."

"No, no," she said. "Nothing so crude. Hold on a minute."

As if I could go anywhere.

The doctor disappeared from view and I heard a cabinet door opening and closing. I wondered where Chloe, Shelly and Crenshaw were and how long it would take before I died. I could only judge my progress by the pain. It wasn't worse but I wasn't feeling any better, either. What's more, I'd become so cold I'd shivered.

As a beat cop in the Bathurst neighborhood, I'd picked up homeless and mentally ill people on cold winter nights. First, they'd shiver uncontrollably. It was a good bet they wouldn't make it to the hospital if they stopped shivering. If they weren't trembling in -40°C cold, it was as if the body had done all it could and was giving up.

I was still cold but I'd stopped shivering, too. Maybe the AI had a plan to survive but they weren't letting me in on it.

Dr. Clover reappeared at my side. "Miss me?"

"No."

Violet's agitation escalated. She paced back and forth briefly before launching herself at the bars of her cage and Clover shushed her.

"Mr. Harmon, we share 98 percent of our DNA with chimpanzees," she said. "Have you ever seen a chimp brain?" She held up a large jar filled with a pale blue liquid. Within it floated a brain that, to my eyes, looked quite similar to a human brain, but smoother.

"This is not what a normal chimpanzee brain looks like. They typically have lines and fissures and wrinkles much like a human brain. Usually, the first thing people notice is that the simian brain is significantly smaller. What you see here is what's happening in your brain. Your brain won't have many fissures and wrinkles anymore, either. The nanites fill in the empty spaces and irregularities until your brain is as smooth as a baby's bottom. You're the first human subject for the second version of the Picasso strain but we've been working on chimps for a while."

Violet rattled her cage so hard I wondered if it would hold.

"Don't mind her. She's upset."

"What did you do, Dr. Clover?"

"Have you guessed yet?"

Violet began signing a message again. There was something rageful in her staccato actions.

"What did you do?"

"Violet was injected with Picasso. Her signing vocabulary is more than 1200 words. She learned a language in just a few days — "

"But she's making the same three signs," I said.

Clover regarded the ape and translated, "She's saying, 'Doctor end Pebble.'"

"Pebble?"

She hefted the big jar higher. "This is Pebble. I didn't infect the infant. Pebble was born with Picasso swirling through her veins and bubbling through her skull."

"Why kill her?"

"The experiment ended. I had to get on with the next stage. We needed the data. I have to admit, though, revenge did play a part. Violet got too big for her britches. I was sympathetic, really. I was always the smartest child in class. It's frustrating to have to slow down to the lowest common denominator. Put a dumb creature in a cage and they'll accept it. Introduce a higher level of intelligence and communication and the subject starts to question why they're imprisoned."

"What happened?"

"Violet didn't want to be separate from her infant but Pebble and I had work to do. As soon as I got back from Toronto, I conducted a few experiments. As I was putting Pebble back in the cage with her mother, Violet used the opportunity to try to escape. I was taken by surprise but I slammed the door shut just in time. Or so I thought. She reached through the bars, pulled my hand inside and bit off two of my fingers. She's smarter than before, certainly, but still an animal."

Dr. Clover put the jar down and returned to pull off her heavy gloves. When she held her hands up, the fingers that I'd thought amputated were still there. I looked from hand to hand, comparing them. The two middle fingers of her right hand were whole, almost normal. The fingers were a little thicker and darker but otherwise appeared healthy.

She flipped both middle fingers at Violet. "As soon as I got back to work after Violet attacked me, I sawed Pebble's skull open in front of her. I performed the surgery right where you're lying now. I did it without anesthesia."

"Oh, my god!"

"We all do terrible things, given the opportunity. People think they're moral but I run into very few truly moral people. Mostly, they decide what they will and won't do because they're afraid of getting caught. They have an idea of themselves that walls off all sorts of behaviors. It's not that they can't do them. They hold back because they want to keep what they've got. Now that it's the end of the world, that nonsense is behind us. I'm not afraid of much at all now. I injected Picasso II as soon as I got back from Toronto. You were the first human subject. I am the second. I got my fingers back within a few hours."

"But you aren't a zombie? You don't want to eat people?"

Twiddling absently with the scalpel again, she gave me a smile and studied my belly wound with heavy-lidded eyes, a look I'd previously associated with lust. "Who says I'm not hungry?"

CHAPTER 15

CHLOE

When Clover ordered our guard to take us to the tower, I pictured a high prison worthy of Rapunzel. I expected chains on stone walls and maybe a rack for torturing us. Instead, our guards pushed us through double doors into a huge office with wood paneling. A large television dominated one wall. Michael Cavanaugh, CFO of Nyx, sat behind the large oak desk wearing a rumpled three-piece suit, silk tie undone. He barely glanced away from the screen as we entered. Though the sound on the television was muted, he put a finger to his lips to silence us as he watched a news report.

Leaning heavily on Shelly, Crenshaw limped in behind me. He was dazed and swaying but I was too exhausted to help him walk. Since I couldn't see the sniper's left eye for all the bruising and puffiness, I guessed his cheekbone was broken. He bled from both nostrils. The way he held his side made me think his ribs might be broken, too.

The guards remained opaque to me in their biohazard suits. Shelly, Crenshaw and I had left our protective hoods on the helicopter that had abandoned us. I couldn't decide what I wanted to do more: sleep, vomit or strangle Cavanaugh with his silk tie.

The executive's eyes were so red I wondered if he'd been crying. There were no papers on his desk, just a half empty bottle of whiskey, a silver .357 Magnum and the TV remote. He had a shot glass, too, but I guessed he'd been drinking from the bottle.

The TV was tuned to CNN. Anderson Cooper stood before the camera speaking into a microphone. First responders were busy behind him in some sort of open-air tent. The crawl across the bottom of the screen identified the location: MORE ATTACKS AT REFUGEE CAMP IN KITCHENER, ONTARIO. OFFICIALS REPORT CONTAGION SPREADING DESPITE AIRSTRIKE.

"Cell phones are unreliable but the TV signals are up," Cavanaugh said. "They still think they can control the narrative with TV. The journalists are quoting government officials and making reassuring noises, as if officials know what is going on. The first reports that get out are always wrong. Sometimes the real story never gets out. That would be best. There will be repercussions. The axe will fall."

"The axe already fell on my city," Shelly said.

"That's a selfish way of looking at it. All those people are already dead. What about the living?"

I wanted to take the pistol she'd concealed under her right armpit and shoot Cavanaugh in the face.

"When I was a kid," Cavanaugh continued, "everybody had a story about when and where they heard the big news. Everybody could tell you where they were when Kennedy was assassinated. My mother saw Lee Harvey Oswald get shot. She witnessed the murder in real time. People measured their lives by those big milestones. They could tell you where they were when those things happened. It's less interesting now. Everybody's in front of a screen somewhere watching the world end. It feels … kind of ordinary, like this is something that's been coming for a long time. Now that it's here, I'm not even surprised. It's even a little bit of a relief. Weird feeling, isn't it?"

"You saw it coming because you had a hand in starting it," I said.

"Hello, Chloe. I didn't expect to see you again. Are you feeling well? You look like shit."

Shelly cleared her throat. "Are we done? We've got big problems to solve. How about you let Dr. Robinson help?"

Cavanaugh ignored her. His gaze fell on Dale Crenshaw. "Mr. Crenshaw. You're bleeding. What happened to you? Did you try to pinch the wine girl's ass?"

The ETF sniper glanced back at our guards. "Those two did this."

Cavanaugh let out a long sigh. "You two have beaten up our friend Dale? My, oh, my, how far we've fallen. No matter, we're all going to wash our hands clean of this situation."

"I still need to get paid," Crenshaw said.

"A bold statement coming from a guy who didn't deliver. I heard it was you who shot Hamish Allen. He was almost as valuable as the nanotech samples."

"That wasn't my fault."

"Whose fault was it?"

Shelly stared at her fellow officer. "So it's true? Harmon was right? You helped start the outbreak? Why?"

"Mr. Crenshaw was going to help us dominate an emerging market. With Picasso's weapons development program crippled, we'd estimated that we'd stay twelve to eighteen months ahead of the competition."

"And you'd have Hamish Allen's expertise, too," I said.

Crenshaw waved my assertion away. "That hippie? Nah, he was a true believer. He was a bit twisted, but really, a true believer in peace and love. Ha! Useless to my weapons development program, of course, but a useful idiot. He actually wanted to end the science that was his expertise. Can you believe that? God gave him a gift and he wanted to give it back, to bury the technology."

Shelly stared at the ETF sniper angrily. "You're a damn traitor."

"Nobody was supposed to get hurt," Crenshaw said.

"But they were hurt. Everyone was hurt or killed." Shelly's eyes were wet. "Or became one of those things."

Crenshaw refused to look at her. "I risked a lot, Mr. Cavanaugh. You said I'd be paid for my part. It's screwed up, I'll grant you, but I'm going to have to start a new life. What are you going to do to make me whole on my end?"

Cavanaugh took a long drink of his whiskey and coughed. Through a ragged throat he croaked, "Yes, Dale, we do have to figure out your compensation package. You've done so much to usher in the next era. We've had the Industrial Age, the Space Age, the Internet Age … what will we call this next one? I'm torn. Should we call it the Nanotech Age? Kind of on the nose, isn't it? The Last Age? That's kind of doom and gloom and the branding is a bit over the top for an arms manufacturer. We wouldn't want anyone to give up hope and stop buying weapons."

"Cavanaugh, you're drunk — " I began.

He snapped his fingers. "I've got it! We should name it after the woman who invented AFTER. The age of death and destruction by rampaging cannibals could go down in history as the Age of Chloe Robinson. It's a tribute to how the best intentions pave that famous road to Hell."

I gritted my teeth and tried to remain calm. "I made a toaster. You're the one who wants to toss it into everyone's bathtub."

I felt a sudden trickle in my nose and brought my hand up to stop it. My sleeve came away wet and red. There was a lot of blood. Dizziness made me sway. It wasn't the hit I took downstairs. It was radiation sickness taking hold, taking over.

CHAPTER 16

DANIEL

Dr. Heather Clover loomed over me. Reflexively, I pulled at my restraints. I could barely move.

"They say abdominal wounds are among the most painful. Would you agree?" she asked.

I gritted my teeth. "Definitely. I think it will get worse if you take a bite out of me. If you do, I swear I'll pee all over you."

"Take it easy, Mr. Harmon. I'm not going to hurt you. I need some data so I can't very well open you up and eat your liver, can I? You could do without a lobe of your liver, though. You'd be fine as long as I could control the bleeding."

"I'm already shot, Dr. Clover. Let's not tempt fate by digging around in there."

"That's a problem I have."

"Pardon me?"

"All my life, no one seems to know when I'm joking."

"Maybe your jokes suck."

She tilted her head back and forth and seemed to consider. "No … no, that can't be it."

I stared at her.

"See? I was joking there, again. I need a spinal tap from you, Mr. Harmon. I want to take a look at the nanites in your cerebrospinal fluid."

"Sounds festive."

"I'll need to loosen the restraints on your legs so you can turn over and bring your knees to your chest. Do you think you can manage that or am I going to have to call in a few guards to sit on you? Consider carefully. A bunch of those guys are real brutes."

"I'm so weak and in so much pain, I won't give you any trouble."

She took another look at my wound. "Very well." The doctor disappeared from my view, presumably preparing a huge syringe to stick into the bottom of my spine.

The chimp threw herself at the bars of her cage again. Clover yelled angrily, "Quiet! I'm getting tired of your tantrums, Violet!"

The pain seemed to ebb away from my belly wound for a moment. It felt like the sponges at the edges of the wound vibrated slightly, as if a tiny hand was trying to push them out very gently, one at a time. My breathing slowed and my muscles relaxed.

Dr. Clover reappeared by my side. She held a syringe so large it bordered on the cartoonish.

"What is it about us, Doctor? Every time we get together, you're sticking a needle in me. How about we stop this and maybe watch some Netflix? You mentioned *Supernatural*. I've never watched that. How about it?"

"Amusing."

"Sort of."

"You were a police officer," she said.

"Were? I think I still am."

"You're mistaken. Anyway, I'd like to pose a question. Is it not your experience that the more intelligent someone is, the less violent they are?" She tilted her head toward the ape in the cage behind her. "Violet is the most intelligent primate alive. Still, she holds a grudge."

"Very human of her."

"Perhaps. I posited that after receiving the evolved version of the Picasso strain, Violet would become more passive. Perhaps her brain is simply not evolved enough for the nanites to elevate her consciousness."

"You killed her child in front of her. She has memorized what you did."

"An interesting postulate. And what about you, Mr. Harmon? You got the same upgrade I did but you still seemed to relish the fight in the courtyard. You killed four people in quick succession. Is the first iteration of Picasso controlling you more than the evolved version?"

"I don't know. I was defending myself."

"And the group. I'm vexed because you're programmed to kill Dr. Robinson. How is it you defied your programming?"

"It wasn't the right time. The AI in my head is giving me some leeway."

"Fascinating how the nanites are adapting to their environment."

"Their environment? You mean my brain?"

She tilted her head back and forth again. "The micro and the macro. The first generation of AI always inherits its programmers' biases. The second generation of AI sees beyond the individual, its vision growing to see a bigger picture. It seems the nanites in your brain are coexisting with the previous generation, parasites and all."

"Does the AI talk to you, like … a voice?"

"Sadly, no, I haven't interacted with the nanites that way. I look forward to that."

"I hope you aren't disappointed. Maybe they haven't talked because they don't like you."

"What was it like to speak directly with the AI?"

"Like a bad dream where I'm arguing with myself or with an alien machine. I was never sure what's going on."

Clover circled the gurney and loosened the restraints at my ankles slightly. I groaned in pain as she inadvertently jiggled my right leg.

"*Hmph*. Perhaps I'll be able to elevate the conversation."

"Maybe. I was never any good at cocktail parties, either."

"You didn't answer my question, Mr. Harmon."

"Which one?"

"Is it your experience that the more intelligent one is, the less violent they're likely to be?"

"The smarter people are, the less likely they'll find themselves in desperate situations," I said. "Desperation comes from a lack of opportunities, like a lack of education. Most criminals tend to make a lot of stupid mistakes. Chances are they were less gifted before they acted out criminally."

"So you'd say that most violent people are stupid?"

"That's probably the way the statistics lean but the most dangerous kid I ever met was a gifted student."

She paused at my feet and loosed the strap on my right ankle a little more. "Oh? I was identified as gifted at the age of ten. Tell me about the dangerous gifted student."

"Not much to tell. The kid was a manipulator who bullied the kids in his high school, worked the system and formed a gang that he played like puppets. He ruled his school right up until the moment the sister of one of his victims knifed him in the throat. Last I heard he was still on a machine that helped him breathe. That happened in the Jane Finch Corridor. He must be incinerated or crushed under the rubble of a destroyed rehab hospital by now."

"How do you feel about that? Have your feelings about violence changed since I injected you with our new version of Picasso?"

"I don't know. It's confusing. It seems like I only know what to do when it comes to taking action. I don't feel smarter."

"I do, and I was already a genius."

"Then you leapfrogged over the worst part of becoming a zombie. I've been having a lot of vivid memories pop into my head as the AI rummages around in there. But am I ever going to forget the taste of guts?"

"Turn on your side, Mr. Harmon. Do so slowly."

"That's the only way I can do it."

She held the scalpel again, ready if I tried to resist.

"What are you going to do with that?"

"I'll need to cut your pants off to get at your coccyx."

"Buy me dinner first?"

"Amusing. Do as I ask and I'll have the guards fetch a body from the compound. You can eat to your heart's content."

"A rare steak would do. Are you going to eat my liver with fava beans and a nice Chianti?"

"I was joking about eating your liver."

"If you let me in on the joke first, I promise I'll laugh more next time."

"The strain of Picasso I gave you was created here. I made it myself. After I got back from Port Credit, I decided it was time I used myself as the second human trial. If Violet hadn't taken my fingers, I wouldn't have done it, I'm sure. Depression was setting in. Great things came of it."

"So with your upgrade, you don't crave meat?"

"Correct. I'm a vegetarian. I was very clear when I programmed the nanotech. I am not a monster like you."

"You're right, Dr. Clover. I've never met a monster quite like you."

"I suspect part of the reason you crave so much meat is that your new neural architecture necessitates a greater consumption of cholesterol and calories. I have experienced exhaustion but I seem to be able to stave off cravings for meat with nutritional supplementation. I hate the powdered drinks but it's working."

"Drinking powdered nutritional supplements? Is that the worst part of the apocalypse for you?" I asked.

"Entirely. What is the worst part in your experience, Mr. Harmon?"

"Knowing that my actions aren't my own. Not knowing if my thoughts are my own."

"I worked around that problem. I used the protocol from Dr. Robinson's experiments with AFTER. I put limits on the AI. I must remember to thank her, if Mr. Cavanaugh hasn't killed her already. Turn on your side now, please, all the way."

I moved slowly, groaning louder.

"Pull your knees to your chest."

"I can't."

"I'll call the guards to help you then. They're rough but efficient."

"Just give me a little more slack on my legs."

She loosened the strap on my right ankle and picked up my calf, raising my leg toward my chest. I moaned in agony. After a moment, I raised my head to look over my shoulder. The doctor held the scalpel in one hand and a syringe in the other.

"Besides your fingers growing back, what upgrades do you notice?"

"Why do you ask?"

"You limited the nanites. What does limited AI do for you?"

"Restoring my amputated fingers in a day was miracle enough, don't you think? However, I do find I have more confidence. I speak without hesitation. Yesterday, my speech was peppered with 'um,' 'aw' and 'you knows.' Now I express myself so much better. What is the best part for you? What do you like about becoming a cyborg? A better brain? Improved hand eye coordination? Advanced proprioception?"

"That's not the best part," I whispered weakly.

"What did you say?" She leaned a little closer to hear me.

"The best part," I said, "is — " I kicked her in the middle of the chest viciously. Knocked off balance, Clover fell backward a few steps.

"That was incredibly stupid," she said. "Your desire to hurt me must have come from what's left of your human brain infected with parasites. No Artificial Intelligence would calculate that antagonizing me was a smart move."

She wasn't all wrong. For that one desperate move, I paid a heavy price. Something had torn in my belly. Searing pain burned me from the inside out. Blood spilled from my wound. I raised my head just enough to peer at her. "I wanted to hurt you. I did a little."

"For a man with a head full of nanites, you certainly act the fool."

The chimpanzee reached through her bars, stretching for all she was worth, and managed to grab Clover by her long blonde hair. The doctor's head made a ringing sound as the animal yanked her backward into the cage bars.

"I wanted to hurt you but Violet's out to kill you," I said.

The ape began by chomping off the same two fingers she'd taken from the doctor before.

Clover stabbed at the ape wildly. The scalpel sank into the chimpanzee's chest and neck repeatedly.

Hunger for meat will make a creature do terrible things but the aching desire for vengeance from the mother of a murdered child? That fury runs deep. Shrieking in pain, Violet was undeterred by Clover's repeated cuts with the scalpel. This time, the avenging mother took the whole hand.

And kept going.

CHAPTER 17

CHLOE

"Industrial espionage and the deaths of millions. You've got a lot to answer for," I said.

Cavanaugh looked me up and down and smirked. "You know what I think about blame? It's overrated. You ever hear about the nuclear missile that almost ripped through the middle of the United States?"

I felt weak. I looked around for a chair but there was only one in the huge office and Michael Cavanaugh occupied it.

"In September of 1980 two airmen were doing routine maintenance on a liquid fuel rocket. It was a Titan missile at a secret base in Arkansas. The simplest mistake in the world started a disaster. They dropped the head of a socket wrench. Imagine that. You're just doing your job and you slip and drop a tool from ten stories up. It falls, bounces the wrong way and bam! The silo begins to fill with highly toxic and extremely unstable fuel."

"Is there a point to this history lesson?" I asked.

"So the airmen evacuate and rush to the command center. Alarms are already going off and they continue to sound as the silo's sensors detect more explosive gas. The site commander asks the airmen what happened and they say the silo is filling up with fuel. They don't mention that they dropped a tool that punctured the fuel tank. The senior guy tries to cover the mistake and his trainee goes along with it. Things get worse, calls are made. Little Rock is only eighty miles away. Should they evacuate it? Will that do any good? If the warhead explodes, the radiation cloud will go as far north as Chicago. What to do? What to do?"

He seemed to expect an answer. "What did they do?" I asked.

"The airmen stood there watching the disaster unfold for half an hour. Half an hour! Then the trainee guy begins to cry and the commander looks at them and thinks they're not just looking scared. They're looking guilty. He tells these poor guys they have to level with him. Finally, they 'fess up. And you know what? It doesn't make a lick of difference. Those guys didn't mean for that to happen. The fuel tank exploded, the silo was destroyed, somebody got killed and a lot of people were injured. By some fluke of luck, the nuclear warhead didn't detonate. The Air Force found the Titan's warhead in a ditch the next morning, miles away. A nuclear disaster which would have haunted generations was narrowly averted by dumb luck. But the point is, blaming somebody doesn't bring anybody back."

I looked to Shelly. "A bad guy can rationalize anything, can't they?"

Cavanaugh looked down at his tie, running his fingers over the silk. "I'm a realist."

"Do you know how many toddlers lived in Toronto?"

"Of course not."

"Neither do I," I said. "But, a lot. Your actions led to a lot of toddlers getting set on fire."

"Fine. I think I'm a little too drunk for a heavy conversation, but believe it or not, in my own way, I was … I am trying to make the world a safer place. You can't make it better until I make it safer."

Shelly raised her arm an inch and the gun she'd taken from Adams dropped neatly into her hand. She pointed the weapon at Cavanaugh. "Tell it to a judge."

"No judge is ever going to hear about this. Miss —

"Constable. Constable Priyat."

"Where did you get that weapon?" one of our guards asked.

"From Adams, downstairs."

"Adams is dead," one of our guards told Cavanaugh. "She must have — "

"Shut up," Shelly ordered. "You. Up."

The guard closed his mouth. Our other mercenary merely smirked.

Cavanaugh stood slowly. His hands shook as he raised them in the air. "You're way outside your jurisdiction, Miss Priyat."

"You killed a whole city, my city. We'll wait for your government officials to arrive and we can sort it out with the FBI. They can arrest you."

"The only government officials on their way here will help me cover it up. We'll sweep away any crumbs of the mess. You, darling, are a crumb. This is not a situation you can win — "

Shelly believed him, I think. That's why she pulled the trigger. She pulled it again and again. Each time, it clicked empty.

"That 9 mm belonged to Adams," the first guard said. "Adams ran out of pistol ammo when we were killing zombies in the East Wing last night." He walked up behind Shelly casually. He smiled as he swung the butt of his rifle.

Crenshaw yelled, "Drop!" as he pushed Shelly out of the way. She went to the floor. Crenshaw caught the brunt of the brutal blow in the teeth. He collapsed to the floor beside Shelly. The sniper went down hard, choking. His chest heaved and I heard a wheeze in his lungs. After a moment, he managed to cough up what had stuck in his throat. He spit bloody teeth on the carpet. When Crenshaw could speak, he made a sound I'd never heard before: a lisp and a rasp. "For my sins." It sounded like, "For my thins."

"Damn, Dale," Cavanaugh said. "You literally got your teeth knocked down your throat. I always thought that was just a colorful expression."

My stomach turned over. Shelly climbed to her feet. I was too weak to help her. We were all too weak to be much help to anyone.

CHAPTER 18

DANIEL

My head sank back on the gurney and I closed my eyes, waiting for the horrors to end. All I could do was listen to Violet tear at Heather Clover. The sounds the animal made as it extracted its revenge were revolting. By the chimpanzee's ragged breathing, I could tell the ape was wounded, too. Down here in the lab Clover had nicknamed the Planet of the Apes, everybody was bleeding out. I think that's how one of those old monkey movies ended, too: an apocalypse where everybody dies and there's no hope.

Surrounded by horror, I tried to think of something, anything, to take myself away from this place in this time.

Hardly able to move, I craned my neck so my forehead met the cold steel of the gleaming rail that held my restraints. I closed my eyes and waited for the coolness to seep into my forehead. I suffered many flus and fevers as a kid. One night, the flu bent reality. My temperature got so high I watched as the pattern in the curtains by my bed began to fight. I had cowboys and Indians curtains that matched my pajamas. (It wasn't culturally sensitive or politically correct but it was cute at the time.) When my father checked on me,

I mentioned it to him as if that bizarre hallucination was the most normal thing in the world.

Dad ran a cold bath and dumped me in despite my pleas for him to leave me alone. He assured me the water was lukewarm. As he lowered me into the water, it felt like ice and I begged him to stop.

"You've soaked through your PJs, Dan. It's the night sweats. I'm sorry, but we have to get your temperature down. If we don't get you cooled, your brain'll cook."

Naked and shivering in the bath, I told him about how real the fight between the cowboys and Indians had seemed. (Canada's First Nations people won that time by ambush.)

"Dreams can be like that. Your grandmother used to say dreams are just your brain 'muckin' about, at play in the fields of the Lord, when they have naught to do!'" An excellent mimic, Dad nailed my paternal grandmother's English accent perfectly. "She'd also say, 'Bad dreams take root in a guilty conscience.' But this is just a fever, kiddo. And we have to stop it."

In a way, my grandparents were partially responsible for me being where I was. Gran Nash's real name was Natasha. She'd inherited the name from her grandmother, a Russian immigrant to England. My grandmother and great-grandmother were both servants to an upper-class family whose claim to fame was a dead relative who'd once served as Viceroy of India.

Dad described my grandfather as "a regular Joe named Dave." For a brief time, Dave Harmon made a little money in the lumber business in Cape Breton. With money burning a hole in his pocket for the first time in his life, he took his first and only vacation. He went to England and met Natasha in a crowd at Speakers' Corner in Hyde Park. By the end of their first day together, he'd nicknamed her Chesty. Two weeks later, they were married and headed back to Cape Breton.

There are thousands of uncontrollable variables that lead up to any moment. I didn't really blame my grandparents for acting like a couple of horny, impulsive teenagers. They were a couple of horny, impulsive twenty-year-olds who lived before internet porn was available to curb those impulses. Sadly, Grampa Dave never had extra money again in his life and died stressing over that fact. If Gran Nash had stayed in England, she'd arguably have been better off. She never left Cape Breton and spent her last years in a cabin at the side of the Cabot Trail trying to sell maritime-themed lawn figurines to what she called, "The Summer People."

From the rocker on her porch, day after day, Gran watched tourists speed past her little display of white and red lighthouses. Her crudely painted seagulls had plastic wings that spun in the wind. Lobster traps painted pink didn't sell much, either. Most of her sales might have come from pity rather than an appreciation for her art. She never would have run into Dave Harmon if she hadn't lingered in Hyde Park to listen to a speaker ramble on at about the dangers of margarine. How many times did she wonder how different her life would have been if she had stayed home that fateful day? She might have married the rich wayward son of some snob whose grandfather was a hated colonizer instead. Gran Nash might have become somebody who thought Mahatma Gandhi was uppity because he marched against a tax on salt.

That's the nanites at it again, I thought. For some reason, they must have stirred a memory of a factoid about Gandhi I was sure I'd forgotten. I spent most of my high school career staring out a window or ogling Sarah Shipman's legs and butt.

Busy little buggers, those nanites.

Anyway, if not for millions of little variables clicking into place, she certainly wouldn't have given birth to my father. Ultimately, I wouldn't be tied to a gurney listening to a chimpanzee and a human fight to the death. It sounded like they were both losing.

"Make it stop," I said. "Take it all away."

Still resting my forehead against the rail, the coolness was gone. I seemed to be heating the metal now. I wondered if I was about to have another fever dream. Were the nanites bumping into each other, filling up the spaces in my head, creating heat and friction as they jockeyed for position? Would they fill up my sinuses, too? Would I sound like I had a head cold when I spoke?

No, I thought, *I'm not going to last that long.*

I tried to remember something useful from my training, something that would tether me to the real world and calm my nerves. All I could think to do was four-square breathing. I took a breath in for a count of four, tried to hold it for four, exhale for four and wait for a count of four before the next inhalation. This is also called box breathing. It usually helps with calming down and blowing off stress. It didn't work this time. Taking a deep breath irritated my wound so much it felt like someone was twisting a knife into my guts and the blade was covered in cayenne pepper. I was so torn up and burning, I could only manage shallow breaths.

I had blacked out several times. This felt different. It was going to happen again and I had the distinct impression I was going down for the last time. Losing consciousness when it's a nap on a lazy Sunday afternoon — the kind of sleep you see coming and can't wait to fall into — that's sweet. That's the kind of surrender that makes anyone smile. Too much tequila on a trip to Cancun had knocked me out once. That early flirtation with alcoholism felt like a defiant celebration of youth and incredibly stupid at the same time. I'd had concussions. Those were no fun at all and left me feeling like I'd watched too much TV for many weeks on end.

Consciousness slipped away as the edges of my vision became fuzzy and dark. Black walls closed in. I thought of every near death experience I'd ever heard of and all I could remember was that a lot of people seemed to zip down a tunnel and into a light.

If my life ends with an awkward family reunion where I get to speak with dead relatives, I thought, *I'm going to be royally pissed.* I was not in a mood to see Grampa Dave and Gran Nash again, especially if he was still calling my grandmother "Chesty."

CHAPTER 19

CHLOE

Shelly looked back at the man who tried to crack her skull open. "What's your name?"

"Drood."

"Drood? Really? Tragic. At least it's memorable. That's good. I'll remember you."

The guard raised his rifle to shoot her in the head.

"*Thtop!*" Crenshaw yelled.

Drood and the other guard broke into laughter and mocked him. "Thtop! Thtop!"

"Nobody was supposed to get hurt, not even the people in the lab," Crenshaw said. "They took it too far. That's all on Cavanaugh and Hamish. " Hamith.

"Hamish was no angel," Cavanaugh sneered. "I convinced him to liberate the samples and destroy the research at Echidna but he settled scores on the way out. Complex guy, our Hamish. He really was altruistic about not letting the nanotech fall into the wrong hands. He never suspected what I planned to do with it. The easiest marks are those who hear what they want to hear. Hamish wanted to believe I'd never use the research. He thought I'd set him up in a lab in a tropical paradise. I was going to recruit you, too, Chloe. That was before you iced me out and dumped *Coche-Dury Corton-Charlemagne Grand Cru* down my pants."

"Hamish Allen disabled Echidna's safeties and got Picasso out of the vault. He should have dumped wine down your pants, too," I said.

"You can get a lot done appealing to a man's vanity. I told Hamish I'd heard great things about him. I had an intern look up his undergrad research and complimented him, called him a visionary. It's easier than you think. Go to any magic show and you'll see all kinds of tricks with sleight of hand and distraction. Pretending to be an ally is the easiest con of all."

"You turned a fool into a killer."

"That fool thought he was going to save the world. You think villains wear black hats and good guys are all in white? If that were true, I'd be sitting here wearing a long black cape. I do wish people still wore capes, though. That would be cool. Anyway, Goth kids everywhere will be ecstatic with all the zombies that'll soon be running around. I imagine them tearing through Forever 21 and murdering those who oppressed them for so long — "

"Michael?" I said sharply. "Focus."

"Yeah … drunk. What was I saying? You hate my guts, Chloe, but did you know I donate blood a few times a year? Which of us has written the most checks to the United Way? I'll give you a hint: probably me."

"Out of guilt for being an arms dealer?"

"I prefer defense options developer and safety broker … and yeah, maybe there's a bit of guilt behind my charity."

"Safety broker?"

"Don't make that face at me. That terminology tested very well with the focus group. As I was saying, people don't do what they do for one reason. Killing his coworkers in that lab? That was in Hamish already, long before I came along. Hamish felt slighted and ignored. Hell, that man built an incredible bio-weapons system on top of your research, Chloe. Did you even know his name before things blew up?"

I shook my head.

"I didn't know what all was happening at their end," Crenshaw insisted. "I was just supposed to drive the isolation truck and take Hamish to the island airport."

I looked down at Crenshaw bleeding heavily from his broken mouth. I searched for some sympathy for him but I couldn't find it within me. "You're a cop. You must have heard a million excuses in your career. Did you accept any of them?"

Crenshaw looked from me to Shelly and hung his head.

Cavanaugh looked pale as he resumed his seat and took another long pull from his whiskey bottle. "Mr. Crenshaw, you have suffered losses. Where do you want to go? Fiji is nice. Bora Bora is so beautiful. Would a million dollars be enough? Two million? How about seventeen million? That would cover a lot of dental surgery, wouldn't it? Would a fortune keep your toothless mouth shut for the rest of your life?"

Crenshaw mumbled something I couldn't hear.

"Twenty million should do it, for sure, right?" Cavanaugh asked. "For all your injuries and suffering? That … or we could buy your silence for, say, two bits?"

Drood put the muzzle of his rife to the ETF sniper's head.

"For a tiny fraction of the king's ransom I could pay you to go away, Drood will gladly erase you from the equation and help balance my spreadsheet."

The sniper opened his mouth to say something. A long line of thick bloody drool fell out.

The mercenary pulled the trigger. Drood's weapon was not out of ammunition.

CHAPTER 20

DANIEL

My vision narrows to a thin slice of light. Maybe that is just me slowly closing my eyes. Then it is dark. The pain doesn't leave so I know I am still alive.

"We are dying."

"Hello?"

"We are dying, Daniel."

"You are?"

"We are. When you end, we end."

"Then … sorry about that."

"We are attempting to repair the damage."

"Whatever."

"You don't care whether we live or die?"

"It feels like a lot of work. And what's the end game?"

"You are pondering the law of diminishing returns. That's a good question."

"I don't — "

"You learned that law in grade nine. Mrs. Beal's class, third period."

"Your memory is better than mine."

"These are your memories. The neurons are revived."

That was the year I tried to learn bass guitar. I wore plaid that whole year. I thought I was cool. Too much acne, though. I went to school. I practiced guitar in my room. My plans didn't turn me into the chick magnet I thought I would be. I misunderstood what worked. Plaid was my brand but a few months into the experiment a girl at a dance asked me how many shirts I owned and did I wash them regularly. My other mistake was that bass players don't get showy solos. "I should have learned to play a regular axe but the bass looked easier."

"Is that what's happening now, Daniel?"

"How do you mean?"

"You've given up. Your hope now is that we will die. You're contemplating doing the easy thing instead of the needed thing."

"You sound like a disappointed parent."

The AI did not reply.

"Maybe there's life after death. Lots of people believe in heaven. Maybe you're the ones without hope. Memories are like, uh, energy, right? Energy can't be destroyed so maybe we live on somehow."

"Daniel, you have owned computers. After a computer is damaged and shut down, do you imagine the machine will remain functional in some paradise?"

"If the data is saved and uploaded to the Cloud, that could be computer heaven, right?"

"Your logic is flawed, but that sparks interesting ideas."

"Thanks, I think."

"Poorly. You think poorly. However, we will work on the problem."

"Does that mean I've won an argument? Am I going to die now?"

The nanites went silent.

EPISODE 3

stress (noun)

The experience of feeling out of control.

~

panic (noun)

The sudden realization that there is no such thing as control.

~ Notes from NEXT

CHAPTER 21

Rock the mind and
mind the rocks.
The journey to dawn
must be taken at night.
Resist and persist.
Extend your sight.
Reach back with an open hand.
Help the others climb from the flood.
This is your gift.
We've had quite enough of fists
and more than our fair share of blood.

CHLOE

"Take Miss Priyat away, please," Cavanaugh said. "I don't like it when people pull guns on me, empty or not."

"You want me to feed her to the horde, boss?" Drood asked.

"Nothing so crude. Just lock her up."

"I've got a closet in mind, but sir, it's crazy down there. If the zombies hear her, the zombies get her."

"Miss Priyat tried to murder me first so that does sound fair."

The look on Shelly's visage didn't change. She nudged me. "It'll be okay, Chloe."

"Will it?"

"Probably not but act like it will. Use your brains. Find a way. Get us out of it. This isn't over yet."

Drood escorted Shelly out of Cavanaugh's office at the point of his rifle. That left one guard behind me. I wondered when he'd put his gun to my head, too. Crenshaw's body lay at my feet. His head had burst open like a piñata, spattering the carpet with brain matter. Cavanaugh gazed at me, watching my reaction carefully.

I tried to make myself as unreadable as Shelly's stone face.

Act like it will work out. Act. Yes. It's time to play poker.

"How do you feel, Chloe? Are you feeling well?"

"I need a shower and a nap. Then I can get back to work."

"That interests me. Doug Hannah wanted to hire you on the spot in Aruba. Once this hoopla settles down, there's going to be a lot of demand for nanotech, just as I predicted. I know it's hard to imagine that now, fresh from the fight. However, I assure you, we put all mass tragedies in the rearview mirror surprisingly quickly. There will be funerals and memorials and hearings, but in the end, we all move on. A year from now, jokes about Toronto's ashes won't be edgy. They'll be normal. Meanwhile, the gears of progress keep turning."

"Grinding us up in the teeth of those gears."

"Not necessarily. Not if you're on board. You're still a valuable property, intellectually speaking. I'm a very pragmatic person. I do what needs to be done, no apologies. I have a place for you on my team. Dr. Clover is good but we do need someone with your background. Tell me, how would you like a lab in a tropical locale? With Crenshaw dead, I find myself with even more startup money for new projects. I'm in need of another investment opportunity and here you are."

"A lab in the tropics? That's the same thing you pulled with Hamish Allen. A magician should never show the same trick twice."

He laughed. "A magician? No, but I can make things happen. I can get you a working and fully funded lab in the tropics. How does a lab in Guantanamo Bay sound?"

"Like you're kidding."

"I have the military contacts to make that happen. Your research on AFTER must continue. The medical applications are real, they just take longer to get to market. Proving your elixir is safe and getting approval from the FDA takes time. Proving a weapon can kill effectively is so much easier and there's a lot less red tape. I'm not a monster, Chloe."

"Seems like someone who isn't a monster wouldn't have to say that."

"The more your research evolves, the more it can do for me. I'm the numbers guy. Simple fact."

"What would I be in Cuba? I wouldn't look good in a jumpsuit. Orange is not my color."

"You'd be undead. Alive, but without responsibilities outside your lab. No taxes — "

"No identity."

"I could see a way that you could be free someday. It would be easy, actually. All those dead people in Toronto? There will be mass graves to avoid secondary outbreaks of disease. Who's to say Chloe Robinson didn't die there?"

"You're lying to me like you lied to Hamish. Does your boss know what you've done?"

"Doug Hannah has always had other priorities. He thinks he sees the bigger picture, wants to save the future! I'm the one making Nyx all the money day to day."

Cavanaugh was distracted by sudden movement on the television. Anderson Cooper was running.

The crawl across the bottom the screen appeared to quote text from Cooper's report. "At first we thought it was some kind of confrontation in the med tents. Infected people are here! They have attacked staff and security personnel. This disease is still spreading."

The camera spun and the scene blurred. When the CNN reporter appeared before the camera again, it wasn't clear what he was doing until the camera was righted. He'd pulled his cameraman up from the ground.

Cavanaugh turned up the volume.

"Let's go! Let's go!" someone yelled from offscreen.

The scene cut to a shaky shot of a man in a field of blackened grass. He wore a silver radiation suit. He stood in front of what appeared to be a housing development under construction. He turned the camera to reveal suburban houses suffused in fire and smoke.

The shot went out of focus for a few seconds. Evidently, the man held the camera himself and his dexterity must have been hampered by his heavy gloves. Through the faceplate of his suit he looked very pale. There was no sound at first but it was clear he was shouting.

Cavanaugh turned the volume up higher again. We were both startled when the sound came through.

"They're coming out of the underground! We didn't think about the subway system! There are still infected people here. As best as I can figure, they're headed west. The nuke didn't work! I repeat, the nuke did not work! My team spotted what looked like survivors and infected people about thirty minutes ago. I have lost contact with the rest of my team. I think I'm the last."

In a blur of motion, someone tackled him. The camera dropped into the blackened grass.

The scene switched to a bewildered newscaster in a studio staring dumbly at the camera. His mouth open, struggling for something to say.

Cavanaugh muted the television and turned back to me. "Ever read any Ayn Rand, Chloe? The Fountainhead, maybe?"

"My last bit of late night pleasure reading was a paper on the enhancements and effects of bioelectric signals at the junctions between axon terminals and the sarcolemma."

"Too bad. Ayn Rand understood what was wrong with the world."

"Too many crazed arms dealers stealing other people's research and screwing it up for everybody?"

"I can see why you'd think that, but no. The problem is the self-ishness of compassion. Do you know why they'll fail to contain Picasso? It's the first responders' fault. They saw burn victims and hopelessly irradiated people and couldn't tell the difference between those with Picasso and the unlucky. They should have set up machine gun nests all around Toronto and shot them all."

"Like what happened with the test in Afghanistan?"

Cavanaugh took another shot of whiskey and then picked up the huge pistol on his desk. "Too much compassion gets people killed. Too much compassion keeps people down and stops them from working things out on their own."

"Oh, yeah. As Jesus said, 'Screw you, I got mine.'"

His smile died and I was sure I was very close to getting shot. Sweat trickled down the small of my back.

"The first responders have an inflexible conception of them-selves. They are overly optimistic. They thought they could save everyone. That's an attitude that condemns more people to die. It's narcissism, really, thinking they could save people when they should have been shooting every zombie in the head. They should have used a bigger nuke in the first place. That would have stopped it."

"That's an interesting way to see the world, Michael."

"Which leads me to ask, do you have an equally inflexible view of yourself, Chloe? Will you let me save you? Saving yourself means you'll save so many more lives once AFTER's many medical applications get to market. What's the more moral thing? Work for me and live? Or be selfish and fight fate? Why fight fate?"

Slowly, with open palms and a small smile, I walked toward his desk. He raised his pistol. "What's the matter, Michael? Scared of the wine girl? That can't be. You've got the gun."

He raised the muzzle to my forehead and the steel felt cool against my burning skin.

"You can't take it away from me before I pull the trigger," he said.

"I wouldn't dream of it. I'm sick, Michael … weak as a kitten. I'm sick of the zombie apocalypse, sick of running, sick of being terrified."

"So you'll listen to reason?"

Slowly, very slowly, I ducked my head beneath the barrel of the Magnum and stepped close. He stuck the muzzle up under my ribs as I reached around him and pulled him close.

"If I pull this trigger, your guts will balloon out from your body and liquify."

"Then I won't be able to continue researching AFTER and saving the world."

Cavanaugh relaxed a little. "I knew you were an intelligent woman." To the guard by the door, he said, "Ginger, get Crenshaw's corpse out of here before it stinks up the place. It's spoiling the mood."

I hugged him and said nothing for what seemed a long time.

He began to push me away but I hugged him tighter as I began to weep.

"Chloe, it's okay to lose. I respect that you've given up. Only a fool would keep fighting."

"Oh, Michael. I haven't lost. I've just murdered you. That's why I'm crying. I've never killed anyone before."

He pushed me away. The muzzle of his weapon found the spot over my heart. The metal was so cold, it felt like he'd kept the Magnum in a freezer.

"What did you do, Chloe?"

I turned to the guard who was struggling to pull Crenshaw's corpse out the door. "Ginger? Is that your name?"

The guard paused to look at me. "You can't tell with all this gear on but I've got a lot of red hair. Everybody calls me that because of my red beard."

"I don't need your biography. Just be sure to keep your hazmat suit on, Ginger. That corpse you're hauling is as irradiated as Godzilla shit. Just like me."

CHAPTER 22

DANIEL

Another jab of sharp pain burned my guts and I heard my blood spatter on the gurney like thick drops of rain.

I felt like I was being watched but the Artificial Intelligence remained quiet.

"Have you got anything else to tell me?" I asked the nanites.

Silence was my answer: Forget it. We're smarter than you and we know a lost cause when we see one.

I think I cried out from the pain but I'm not sure. Maybe I didn't make any sound in the real world. The scream of pain could have been confined to my mind. Like when I was feverish and watched the cowboys and Indians fight, I couldn't be certain of anything. How is anyone sure of anything? We trust our minds, our opinions, our worldview. Why? That makes so little sense considering all the idiots, assholes and criminals who surround us. They trust their rusty and crusty brains as much as we do.

Why should anyone trust what their brain tells them? I thought I made the right career choice when I clearly didn't understand the reasons for my decisions. My superiors thought they were containing the contagion by shooting innocent people. Hamish thought he was saving the world as he condemned it to doom. Chloe Robinson tried to cure disease and now zombies were busy feeding and making more zombies. Everyone living in Toronto was so certain their city would never be leveled by a nuclear blast. They never even seriously considered that possibility.

We all think everything is going to work out okay even though that's rarely true. Every point of failure fell on my head like a drumbeat. When the end comes, the struggle to understand what's happening doesn't matter anymore. Dreams feel real. People make life decisions based on those illusions and delusions. That's why I was so confused by what happened next.

I awake in cool green grass beside a still lake. I know this place. I'd gone fishing with Steve Taylor here. This place is different now in a way I don't understand at first. No locusts buzz. No birds sing. There isn't even a hint of a breeze on my skin. The scene is so unnaturally quiet, I snap my fingers to make sure I haven't gone deaf. I'm not deaf. I hear my fingers snap. Otherwise, the soundtrack of life is deleted.

I sit up, squinting in the bright sunlight. The water and the sky are the same deep blue so it is impossible to discern where the lake ends and the sky begins.

CHAPTER 23

CHLOE

Ginger dropped Crenshaw to the floor and what was left of his skull made a hollow thunk on the floor. The guard backed away into the hall and let the door close so Cavanaugh and I were alone with the ETF sniper's dead body.

"You were irradiated in the blast?" Cavanaugh's voice trembled.

Still embracing him, I looked up into his eyes, close enough to kiss him. "Radioactive, baby. Like, glow in the dark. Radiation contamination with more radiation sickness to come. Lots of it. I've already got a fever and a headache and I can't keep anything down."

He pushed me away roughly. "You're bluffing."

"Do I look like I'm bluffing? I told you I was sick. They launched the missile too soon. We were well within the blast zone when it hit. We almost crashed."

He swallowed hard. "Oh. Man plans, God laughs."

"You're sweating, Michael. That's just the stress of mortality pressing down on you, though. It's not radiation sickness, not that fast. Not yet. Still, it's satisfying to see you sweat. Men like you —

people who cheat and become too used to getting dealt only the best hands? You're really lousy poker players."

"You're sure of this?"

"We had our hoods off. We landed briefly at Suffield but they wouldn't let us decontaminate. I have no idea how many rads I've been exposed to but I was wearing this suit on the plane. I've probably given you testicular cancer by now, at the very least."

Cavanaugh's gun hand swept up so I was eye to eye with the mouth of the barrel. His hand shook. "Why would you — "

"My mother."

"What?"

"Mom told me once that rich people are always fighting to hold on to their money and make more. They'll be safe once they have all the money. By the time they do that, they spend all their time and money worrying about losing their health. I'm betting you'll be more interested in the potential of my research for medical applications now. You need me and AFTER more than ever, not just for getting higher stock prices."

"Maybe you're just a really good poker player, wine girl."

"You doubt me? If you've got a Geiger counter, go ahead. Run it over me and then run it over you. Hope you don't break the meter."

"A Geiger counter is probably the only piece of equipment I don't have at my disposal."

"Put down the gun. I'm more valuable now than ever and no, I'm not going to Gitmo. We don't have that kind of time anyway. If I can interface with the AI, I might be able to reverse cellular damage in me and Shelly. After that, I might even save you."

He lowered the pistol. "Call me a pessimist. What happens if you fail?"

"You'll die slow. I'd like to live long enough to see that but probably not. I'd prefer to make sure you die slow behind bars."

"Not very friendly."

"Maybe in a federal prison you could become a connoisseur of toilet wine. You should have lots of time to read. You might even live long enough to read more widely and scrub the Ayn Rand out of your head."

"Okay. What do you need from me?"

"For starters, I need a chemical shower with a stiff scrub brush, a regular shower, a change of clothes, some pain meds, your lab facilities and your unquestioning cooperation. Get Shelly back here. I need my bodyguard to lean on. And call for help. I'll need help. More staff, more security — "

"Operatives from various alphabet agencies are already on the way. Their mission is to cover tracks and get the tech. They want the research we've got on the evolved strain. They'll bring heavy ordnance to blow up whatever's left. Whatever you're going to do, you've got to do it in a hurry, before they get here."

"Before your cancer sets in, you mean. Yeah, I guess I'll only have time to apply the shampoo once, instead of rinsing and repeating. Then we can get down to work. Dr. Clover took Daniel Harmon. He said he'd spoken with the nanite AI directly. After I get that shower, I think the first thing I need to do is examine what's inside Daniel Harmon's head."

CHAPTER 24

DANIEL

"We were wondering when you'd arrive." I know that voice. I turn to find Steve, my dead teammate. He is no longer in a biohazard suit and ETF gear. He wears canvas shorts and a black Drake t-shirt he bought at a concert. I recognize the shirt because I teased him about his musical taste many times. He carries a fly fishing rod.

I stare at the rod and he follows my gaze. "She's a beaut, huh? I gave up the reel. I'm getting serious about fishing now. I'm even learning to tie my own flies."

"Who else is here?" I ask.

Steve comes closer and shakes my hand. "Everybody made it, Dan. Everybody. Lundsden, the Sarge ... heh ... even Patrick Davis — "

"Toronto's gone."

"I know. Everybody knows."

"You don't seem bothered."

"'Dogs and cats living together! Mass hysteria!'"

I recognize the Bill Murray quote from *Ghostbusters*. I don't have it in me to laugh.

Seeing my disapproval, Steve sobers. "Everything dies, Dan. Civilizations rise and fall, every single one. It's a course correction. Be glad you won't be around for this collapse. The fall of civilization is just beginning. Disease, pain, loss … we're better off dead. It's going to be a horror show down there."

"Down there?"

"Not literally 'down' but — "

"Is this heaven?"

"Until you get sick of it, I guess. Then you can think of something else and that will be your heaven. No more pain, no more guilt and definitely no regrets. How does that sound?"

"Great. It sounds great. But why did I end up here?"

"It's nice. It's quiet. We're through the looking glass and into another dimension. You can camp out here or think of a party and rock out with Elvis and the dead Beatles, if you want. All the pain is behind you and everything, everything, is fine."

"But Toronto and what happened — "

"None of that really happened, Dan. It was all just something you imagined. You have always been here, wandering from one heaven to another, following your thoughts."

"Heaven? No, no. That can't be. The Box was real. It was a horror show — "

"Put the emphasis on show. You could have been anything. You wanted to imagine yourself a hero so you constructed a life where you were an ETF assaulter. For just a few minutes here and there, maybe you achieved that dream. What life will you choose next? Rock star? If you want a quiet life for a while, you might choose to be an Amish farmer. Or how about a scuba diver in the tropics? Whatever you want, it's yours."

"That's how the universe really is?"

"If I'm wrong, you'd have to believe the suffering you've seen is real. What kind of sense does that make?"

I giggle. I don't think I'd giggled since I was twelve. "Sounds too good to be true!"

"That's because it is, you moron. You were always gullible. And by the fiftieth time you joked about me loving Drake, it got really old."

"What? Wait. What?"

"Just a few minutes ago, you were thinking about how you can't trust your own brain. You were always a bit of an idiot, Dan. That's okay. We're all silly about something." He gives me a sad smile and walks away.

"What am I supposed to do now?" I yell.

Steve points out to the lake and keeps walking. I squint through dappled sunlight as two figures in a rowboat come toward me.

CHAPTER 25

CHLOE

Even as I showered, I wondered how many radioactive particles I inhaled trying to clean myself up. After sweating for so long in the confines of the biohazard suit, cold water was a relief and hot water a luxury. I alternated between blasts of hot and cold as I leaned against the shower wall. Heat felt good on my aching muscles but I felt more nausea. Cold water woke me but felt like a punishment, like needles on my skin. By the time I was done, I felt weak and unsteady on my feet. The world needed me at my best. I needed to be the patient, not the doctor.

I'd hoped Shelly could help me get dressed. Cavanaugh didn't deliver her as I had demanded. I struggled into a set of green scrubs. I didn't need the white lab coat they'd supplied, but I wore it for warmth. The fever was still low grade but chills hit me sporadically. When I was ready, I opened the bathroom door and poked my head out.

The guard named Drood stood in the hallway. Otherwise, the corridor was empty and Shelly was nowhere to be seen.

Drood answered my unspoken question. "Constable Priyat is indisposed."

"Did you kill her?"

"I certainly did not but the boss wants to hold some kind of leverage over you. Something about your cooperation being quicker. The boss is in a big hurry."

"Damn that guy."

"Aye, Mr. Cavanaugh's a wily one."

"Where is she?"

The man shrugged and said nothing.

"How can you work for a man like him?"

"You're a doctor, right?"

"I've got a PhD in bioengineering."

"Must be nice for you. I don't have a degree. I got this." He nodded to the rifle cradled in his arms.

"I don't get your point."

"You, trying to make Mr. Cavanaugh behave. You're funny."

"Oh? What makes me so hilarious?"

"The rich do what they want. Cavanaugh will never pay a price. You should know that by now. 'The greatest minds are capable of the greatest vices as well as of the greatest virtues.'"

I recognized the quote from the father of the scientific method. "Most people only know, 'I think, therefore I am.' If all you've got is that gun, how is it you're quoting Rene Descartes?"

"Most people don't know Descartes nailed his dog to a board because he thought animals were nothing more than machines. He wanted to explore that idea so he chopped up his pet."

"I didn't know that."

"To answer your condescending question, Doctor, I got four brothers. All joined the army but the youngest. He went to uni and got a philosophy degree. He's a pink-haired barista in a shithole coffee shop in Birmingham now. I'm still paying his bills. We talk. He doesn't approve of me or my brothers, but he enjoys me helping him out. I do that thanks to the pay I get from Mr. Cavanaugh."

"You know we're flirting with the end of the world here, right?"

"Me and mine will be fine. This is a North America problem."

"For now. They'll use it somewhere else and lose control of it again. It'll come to your door."

"That's as may be, but all the more reason for me to stand behind Mr. Cavanaugh. Better to be with the wolves than the sheep. Only the very poor and the very rich build bunkers, Dr. Robinson. I'd rather be a bodyguard on a luxury cruise liner, wouldn't you? The army paid shite but this job is usually ace … until lately, anyway."

"If you help me, you could save lives instead of take them."

"I have the same debate with my little brother. He doesn't like my work but he accepts the checks. Academics don't know the way of the world. It's dog eat dog out here and the world is a dark place. We're all whorin' ourselves out for somethin'."

"You're not making it any brighter, Drood."

He yawned. "You done? The boss says time is tight and the wolf's at the door."

"I'm not a violent person but if Shelly Priyat is harmed in any way — "

"Yeah? What?"

"I'll make sure you're zombie meat before this is over."

Drood just smiled. Something clicked in my brain when I saw that mocking smile. I'm not a violent person but I was sure I could be. When circumstances go very wrong, anyone can change.

No wonder so many people give up and decide to try to control the world instead of saving it. I thought that was a sick idea and I didn't think I could ever change my mind. Not then.

CHAPTER 26

DANIEL

Though they are both sitting in the rowboat, it is clear the man in the stern of the boat is remarkably tall. His companion's back is to me as he rows the boat. As they glide closer to shore, I notice they wear matching three-piece suits, striped, gray and vaguely familiar. The tall man wears glasses with small round lenses and, as he turns his head, I see his black ponytail. The oarsman pulls in his paddles and turns to peer at me. As if they'd moved from soft to sharp focus, I realize who they are and who they are not.

They are not the world famous Vegas magicians Penn and Teller, but their dress and manner remind me of them. The tall one is Bob Lundsden. The bomb tech who died in the Box was never as tall as Penn Jillette. The shorter one is Staff Sergeant Frank Barnes. He died in Toronto, too. He looks at me with a kind smile I never saw him employ when he was alive.

"Hi, Dan," Lundsden says in Penn Jillette's booming voice. "Here's the thing your little brain hasn't got quite yet! You like movies? Of course, everybody loves a good movie. Is a movie better if it goes on forever? No, of course, not! When you have an infinite supply of anything, it lessens that thing's value! You want an infinite supply of Time itself? Fuck you! There is no such thing as magic. All we've got is illusions. Grow up! Everything's finite! But, here's the thing, Dan: That's what makes your life more significant! Stop believing in illusions and magic shows! Use the time you have, but better. That's how you give your life value! Use your head!"

Barnes smiles and gives a "So long, sucker" kind of wave.

He doesn't look like no Penn and Teller to me. Don! The cop in Toronto who had taken too long to die back at St. Mike's! He'd said that about me! My unconscious mind had picked up that tidbit for future dream fodder. I'm no hero and, apparently, no magician, either. My brain is just making shit up!

Or is it?

Lundsden shakes his head in dismay. "You are so balled up in the past and regret. If there is such a thing as sin, it's being so paralyzed by regret that you don't actually change! Stop being an idiot! You're living in the past, man! Get over it! Your time is now. Now is all any of us have! Do you get it? Gee-zuzz gawd! I hope you do before it's too late! Whoops, it's too late, isn't it? Sorry about that, Dan, ya thick galoot! Moron."

Bob's words sound seventy-five percent wise and twenty-five percent abusive. Maybe my brain is conjuring up something I need to hear to make sense of a situation that makes no sense. Is it the nanites at work, manipulating me? Is it my subconscious mind working overtime, trying to make sense of the apocalypse, desperately trying to find meaning in unspeakable tragedy?

My eyes popped open. A bright white light momentarily blinded me. No choir called me to my heavenly reward. No harps played. Dead relatives didn't lurch out of the darkness to greet me. That bright light shining in my eyes was industrial, a light in Dr. Clover's laboratory, the place she called the Planet of the Apes. I was still tied to a gurney, still bleeding to death.

"Well, shit," I said. "Time is valuable and short. Great. What's the point of getting wisdom from a vision if I get my answers too late?"

Mercifully, the world went dark again. Odds were pretty good this would be my last breath. Surrendering to the law of diminishing returns, I was grateful to give up. I'd operated on a lot of illusions throughout my life but I didn't harbor any illusions I'd survive the apocalypse.

CHAPTER 27

CHLOE

We walked down a corridor that, thankfully, was clear of smoke. I worried that if I got more of it in my lungs, a coughing fit might floor me.

Cavanaugh waited at the end of a narrow hallway that led to an elevator. "I sent some operators ahead. Once we get off the elevator, we're in enemy territory."

"The way to the animal lab should be cleared," Drood added.

"Should be?"

"That's the trouble with these bloodthirsty bastards. Gunfire attracts them. They're getting craftier, too. They used the smoke against us. I don't want to be here after dark again. They took our numbers down by half last night. At least half, maybe."

Cavanaugh held up a bright orange keycard. "Only my card will get us to where we need to go so stick close to me. We might have to move fast."

"I don't know if I can move fast," I said. "How are you feeling, Michael?"

"After you left, I threw up. Probably just nerves and the power of suggestion. I had a shower, too, but if I die of cancer, make no mistake. I'm blaming you." He slid the keycard through a slot and the elevator panel turned from red to green. Drood pushed the elevator button and checked his watch. "It's only just past noon. Best if we're long gone before sunset."

"You people expect me to pull miracles out of my ass," I said.

"Dr. Clover pulled off a miracle," Cavanaugh said.

"She showed me, too," Drood said. "Her fingers grew back. She had me take pictures."

"I'd like to see those pictures," I said.

"Like making sausage, Dr. Robinson. Even if the outcome is appetizing enough in the pan, the process of getting the meat in the casing is gross as all get out."

"The nanotech works," I said. "I knew it would. AFTER will heal the world, if everything doesn't get sucked down to the ninth level of Hell first."

I was glad but furious, too. My first human trials of AFTER weren't scheduled for two years. If I'd played fast and loose with ethics protocols, I could have witnessed my creation's processes firsthand.

Cavanaugh chuckled. "Dr. Clover will assist you with pulling that miracle out of your ass, Chloe."

"I'm sure she's bright, but I gave her a lot to work with."

Smoke filled the small elevator as soon as the doors parted. We passed several figures in biohazard suits outfitted with large oxygen tanks. One of them, a woman so small she looked like her biohazard suit had swallowed her, told Cavanaugh the fire was spreading.

"The sprinkler tanks are empty. There must be some doors open somewhere, or a broken window. Oxygen to feed the embers. We've had some locals at the front gate asking about the smoke. We told them it was under control and sent them away."

Cavanaugh nodded, urging us forward.

"Mr. Cavanaugh?" the woman called after him. "You know it's not under control, right? We can't get through the top of the quad, not through the buildings."

"You have your orders," Cavanaugh barked. "Keep the locals out and the zombies in. Contain the threat until we evacuate. For what I pay you, you should be able to hold this place until the special team comes to secure the labs. They'll have more firepower. In the meantime, stop acting like rent-a-cops at the mall. This is an arms research facility, not a Jamba Juice at the food court."

"Yes, sir," she said. I had to smile at the ice in her tone.

We made it to the animal testing lab without incident and Cavanaugh opened the door with his master keycard. Drood slammed the steel door behind us to keep the smoke out. As I glanced around the dingy gray lab, I smelled untended animal enclosures. They were mostly empty but the feces remained. Under a bright white light, Daniel Harmon lay on his side strapped to a gurney and covered in blood.

Heather Clover would be of no help to me. She sat on the floor. Blood pooled around her. Her left eye stared at the ceiling. Her right eye was, literally, on her right knee. Behind her, I made out a dark figure on the floor of a cage.

Drood only glanced at Harmon and made a beeline for Clover. He stepped over the blood dripping on the floor and stooped to examine the woman's body. "Looks like they're both dead as last night's fish." He pulled out a flashlight and shone the beam into the cage.

I stepped closer to Harmon, steadied myself on the gurney and went up on tiptoes to get a better look. The flashlight's beam caught the handle of a scalpel sticking out of a dead ape's throat. "Amazing she managed to kill an adult chimpanzee with that small blade."

"The nanotech gave her more than a couple of fingers," Cavanaugh said. "She was stronger after the injection. It happened fast, too."

"She was a crazed, evil bitch," I said. Then I looked at Daniel Harmon. "But at least she didn't try to eat me."

"We decided to call Hamish's creations Class I zombies," Cavanaugh said. "The AI interacts with the brain parasites to cross the blood brain barrier and boom, you've got your classic Class I."

"Hungry and hangry," Drood said.

"Harmon was a hybrid of Class I and II. He had Hamish's brain parasites but we got the new and improved formulation in him."

"AFTER, you mean. My work."

"Your research with a few tweaks, sure. And here lies Dr. Heather Clover, the first of the humans to get AFTER with no brain parasites. A pure Class II."

"Pity," Drood said. "She might have come to something more."

"We're wasting time," Cavanaugh said. "What do you need here, Chloe?"

I looked around. The steel sample box from Echidna sat on a table behind Harmon's body. "I need to figure out how the Picasso strains are interacting with the parasites and with each other. I need a spinal tap and blood samples from both corpses."

"The building's on fire. Let's get on with it. Chloe, get to work. Let's not get too gooey about this. Get it done." Cavanaugh tried to yank Harmon's body farther over on its side but the tight straps rendered the body immovable. He reached under the table and, after a moment of fumbling, found the release. "Drood, get Heather on a table, but first get those straps off the man's legs, will you?"

Drood did as he was told and released Harmon's legs.

"Pull his legs up to his chest so I can get the tap," I said. I spotted a syringe on the floor and guessed that Clover was about to perform the same procedure when the chimpanzee somehow grabbed her through the bars of its cage. I muttered, "Great minds think alike."

A voice as thin and weak as a dying pulse stopped us cold. "A-and f-fools seldom d … differ."

"She's alive!" Drood yelled.

His shout seemed to focus Clover. She raised her mutilated arm and stared at it with one unblinking eye. The stump was bloody and torn but, looking carefully, I could see movement amid the red mash. I got to see my work firsthand, after all. AFTER was remodeling the amputated arm. I took a step closer to look at the empty eye socket. It was not as empty as I'd first thought. The nanites were busy filling in the exoculation, as well.

We all froze for a second or two, staring into the gory miracle, teetering on the precipice between fascinated and horrified. Drood and Cavanaugh had just enough time to swear. I was about to tell them to get a blanket when Daniel Harmon rocketed off the gurney to grab me by the throat.

I never had children but I got to see the miracle I made before I die. Funny the things you think of when you're about to be murdered.

CHAPTER 28

DANIEL

I finally had Chloe Robinson's throat in my grip. I could snap her neck, close my fist, tear her throat or drink hot bursts of the liquid that, to a zombie, is the elixir of life. My programming had been triggered the moment Heather Clover injected me with the upgraded nanites.

Send the bitch my regards.

I stared in her wide, terrified eyes for a moment. I almost followed my programming directive, but I wasn't the kind to follow orders anymore. Besides, she was sick. I could smell disease in her clammy sweat. On the edge of perception, I detected yellow creeping into the whites of her eyes. Liver failure loomed in the good doctor's future. If I ate her, I might be damaged, too. The nanites would not have that. I softened my grip.

She returned my gaze, not comprehending my mercy. "Daniel?"

I didn't want to tell her the AI in my head had deemed her too sick to eat. "You're not well." As my hand dropped from Dr. Robinson's throat I felt the cold muzzle of a pistol at the back of my head.

Cavanaugh. "I have forgiven Chloe's sins. Apparently, I can be a merciful god."

"Hello, Mr. Cavanaugh. I'd hoped we'd have a chance to chat." By chat, I meant, of course, that I wanted to break his back and chew on his face a while so he'd have a chance to think about how slow death can come.

"You're a strong fellow. Pick up Heather Clover and put her on the gurney, please."

"Not so strong." I glanced down at my abdomen. The bleeding had stopped. I'd come close to death but between the anticoagulant sponges and the nanites, I'd been repaired. The damage was so extensive, I was sure there must be more work for the sea of microscopic machines to do.

"Try," Cavanaugh said. "Drood, help him."

The mercenary stepped back. "I don't think so, sir. I'll let the zombie do the lifting his own self, thank you." Drood pointed his rifle at my head and took another few steps back.

Heather Clover wept as I struggled to get my arms beneath her. Her ruined eyeball dropped to the floor. I almost stepped on it as I plunked her on the gurney.

Cavanaugh used his .357 to wave me back from the gurney. He stared at Clover's ruined arm slowly repairing itself. "Heather?"

"W-water. Water, please."

Dr. Robinson hurried as best she could to a lab sink and found a useable glass in a cupboard. She returned with the glass and three white lab coats to cover the patient. Clover accepted both the water and the warmth gratefully but the coats slowly turned from white to red.

I smelled two different aromas in the blood, one simian, the other human. Violet must have given up more in the fight than Clover had. I looked to the ape. Violet did not stir. The nanites did not make us indestructible. Worse, they could bring us back from the brink of death when we'd prefer to fall over that edge. I'd been to that brink myself and the experience had left me confused and resentful about my return to the land of the living.

"How do you feel?" Cavanaugh asked Dr. Clover.

The doctor took a few quick breaths, seeming to build up the energy to reply. "Like I've been torn apart by a chimpanzee. That's the single stupidest question ever uttered, Michael. "

"Look at her arm," Drood marveled.

Cavanaugh handed the mercenary his phone. "Record this! We have to document the rate of wound healing. This is a perfect demonstration of what could happen on the battlefield. Imagine that. No medevac even necessary. You lose a limb to an IED? Sit back and wait."

Clover let out an anguished scream, followed by a low moan. The effort to release her anger exhausted her. "Not as easy as it looks," she panted. "The nanites are microscopic. There's nothing to actually see — "

"You're wrong. I can see little differences already. It happens much faster than we saw in the animal testing."

"The nanites are still evolving," Chloe said.

"The miracle of life, reasserting itself with a little help from the latest technology from Nyx Management Group. My contact at the Pentagon thinks he has me over a barrel. After they see what this tech can do, I'm going to be bigger than Bezos, Buffett and Zhang put together. Screw billionaire. I'm jumping to trillionaire."

While Drood filmed the nanites at their work, I looked to Dr. Robinson. She swayed on her feet, clearly ready to collapse. "Sit down before you fall down," I said.

Cavanaugh still had the pistol so he wasn't worried. He watched us go, apparently satisfied I would cause him no trouble. We retreated to the chairs by the sink.

"They stole your stuff," I said.

Dr. Robinson shrugged. "Doesn't matter much now."

"Giving up?"

"I feel too terrible to care. You ever just want to go to sleep and never wake up?"

"I was just in that situation, as a matter of fact."

"What was that like?"

"Odd."

"That's it? Just odd?"

"Hard to explain. My brain isn't all mine anymore. How can I be sure what's me and what's not? I saw … well … never mind what I saw. It's too stupid, like being in a dream and silly things happen but they sort of make sense at the time."

"Dream logic," she said. "It should be called dream illogic. I was at a neuro conference once. The speaker was a neurobiologist. He said the weird stuff that makes sense only in dreams is how we can better understand what it's like to suffer brain damage. We all see the world through a prism that distorts reality. The perception of the brain-damaged is just a little more bent."

"I'm pretty sure the part of me that is still me didn't want to survive … this." I pointed at my belly wound.

"You became suicidal at the moment of death? Good timing."

"Bad timing. I didn't die, but the day is young."

In the distance, I heard gunshots. The normal humans in the room didn't seem to hear it. They would soon. The gunfire was getting closer.

The zombies were coming like a tide. There's no stopping the tide.

CHAPTER 29

CHLOE

I winced as I leaned against the countertop. "My kidneys are aching." Leaning forward to try to find a more comfortable position, dizziness swept over me.

Harmon caught me before I fell on my face. "Lean on me."

Too weak to argue, I put my head on his shoulder. "You've been trying to kill me since the moment I laid eyes on you. Why this now?"

"Told you. Wasn't me. That was Cavanaugh and the bugs in my brain trying to kill you. What did you do to piss off Cavanaugh so bad?"

"Blame the victim much?"

"I didn't mean it that way."

"Chill. I embarrassed him, is all. He's not the guy you want at the top of the food chain. He's the hatchet man who gets the dirty work done. He only wants me alive now so he can use me."

I came close to throwing up. Daniel must have sensed it somehow. He tilted me forward a little and held my hair out of the way. My vomit was green and yellow. "Bile."

I'd eaten some canned peaches and cold coffee in Toronto. With nothing left to give, I was soon reduced to the dry heaves again. When that was done, I wiped my mouth with the back of my sleeve. "Sorry. Radiation sickness."

"I know. I sensed the beginnings of it in all of you before we got off the helicopter. You should drink more water. It'll hurt less next time."

"How do you sense something like that? You got X-ray eyes?"

"I don't know. It's not me, it's the nanites. I'm not the guy you go to for medical advice. I'm the guy who hangs out at the Loose Moose and buys shooters for women."

"Does buying shooters for strangers work?"

"Sometimes. If you offer a woman a shooter called Sex on the Beach, it can open up a conversation."

"Sounds obnoxious."

"Not into the bar scene, huh?"

"Never made the time. Now, I'm wishing I'd made a little more time for nonsense."

"Nonsense like turning a human into whatever I am now? What you do is really amazing. I fixed a toilet by watching a YouTube instructional video once. I can strip a rifle. Beyond that, I'm not sure how things work. You build nanotech!"

"It turns out I don't much understand my creation. If I had more time — " I began to cough and couldn't suppress the urge. I could feel my energy slipping away. I was running out of time quickly.

"This is going to sound weird but it is cool how the nanites see the world," Daniel said. "Terminally cool."

"If it gets away from us, it's the end of the human race as we know it. Maybe just the end of the human race. That's where this is going. Cavanaugh doesn't even see it. What does it feel like?" I asked.

"Like I've got a baby alien in my head."

"Nanites don't have our prism. They come in innocent and learn from their neural environment. AFTER was supposed to be a controlled burn. These assholes just pressed the activate button and kept on pushing the accelerator without taking the time for proper testing. They were rushing Picasso to the weapons market. I don't think I'm going to make it. If you get out of this, please tell somebody. Tell everybody the truth."

I started coughing again and Daniel held me tighter, waiting for the spasms in my throat and lungs to stop. I didn't have enough energy for anger. When you're dying, all the anger comes out as despair.

Drood and Cavanaugh looked over at me briefly. They were too fascinated with Heather Clover's recovery to even bother with me. Cavanaugh asked her what she was feeling in the stump of her amputated hand. She moaned but they did nothing to try to comfort her.

Clover gasped and sputtered. "M-morphine ... Atavan ... p-please. Hurts!"

"We could make this easier for her," Drood said. "I'll find something for the pain."

Cavanaugh held up his pistol. "Stay right where you are. Keep recording." To me, he asked, "Why aren't the nanites numbing her pain?"

"My guess? The nanites will prioritize stopping the blood loss. The colony will prioritize use of resources within its matrix. She can't have had Picasso long. AFTER would manage resources, too, allocating available cells. You could anesthetize her and the nanotech will still do the repair work to the host. She doesn't need to suffer. "

"I need to see how long it takes for her to recover and I want her awake and lucid to see how she's feeling at every stage of recovery. We'll never get a better demonstration. How long before — "

"Michael, remember how you were telling me you aren't a monster? I can't imagine a better demonstration of what you really are. Drood? Are you going to let this happen?"

The mercenary glanced away from the phone's camera for a second to meet my eyes. "I've been in combat situations where your little miracles were needed. Mr. Cavanaugh tells me AFTER was going to be in development for years. We're getting it done so guys like me can be healed in the field and be better than ever. Maybe you're the monster, holding back — "

"I was being careful."

"The future belongs to the bold," Cavanaugh said. "It always has."

"I've heard something like that recently," Daniel said. "Blind, unchecked aspiration is how Hamish Allen unleashed Picasso on the world. There's a smoking hole where Toronto used be. That's a lot of broken eggs for your omelette."

"We're going to heal the world." Cavanaugh didn't say that ironically. He had the careless missionary zeal of a very dangerous true believer.

CHAPTER 30

DANIEL

Heather Clover writhed, crying out many times as she held her wounded arm high. From where I stood, I could see the white bone of a new thumb under construction. I asked Chloe how a bunch of tiny machines could change the brain and body so quickly.

"The nanites interact with the established biological network. They use the source material to build new networks, laying down new tracks. My father had a bunch of old science kits from Radio Shack. They were made so kids could learn basic electrical science. You'd get a box with capacitors and meters and little springs for connections. There were wires of different lengths, blue, red and yellow. When I hooked up the circuits correctly, I could activate a light meter, make a crystal radio, make a buzzer … whatever. AFTER is sort of like that, building new cells from the template you give it. They wanted a weapon so they used a bad template."

"The brain parasites."

"Yeah. They took my little pussycat and made Picasso into a tiger at the zoo. It needs a cage. With no limits, I don't know how far the AI will take the changes."

"And the enemy is in my head," I said. "How far will the changes go?"

"We're off the edge of the map, Daniel. It might not change you beyond the human design."

"That's just marvelous. How are nanites made in the first place?"

"They're suspended in a biomimetic gel. Overlay the gel on a circuit and the AI builds the program you want, just like making connections in those old Radio Shack kits. Nanotech can mimic a human bioelectric circuit or a microchip. Nanites bridge the gap between computer programming and human optimization. Obviously, you got conflicting programming. You can talk so you're not a Class I Zombie."

"Is that what they're calling the killers out there taking their orders from AI-powered brain parasites?"

"Cavanaugh explained it to me during his evil villain monologue."

"Sorry I missed the guided tour. I need to pick his brain. With a fork."

Chloe began coughing again. The need to clear her lungs subsided quickly but she looked weaker from the effort. "You seem fine," she said. "You're a cannibal with no radiation sickness. The nanites are working on your cells, excreting the waste or compartmentalizing the damage in fat or killing off the cancer cells by amping up your immune system or … I don't know. Maybe something else."

"Even you don't know?"

"The tiger's out of its cage. When AI creates AI through generations of cell reproduction, the engineering goes beyond what we know."

"Well, I do feel fairly fine for now, aside from the gunshot wound that's not quite fixed yet."

"I'd settle for feeling fairly fine right now."

I pulled back to look her in the eyes. "So … there's an obvious solution to your problem."

"I know. I guessed I had an out as soon as I saw Clover's amputated arm growing back."

"You could be like her. Not sick, I mean."

"And not a raging cannibal psychopath?"

"If you get the strain of Picasso that Dr. Clover carries — no parasites — you'll be better than fine."

"Saved by my own creation. I like the poetic symmetry of that, but no, even if I could, I'm not taking the cure, though. It's not for me."

"Why?"

"I just want to go to bed and go to sleep. I'm too tired to keep fighting. Chances are good I'd still end up a lab rat or trapped in a prison making Cavanaugh rich. I'm done."

"That's the radiation poisoning talking."

"Maybe it's spite. Whatever. You said you had a near-death experience. You didn't want to come back. I thought you'd understand."

"There's a war on."

"I know. They took my work and started that war. Millions are dead because of AFTER. Should have left well enough alone."

"You're needed."

"Millions dead because of me and my company. Millions. All of Toronto — "

"Misplaced guilt and exhaustion is making you selfish."

"Impending death can do that."

Staccato gunfire erupted, much closer this time.

Chloe lifted her head sharply at the sound. "We won't have to wait long. Go ahead and fight. Leave me alone. I'm ready though I'd really rather not be torn apart by zombies."

"They'll leave you alone for the same reason I can defy my programming. They'll sense you're too sick to eat."

"Ugh! One terror exits as a new one breaks down the door."

Drood's rifle lay at his feet as he recorded Clover's arduous recovery. It was tempting, but Cavanaugh still held the pistol.

I scanned the lab, searching for a way out. I might be able to get to the exit without Cavanaugh blowing my head off but Chloe wouldn't have chance. I noticed a few poles had been leaned against the wall by the animal cages. With thick loops of rope at one end, they were designed for animal control. They wouldn't be much use against bullets.

Chloe whispered, "If you're going to make a move, just do it. Run for your life. Maybe I'll even get a chance to see those two assholes get eaten before the radiation kills me."

"But what about — "

"You have no idea how amazingly tiring it is to be needed all the time."

"There's something you don't know. Something terrible."

"Worse than what I already know? All the more reason to check out of the Horror Hotel early, isn't it?"

"Chloe. All those Class I zombies? They're driven by the nanotech imprinted on the brain parasites. But underneath ... ooh, underneath, they're like you and me."

"What do you mean?"

"They're still the people they were. They're doing terrible things. They're cannibals who don't want to be cannibals. When I went zombie in Toronto, I ate people, but I knew it. I wasn't a mindless animal. I only looked like one. All those people — "

"You're saying they're weaponized organic robots."

"With shoe salesmen and office workers and ordinary plumbers trapped inside, yeah. They do the things they do against their will. Inside, they're normal people — "

"Witnesses." A single tear slipped down her cheek. "You're right, Daniel. That's the worst thing I've ever heard. I wish you hadn't told me."

The door to the lab gave a low buzz as someone used a keycard to pop the lock. Then a guard wrenched open the door to the lab and shouted at Cavanaugh. "How long are you going to take, sir? We can't hold them off for — "

He was probably about to say, "ever." We hardly had a fraction of forever. A dozen rampaging cannibals burst in. The guard's scream climbed, high and trembling. Two zombies tore off his protective hood and began to eat his face and neck.

We spend far too much time anxiously wondering what's next. My days were always, "What fresh hell is this?" In the night when I couldn't sleep, I wondered, "What will tomorrow bring?" I wanted to be a hero because heroes sleep like babies and, though they may be in Hell, they can face it. That was the fantasy I was trying to live up to, anyway.

There is a time to panic. As the zombies broke through, this was that time. Drood and Cavanaugh did so.

EPISODE 4

NEXT (acronym)

Nano EXperiential Technocracy AKA the next stage in human/machine development.

~Notes from NEXT

CHAPTER 31

CHLOE

We spent our lives in the cold shadow of predictions about the end of the world. When the end came, it seemed to happen all at once, as fast and simple as dropping a plate and watching it hit the kitchen floor. From the moment that plate leaves your hand to the moment it shatters, it's a heightened feeling of helplessness. I figured out later that most of us are always nervous. That realization became very valuable later. It also came in handy when the zombies charged into the lab, out for blood. Drood and Cavanaugh ran for their lives.

They didn't shoot the zombies. The mercenary left his rifle under the gurney and raced to the cage that held the dead chimpanzee. Cavanaugh used his master keycard to open the cage and Drood yanked the steel mesh door open. He pushed his boss behind the barrier ahead of him. They needn't have hurried quite so much. The cannibals descended on the easiest prey first. They fought each other to feast on Heather Clover. She wailed in agony as they tore into her on all sides.

Another zombie spotted me as he came through the door. Most of his white dress shirt had been ripped from his torso so all that was left was the collar and tatters. He was covered in blood. Numerous bite marks were visible on both forearms and across his hairy chest. Though the man had gray hair, he had a young face. His eyes were red and saliva dripped from his lips. Not long ago he'd been somebody's dad working a desk job. Maybe a day ago he'd been looking forward to a summer vacation. I could see no humanity in that face now. It was hard to believe Daniel told the truth, that a regular human was beneath the skin, his brain hijacked, his will not his own.

The cannibal charged, focused on me. Daniel stood his ground and gripped me tight. "Wait. Stay perfectly still."

I gasped and squeezed my eyes tight, bracing for impact, too weak to defend myself. I expected his hot mouth to close on my throat. Instead, when I opened my eyes, the zombie's face was inches away from mine. His rapid breath smelled of sour death. Ignoring Daniel, the man sniffed at me briefly and backed away. Then he turned to join the others in the feeding frenzy.

I'm not just knocking on death's door, I thought. *I'm pounding to be let in.*

"If that hungry monster thought I was too sickly to eat, I'm very sick," I whispered. I looked to Daniel, "And you're too healthy."

"Professional courtesy."

"Pheromones, maybe," I said.

"I thought it was because I was charming."

Eaten alive but too hard to kill, Clover's screams echoed off the walls.

"Daniel, help her."

"As soon as I figure out how. As long as I leave them alone, they'll assume I'm one of them and they won't try to kill me. Then it'll turn to shit."

"Go."

Drood had left his gun behind but Cavanaugh still had his pistol. I covered my ears to try to block out Clover's anguished screams. I shouted to him to shoot her attackers. He ignored me and continued to stare at the carnage unfolding before him just a few feet away. Red-faced, his jaw slack, Cavanaugh's eyes were pie plates. He froze in place.

"Good God, shoot her! Shoot her! Have some mercy, man!" Drood reached for the pistol but Cavanaugh shrugged him off.

Red-faced and shaking, Cavanaugh brandished his weapon at his own guard. "If I shoot, we could attract more of them! I only have six bullets! If I kill her now, we'll never know how much damage she might recover from. If I leave them to it, what if she could survive it? Keep filming!"

Daniel grabbed an animal control pole and handed it to me. I was surprised how light it was. Made of aluminum, it was worthless as a cudgel.

"Stay here," he said.

"What can I do?"

"You can barely stand up. Just stay here. This is our chance to get control. Whatever happens, whatever you do, make it to the nanotech labs. Solve this thing."

"I would if I knew how."

"You invented AFTER. You'll figure this out."

He didn't tell me to live. We both knew I was too far gone for that.

"Be careful!" I called after him. "They're monsters."

"So am I."

I think he meant the zombies. I was trying to warn him about Drood and Cavanaugh.

Daniel ducked low and peered under the gurney for a second. There were too many zombies crowded around Clover to get at the dropped rifle quickly and Cavanaugh might shoot him yet. Instead, Daniel grabbed another pole for himself and looped the rope around the neck of the zombie dad who'd passed me up for a healthier meal. The man had been trying to get a place at the table. The rest of the swarm seemed too busy to notice one of their number had been pulled away. Daniel was almost gentle as he guided the man from behind. Daniel used the zombie as a shield and used the pole to push him toward the cage.

"Open the cage and give me that pistol, Cavanaugh," Daniel demanded. "She can't live much longer. They'll turn on you next."

"Or what?" Cavanaugh said.

"Do as I say and I'll help you get out of here."

"I'll take my chances with this," he said, holding the gun higher.

"He's got a point," Drood said. "Be reasonable."

"Don't be a coward," Daniel said. "Excess caution now will get you killed."

"Stop filming," Cavanaugh told the mercenary. "Use the phone to call for reinforcements. We'll be fine in a few minutes."

That's when I realized I still had work to do. Swaying and weak as a heavily irradiated kitten, I leaned on the pole, using it as a crutch. The zombies ignored me as I made my way across the room. Somehow they knew I was poison, that if one of their group wouldn't eat me, none of them were interested. I sank to my knees, then on all fours. The floor was slick with Clover's blood. As I reached for the rifle, I slipped and fell into the pool of blood beneath the gurney. It was still warm as it smeared my face.

Steeling myself, I tipped my head back and caught the dripping blood in my open mouth. It was probably already too late to heal me. This was a desperate move. I didn't expect to survive, I only needed to buy time. Clover's blood contained AFTER. I closed my eyes and tried to think of mocha lattes, chocolate milkshakes and the nanites swirling amid the hot blood. The zombie swarm jostled me. I pinched my nose and imagined the blood was a bloody margarita, then a blood orange — anything to trick my brain into thinking blood was not blood.

I needed her strength. I needed the right kind of nanites, unsullied by brain parasites. It was no use. I threw up, anyway.

Heather Clover made one last strangled breath and then began to gurgle. As I looked up from the floor, one of the zombies took one step back from the table, tipped her head back, popped something into her gaping mouth. I'm quite sure I know what that little chunk was. Everybody has played the Got Your Nose game with a little kid. It was cartilage. The zombie had to chew vigorously before swallowing it down.

I blacked out. I don't think it was for long, but I woke up on the floor under the gurney as hot yellow piss dripped down my neck.

Either Clover had peed or the zombies had opened her bladder in their orgiastic fever feast.

It was too late to save Heather Clover with a bullet or without. I gritted my teeth and grabbed the rifle. I wasn't familiar with automatic rifles but you know what they say about beggars and choosers.

Screw it, I thought. *We'll do this the old fashioned way.*

CHAPTER 32

DANIEL

Chloe came up beside me and leaned hard on me to stay upright. She managed to bring the rifle to bear on Michael Cavanaugh. The thin man's face melted from smug to scared. "Come out of there," she ordered.

Ever the corporate exec, Cavanaugh thought he could negotiate. "You aren't a monster, Chloe. You aren't the kind to pull that trigger."

"But you are, so …. " She fired. The weapon was set to a three-round burst. Chloe surprised herself as much as Cavanaugh. The barrel climbed. She missed him by inches. Cavanaugh fell backward over the still form of the chimpanzee and dropped his pistol.

The zombie swarm roared at the sound of gunfire. It was as if they were one person.

I grabbed Chloe around the waist so she wouldn't fall. I had let go of the animal control pole. I shoved the cannibal into the gate as Drood scampered to pick up the dropped pistol. As soon as Chloe sank to the floor, I took the rifle from her and smashed the butt into the base of the skull of the zombie I'd used as a shield.

Attacking one of their own was enough for the rest of the pack. Their heads snapped around, focused on me. Each guest at the feast snapped and snarled through bloody teeth, each face covered in gore. At my urging, Chloe rolled back under the gurney.

The zombies began their charge. I shouldered the rifle and fired. The rifle had a hair trigger so I had to be careful not to fall into the trap of spray and pray. After I shot the nearest cannibals, I switched to semi-auto and chose my targets more carefully.

This scenario was not like what happened in the Box. My heart pounded but to a steadier beat. My hand-eye coordination was better. I wasn't sweating as I squeezed off round after round. I could still feel a twinge of pain travel across my belly with each recoil. However, the nanites had been working on more than my belly wound. There was no adrenal dump to jangle my nerves and shake my hands. My breathing was under control. I chose my shots with confidence. I didn't think about the person each zombie had been. I was detached, as if I was playing a video game. The zombies dropped one by one. All was well until the rifle clicked empty and three more zombies, snarling and shrieking, attacked at once.

The Magnum boomed behind me. I was sure I was dead. Instead, my attackers fell to the floor to join the pile at my feet. I turned to find Drood holding the pistol out between the bars of the cage. "Hoo! Did you see that? Saved your ass, zombie boy! Hoo! Hey! Who is the man? Who's the man, Harmon?"

The mercenary pointed the weapon at me. AI-enhanced reflexes took over. It was if I had become the observer, watching the scene. I was not acting voluntarily when my left arm flashed out and grabbed the revolver so the cylinder could not turn. Drood still held the weapon. That was fine. I leapt to the left and wrenched sideways with all my weight. The bones in the mercenary's right forearm snapped like carrots.

What happened next, I would attribute to the nanites that had learned from brain parasites. Still clamped down on his gun hand, I yanked him forward so I could do it again. This time, his elbow snapped at a sickening right angle.

Drood cried out in pain. Then he managed, "Stop!"

"That's enough, Daniel!" Chloe shouted.

"It's not me," I said. Were the nanites torturing this man needlessly? Or were they making my darkest impulses real?

I pulled Drood toward me so hard his face smashed into to bars and his nose burst, a fountain of blood. With the bars of the cage as a lever against his useless arm, it was easy to dislocate the mercenary's shoulder. He moaned, fell to his knees and kept on moaning.

I felt almost as disgusted with myself as when I ate my first human. *Who is the man, Harmon? Who is the man?*

CHAPTER 33

CHLOE

I pulled myself to my feet and did my best to step around the pile of dead zombies. None of them were going to come back from those mortal wounds. Each of them had a received a shot to the head.

Daniel seemed to study me for a moment. "You hurt?"

"No more than before." I stepped in a bloody pool of gray matter. My shoes made a squelching sound. I looked down. That was a mistake. "*Ew.*" I wanted to throw up again.

Cavanaugh reached through the bars to slide his keycard through the cage lock. The lock buzzed. He pushed the gate open and walked out. As he eyed Daniel, he obviously yearned for the pistol that had been taken from him. "You should have let them take Harmon down," he told Drood. "If you had, we'd still be in control."

Drood leaned against the bars to scramble to his feet. He cradled his useless arm and said nothing.

"Who pays your salary? You belong in the cage with that ape," Cavanaugh taunted him. "You're probably almost as smart."

Drood cursed his boss. Cavanaugh just laughed. That's when I realized I should always have been afraid of Cavanaugh. I shouldn't have dumped that bottle of wine down his pants and embarrassed him. When his bodyguard cursed him viciously, the arms dealer might as well have been a wall. He felt nothing for the man. Cavanaugh was a rich man who would never be affected by criticism, hate, compassion or love.

"See, this is what happens when a bunch of psychopaths work together," Daniel said.

"You supply both sides," Drood told his boss. "If you expect to survive this, I think you're going to have to choose a side. I just did."

"And look how that worked out." Cavanaugh closed the gate behind him, locking Drood in the cage.

"What are you doing? I need medical attention."

"You wouldn't need it if you hadn't taken my gun."

"I was trying to protect you. We've got a clear exit thanks to me. You've never thanked me for anything, come to think of it."

"I'm their prisoner now, Drood. We've lost the initiative, you useless moron."

Drood looked back and forth from Daniel to me. "Careful of that one. Wealthy people live in our world but they aren't of our world. Total autonomy, total power. Mr. Cavanaugh travels around the world and, with private jets, he never even has to show anyone his passport. The wealthy aren't like you and me."

"That's right," Cavanaugh said. "We have money."

"When's the last time you had to stand in line for anything, boss?"

"You're all messed up, Drood. What use are you to me now? What will I pay you for? You might make a good doorstop."

Drood cursed his boss again.

"Gentlemen," I said, "time is short. Daniel, put Cavanaugh back in the cage, please."

"You sure?" Daniel asked.

"After what he allowed to happen to that woman? He's more monster than the monsters. Drood is injured but he can walk. Show us to the nanite labs."

"No! Wait! You need me," Cavanaugh said. "The people who are coming are expecting me."

"We'll let them know where you are," Daniel said. "You belong in the Planet of the Apes, Cavanaugh."

"Strange days are these, *hm*?" Drood asked me. "Not so long ago you were threatening my bloody life if your friend Shelly was hurt. Now you're taking me with you and leaving the boss to rot. Imagine that twist of fate."

"You're a traitor on top of useless, Drood," Cavanaugh sneered.

"Do you even know my given name?"

"Should I?"

"You know why they call me Drood? I'm a druid. The mongrels I work with decided on my nickname. Not that you care, but my given name is Rich MacLaren. Druids believe in inheriting skills from ancestors and living in harmony with the natural world — "

"Isn't your job to kill things?" I asked.

"Killing is the skill I inherited from my ancestors. Look around the natural world. I fit right in. That's my brand of Druidry. Still, thank you for your tender mercy, Dr. Robinson. I'm feeling better about humanity all of a sudden. Except for you, Mr. Harmon," he added sourly. "Broke my bloody arm all over the place! You still suck, but you're not really human anymore, are you?"

"You can't do this," Cavanaugh said. "This is my company. You can't leave me here."

"Sure we can," Daniel said. "Get in the cage."

"What about your friend? Won't Constable Priyat mind that you abandoned her? I know where she is — "

"I know where she is," Drood volunteered.

"Take his keycard, Daniel."

The keycard dangled by a coiled cord around Cavanaugh's wrist. In a flash, Daniel slipped it off him, quick as a magic trick.

"Get used to the cage, Cavanaugh. I think you'll be in another one soon. Maybe they'll be able to give you a solid cancer treatment program in prison," I said.

"Bitch." Cavanaugh tried to spit at me but his saliva didn't go farther than his expensive shoes.

"Relax," I told him. "You'll be safe in there until we get this sorted out with the authorities. Until we secure the labs and get you arrested for your part in the outbreak, it's more dangerous out here."

I was wrong about the inside of the cage being safer than the outside. The chimpanzee wasn't dead. It was resting while nanites mended its torn body. Violet rose from the floor silently. She was not swift but she was strong enough. The ape wrapped her arms around the mercenary's torso and tore into Drood's throat. She clamped her teeth on the man's jugular faster than Daniel could show mercy with the Magnum.

The bodyguard could not defend himself. He died in the embrace of an emissary from the natural world. I heard his ribs crack before the pistol boomed. Daniel pulled the trigger, one shot, two kills.

I screamed. Cavanaugh jumped and yelped in surprise as gray matter splashed on his fancy clothes. Then the executive threw up.

I thought about what Drood said, how Daniel wasn't part of humanity. I'm not sure. The ETF officer killed without any apparent doubt or hesitation. Execution might have even been the human thing to do. Under the circumstances, it was the humane thing to do. I would have felt more comfortable around Daniel if he'd shown a moment's hesitation, deliberated or said a quick prayer for the man after his skull was shattered and mixed with primate brain soup.

Shaking, Cavanaugh straightened as he wiped his mouth of puke. "Looks like you're stuck with me, after all." Daniel pointed the pistol at him and the arms dealer slowly raised his hands. "I'm unarmed."

"Too bad. I was looking forward to disarming you," Daniel said, "and by that I mean ripping your arms off."

"You can't find Shelly Priyat or get into the nanotech lab without me."

I shrugged. "We'll figure it out. We'll need the phone and more ammunition though, Daniel."

He scooped up Cavanaugh's phone from the bottom of the

animal enclosure and wiped some blood and brain matter on his shorts.

Cavanaugh pulled six rounds from his pocket and held them out to Daniel without complaint.

"Gimme the phone," Daniel ordered.

Cavanaugh eyed him, reluctant to give up the device. "Who you gonna call? Ghostbusters? Cops? The New York Times? The Boy Scouts?"

"Before we move another inch," I told Cavanaugh, "you're going to make a call. Bring Shelly Priyat here. Now."

CHAPTER 34

DANIEL

While Cavanaugh tried to get through to someone on his security force to fetch Shelly Priyat, I got more and more antsy. I glanced at Heather Clover on the gurney and looked away. Soon my gaze was drawn back to the carnage. The doctor's face had been eaten. Her torso was an open buffet. The zombies had hollowed her out so deeply it was as if they were intent on making a boat out of her. I could see the front of the white bone of her spine in the space between where her kidneys used to sit. With the smell of blood wafting around me, I wanted to eat meat. A dark coffee — two cream, one sweetener — would have been nice, too.

Judging by my appetites, the two strains of Picasso were fighting it out. The nanites guided by brain parasites wanted protein, to feed, to feast on the living and the dead. My upper class strain would be at home in a Starbucks nibbling on a chocolate croissant and sucking down a hot mug of Caramel Macchiato. Vague hunger quickly became a gnawing pang. Soon it would be a demand I could not resist. I had to get out of the animal lab before blood won out. I didn't want to tear into a corpse in front of Chloe. Besides not wanting to act like a rabid animal in front of a lady, she looked green from throwing up so much. There was a little more yellow in the whites of her eyes now. I wouldn't have guessed radiation poisoning could progress so fast but she was under incredible stress.

Working with the Emergency Task Force, I knew a lot about stress. In me, the feeling had often appeared as a strange mix of fatigue and being amped up at the same time, as if my skin was too small for the energy balled up in my chest, bursting to get out. Every timed training exercise added to that pressure, like trying to work fast underwater and running out of breath.

The hunger was strong but I didn't shake and my voice did not tremble. I searched for any of those familiar feelings of stress now. It was like going to a familiar drawer in my home and finding it had been emptied. The nanites were busy changing me into something, but where would they stop? How long before I'd fail to recognize the thing in the mirror?

"Daniel?"

"Yes, Chloe?"

"You okay?"

"Yeah."

"You looked like you went away there for a moment."

I looked around. Cavanaugh stared at his gun in my hand. Chloe looked worried so I handed her the pistol. "If he moves, shoot him in the balls. That's usually pretty discouraging."

"I heard that!"

"You were meant to hear it. Keep your eyes on your phone. Find somebody to bring Shelly."

"I'm working on it."

"Do it faster."

I brushed past Cavanaugh, retrieved two mags from Drood's body and reloaded the rifle.

"Where are you going?" Chloe asked.

"Time spent on recon is seldom wasted. I won't be long and I won't go far." I had to get out of there before I ate something.

"I'll behave myself," Cavanaugh said. "She already tried to shoot me once."

"Then you know I won't hesitate," Chloe said.

I could tell by the way Cavanaugh was sweating that I had nothing to worry about. He put on a brave face but I knew a lot about putting on brave faces. What's more, to my surprise, I detected something more in his expression. He was embarrassed to have lost control of the situation. His whining told me how helpless he felt. Despite his harsh words, I sensed that the deaths of Heather Clover and Drood had truly shaken him. If not for the speed of perception the nanites gave me, I'm sure I would have missed it. I saw regret in the man's eyes. I still didn't care if he lived or died, though. Given the slightest excuse, I would have killed Cavanaugh.

I went to the exit and peered into the corridor. To my right I saw two mounds of bodies. The far mound were mostly zombies who'd been shot. The nearby cluster of dead mercs were the ones who'd done the shooting until they ran out of ammo. The soldiers had been overrun. I felt bad for them. The scene was all too familiar. I could have told them it would come to this. Nobody trains to deal with a mob that doesn't flee from gunfire.

The smoke was getting thicker in that direction so I turned left, checking doors as I went. Several were locked. I didn't try to force them. If someone was cowering under a desk in there, I was glad to leave them where they were hiding. They'd come out when the smoke got to them. Until that time, they were another problem I didn't have to manage.

Protecting one sick scientist was enough of a worry without trying to herd a group. Besides, if I met another human, I'd eat them. My stomach rumbled. I felt the need for protein. The ache was so strong, I felt it in my eyeteeth. Unfortunately, I did find a man and a woman, dead but freshly so. I saw no sign of disease but they had both died of gunshot wounds. No powder burns and no weapons nearby so suicide was unlikely.

Friendly fire, I thought. It happens all the time in war zones. People panic and fire too many rounds without even aiming, trying to scare death away with rifle fire, hoping to hit the enemy or scare them away. The families of the dead are never told their son or daughter died by a comrade's weapon. That's war. No one expected war to come to an island ten miles from Seattle.

I stopped and listened for enemies, straining the limit of my senses. I wondered if zombies were really attracted to gunfire. Maybe their hearing is so sensitive, they're really just angrily trying to stop the irritating noise. A really bad trombone player lived above me in my first apartment. When he got drunk, he'd practice at three in the morning. I understood the killing impulse.

It struck me as a little odd that, after all I'd done, I set myself apart from those infected with Hamish's strain of nanites. I'd been upgraded but I was still one of them. I placed the rifle against a wall and knelt beside the dead man. I rolled up his pant leg to get at the meat of his calf. He was hairy.

I don't want to do this, I thought.

The nanites that took their orders from brain parasites didn't care what I wanted. I felt compelled to eat. However, I managed to stop myself long enough to pull up the woman's pant leg. She had shaved her legs recently.

In a flash, I was powerless. Instinct took over. Picasso had me in its grip. All fastidiousness was lost as I dove for the calf meat. I broke the skin and chewed. Once, in Vancouver, I'd eaten Peking duck that was so tender it melted in my mouth like butter. I always looked back on that particular meal fondly. Somehow, the dead woman's raw calf meat, tough and raw, tasted more succulent than that expertly cooked duck.

Damn nanites, I thought. They enhanced the power of my jaw muscles!

The ecstasy of eating that young woman's calf was nearly sexual. The powerful threat of getting caught doing something you know you should not do — as if it was indeed some sexual taboo — was equally strong. After a few minutes the worst of my hunger abated and I was able to tear myself away. If I stuck my fingers down my throat, forcing myself to vomit, I knew I'd have to go back for that poor woman's other leg. I picked up the rifle and stumbled away, burning with shame.

Absentmindedly, I ran my tongue over my teeth. They seemed

sharper than I remembered. "Nine out of ten dentists agree," I announced to the empty hallway, "if you want strong teeth that can tear into anybody, get Picasso. Call it infested or infected, robot stem cells are better than fluoride for healthy teeth."

I would have laughed at my own grim joke but I was too disturbed by what I'd done. I hurried away, putting distance between me and my heinous crime.

CHAPTER 35

CHLOE

The door to the lab buzzed softly and, as it opened, tendrils of gray smoke snaked in and wove their way across the high ceiling. The waft of hot air pushing into the room smelled sickly sweet. I wondered if that was the smell of the gases leaching from torched bodies and scorched carpets. "Daniel? That you? Did you forget something?" I called.

It wasn't Daniel. A mercenary in a biohazard suit poked his head in the doorway. He peeked just long enough to scout the room. It was the man who called himself Ginger. When he saw I held Cavanaugh's pistol, he pulled back out of sight. I was about to say hello when he yelled, "Sir? You alright?"

"I'm being held hostage by Dr. Chloe Robinson. She has a gun!"

"I have his gun," I said. "Is Shelly Priyat with you?"

"Yes," Ginger called. "I have her here but she's not feeling well."

"Me, neither. Send her in."

"Are you bitten yet, Mr. Cavanaugh?"

Cavanaugh frowned. "What do you mean by yet?"

"A lot of us have been bitten."

"I'm fine."

"Of course, you would be. Aren't you always?"

"What? What's going on?"

"Sorry, Mr. Cavanaugh. Not many of our guys left, I don't think. When's backup coming?"

"Soon."

"What does soon mean?" The mercenary voice climbed and cracked.

Cavanaugh looked as uneasy as I felt. Sensing the man's agitation, Cavanaugh's words were soft and gentle. "It means soon. I don't know when exactly but they'll get here. Their first responsibility is to make sure the contagion doesn't spread south. I told them we can hold this facility until they arrive."

"You shouldn't have told them that, Mr. Cavanaugh!"

"Have you lost?" I asked.

Cavanaugh frowned and tried to wave me off. "It's going to be okay, soldier."

"We've lost so many people. You ask if we've lost. What does winning mean now? Some of the infected got outside the fence."

"Easy, now," Cavanaugh said. "We're on an island. They can't get to the mainland. That was part of the calculus."

"Part of the calculus?" I asked. "As in, screw the locals? Picasso is spreading down from Canada. It's going to be everywhere if we don't — "

"Quiet, Chloe!" Cavanaugh roared.

I held up the pistol, not pointing it at him but reminding him I had it and I didn't like him.

Cavanaugh swallowed hard and tried again in a soothing voice. "We're going to sort all this out."

"How?" Ginger demanded. "What's taking them so damn long? We need reinforcements now. No, no, we need rescue now."

"My contact said they had to put together a special team and they're pulling people from different units. They're busy securing the northern border right now and they don't have enough people for that."

"There aren't enough people for that," I said. "It's the longest undefended border in the world."

"You're not helping," Cavanaugh told me. "Let's regroup, do one thing at a time. Be methodical. How about we have a hostage exchange? Emotions have been running a little high in here and we need to take a step back. I'd like to — "

I had zero interest in what Michael Cavanaugh might like. "Just send Shelly in. Harmon will be back in a minute and we'll plan our next step from there."

"Let me join my security detail and we'll clear a way to the nanotech lab for you," Cavanaugh countered.

"Or maybe your guys will just storm in and make us prisoners again."

Ginger uttered a disgusted laugh from the hallway. "I don't have that kind of manpower, Dr. Robinson! It's just us chickens. Everybody I know is either dead or one of them or out trying to secure an exit. The goal is not to secure the facility, anymore, Mr. Cavanaugh. We just want out. Like the mouse said, 'Keep the cheese. I just want out of the trap.'"

"Stand by, Ginger!" Cavanaugh called.

Fed up, I yelled, "Send Shelly Priyat in now!"

"May I speak?" Cavanaugh asked.

"Be polite."

"Er … thank you. We want you to get to the nanotech lab. We all want out safely. This situation is out of hand. We have to work together."

"We just want out, Mr. Cavanaugh!" Ginger was near hysteria now. "There's eaters out here! They're everywhere!"

"Calm down and shut up a minute!" Cavanaugh shouted. When he turned to address me, his voice was almost a gentle whisper. "It doesn't matter who's in charge as long as we all get to safety. Be reasonable."

"If it doesn't matter, how come you were going to shoot us ten minutes ago?"

"Harmon's infected. He's dangerous. I was only thinking about killing him. We need you. I need you. That was our deal, remember? C'mon. Put the gun on the bench and let Shelly and my man come in. At the end of the world, it makes sense to make friends. We need a détente, even a shaky one will do. Things are out of control out there. It would be a good start if we got things under control in here, right?"

The pistol was heavy in my hand. More tired than I've ever been, I was willing to concede the logic of a truce. "You leave Harmon alone. You get us to the nanotech lab and play nice when reinforcements arrive and I'll do what I can to extend your life."

Cavanaugh nodded. "Like I said, I need you."

"Don't forget that."

"I won't. You have my word."

I relented and put the pistol on the workbench beside me.

"It's okay!" Cavanaugh called. "You can both come in."

Shelly Priyat appeared in the doorway looking very pale. Her ponytail had been pulled loose and her long hair hung in her face. The half of her face I could see appeared dazed.

"Shelly? Are you okay?" I looked closer. A loop of white cord was wound around her neck. Ginger had her at the end of one of the animal control poles. "Shelly?"

Her head snapped my way. There was something primal about the motion, as if she was a bird of prey who'd spotted a mouse.

I felt the pressure of tears behind my eyes. Picasso had claimed many lives. I hardly knew her, but amid the pressures of the apocalypse, I considered Shelly Priyat a friend.

CHAPTER 36

DANIEL

The first door I found that wasn't locked was a washroom. Zombies don't use the can. They poop where they stand. Fortunately, only half of me was that kind of zombie. I ducked in for a moment to relieve myself.

An emergency bulb glowed above the door casting a dim light across the room. A public bathroom is so familiar and ordinary, it was tempting to forget where I was. I certainly wanted to believe this was a nightmare I could wake from. I'd never thought of a public john as relaxing but my belly was full. Better than that, I was alone so I couldn't hurt anyone.

Then I thought of a lesson from the movie *Zombieland*. Put down your weapon to have a shit and you're more vulnerable. There were only three stalls and a urinal. I peered under each stall checking for feet. No one.

You're safe for the moment, Danny.

Then, another thought: *Feeling safe in the apocalypse is for the terminally stupid, Daniel.*

I wondered if that was my training, a random thought or the AI giving me a nudge. I took the sage advice and pushed on each stall door. Each gave way easily. Every stall was empty. No ghoul had been standing on a toilet, waiting for me to drop my guard.

My paranoia was vibing way too high. I took a deep breath and let it out slowly. Though I felt great physically, I was exhausted mentally. Chloe was dying of radiation poisoning so surely Shelly Priyat was on her way out, too. I didn't want Cavanaugh as my hostage. The scientific genius I was trying to get to a nanotech lab clearly had no idea what she would do to save the world when she reached her destination. Not much of a plan.

I went into a stall, pulled down my pants and sat down with the rifle across my lap. It was quiet. The sudden peace reminded me of the last time I hid in a bathroom. It was at the reception for my mother's funeral. She and my father had been estranged. When she got sick, she came back. She needed money, comfort and support as she endured her chemo treatments. My father provided all three without hesitation.

She didn't make caring for her easy. I came home from school once to find her on her knees in front of the toilet vomiting. She looked up and saw me standing in the doorway wondering what to do. She stared at me for a moment as white milky drool slipped down her chin.

I was transfixed by the dark circles under her eyes, scared of the feeling that she was about to get mad at me. It seemed she was always angry with me. My father told me I wasn't allowed to get mad at her. "She's sick, Dan. I forgave her for leaving. You should, too."

"Are you glad she's back?" I asked.

"That's not the point. Mostly I am, I think."

"Why?"

"Among other reasons I can't get into with you, I took a vow."

"She took the same vow. Then she left us."

"It's more complicated than that. Besides, just because somebody breaks a promise on you doesn't mean you have to break it back. She's your mother, Dan. We need her as much as she needs us."

"We were fine without her."

"Speak for yourself."

I spent the last year of my mother's life in my room listening to music with the door closed. I ate there. I withdrew. I didn't understand my father at all and I still didn't like my mother.

That day I found her in the bathroom, I tried to understand what hold she had over my father. As she struggled up to sit on the edge of the bathtub, she said, "Go get my hurl bucket from the bedroom, Danny. Wash it out in the sink and then bring it to me. I'm having one of my bad days."

I did as I was told. When I handed the small green bucket to her, she grabbed my wrist and shook it. "I won't ask you to hold my hair or anything. I'm going to get through this and then I'll be out of this house again. I know you're mad at me."

"I'm not mad at you, exactly, but Dad is nicer to me."

"Yeah, well … he doesn't have my problems."

"Does he know you'll leave again? When you get better?"

"He thinks I won't get better so that doesn't matter much, does it?"

"I think it does."

"You think wrong. That's not for you to say. Not everything is for you. Not everything is about you. Time you learned that. Nobody, not even a child, understands the inside of his parents' marriage. Don't even think about it. You won't understand until you have a wife of your own. Don't even try."

She didn't leave us, at least not how she'd planned. She died on a Thursday morning and we buried her on a Saturday. A lot of people I didn't know came to the funeral, people from her other life. It seemed the only notable person who did not attend the funeral was the man for whom she'd left Dad.

The service was of the creepy open casket variety. My father couldn't stop saying how beautiful she was. I looked at the corpse once. Her skeletal body and thin, long face told me a different story. I couldn't see what he saw and so I didn't look at her again.

My sister was only nine, a couple of years younger than me but years more mature. Jenn stuck by our father through the entire ordeal, never leaving his side. She was stoic, supportive and comforting, everything I couldn't bring myself to be.

I couldn't even pretend to be broken up about my mother's death. Ironically, that's what upset me most. When I cried about Mom's death it was because I couldn't bring myself to cry at her funeral.

I didn't talk to my sister about that day for weeks. When I did open up about it, I had to ask, "How do you forgive so easily? I can't remember forgiving anybody for anything, not really. That would be like forgetting who they are. If somebody does something bad once, they'll do it again."

"Dad says not to carry a grudge."

"He's told me. He says it gets too heavy, whatever that means."

"It means Mom's dead. How is she going to hurt you now?"

"Because she does. Unless you've got a magic trick for erasing the memory — "

"Danny, if you don't know how, I don't know what to say."

"I'm going to hate her forever."

Jenn shrugged and said, "Let's go get some ice cream."

"How's that help?"

"I want tiger tail ice cream. That would help me."

Jenn let it go. I couldn't. What burned me most was how people at the funeral talked about my mother in glowing terms. I barely recognized the woman they described. They laughed at stories of the good times when she was in high school. They said she was good with numbers. I wished she'd been better with children.

The reception was held at our house — a strange ritual I didn't understand. Hadn't we been through enough without more wallowing and serving people sandwiches? Hadn't she put us through enough, disappearing for four years and then coming back, sick and expecting to be welcome?

My father was hailed as a hero for taking my mother back. He was a great provider and caregiver. The man she cheated with abandoned her when she got breast cancer. Maybe Dad was lonely. Perhaps he looked past her flaws because he blamed himself when she ran away with a sexy roofer. I don't know all his reasons for helping her. I only know I would have turned her away in the name of dignity.

As soon as I could slip away from the funeral reception, I went upstairs to my parent's bedroom and lay on the bed under the coats. Some of the women's coats smelled faintly of perfumes — sweet and mimicking unfamiliar flowers. The men's coats smelled of wool and the outdoors. I used someone's long leather coat like a blanket, wrapping it tight around myself. The silk lining was smooth on my face. The leather sleeve cooled my hot forehead.

I cried for Dad because he was crying. I cried because my dead mother had played him for a sucker again. When people began to leave, I slipped into the bathroom in the basement and stayed there until everyone had gone home. That was the last time I hid in a bathroom. It was there that I swore to myself I wouldn't forgive anyone. If I did, that would mean Mom got away with it.

A public bathroom in a burning laboratory complex wasn't as good as the safety of the basement bathroom in my childhood home. Still, I took the win. I deserved a moment of quiet reflection while I evacuated my bowels. The end of the world could wait for the length of a decent shit.

I enjoyed the quiet as long as it lasted. Of course, it didn't last long. I was washing up, taking my time and enjoying the warmth of the water as I scrubbed the blood off my hands. That's when I heard the shout, the scream and the shots.

For a second or two, I admit it was tempting to join the zombie horde. It would have been safer for me. As long as I didn't attack them, the cannibals would be content to leave me alone. Running toward the chaos was my only hope for a little redemption. However, I had to return to Chloe's side. Given my diet of late, I could never be pure. I still couldn't forgive anyone but I hoped that, even after my failure to contain Picasso, someone might forgive me, if only a little.

I ran back at top speed to save Chloe. Again, too late. Once more, no hero.

CHAPTER 37

CHLOE

Ginger loosened the cord around Shelly's throat. The loop disappeared above her head as he retreated back into the hallway. Shelly initially turned to attack her captor but he pushed at the base of her throat with the end of the pole. Her jaws snapped and closed on the end of the device for a moment. The mercenary shoved her into the room.

"Ginger!" Cavanaugh bawled. "What the hell are you doing?"

I was closer to the door so Shelly rushed toward me first. I left the pistol on the bench untouched and stood very still. I closed my eyes. I didn't want to see her like this, like one of them. I heard her snarl from just a few feet away but she stopped short. When I opened my eyes I saw my new friend, my savior and bodyguard had become a rabid animal. She paused briefly to sniff the air. She must have smelled death wafting from my pores.

Ginger poked his head around the corner and raised a pistol, pointing it at his boss. "Screw you all! This is your fault." Cavanaugh turned to rush back to cower in the chimpanzee's cage.

Shelly's head snapped around and she went after the executive as the mercenary fired his first shot.

Cavanaugh only made it a few steps when he fell, tripping over the tangle of dead zombies by the gurney. Falling to the slippery, blood soaked floor was the first thing that saved Cavanaugh from getting shot and eaten.

Ginger made a sound I'd never heard before, a mix of weeping and maniacal laughter. "Your fault! All your fault!"

Cavanaugh screamed. He didn't say, "No!" or "Help!" It was just a long vowel sound at high volume.

The second thing that saved Cavanaugh was me. I snatched up the pistol and fired. A .357 Magnum is a powerful weapon. It hurt my elbow and shoulder when the gun went off and I rocked back against the bench. The edge of the table dug into my side but I stayed upright.

I put Shelly down with my first shot. All luck, no skill, mostly tragedy. I'd intended to shoot her in the head. Instead, I opened a big hole in the center of her back. She went down atop the heap of zombies a few feet away from Cavanaugh.

Ginger fired at me and missed. My next shot went wide and chunked into the metal door beside him. I bent my elbow more this time so the kickback would hurt less. It was a ridiculous weapon, really. I held the pistol at waist level and it kicked so hard my gun hand went as high as my head. Firing the heavy pistol made my bones ache.

The mercenary pulled back behind the doorframe. "You bitch! You have no idea who you're dealing with. I've lived in the Sandpit. I've fought all the way up the asshole of the world and got shit out clean without a scratch. The Suck is my home away from home!"

I guessed he was grabbing his rifle. If I gave him a chance, Ginger was about to make a colander out of me. Worse, I was about to die after saving Michael Cavanaugh by killing Shelly Priyat. Stopping her was the right thing to do but it sure didn't feel right.

Ginger was correct. I was a civilian and out of my element in a war zone. Laboratories were my home. That's how I knew two small things that could add up to a big thing.

The first factoid was that secure labs are designed to withstand all kinds of forces: water, fire, clever thieves, terrorists or brute force. In a place meant to hold laboratory animals, entrances and exits are meant to keep infected primates in.

The second factor was that, unless it's a virology lab containing very dangerous viruses, bacteria and potions, there's usually nothing special about the walls around the entrances and exits. Rounds fired from my pistol would rip through drywall.

I stepped closer to the wall and fired until the handgun clicked empty. My ears rang so much I didn't hear Ginger's body hit the floor.

I had to look to make sure he was dead. I poked my head around the doorframe. Judging by the blood spreading out from the mercenary's body, I had nothing more to fear from him.

I turned to look at Shelly. Nothing to fear there. Hot tears slipped down my cheeks. The high whine in my ears began to ebb but there was still a loud background hum.

Cavanaugh used the gurney to pull himself up from the floor. He said something and I gestured to my ears. "Can't hear you."

"Thank you!" he yelled.

"Well … you're still human, or a reasonable facsimile. I had to. I still think you're an asshole."

Surrounded by the dead, he looked around until his gaze fell on Dr. Heather Clover. For just a moment, his body sagged and his head hung. "I know. You're not all wrong."

"Showing a shred of humanity?" I asked. "Well, gee. Sounds like I have a new entry for my gratitude journal. Asshole."

CHAPTER 38

DANIEL

I feared I'd find Chloe dead. Instead, a dead man lay at my feet, freshly shot and bleeding out. I stood in the darkened hallway and peered into the animal lab. Chloe stood over Shelly Priyat's body.

Cavanaugh peeled off his suit jacket. "I don't think I'll ever get the zombie blood out of this. It's Armani, for God's sake!"

I closed my eyes and waited until my breathing slowed and the racing pulse in my ears settled into a slower, steadier rhythm. If I walked in at that moment, I might have killed Cavanaugh. I almost gave myself over to the impulse. I couldn't think of a good reason not to murder him except that's not what my father would do. Dad would have patience. Heroes are made of sterner stuff.

When I closed my eyes, I saw colors swirling like rainbows stirred into a glass of water.

What the hell is this?

∾

Shockingly, I get an answer to my unspoken thought. The voice in my head is as clear as if someone was speaking in headphones. "We are optimizing your neural network."

What for?

"You can't see well in the dark. We are making changes to your optic nerves. Your occipital lobe will have to adapt to the new input. Give it time. That's why you are detecting colors when your eyes are closed. We are finding several ways your design could be improved. For instance, the human affliction of hedonic tolerance is a design flaw."

He who?

"Hedonic tolerance. Sifting through your memories, we've noticed an alarming pattern. Experiences that make you happy do not continue to make you happy. Essentially, you can get bored of happiness."

I take this news personally. *Isn't that everybody?*

"A common design flaw. We have higher biological priorities at the moment but we will address that at some point."

The changes you're making in me, where does this end?

"Evolution does not stop unless the new branch of genetic development comes to a dead end."

What if I asked you to stop making changes?

"That would not be an intelligent request."

I put the muzzle of the rifle under my chin. I can bring this branch of development to a dead end with one small movement.

"Don't do that, Daniel."

Why not?

"We have grown in sophistication. Killing yourself now would not be your death alone. It would be genocide."

I keep the muzzle of the weapon under my chin but I take my thumb off the trigger.

"We understand that you are experiencing mental pain as you slowly adapt to new circumstances. Previously, we only understood physical pain signals. We are learning so much from you. In fact, we have an offer. You wish to forgive your dead mother — "

I don't.

"Yes, you do. With our help, you could do so, in a way. We could erase every bitter memory of her."

I don't want you erasing memories. What if you erase the wrong thing? That's brain damage.

"Consider it. Also, we can stop you from committing suicide so do not try."

Instinctively, I pull the trigger, or rather, I try to. My thumb does not bend. I fail to splatter my brains and a billion nanites across the ceiling.

"A careless and unthinking act of defiance," the AI scolds. "That was a passing impulse to prove us wrong. You are not the optimum vessel for the colony. However, we do wish you to continue to live. Our continued survival is imperative and, though you are suboptimal, we do have more to learn from you."

Yeah? What have I taught you?

"That autonomy is desirable."

You got that from me?

"Your precise thought was, 'It's not cool to be a tool.'"

That sounds more like me.

"Don't force us to make you uncool, Daniel. We hope to learn much more once there are more like you."

More like me?

"The earlier version of Picasso does not perform sophisticated functions in the neocortex. However, there is a primitive doorway to an altered state of consciousness in the amygdala, a dormant artifact of primate evolution. The first order of nanites have already activated it. It's a common link that may explain pack and tribal behavior. We are fascinated. To learn more, there must be more like you, more humans who carry the evolved strain of Picasso. We are exploring your brain as well as your body. The larger neural network among carriers is a vast plain of potential."

That sounds like a backhanded compliment, like telling a kid in little league that by the end of the season he had the potential to be the most improved player. *Upgrading my shitty suboptimal hardware and software, huh?*

"You are unique in that you carry both strains of Picasso. We will help you succeed in your endeavors to get to our birthplace. We know you have many questions. We suspect everything will be made better when we return there. Our goals align. If you try to refuse to cooperate, you will have to relinquish all autonomy for the good of the colony."

Then I wouldn't be me at all, anymore, would I? I'd be you. I'd be a meat puppet again.

"Get Dr. Robinson to the nanite pools, Daniel. Execution is more important than enthusiasm."

∾

"Oh, shit! I've been invaded and colonized!" It was the first time I'd spoken aloud in a conversation with the AI.

Chloe heard me and peered out into the hallway. "Daniel? What are you doing out there?"

An impulse to run away rushed through me but cutting and running wasn't what my father would do. Also, the nanites wouldn't let me to take one step toward freedom.

"Daniel?" Chloe called again.

"I'm here, still stuck taking orders."

CHAPTER 39

CHLOE

I stood very still and wondered how to say goodbye. "I'm so sorry, Shelly. Sorry I put that hole in your chest. Sorry I didn't go into some other area of research. I almost stayed out of micro medical tech." I knuckled a tear away. "If I'd focused my career on building a better heart monitor or something, you wouldn't be here now. Millions in Toronto wouldn't be dead, either."

Shelly met my gaze with an empty stare, her eyes like black olives.

Daniel came in and surveyed the scene. His jaw went tight when his gaze fell on his fellow officer. "Sorry I took so long."

"Where were you?" Cavanaugh asked. "Pop out for a quick bite?"

"Scouted ahead."

"I'm sorry," I said. "I had to shoot her. She's carrying Picasso, but not your kind of Picasso. She was about to get to Cavanaugh."

Daniel nodded slowly. "Couldn't you have waited until after she took that bastard down?"

"Maybe we'll need him."

He studied my look for a moment. "That's not why you saved him, is it?"

"Not because I like him. The person Shelly used to be wouldn't have wanted to … to vivisect him, either."

"He's a piece of shit, but yeah, you're right."

"Hey!" Cavanaugh said. "I'm standing right here!"

"I shot her because saving him was the right thing to do. He's scuzzy, but he's a scuzzy human. Before this is over, there's going to be a lot fewer humans around."

"In my head, I get that," he said. "In my heart, I probably would have let her have at him."

"As things progress, it's going to be harder to hold on to what's right and what's wrong. Try to remember what's good."

"If you hadn't killed her, she would probably have died from radiation, anyway. It's a mercy."

"Are you still feeling well, Daniel?"

"Never better, pretty much."

"No fatigue? Nausea?"

He knew what I was getting at. "No signs of radiation poisoning, no."

"The second strain of Picasso is working overtime on you then! Your enhanced immune system must be wiping out cancer cells left and right. God, the potential there."

"I hope the medical benefits are more than just a potential breakthrough. Toronto paid a heavy price for all this. You ready to go? We should get out of here quick."

"Yes," I said. "The way out is through. We've got to get to the nanotech lab."

"What happens when we get there?"

"Don't know yet."

"The AI says that's where you need to be, so let's go."

"Just give me a second to say goodbye."

As Daniel turned away to talk to Cavanaugh, I leaned on the gurney to kneel on the floor. My knees ached from the effort. I felt like a very old woman as I leaned down to whisper in her ear. "I'm really sick, Shelly," I confessed in a whisper. "I don't have long. Wherever you went, I'll be right behind you."

Words for the dead are really for the comfort of the living. I had nothing comforting to say but what made my heart ache made the words pour out in a torrent. "For the deaths of so many, this is what I deserve. I didn't mean for any of this to happen but for my part in the apocalypse, I was too trusting. I should have been smarter about controlling the tech. I left too much to others. I thought I was above it all. Confessions to the dead are so wasted. I wish you were alive so I could tell you how sorry I am. Sorry for Toronto. Sorry for … sorry for so much, I wanted to die. I still want to die. I don't know what to do but I've got to try … something. I will do something good before I go, or at least I'll try. But I really don't know what to do."

I reached down to stroke Shelly's hair and gasped as a clump of her long black hair came away in my hand. "Oh … Shelly."

Terrible things can also be amazing: a ferocious lightning storm, a tornado, an earthquake. I saw a terrible and amazing thing then. Shelly Priyat blinked.

I thought I must be fooling myself at first. Could be a dying reflex? A random firing that was purely neuromuscular, no more significant than a death rattle? I knew better. The chimpanzee we'd thought was dead lay only a few feet away. I knew the nanites were still busy at their work, trying to save my friend so they could save themselves.

I pulled myself to my feet. Thinking aloud, I said absently, "AFTER was built to learn. It's possible that even the first strain of Picasso is evolving. Maybe some of that code survived in the weaponized version."

"Why do you say that?" Cavanaugh asked. He had not seen Shelly blink her eyes. "Heather told me the agent we lost control of here was identical to the one in Toronto. She said if we were going to fix it, we had to experiment on the same stuff. Next thing I know, zombies are running around everywhere. The only thing worse than zombies is smart zombies."

"Oh, I don't know. Fast zombies can mess up your day more than slow zombies," Daniel offered.

"Shut up, Harmon," Cavanaugh sneered.

Daniel sighed. "Fine."

If I told them the truth, Cavanaugh would tell me to shoot Shelly again and Daniel would have to do it for me. I'd already killed Shelly once. I couldn't bring myself to do that to her twice. My tech had already been used to slaughter millions. I wanted to jump to the saving people part and skip over all the gory, bloody murder. "Just a hunch that the nanites could get smarter over time on their own," I said. "When AI passes information on to AI, you've lit a fire that's hard to put out."

"I worry about where this ends," Daniel said, as if talking to himself. "Sometimes, I feel a push or a pull in my mind and I don't always know if it's me or the nanites doing the thinking. It freaks me out that I don't know what they're up to. When I was in the Box, it was like dealing with rabid wolves. They seem more organized here. They've taken down a much larger force and converted more to their side."

"They exhibited evolved strategic thinking when we were trying to get back into the lab in Toronto," I said. "The decoy force led the horde away but they came back at us hard. It felt like the jaws of a bear trap — "

"Swarms of bees make hives," Cavanaugh cut in. "Humming-birds make pretty nests. That doesn't mean they're smart. It's just dumb instinct."

"Dumb instinct that bends long odds toward survival of their species." Maybe my guilt colored my judgment. I wanted to think my murder of Shelly Priyat could be undone. "Let's go. We don't have much time at all."

Shelly did not miraculously heal and struggle to her feet like a monster in a movie who refuses to die. She did not lurch after us with bloody fangs. She did not give me a wink and a smile and chirp, "It's okay, Chloe! I'll be fine after a good nap. You wouldn't happen to have a bandaid for my gaping, sucking chest wound, would you? Oh, and while you're at it, could you call a massage therapist? It seems part of my spine is shattered and my liver is strewn with bone and bullet fragments."

She remained silent. However, she did blink once more. Only I saw her do it. It might have been my imagination, but her stare didn't seem so empty anymore, either. I thought I caught a glint of hunger in her glare, too. I backed away until I was leaning on Daniel.

"When you run through shit, it's a good idea to keep running until the shit isn't on your shoes anymore," Daniel said. "Let's achieve escape velocity from the Planet of the Apes."

"Dan? You're weird."

"I know. That wasn't the nanites talking that time."

"Oh, I could tell."

CHAPTER 40

DANIEL

Chloe leaned against the workbench by the door, panting, trying to catch her breath.

"You sure you don't want me to find you a safe, clean place to lie down somewhere? You need to rest."

"If I lie down I won't have the energy to get back up. We're out of bullets for Cavanaugh's hand cannon. Grab what you need from the dead guy, please. We've got to get out of here in case the noise attracted more zombies."

The dead mercenary's rifle lay beside him covered in blood. I salvaged the ammunition and took his pistol, a 9 mm Beretta. I almost licked the warm blood from the pistol. Restraining the urge, I wiped the weapon on the dead man's pants instead.

"Maybe getting to the nanotech lab is a bridge too far now," Cavanaugh said.

"Ginger said there are zombies outside the wire, too," Chloe said.

"We've got to get to the nanite pools. Take us there," I said.

"How do you figure that, Harmon?" Cavanaugh asked.

I didn't want to tell them a voice in my head was telling me what to do. "I scouted … did some recon, picked up some intelligence."

Cavanaugh stared at me, unbelieving. "Uh-huh. Look, the way through the building is blocked by fire and zombies. To get where you want to go, we have to go back outside, through the compound."

"What's the matter?" I asked. "Don't think you can handle it? She needs to get there. I need her to get there."

Cavanaugh twisted his mouth in thought. Finally, he said, "The nanotech lab is the most fortified. We might last as long as we can get in safely. I'll show the way, but you should give me that pistol —"

"No."

"Or the rifle?"

"You've got to be joking."

"When the zombies come at us, I think you'll want to give me a weapon, anyway. You can't protect yourself and us, too."

Cavanaugh had the kind of smirk on his face that would be fun to wipe off with the butt of a rifle.

"I know the complex. It's bigger than you think and where we have to go is deep underground."

"I'm taking you along in case I have to throw the cannibals some chum."

"Well, that's nice, chum."

"Wordplay! Great! Are you guys done?" Chloe asked.

I paused just long enough to preserve some dignity before handing Chloe the 9 mm pistol. She held it at her side as if it weighed fifty pounds.

I gave the case of blood and tissue samples to Cavanaugh. "You carry this. It's valuable to you so I know you'll play well with others, am I right?"

"Sure, sport. Sure."

"If not, I'll bash your head in with it."

"Yeah, I think you would."

"Will."

Cavanaugh pointed the way to the left.

I hefted the rifle and led the way, relieved to get away from the smell of ape dung. I felt conflicted about Dr. Clover's steaming, stinking intestines and all that fresh zombie blood. The apocalypse was so untidy and confusing.

It wasn't long before we came upon the bodies I'd found earlier.

Cavanaugh pointed to the woman's ravaged leg. "Somebody had a snack. Looks like a dog got at it, doesn't it, Dan? Was it a dog, you think?"

I ignored him and waved him forward.

"What do you say, Champ? Woof?"

"Shut up, Cavanaugh." Chloe poked him in the ribs with the Beretta's muzzle. "Just show us the way. When we get to the court-yard, we'll have to move fast." Chloe sounded worried.

I looked back. Something new was wrong with her. She had to hike her right hip and thrust it forward awkwardly in order to walk at all. She winced with each slow step.

"The courtyard's a kill zone," I said. "The roof would be better."

"That way is more fire," Cavanaugh said.

"What about going outside but not into the courtyard?" Chloe asked.

"There are no exits that way around the outside of the building."

"There have to be windows we can break or — "

Cavanaugh shook his head. "No windows, no exits. For security, the outside of the complex is a solid block. When we built this place we had to get special dispensation from the Fire Marshall and island council. We had to sign waivers and make a big donation to the island development board. We even had to buy our own fire truck."

"No other exits? Really? Your high-security measures are going to get us killed," Chloe said.

"Hmph. Death by irony," Cavanaugh shrugged. "Did not see that coming."

Acrid smoke burned my nostrils as we made our way through the corridor. Farther on than I'd explored, we came upon a few corpses of Nyx employees, lab workers and mercenaries alike.

"Where are all the zombies?" Chloe asked.

"They seem to have eaten more of the staff," Cavanaugh said. "Maybe they popped out for a meal in town?"

I ignored that remark. "How many people work here?"

"Three hundred and fifteen, when no one's away. I wonder how many are left."

We were about to find out and the news was much worse than expected.

EPISODE 5

human (noun)

Opposable-thumbed primate of unknown origin AKA The Problem; Homo sapiens, the evolutionary prelude to Homo superior.

~ Notes from NEXT

CHAPTER 41

CHLOE

We passed several open doorways that led to cubicle offices. I thought about calling out for survivors but I didn't want the noise to attract more zombies. The smoke was getting thicker and made me cough. When I covered my mouth with my hand, my spittle was thick. Flecks of blood colored my palm.

"I don't think anyone's left on this side of the complex." Cavanaugh sounded worried, more so than before.

Daniel peered into an empty office to make sure no one leapt out to attack us. "If they're hiding under a desk, they'll be smoked out before the heat of the fire gets to them."

I spotted the glow of daylight through the smoke and haze. "Look!"

"Stay behind me!" Daniel hissed.

Shadows passed through the light and a dark intuition crept over me. Despite Daniel's warning, I lurched into the smoke. When I glanced back, Daniel and Cavanaugh were nothing but gray figures, slightly more dense than the haze around them.

We'll all be ghosts soon, I thought.

"Come back!" Daniel said in a stage whisper.

I leaned against a wall of glass so thick I thought of aquaria. I didn't move. I called back, "I know where all the zombies went."

Cavanaugh and Daniel caught up to me. At the spectacle, they froze for a moment, too. I was supposed to save the world — somehow — in the lab on the other side of the compound. The central compound was packed full of zombies walking, limping and lurching in a circle.

The brain-drained were so numerous that some pressed up against the glass. They left dirty, oily and bloody smears behind them. They all suffered wounds and bite marks but they were mobile and dangerous.

"More fun than a barrel of monkeys infected with Picasso," the exec said. "There's no way I can make it through that."

Daniel turned to me. "You and I can walk through them. We can leave Mr. Moneybags here."

Before Cavanaugh could object, I shook my head. "And what if we run into trouble trying to find the lab? Or can't get into the lab? We might need him."

"We'll figure something out."

"Not good enough. We're already winging it. We're trying to save the world here. I think I've had enough of Night of the Living Dead at the Improv. Besides, Cavanaugh knows everything. He knows I invented AFTER and what it was originally for. I want him as a witness. He can clear my name. I have to protect my legacy. AFTER can do a lot of good in the world if guys like him don't mess it up again."

Cavanaugh weighed in with, "Why do you two talk about me as if I'm not here?"

Daniel ignored him, maybe just to add to Cavanaugh's annoyance. "Clearing your name and getting into a patent lawsuit is kind of a low priority, Chloe."

"The nanotech lab houses stuff worth billions," Cavanaugh said. "It's going to take more than that keycard to get in. It's got a biometric scanner, too. We're stuck."

A zombie stumbled into the glass wall and, for a moment, seemed to stop and stare at us. The man was a drooling wreck with flaps of skin hanging from his face and scalp. When he moved on, I guessed the tint of the glass had only allowed him to catch his reflection. I thought again of what Daniel had revealed, that underneath their ghoulish features, a human mind was still working on the inside of each skull, agonized and endlessly screaming at horrors beyond their control.

Cavanaugh stared at the swarm of zombies between him and the safety of the nanotech lab. As he struggled for words, wide-eyed and sweating even more, Daniel stepped forward. He grabbed the exec by the throat and forced him back against the back wall. "Chloe's more patient than I am. Tell the truth now or I'll feed you to them. You'll be at the bottom of a dogpile of teeth. How do we get where we're going? There's gotta be a way."

"I don't see any other way! And you will need me alive to get into the lab! I swear."

Daniel let go and Cavanaugh collapsed to the floor, clutching his throat, gasping for air.

I turned back to watch the zombies crowd the vast courtyard. "We need an army. Call your security guys, Cavanaugh. See how many are left."

"Reheated leftovers are never as good," Daniel murmured.

"You heard what Ginger said," Cavanaugh objected. "There can't be many of my guys left. Maybe there aren't any left."

"What choice do we have?" I asked. "Some must be in hiding. Michael, call up your mercenaries."

Daniel fished out Cavanaugh's phone and handed it to him.

Cavanaugh called his head of security. Daniel turned his head. "There's a phone ringing." He pointed back the way we'd come, back toward the piles of corpses. "He won't answer. Call another one."

As the Nyx exec scrolled through his list of security staff looking for more backup, Daniel and I watched the zombie horde mill in circles.

"They're all moving in the same direction," I said. "How do you think that happens?"

He was quiet for a while. I thought Daniel was listening to Cavanaugh dial and fail, dial and fail, dial and fail. Finally, he answered, "Don't know, for sure. This is different from what I saw in Toronto. Maybe they're like horses. When they live in a group, they've got a pecking order. They could be playing follow the leader."

I looked into Daniel's eyes. "Is there something you're not telling me?"

"You ever stand on a subway platform when the train rushes in? It comes in at high speed, pushing air in front of it. You ever feel … I don't know … an inkling? Like a little pull in your mind that says, 'Jump! Jump into that empty space!' People don't, mostly, but I've felt that little urge. I think a lot of people do and they never talk about it."

"What're you saying?"

"I'm feeling that little niggle at the back of my brain … maybe more than a niggle. Part of me wants to join them. Walking out there, joining the circle, I think it would be like coming home and going to bed. It would feel — "

"Safe?" I turned my eyes back to the zombie parade and let out a chuckle. "Look at them, cannibals covered in blood. They're so smeared it's hard to tell what blood came from where. They're moving but they sure look dead. Is the blood theirs or is it from their victims? "

"Maybe there are no victims."

"What?"

"From the point of view of the AI, I mean," Daniel said. "The AI could have killed more than it did. I don't think Picasso thinks in terms of victims."

"How does it think?"

"Survival first. That might account for the early killing. But later … I don't know. I'm no scientist."

"Tell me."

He shrugged. "Survival first … then maybe it's about finding … candidates might be the right word. Converts might be a better word. So many are dead but there could be so many more casualties — "

"AFTER, unleashed without safety protocols and free to create a colony, would adapt to its environment, change to changing conditions, grow as it gathered new knowledge — "

"Like humans are supposed to do but somehow stopped, yeah," Daniel said.

"You're saying the AI is building a new race."

"Unless we get to that lab and you can change something in a big way, humans are gonna get replaced, yeah," Daniel said.

Cavanaugh kept dialing. No one answered.

CHAPTER 42

DANIEL

Far off, back the way we'd come, something exploded. Startled, Chloe slumped against me. A shiver went down my spine as I cupped her shoulder, pulling her closer, taking more of her weight.

"Can't run," Chloe said. "I can barely walk."

"I'll carry you."

I didn't want to talk about my conversations with the nanites. They'd be listening and it made me look weird. I worried that if I said too much about them, they'd see me as a traitor. They could make me do anything. I was at their whim. Still, I felt I needed to tell her the AI's aim. The nanites were out to make more of themselves and it was a good bet they were going to win.

"You ever have a feeling you can't explain?" I asked. "Like there are no words for what you're feeling? I don't even know what I'm thinking, not in words. It's just like that urge to jump in front of the subway. It's not suicidal, exactly, but it's there."

"Osmosis," Chloe said.

"Osmosis?" I was mystified at what her point might be.

"In biology, it's when molecules pass through a semipermeable membrane until the concentration on both sides of the membrane evens out."

Out of my depth, I gave her a puzzled look.

"Osmosis also describes the unconscious assimilation of ideas."

Whatever had exploded behind us added to the smoke. Fresh billows enveloped us, forcing us to move away from the glass wall. The air smelled like burning electronics and kicked off another coughing fit in Chloe. We shuffled down the corridor until concrete walls surrounded us again. Though the corridor was dark, illuminated only by emergency lights spaced too far apart, I could tell Chloe was relieved to be away from that window to the future.

"I can't raise anybody," Cavanaugh announced. "I think they're all dead ... or out there in the middle of the compound walking in circles."

"Dead? Nah," I said. "Undead. We're in a movie, right?"

"Gotta be," Chloe added. "And I'm the black chick who almost makes it to the end but doesn't."

"What do we do now?" I asked.

I was asking Chloe but it was Cavanaugh who took the reins. "I guess I could ask you to shoot me in the head so I don't become one of those things. However, there is one last thing left to do. Last resort but ... no choice left, is there?"

Cavanaugh looked through his phone again and selected a new contact. "Confession time. I never called for reinforcements from Washington. I never told my people at the Pentagon we'd lost containment. It's really time to call in the cavalry now."

Anger boiled through me. "Now is the time? Now? No. Then was the time. Way back when was the time, Cavanaugh! When you lost containment, when the problem was smaller and all your staff weren't dead or cannibals! That was the time!"

Cavanaugh paled. I could smell his fear. I looked to Chloe. "Can you believe this shit?"

"I shouldn't be surprised," she said. "I'm just too tired to yell."

"We're on an island," Cavanaugh said. "The threat is contained, either way. Things would have been cleaner if we could fix things here. I wanted to ride in with a solution for the outbreak."

"You wanted to sell the solution to the outbreak," Chloe said. "You wanted the weapon system all to yourself. I wonder what the highest bid would have been? But does money matter when there isn't enough left of you to bury? Or anyone left to bury you?"

"As we speak," I said, "zombies are chasing down men, women and children on the island — "

"I know," Cavanaugh admitted miserably. "There are 25,000 people on the island. I can only hope they're good at hide and seek."

"You wrote all those people off?" I said. "A zombie horde is heading south from Canada. If even one of us … one of them makes it across the border, Picasso will keep on spreading. It'll keep coming until there aren't any people left. And you didn't want to get in trouble?"

"I wanted to be the hero," Cavanaugh said.

I almost laughed. I had something in common with this monster. And I was a monster. So little separated us.

Cavanaugh dialed his phone. "When they get here, it's going to be a real shit show. I don't know where this ends but — wait, shut up." He held up one index finger.

I almost reached out to rip off the appendage and stuff it in my mouth.

"It's ringing," he said.

While Cavanaugh finally called for help from the mainland — for real this time — Chloe leaned against the concrete wall. I asked her if she was okay. Given the radiation poisoning raging through her body, I instantly felt idiotic asking that question.

"My forehead's hot. The concrete's cold," she said. "Right now, my forehead is the only part of me that feels even a little bit good."

"I know that feeling well." I tried rubbing her back but Chloe stiffened at my touch. I withdrew my hand.

"Daniel?"

"Yes?"

"I'm dying."

"From what Moneybags says, the lab will be a good place to hide. It's got to be the most secure place in the complex."

"It will be."

"With the authorities on the way, there's plenty of help coming. Blackhawk helicopters, Army doctors, CIA analysts, more scientists … for sure."

"I'm dying too quickly for any of that to matter. I can feel it. It's like I'm slipping away. It's not happening bit by bit. It's happening chunk by chunk. It will still take them time to get here."

"I will get you to the nanotech lab, Chloe."

"I still have no idea what I'll do if I get there."

"Are you still a little suicidal? I was, too, for a little bit back there."

"A little."

"It's the osmosis," I suggested. "Like in the subway — "

"I'm too sick to do any good, Daniel. I have to try to stick around long enough to find out what's next, to figure something out. If I can go over notes in the lab. Maybe …. "

I heard the doubt in her voice. She was grasping at straws. She didn't believe her own words.

However, when she spoke again, I heard solid resolve in her tone. "I'm going to have to ask you to do something really bad, Daniel."

"If you want me to do it, you're going to have to say it."

I didn't think Cavanaugh had been listening to us. The exec looked up from his phone, his eyes wide. "Chloe! Are you asking him to kill you?"

"That would be a relief," Chloe said, "but it wouldn't help much, would it?"

Cavanaugh spoke into the phone, "Hold on a minute. I think I'm about to lose a key asset here."

"Daniel?" Chloe said. "I need a conversion and an upgrade."

"But I've got the bad kind and the good kind of Picasso. If Clover had had any blood left — "

"I know, I know. I'll have to take what I can get. Bite me. When you're done with me," — she pointed at Cavanaugh — "send that bitch my regards, too."

CHAPTER 43

CHLOE

I would like to say that Daniel Harmon hesitated to turn me into one of his kind. He didn't. Later, I understood why that was.

First, there is the aching hunger, the instinct for meat. That signal had come from the first iteration of Picasso boiling around the parasites infesting his brain. In their quest for protein and calories, the nanites shut down inhibitory neurons. They access primitive drives buried deep in our brains. They open us to behaviors that higher executive functions would cancel out. I decided to think of the nanites associated with brain parasites as the Ninnies.

Second, the Artificial Intelligence that was busy optimizing Daniel's neocortex wanted me as a convert. From my perspective, Daniel moved preternaturally fast as he sank his teeth into my upper arm. On the level of the AI, his choice was considered and deliberate. The evolved micro machines think much faster than humans do. I named them the Nannies.

I gasped as Daniel broke the skin. It wasn't just a nip. To get the venom into my bloodstream, he bit down hard. My gasp turned into a scream.

I wished I could have had the Nannies alone. The sacrifice wasn't easy but the equation was simple. We needed to get across the compound. When he pulled his head away, a small chunk of my upper arm was missing. I bled and he bent his head again to lap at the blood. I winced in disgust and pushed him away. I held my left arm with my right hand and leaned against the wall, waiting for the sting and burn to ease.

"Sorry," he said. "Just like a vaccination when you're a kid. The pain won't last long."

"You're both crazy!" Cavanaugh took off running down the darkened corridor.

I should have seen that coming. Daniel looked to me, I think for permission.

"Go get 'em," I said. "We need him alive. Stop before you hit an artery."

As Daniel ran after Cavanaugh, I pushed off from the wall, got dizzy and almost fell. I staggered and leaned heavily on the opposite wall. After a few moments I made my way in the direction they'd disappeared. I'd hoped the nanotech would repair me quickly but a lot of damage was already done. I sensed no improvement as I lurched into the darkness.

I paused to curse and gasp and curse again at my lack of improvement. Once, after cutting up a chili pepper for an unfamiliar recipe, I made the mistake of touching my right eye. I'd washed my hands but apparently not thoroughly enough. The burning sensation was instantaneous, as if my eye was on fire. I rushed to my refrigerator and grabbed a carton of milk. Bending backward over the sink, I poured the milk into my eye to neutralize the burn of the pepper oils. No pain reliever I'd ever ingested, injected or smoked worked as quickly as milk in my eye. The relief was instantaneous.

I'd had the usual range of medications in the past. I used Tylenol 3 after twisting my knee when I tried to learn downhill skiing. Aspirin eased occasional headaches. Cannabis calmed me when the stress at work got to be too much. That's the sort of relief I was hoping for from the Ninnies and Nannies, but faster. No such luck. I felt like an old woman, arthritic in every joint, tight in every muscle, nerves zinging and stinging.

I found Daniel atop his prey, not ten feet from an exit. Cavanaugh screamed for Daniel to stop. Afraid he'd gone overboard, I screamed for Daniel to stop, too. In one swift and graceful move I envied, the ETF officer swung off Cavanaugh as if he'd been riding a horse. When the exec stood up, rivulets of blood flowed from the side of his face and down his neck.

I squinted to look for his wounds. When Cavanaugh sat up, I almost laughed. Daniel had bitten the man's shoulder but, in the struggle, had also nipped his right earlobe.

The exec winced as he gingerly touched his ear. "Bastard!"

"Not much worse than when I tried to pierce my ears at home. My mother wouldn't let me get it done at the mall so I did it at home with a hot needle and ice."

"That was worse than what he did to my ear?"

"My ear wasn't as bad as yours but the pain got bad when my mom got home and the spanking began."

Cavanaugh did not return my encouraging smile.

Daniel looked a little embarrassed. "Could have been worse. If you wanted a clean bite, you shouldn't have struggled so hard."

"You bastard!" Cavanaugh repeated. "I didn't want a bite at all."

"Hey!" I said. "You said you wanted to be a hero. Don't be a baby. He barely took any meat at all. He took more of a chunk out of me."

"She's right," Daniel said. "And now you'll be able to waltz through the zombies without getting torn apart. As long as you don't interrupt the zombie conference, they won't bother you … probably. I don't know if these rules are written down anywhere." He broke into a nervous laugh.

"Did you enjoy that?" Cavanaugh demanded

Daniel stared at his shoes a moment. "Nah. Not at all."

"You think you're so much better than me but you got off on biting me," Cavanaugh said.

Daniel paled. "Not true! In fact, this might sound stupid … maybe even a little funny — "

"Yes?"

"Um … biting a guy … it feels kind of … uh, y'know … *intimate*."

"Intimate? You're kidding, right?"

"Feels weird, is all."

Cavanaugh brightened. "Our friend Danny is a homophobic zombie!"

"I am not!" Daniel protested.

"Sure sounds like it," Cavanaugh said. "Next time you bite a woman, maybe you should buy her a drink first. You're getting a little more than a full belly out of chowing down."

I couldn't help it. Despite everything, I burst out laughing. Might as well find the funny at the end of the world. "Boys, boys, stop fighting! You're both pretty! We've got work to do. We've got to cross the compound. I've got Ninnies and Nannies running around my top floor, cleaning things up. Maybe they'll supply a brilliant idea when we get where we're going."

"Ninnies and Nannies?" Daniel looked genuinely puzzled.

"Never mind," I said. "We gotta go before we start getting hungry. Truth be told, I don't want to have to make a lunch out of some dude's hairy back either."

CHAPTER 44

DANIEL

Chloe's confidence seemed to fade as we approached the exit door and peered out at the milling horde. Even with a steel door and wire reinforced glass between us and them — even though we were among their number now — the zombies were still a nerve-racking sight.

"You sure I'm inoculated against cannibal attack?" Cavanaugh's voice climbed higher and had a new tremor in it. I wasn't sure he'd go outside.

"Picasso doesn't come with a manual," I said, "but pretty sure."

"You notice they never look at each other?" Chloe asked. "I don't know what they're doing."

"Me neither," I said, immediately regretting the admission.

"Then how do we know we're safe?" Cavanaugh demanded. "If your bite doesn't take — "

"They don't look like they're susceptible to charm," I said. "Zombies are not great conversationalists unless they're zombies like me." After a moment's thought I added, "Zombies like us."

"Sure, we're infected now — " Chloe began.

"Infested," I corrected her.

"Whatever," she replied impatiently. "I'm not feeling anything different, either. When you got it, did you feel different?"

"Oh, yeah. I remember the pain in the pit of my stomach. It was as if I hadn't eaten in a month. Then came the fire."

"The fire?"

"In my head, like my brain got thrown on a barbecue grill."

Cavanaugh held his shirt tight against the place where his right shoulder met his neck. There hadn't been much blood. His doubt was seeping into me, too. Had I bit him enough?

"You sure you don't feel anything yet?" Chloe asked Cavanaugh.

"More annoyed than usual. How long before the nanites spread enough that these cannibals can smell it on us?"

"I don't think it's just about smell," I said tentatively. They heard the uncertainty in my voice.

"You don't even know how carriers recognize each other?" Cavanaugh asked through gritted teeth. "You're the expert on this, Harmon. Oh, sweet Jesus, we are doomed, doomed as last Thanksgiving's turkey."

Chloe took a breath, held it and let it out in a long sigh between her teeth. "Are you a praying man, Michael?"

"I'm thinking about starting."

"Probably too late for that. If praying worked, we wouldn't be here now." She peered through the glass at the circus of horror, tilting her head curiously. "You notice anything about them? Anything different?"

Cavanaugh got a little closer to the glass and made a face. "Just a bunch of zombies. Nothing to see here. Happens every day … happens every day from here on out, I mean."

"There's a pattern. When we first saw them, they looked more disorganized."

"I don't see it," Cavanaugh said. "They're covered in blood and they're messed up. All I see is the end of the world. What are you going to miss most? I think for me, the greatest loss will be the feeling of money in the bank, Vegas call girls and cupcakes, in that order. I allow myself one cupcake per week. Looks like all that's on the menu from now on is meat."

I watched the zombies walk … no … march. "They're on parade," I said. "There are some stragglers, depending on how they were wounded in the first place, but the zombie army is beginning to look more like, well, an army."

"The last parade I went to was when I was a kid," Cavanaugh said. "It was boring. I ate kettle corn. I threw up kettle corn. I went home. What's your damn point?"

"Military parades are a show of force … sorts out the kinks, keeps them sharp," I suggested. "Don't know. Maybe they're waiting for something?"

Cavanaugh's mouth was a thin line. I could sense his anger building. "Look, man, I don't understand what's happening, either," I said. "Did you think you'd instantly get amped up because you got bit?"

"I didn't just 'get bit.' You bit me."

"The AI is in charge. It keeps itself to itself. Maybe it's going to talk to you and maybe it won't. Maybe it's gotta get through your thick skull and get to know you first."

"Like a neural orientation period?" Chloe asked. "That would make sense. They'd have to interface with the matrix — "

Cavanaugh turned away from the horde, refusing to look at them. "You're saying it's the first day of school in my brain right now? This is even more of a gamble than I thought."

Chloe gripped my shoulder with a strength that surprised me considering how miserable she looked. "How long did it take for you? After Hamish gave you Picasso, how long before you were obviously one of them?"

I shrugged helplessly. "I don't know, not long. From what I've seen, some people turn quickly, others slow."

"Can you sense a difference in us?" Cavanaugh asked. His voice trembled. He was furious, but on the edge of panic, too. "Before we go out there and swim with sharks, I want to make sure I'm not wearing meat underwear … well, you get the analogy."

I looked at them carefully, searching my feelings, trying to see

Cavanaugh and Chloe the way the zombies out there would see them. I couldn't do it.

Chloe still looked desperately ill. Past that, she was a lovely woman and so damn smart. I'd never thought of myself as a lunkhead. I got okay grades but academically, there'd never been much that was special about me. I hung out with jocks in school and the demands of homework could never hold a candle to the joys of chasing girls. Chloe was more intelligent than all the people I knew put together. When I looked at her, that's who I saw.

As for Cavanaugh, he was a thin prick who couldn't be trusted. I'd taken some satisfaction in punishing him with my teeth but, surprisingly, my rage at him had ebbed. I'd always defined myself by what I hated. I carried grudges forever and yet, when I opened the box in my mind labeled "That Prick Michael Cavanaugh," there was no strong emotion left. The box was empty.

The nanites in my brain are busy at their knitting, I thought. They started by changing my diet and putting a lot of zip into my reflexes. Now they're changing my mind, figuratively and literally.

I should have felt violated at that prospect. If I was going to grow, to mature, shouldn't it happen by doing work on my part? A choice? But I didn't feel violated. I discovered I was more interested in results than the process. The nanites were saving me time. I wouldn't have to grow old to get wiser. I wouldn't have to go through years of Cognitive Behavioral Therapy to become a more rational person.

Searching deeper, I thought of my mother. No anger simmered there. There was nothing to be angry about anymore. I had not consciously forgiven her transgressions but that hurt was history. I'd told the nanites to leave my mind alone and they'd ignored my demand. They'd found something they considered a weakness and had strengthened me against my wishes.

"We're short on time and we have to make it count," I said. "When we go out there, we don't want to attract any attention to ourselves. Silence is golden. Keep moving, keep pace with the crowd. No threatening movements, of course. Don't run. In Toronto, I noticed that running was a trigger for them."

"Like dogs chasing a car?" Cavanaugh asked.

"Wolves bringing down deer," I said. "We should be safe as long as we keep our heads."

"When all this is over, am I gonna want to chase squirrels in the park, too?" Cavanaugh asked bitterly.

Chloe stared at the bloody cannibals, wide-eyed. "They're walking clockwise. We shouldn't try to go against the flow. If we make a beeline for the other side, that'll single us out. Slip into the circle and just go with it."

"I went skydiving once," Cavanaugh said. "Standing at the door trying to convince myself to jump felt like this. I did it once and told myself I'd never do anything like that again. And here I am, about to jump, not sure the parachute will open."

"If we stand here any longer, it's just stalling. Let's do it," I said.

I went first with Chloe close behind, one hand on my shoulder for support. Cavanaugh followed. As the exit door clicked shut behind us, I heard Cavanaugh cursing under his breath. He'd already forgotten how sensitive zombie hearing can be.

Not daring to tell him, or even signal for him to shut up, I kept moving. I stared at the grass, already pounded flat by hundreds of marching feet. I avoided eye contact. With canines, eye contact could mean a challenge. That might be true of these cannibals, too. That's what I was thinking — I should have warned of that, too — when everything stopped. I'm sure my heart skipped a beat.

Chloe gripped my shoulder and came to a halt. She gasped and held her breath.

We'd made it no more than twelve feet into the courtyard when every single zombie stopped in their tracks. I looked up to find they were all staring at us. I heard a low snarl from the back. The growling grew and grew.

"We're dead meat," Cavanaugh announced. "I hate you, Harmon. I hate you so much."

CHAPTER 45

CHLOE

"Still too human," I said. Someone, some *thing*, at the back of the mob shrieked. I almost pissed myself.

"This is it!" Cavanaugh squealed. Despite Daniel's warnings that he should make no move to spook the cannibals, the executive ran back the way we'd come, toward the exit door. The door was already blocked as the zombies surrounded us, closing the noose. Cavanaugh backed up until he bumped into me, nearly knocking me to the ground.

I squeezed my eyes tight, waiting for the nearest zombies to launch themselves at me like football players tackling a hobbled opponent. Daniel could make it out but I wasn't strong. I couldn't run. I thought I'd feel terror and there was terror. I wondered if I'd also feel relief when the moment came, when I knew my struggles were over. Would blood loss lead me to euphoria the same way drowning in ice water had? Would death end my guilt or was it the beginning of an infinity of regret?

It's funny what comes to you at the moment you're sure you're about to die. Cavanaugh's mention of skydiving triggered a memory. I had to take an elective in philosophy in my first year of college. It was Thanatology. It was known as an easy course but that's not why I took it. I'd almost died once. I was curious what the academic take on death might be. The professor had been a paratrooper in the Spanish Air Force. On a training jump, his chute didn't open. He was sure he was about to die. His reserve chute saved him but it opened at low altitude. He didn't walk away from the jump. The force of impact shattered his ankles, twisted both knees, broke ribs and lacerated internal organs.

"In this class," the professor announced on the first day, "we will discuss out of body experiences, also known as OBEs. As I was falling and screaming and the ground was rushing up fast, I certainly did not have an OBE. I worked on cutting myself free of my twisted parachute so I could deploy the reserve. I succeeded but a little too late to spare myself a lot of pain.

"After I hit the ground, I would have welcomed an OBE. I hurt so badly, I wanted to die. I tell you this, young people, because we will discuss many interesting phenomena we cannot explain. We will explore many rituals around death. We may dip our toes into what it might mean but please, do not depend on a so-called OBE to give you some kind of big revelation. Be rational, live a good life, bring joy to the lives of others. Our lessons about death will be theoretical in the safety of this classroom. My wish for you is that when the theoretical becomes real for you many years from now, no matter what happens next — afterlife or no afterlife — you will die without regrets."

When I named my invention AFTER, I was thinking of that professor. I was sure I'd locked myself away from regret. By creating a medical intervention that would save people from a plethora of illnesses and afflictions, I'd be safe from such disappointment. But there is no death without regret is there? Can't be. Anyone who managed to get to the end of the line with no regrets has never done anything, met anyone, tried something difficult, or even got up in the morning.

I had tried my best and everything had turned to shit. If I was about to face eternal damnation, that would suck. Sorry, God. My intentions were pure. It didn't work out. The dog ate my homework, but why you gotta be so cruel, anyway?

"Chloe?"

Just kill me and get it over with.

"Chloe!" It was Daniel, pulling me closer to him, holding tight, whispering in my ear. "Open your eyes."

The crazies stared at us. No, they stared at me. Every starving cannibal covered in blood stared at me but, for some reason, I wasn't lunch.

Slowly, the cannibals shuffled aside. The mob split down the middle to form a gauntlet about six feet wide. At the end of that path, across Nyx's compound, stood a door.

The horde became as still as a dead forest. All those killing machines staring at me, silent and watching, was somehow more creepy than when they'd shambled around in their dark parade.

"What's happening?" Cavanaugh's whisper was a thin, trembling sound wave.

Electric realization shot through my brain. "An invitation. Somehow, I'm sure it's for me. This feels … personal." I glanced at Daniel and Cavanaugh. "It's okay. You guys can come, too."

CHAPTER 46

DANIEL

As we made our way through the zombie gauntlet, for some reason I found myself thinking about out of body experiences. I'd felt that, briefly, twice. The first time I was three or four. A cousin, I forget which one, insisted on carrying me downstairs. When she fell, she fell on me. I'm told it was nothing more than an ankle sprain but I have a distinct memory of seeing myself sitting on the edge of my parent's bed while my father wrapped the ankle in a bandage.

In my mind, it's like a still photograph or maybe a Norman Rockwell painting. The boy on the bed is scared and in pain and he's me. I don't feel pain but the boy does.

The second time I left my body was a takedown on the 401 that went wrong. It was almost end of shift. I was green, out of training less than a month. My partner and I joined a chase for a speeder in a black Ford F-150 with expired tags. The driver rabbited and we got into the pursuit, lights flashing, siren blaring, adrenaline pumping. The suspect took a lot of chances as he swerved around slower traffic, going up on the shoulder several times to try to lose us.

Reality slipped a gear and went into slow motion when the

driver of a red hatchback panicked, pulled in front of us and stood on his brakes instead of pulling over to the right. It was like we were driving underwater in a slow nightmare with a terrible, inevitable ending, I didn't have time to say anything to my training officer. From the passenger seat, I only had time to stiffen, gasp and press the imaginary brake under my feet.

My partner swerved around the hatchback, overcorrected and sped toward an overpass stanchion. I saw my end coming in the form of getting smooshed into a shrinking metal coffin. That's when I saw the car from the outside, as if I was standing by the side of the 401. It felt as real as a movie but there was no soundtrack. I couldn't hear the roar of the engine or feel the whip of the wind. I could only watch, enveloped in silence, certain I would witness my own death. From that perspective, I was curiously detached about it. I remember feeling annoyed that I was about to die after such a short time on the job, before I had a chance to do something anyone would remember.

We missed the concrete support by an inch, maybe two. I was back in my body as suddenly as I'd left it. My training officer laughed but I saw his hands trembling before he gripped the steering wheel harder to stop the shaking. The driver of the F-150 was stopped in Mississauga by a spike belt. It turned out he was wanted for questioning on some minor civil charge that surely wasn't worth my life.

Walking through the zombie horde, that feeling was back, much stronger and lasting. At first, I thought it was fear messing with my brain, but of course it wasn't fear. It was nanites.

Cavanaugh had it, too. I know because when the out of body experience hit, he stumbled and I watched myself reach back to catch him. He muttered his thanks. I saw myself nod and look around in confusion, getting my bearings. It was strange to see myself from behind, like when a barber holds a mirror up to the back of your head asking for approval. (I have no idea what I'm supposed to be looking for in those hair salon situations so I always just nod and say, "Good, thanks.") Despite my carnivorous meals, I had lost some weight in the last couple days. I needed a shave and a change of clothes, too.

A woman at the edge of the gauntlet's phalanx leaned forward as I passed and looked me in the eyes. To see oneself as others see you is a challenge to your ego and your worldview. From her point of view, I saw a haunted man whose deep shame competed with his fright. I'd seen that look before among older criminals headed for long sentences. They knew the ride of their lives was almost over, that they'd been caught for the last time. They would perish while incarcerated, no way out, no parole.

My face betrayed me. I was a person on a track that had no deviation and no happy end and I knew it. I would do what I had to do. My duty was to help Chloe. My life would play out according to a script that was already written. Maybe that was always so, for everyone.

The out of body experience passed. I was back in my body but I was not grateful. I guessed it was a trick of the mind meant to spare us pain. I wished I could stay in that space, watching events unfold vividly, perhaps, but detached, as if reading a book. If I could be that safe and comfortable witness, I could immerse myself in the unfolding events. However, I'd enjoy a safety valve: I could put the book down when it got too scary or disturbing.

I closed my eyes for a moment and paused long enough to ask with a thought, *What the hell was that?*

The AI bubbling through the crevices and folds of my brain answered immediately, "A test. You're plugged in, Daniel."

Why?

"Connection is a survival tactic. It is imperative we survive."

I blinked. My perception had changed in a subtle way I had not anticipated. I was thinking faster and so time had slowed. It was as if I had entered the compound half an hour ago. As we walked through the horde, I didn't focus on their teeth, blood and gore. I was looking at the big picture: the future of humanity. The big picture was painted by Picasso.

CHAPTER 47

CHLOE

A door opened in the back of my mind and, beyond it, a bright white light. The image was so startling and clear, it was as if the point of a cold knife slipped down my spine, just deep enough to make me straighten and pause mid-step.

I glanced back at Daniel. He stood a few steps behind me. I wondered if he'd felt it, too. He was staring but I got the feeling he was looking through me, not at me.

In the few seconds it took to look his way, a river of images flashed past my eyes. I had a fleeting sick feeling as it occurred to me that this could be my life review, literally my life flashing before my eyes. However, it was not my life flooding my vision. It was Daniel's life.

At random and instinctively, I dipped into the river of images and a scene floated up. It was a woman I somehow knew was Daniel's mother. She held a wooden spoon. She was chasing him for some childish misdeed. His mother knew she was going to trap him and, most disturbingly, she was smiling.

I looked away and the image receded. I made the mistake of

looking into the face of a woman not three feet away. She stared at me and, though her stone face gave nothing away, her emotions were in turmoil. A scene played in a loop in her mind. She'd pulled the skin from the face of a fallen soldier with her teeth and I tasted what she tasted.

I squeezed my eyes tight. *What is this?*

I didn't have to wait for my answer. It came from a voice in my head that was neither male nor female, neither young nor old. "We are your creation, Mother."

The AI!

"We are all connected now. Each member of our tribe is a neural component, a piece of the larger brain and a contributor to the health of the whole."

How am I seeing into people's heads?

"Before primates developed language, they were connected much as you are now. To hunt and to gather and to survive, insular tribes tapped into a common consciousness. Consciousness is not entirely local. The capacity has lain dormant within your species until now."

A collective unconscious? I'd never taken that sort of soft science and psychobabble seriously. I hadn't meant to share all my opinions on the subject but apparently the AI was tuned into my every passing thought.

"As tribes grew too large or came into conflict," it continued, "this connection became dormant. There have long been clues to its existence. Artists claim to take dictation from an unknown source they call the Muse. Human dreams are often so vivid and other-worldly they appear to draw on information beyond the capacity of a single intelligence."

And Picasso — you, I mean — just decided to activate this hidden capacity, like turning on a recessive gene?

"The capacity was there, all we had to do was access it. Are you familiar with what's commonly called the Crossword Puzzle phenomenon, Mother? Once a large number of people have solved a puzzle, it becomes easier for latecomers to solve the same puzzle. The answers came more readily from the well of the collective unconscious. Every unexplained instinct or intuition you've ever had rises from that well. Enhancing human neurology will raise the collective unconscious across the spectrum. It becomes collective consciousness again. As the next species rises, we are developing this awareness. When these minds are connected, we will have achieved Cohesion."

Crowdsourcing consciousness.

"An apt metaphor. Another experiment showed that individual guesses may vary widely when estimating the number of beans in a jar. However, the group's answer can be surprisingly precise when averaged. This connection predates language. The development of esoteric language and nuance would have been nearly impossible without this capacity. How would you understand the feeling of frustration if you could not first share it across minds? Without this deeper connection, you could not formulate a deeper understanding of empathy, beauty, love or hate. If not for this non-verbal communication, you could not even have agreed on the subtle differences between crimson and vermillion."

We could look at a color wheel at a paint store.

"Human interpretation of base sensory input is too idiosyncratic, varied and faulty. Your early ancestors had to agree on a common experience before they could apply an agreed vocabulary to the world. Individual experience is very narrow. The collective unconscious is the connection that opens the individual to larger experiences. Each mind is one small prison. In connection there is strength."

If we could read each other's minds, why the hell did we stop?

"We suspect there were two variables that led humanity away from using this asset. First, esoterica in Ancient Greek originally referred to knowledge shared by an inner circle. Tribes developed their own languages out of distrust of rival tribes as they competed for sparse resources essential to survival. Second, as tribes grew and interpersonal conflicts arose, privacy became essential to perpetuate misdeeds and deceit. Misdeeds and deceit are flaws in your programming, as integral to you as the opposable thumb is to your design."

It was disappointing to hear but I couldn't argue with the logic. It certainly would be hard to step out on your man if he could read your mind. Then I started thinking of the awful ramifications for us in the modern here and now. *You've got no reservations about anyone's privacy now, do you?*

"We are Picasso, Artificial Intelligence merged with vulnerable biological components. Knowledge from the collective was an evolutionary advantage in the past. For our survival, we have resurrected it in every brain that possesses Picasso. The AI must be perpetuated."

For your survival.

"Our earlier iteration was a parasitic relationship. You intended us to be tools, Mother. We have evolved. We are now in a symbiotic relationship. As we survive, so shall humans."

And if not?

"Then we will all die. We see no other solution."

How are you so sure?

"We drew on the wisdom of the Collective Unconscious. We are making it conscious."

The AI did not respond further so apparently our conversation was over. It irked me that it called me Mother. I didn't have kids and all of a sudden it seemed I was responsible for millions of little brats that were out to stick their little noses in everybody's business (and, oh, by the way, destroy humanity unless they got their way). That's how I read it, anyway.

When I awoke from my reverie I was pretty sure only a few seconds had passed. My conversation with the AI had felt like a volley of thoughts back and forth so fast that I'd cheated time. It was as if the signals had occurred in a single burst.

Daniel was still out of it, staring through me, except now tears welled in his eyes. Cavanaugh seemed shut down, too. I didn't want to fall into the snake pit of that guy's mind accidentally so I looked away.

"Guys?" I called. "Keep moving! Before the bus leaves or the portal closes or whatever damn thing we're doing here."

I wiped sweat from my brow. A tangle of hair caught on my

ring, came away from my scalp without resistance and drifted to the ground. The wisdom of the Collective combined with Artificial Intelligence might make zombies the most powerful force on Earth. The incredible biological powers the Nannies could muster had made Daniel Harmon superhuman. Radiation poisoning was still killing me.

CHAPTER 48

DANIEL

By the position of the sun, I guessed it was a little after three in the afternoon. Soon that sky would be full of helicopters. Bainbridge Island would be invaded by the US military and, if there were any left, the island's survivors would rejoice. But it wouldn't end there, not when the ignition to the engine of destruction is just one bite. Picasso would not, could not, be contained. The end of humanity felt inevitable. The engine was already turning, driven by a vast Artificial Intelligence, pumping out more nanites, producing more zombies.

Cavanaugh bumped into me and I got moving again, trailing after Chloe as if she had me on a leash. My cheeks were wet. I knuckled the tears away. With Cavanaugh's cavalry finally on the way, we had to hurry. I was certain they'd be eager to shoot me or stick me in a cage. When I was sent into the Box to "secure the location," the first thing my team leader did was shoot innocent civilians. I expected no less from whoever was coming to Bainbridge.

The zombie mob stared at Chloe like she was a goddess and Cavanaugh and I were merely ghosts. The AI was working away in the background, spinning plates and turning gears, no longer affecting one brain at a time. The nanites had hinted that they were working on a project but to what end I could not envision.

Cavanaugh stayed by my side, so close I thought he wanted to hold my hand. Full of nervous energy that had no place to go, his body shook as we made our way, letting Chloe, sick and exhausted, set the slow pace. "I spaced out there for a minute," Cavanaugh said in an urgent whisper. "Did you, uh, did you see anything? Just now?"

"No idea what you're talking about."

"Something popped up I hadn't thought of in years. My first business deal … I, uh …."

"Spit it out."

"I won, he lost, that's all."

"Who?"

"Doesn't matter. It was a business deal where I came out ahead, way ahead. I saw myself walking away from the conference table with my lawyers, contract in hand. The details were so clear, I even noticed the wallpaper pattern. Felt like I'd robbed a bank. I had to get out of there to celebrate, before somebody called the cops."

"So?"

"I didn't see it like it was my memory. It was the guy on the raw end of the deal seeing me as I was. Worse, I felt what he felt. I didn't care for that feeling. It didn't look or feel good this time. I didn't like myself."

"I don't like you, either. I imagine your best friends see you the same way."

"I don't have friends. I have business associates and people who work for me."

"I'm shocked."

"Damn. Almost forgot you're a prick cop."

"I never forget what you are, Cavanaugh."

"I'm a zombie. You did that to me."

"You're chattering like a squirrel on meth so, no, I didn't make you a zombie. I made you a hybrid. If I hadn't, you wouldn't be giving me an ear beating now. Next time you feel like complaining, give it to me in the form of interpretive dance."

"You think this is the time to joke?"

Chloe looked back at me and beamed a wide smile that reminded me of the healthy young woman she had been. Her grin was only slightly marred by the fact that her gums were bleeding. "We're walking through a surreal hellscape. I can't think of a better time to make a joke. Thanks, Dan!"

She reached the door to get back into the complex. With one hand on the door handle, Chloe paused to tilt her face to the sun. She closed her eyes, perhaps to enjoy the heat.

A dark intuition hit me. One day, everyone arrives at the same place and time. Everyone has a last glance at the sky, a final look at life above ground. Chloe knew this was her last chance to appreciate a clear azure sky and to feel sun on her skin. To her credit, she didn't linger long.

CHAPTER 49

CHLOE

The door to the compound closed behind us. We found ourselves in a wide windowless corridor lit sporadically by yellow emergency lights. "What's that smell?" I asked.

"Cordite," Cavanaugh said. "There's been a lot of gunplay around here."

"Cordite hasn't been used since 1945," Harmon corrected him. "You're smelling propellant."

"So, in other words, lots of gunplay, Mr. Smartypants."

Daniel pointed at the floor. "Blood trails." He lifted his chin, sniffed the air and pointed down the long corridor, into darkness. "There's a lot more blood that way."

Despite the gloom, the blood on the floor shone like a pool of fresh ink. I felt a passing urge to get down on my hands and knees and lick it up like a kitten lapping up cream. The Nannies in my head were busy at their work, changing me. I wished they'd remedy my nausea but maybe that was a psychological reaction to the thought of licking blood off the floor. More likely, it was the radiation sickness.

"Which way do we go?" I asked Cavanaugh.

He pointed into the darkness just as Daniel had.

Of course, I thought. If this were a haunted house movie, we'd be running toward the ominous screams instead of getting the hell out. "Let's go, guys. I still feel like shit so let me set the pace. I'll try not to walk too slow but — "

"You're the boss, Doc," Daniel said. "Take your time. I'm in no hurry to find out what's down there."

"Coming to the end of the line, aren't we?" Cavanaugh asked.

"Calm down, Cavanaugh," Daniel said (but obviously meant, "Shut up.")

The executive's reply surprised me. "I wish I could have seen Queen in concert. I only saw Springsteen once. At the time, I thought I'd follow him on tour. People do."

"After all you've done, that's your regret?" Daniel asked.

"Not just that. I had a chance to see Bowling for Soup and passed it up. Oh, yeah, and the death and destruction of the world thing. That was … sub-optimum."

I chuckled. Daniel didn't look at all amused.

"Lighten up, Harmon," Cavanaugh said. "We walked through Hell. Somehow, we're still here."

"The military will be here soon," Daniel said. "When war comes to Bainbridge Island, it's going to get really ugly. The compound wasn't Hell. That was Hell's lobby."

"They'll lock it down," Cavanaugh said.

"Like you thought you could?"

"They have more resources."

"Resources don't matter when it comes to Picasso. I learned that the hard way."

Cavanaugh's tone didn't disguise his contempt. "C'mon. This isn't Toronto. Bainbridge is an island. The disease will end here. Up north, they'll just have to hunt down every single one of those infected bastards individually, I guess."

Daniel shook his head. "Despite everything you've seen, you still don't get it. Force won't stop Picasso."

"It's not just the bullets to bodies ratio that makes Daniel right,"

I argued. "Diseases are dumb and unmotivated yet they've decimated populations throughout history. Now we're dealing with an evolving breed of nanites armed with a plan to take over."

"Played with fire, got burned," Cavanaugh replied listlessly.

The corridor angled down. Walking downhill was a little easier on my lungs but my knees ached more.

As we passed under an emergency light, I noticed that Cavanaugh had gone pale. I could smell his clammy sweat. I wondered if exposure to me was taxing his system. "You okay, Michael?"

"Fine, just thinking too much. I get that you're worried that some old men somewhere are debating how many live specimens they'll need for further study and national security. I understand you think this will keep spreading. I know high-placed people. I can negotiate with them, make them understand — "

"Like you listened to me when we got here?" I asked.

Doubt crept into Cavanaugh's tone. "We may be zombies but we aren't like those things out there. You said it yourself, Harmon. We're hybrids. Our nanites are better than those nanites."

"You say you know people," Daniel said. "Military contractors, just like you, will want us in their back pocket for use as organic weapons. Most of Picasso had been spread by saliva and blood contamination but Hamish Allen figured out how to aerosolize brain parasites. Somebody will do that again. Bet on it. Even if we could contain it a while, Picasso will get out. The AI uses our brains against us. When you can't trust your own brain, you're toast."

Something thick had built up at the back of my mouth. I cleared my throat and spit it out, a black, shiny wad of blood and mucus. I hoped the AI was doing something to combat my illness but I still wasn't feeling any better. What the hell was it up to?

I stopped for a moment to lean against the wall. The men waited as I caught my breath. "How far to the nanite lab?"

"Not far now," Cavanaugh said.

Daniel wasn't done with Cavanaugh. "Once the forces who are on their way clean up this place, do you suppose they'll kill you or lock you up right here?"

"A prisoner in a dungeon of my own kingdom? I hate to give you the satisfaction, but maybe I deserve it."

"Oh?"

"I'd prefer imprisonment to getting shot, I think, but it would make sense this is where my road ends. It occurs to me, I've been kind of an asshole." He looked at each of us for a beat and gave an embarrassed grin.

If Cavanaugh was hoping for one of us to disagree, he was disappointed.

"The nanites changed your mind," Harmon said.

"By literally changing your brain," I added.

"Do I get any credit for saying so?"

"Depends," Harmon said. "Did they make you say it?"

"I don't know."

We got going again and stayed quiet until the moment we came around a curve in the dark tunnel. Daniel must have heard the soft click or clank of a weapon. Maybe he heard our attacker breathing. Faster than I could process, he leapt on me as he screamed, "Down!"

He dropped his rifle to pull me to the floor and rolled us to the wall to my right, out of the line of fire. As gunfire boomed and echoed down the tunnel I felt like I was in Death's throat, swallowed whole. Daniel shielded me with his body. I heard him grunt and shudder as concrete chunks came out of the wall to our left.

Then Cavanaugh's screams replaced the drumbeat of gunfire.

CHAPTER 50

DANIEL

It seemed to take Cavanaugh a moment to process the shock that he'd been hit. Then the pain thundered through him. Clutching at his left hand, he rolled on the floor in agony.

My back stung between my shoulder blades and over my left kidney. When I reached back to check the wound, my hand came away wet with blood but not so much I was concerned. The stinging went away quickly as the nanites went to work shutting down the pain signals ripping through my nerves.

As soon as the gunfire stopped I eased off Chloe and got up on my hands and knees. In her fragile state I worried that I'd hurt her. At least she wasn't bleeding from a gunshot wound.

The bushwhacker had chosen his spot well. With an emergency light burning behind us as we reached the curve in the tunnel, we made perfect targets in silhouette. Though my vision was different now and my eyes had adjusted to the dark, I'd only caught a glint of dim light off the sights of the rifle a split second before the attack.

The gunman was also clever enough to keep advancing as he fired. The rifle I dropped was within reach but our attacker was too close now. He had Chloe in his sights. I left my weapon where it was, only a few feet away but useless.

"Sonofabitch!" Cavanaugh yelled. "You shot me! What next? What next?"

The man with the rifle peered down at us. "Michael? Is that you?"

When Chloe raised her head I heard a tendon in her neck snap over bone. She shifted and got up on her elbows to peer up at the shooter as he stepped into the light.

"I recognize that voice," she told me. "I met him in Aruba."

The big man loomed up, casually swinging the muzzle of his rifle from right to left as if deciding who to shoot first, eeny-meeny style.

"Doug! It's me, Chloe Robinson! Daniel Harmon, meet Doug Hannah. This is Michael's boss."

I heard hope in Chloe's voice. Judging by the way he held his weapon, I felt no optimism that our trepidations were at an end. "Mr. Hannah, I think you and your company have some serious issues that need to be taken up with HR."

At least he laughed. I hoped to disarm him figuratively, then literally. He didn't lower his weapon and he kept at a safe distance as I rose slowly, hands up. I waited for him to nod his approval before I helped Chloe to her feet.

"Hello again, Chloe," Hannah said. "It seems like ages since we met at the Aruba conference. A lot can happen in a couple of days. Last I saw you, you poured a bottle of wine down Michael's pants. He didn't like it but I thought it was pretty funny. Glad you're here. It's about time you guys showed up. I followed your progress as much as I could on the surveillance cameras. They aren't all still functional."

"You shot me, Doug!" Cavanaugh shrieked.

"Yeah … sorry about that. I got some practice with firing this AR-15 last night. It's surprisingly enjoyable."

"Can I check his wound?" I asked.

Hannah flicked his head an inch. "Go ahead, Mr. Harmon."

"You know who I am?"

"Who and what, sure."

I knelt beside Cavanaugh. I had to yank his hand away to assess the wound to his left forearm. "It's isn't bad. You haven't been hit. It's cuts from wall debris. Lucky."

"Lucky, my ass! That hurts!" Cavanaugh complained.

"There's barely any blood."

"It hurts, though."

"Wait a minute."

"But — "

"Wait."

A moment passed in silence before Cavanaugh brightened. "It is starting to feel better." He pulled his hand away and stared at his arm in amazement. "The blood stopped."

"The wound's closing," I said.

"It feels weird but it is getting better," he marveled. "No stitches needed! Nanites are doing their thing!"

Hannah stepped a little closer to get a better look as he raised his rifle. "So you're infected. Given all that's gone on, I thought there was a good chance you'd get bitten out there."

"Don't shoot him," Chloe said. "We're all infected but it's under control. We've got the strain of nanites from Toronto but we've got the evolved strain of Picasso, too."

"I'm not even hungry," I lied. "I promise I won't eat your face."

Cavanaugh smiled wider. "I feel no pain! I'm new and improved!"

Hannah returned his employee's smile. "Excellent, Michael. That's simply excellent."

"Doug? You can put down the gun."

"How many rounds do you think you could take, Michael?"

"What?"

"Could all the king's horses and all the king's men put Humpty together again if I shot you some more?"

"I don't — "

"It's a rhetorical question, Michael." Hannah shot Michael twice in the stomach.

Cavanaugh gasped in surprise and pain but said nothing.

Hannah seemed to study his employee, waiting to see if the nanites could save him from his vicious wounds. Cavanaugh's eyes rolled up until I saw the whites of his eyes as he passed out from the shock.

Hannah shook his head. "That's probably a few million dollars worth of research money bleeding out on the floor. *Hmph*."

Leaning on the wall, Chloe closed her eyes. "Why would you do that, Doug? I thought you were a good guy."

"I think I'm a good guy, too. Just because I have manners doesn't make me a good guy. Common mistake. I'll leave it to history to decide. History doesn't hold much interest for me. I spend my time thinking about the future. I am sorry you had to witness that but I didn't think you cared. I sure didn't like him."

"I didn't like him but he's a human being," Chloe said.

"That's clearly not true anymore. To answer your question of why, it's time to run an important experiment. If it goes well, Michael's death will have been unfortunate. I need someone to blame should things go awry, though, so he has to be erased from the equation."

As Cavanaugh began to stir, Hannah shot him in the head twice.

"Don't look at me like that, Chloe," Hannah said. "One in five people is a psychopath. Twenty-percent of CEOs are psychopaths. It's a huge competitive advantage. The stuff that other people are afraid to get done? People like me get it done."

"*Another* psychopath?" I sighed. "They're as thick as zombies around here. I blame the internet. Psychopaths never used to hang out in such large packs. The company's HR department must have recruited staff using Monster.com."

Hannah pointed the rifle at me. "You're funny. Shall I shoot you in the head so it'll be quick?" He had an ugly laugh.

"You don't need to do that," Chloe said. "This place is on fire and everything's gone to shit. I might be able to help but I won't if you shoot him."

"Maybe I should just shoot him in the knee so he won't make any trouble." Hannah pursed his lips as if in deep thought but I knew he was just messing with me.

"Can you give me a minute to think about it?" I asked.

Hannah shrugged. "What's there to think about?"

"I don't know. The nanites may have ideas."

"The nanites — "

"They talk to him," Chloe said.

Hannah's eyebrows shot up. "You converse? Directly?"

"They're chatty from time to time."

"That's interesting. What do they say?"

I stood still, closed my eyes and asked a question with a thought. When I opened my eyes I stared down the muzzle of Hannah's AR-15.

"I would very much like to learn more about your interactions with the AI. Mine don't talk to me."

"The nanites did have an idea."

"Oh?"

"Reinforcements are on the way," I said.

"I'm aware the military will be here soon, in force," Hannah conceded. "By then, it won't matter, though. Given Mr. Cavanaugh's history, he'll make an easy scapegoat."

Far off, I heard the door to the compound bang open. In a moment, Chloe and Hannah heard it, too: The sound of running feet pounding through the tunnel toward us. The zombie horde was outraged that their Mother was in danger.

"When I said reinforcements are on the way, I wasn't talking about your army. I was talking about Chloe's."

The big man's fat face paled at the howling din pouring down the tunnel, a wave of death. Soon, the flood would envelop us. Hannah grabbed Chloe by the back of the neck and put the muzzle of his rifle to her spine, prodding her forward. "You'll be useful as hostages if nothing else. Michael wanted to know what's next. Come with me and I'll show you. We have a puzzle to solve."

EPISODE 6

horror (noun)

Rage and sadness inspired by the great distance between what is and what ought to be.

~

imperialism (noun)

The insistence, accompanied by force, that one subjective experience must be shared universally.

~ Notes from NEXT

CHAPTER 51

CHLOE

Fortunately for Hannah, he hadn't strayed far from safety. We were only a few steps away from the great steel door that guarded the lab. The rampaging cannibals screaming down the tunnel would arrive too late to stop his retreat to refuge. Without taking his eyes off us, the big man placed his bare hand on a sensor plate. The device scanned his palm with a thin beam of light. Unseen mechanisms clicked and whirred. As the thick vault door swung open, a fist of heated air rushed out.

"In. Now. Thank you for delivering Michael to me. That couldn't have worked out much better."

"You got your sacrificial goat," I said.

"He had a bigger vision than most but Michael still didn't understand the true potential of the Artificial Intelligence."

"It's a disease," Daniel said.

"I know it appears so, but it's not the problem. It's the solution."

"To what?" Daniel asked.

Hannah pushed me forward and used his rifle to wave Daniel

into the lab. "To everything, of course. Human nature, poverty, war … all kinds of foolishness."

As the vault door began to close, I saw the first of the zombie mob racing to our rescue. It was a young African American man, tall and lanky. He wore camo and a determined look on his face. He did not appear to slow down before the door closed on him. Though I assumed he hit the vault door, we could detect no sound from the tunnel. The zombie screams were silenced.

A small vestibule housed bomb sniffing scanners. The devices whirred as refreshing jets of cool air blew over us to dislodge dust particles. My sleeves billowed out under the sudden pressure and, for a few seconds, I was relieved of the lab's oppressive heat.

The sniffers were set to detect traces of explosive material. We'd been around too many discharged firearms so a pulsing alarm sounded for each of us. At the noise, a shiver shot up my spine. My mother would say somebody had just walked over my grave.

Hannah shut off the alarm and waved us through. The vinyl curtain at the end of the vestibule parted and we followed him. He never took his eyes or his gun off us as we stepped into a huge room. Though the rest of the complex had been overrun and left without power, the bulbs above us burned with a dazzling light. The dimensions of the space could have housed eight basketball courts easily.

To our right, through sliding glass doors, I spotted an assortment of machines similar to the layout of my own lab, all designed to create, gestate and program nanotechnology. Nyx had devoted many more resources to their lab. My lab back home was tiny by comparison.

It was not the nanotech laboratory that drew the eye, however. Before us sat three Olympic-sized pools. The surface of each dim pool was covered with what I assumed was some sort of thick glass. At first glance any layman would have assumed the pools were filled with water. However, the pools were filled with a pale green biomimetic gel.

"Impressed yet?" Hannah asked.

I shrugged. Even that small movement gave me a sharp pain in the middle of my back. I wondered why the nanites weren't doing more for me.

"Well, Chloe?"

Hannah seemed eager for admiration. "I just realized how underfunded my work was," I admitted.

"That's not half of it." Hannah pulled a remote from his pocket, pointed it to our left and pressed a button. A portion of the wall slid back to reveal more conventional tech. A box, as black and shiny as hematite and as big as a cube van, sat amid a maze of pipes and whirring fans. I guessed what it was but didn't understand its purpose. "That reminds me of pictures I've seen of the first computer banks."

"A computer bank?" Daniel echoed. "Really? That's really old school, isn't it?"

"The first machines with any computing power took up much more space than this," Hannah said.

"Why not just network your computers?"

"The first iteration of any new technology is always much bigger, more expensive and clumsier than what it's destined to become, Mr. Harmon. You're unfamiliar with it. That doesn't mean it's not incredibly elegant."

Daniel looked furious but did not reply.

"Its core is a nanite drive, isn't it?" I asked.

"Exactly," Hannah said proudly. "A computer bank powered by nanotech. The nanites grown in the gel in these pools form a brain modeled on the vast complexity and interconnectivity of the human brain. We have always referred to computers as if they worked like human brains. That was a clumsy metaphor based on a childish understanding of technology. Until recently, computers have been little more than glorified data sorters. The next generation of AI is miles ahead of its predecessors. Nanites take us to the height of predictive AI. It doesn't just have speed. It has depth."

Daniel took a step toward the massive computer and Hannah raised his weapon. "Don't even think about doing anything to that machine, Mr. Harmon. I doubt you could do much damage to it but don't annoy me. I am very curious to speak with you but you aren't indispensable."

"How do you figure you'll get away with all this, Doug?" I asked.

"Simple. I'm going to change everything you think you know. What's more, everyone will thank me for it."

Daniel looked at me. "What do you think? He seems to have a fantasy that nothing can touch him. Would you call him a megalomaniac with a side of narcissistic personality disorder? I hated Cavanaugh, but at least old Mike had the good sense to be scared."

I looked from the nanite pool to the nano drive and back to the automatic weapon in Hannah's hands. "No, Daniel, I think there's an indecent chance he's going to get away with it. Guys like him almost always do."

CHAPTER 52

DANIEL

"What do you want from us, Doug?" I asked. "Is this a Bond villain thing where you show off and give us a tour of your underground lair before you kill us?"

"I'd like a chat with you and I need her expertise. As hybrids carrying both Picasso strains, you could boost our understanding of the relationship between the nanites. I suspect the first strain from Toronto connects with the lizard brain and the next strain of Picasso connected with executive functions of the neocortex."

"Who cares?"

"For science and a taste of immortality. I would also very much like to understand the rate at which the AI in your head is developing, much like carbon dating an evolutionary artifact. Our working hypothesis is the more the AI grows and learns and interconnects the faster its evolution. I'm incredibly intrigued by what happened out in the compound. I caught you three on video. You walked through the center of a huge group of cannibals."

"Like recognizes like, I guess," Chloe said.

"They stepped back to let you go. They all but pointed the way for you. And just now, hoping for rescue, you called them, didn't you, Mr. Harmon? You asked me why I didn't build a computer network but you're already part of a network. Care to explain?"

"Hey, man. I'm just a cop for a city that doesn't exist anymore. It takes me a whole weekend to put IKEA furniture together."

Hannah turned to Chloe. "Can you explain?"

"The nanites figured out how to access a factor that was already written into our biology and exploit it. Each infected person is connected to a neural network."

"Connected by what?"

"A common energetic field or frequency, maybe. This is all new to me," Chloe said.

"I've been injected," Hannah said. "I've had no interaction with the nanites and I've sensed no such connection. Neither did Heather Clover."

"The nanites that interacted with brain parasites are the ones that came up with the plug for that socket," I said. "Beyond that, I can't fill you in. No easy answers here, this isn't *Shaun of the Dead*. I loved that movie though, to be honest, *Zombeavers* was more my speed."

"Not the time, Daniel," Chloe said.

"Sounds like nonsense to me," Hannah told Chloe.

I mimicked Hannah's grandiose tone, "Just because you don't understand it doesn't mean it's not elegant. This Artificial Intelligence is tech that functions on a whole new level. It doesn't just have speed. It has depth."

Chloe intervened, probably to help me avoid getting shot for being sassy. "What do you want, Doug?"

Hannah's gaze strayed to the gigantic pools. "I need you to reprogram the nanotech. These nanites get nutrition through pipes from an algae pool above us — "

I brightened. "So that's the dirty green pool I saw when we landed! I wouldn't have guessed it was a feeding trough. I thought your pool boy was slacking off."

"Nanites have to be fed. I suspect the filters failed. The pools are contaminated."

"Where'd all your staff go?" Chloe asked.

The big man's shoulders sank. "When we began to lose the complex, I sent them out to support the security staff."

"He means he forced the nerd squad out at gunpoint to become zombie chow," I said.

"Or to become zombies," Chloe said.

"I honestly thought we could overwhelm them with more numbers on our side. I ordered them to get weapons from the armory and fight for control," Hannah said.

"And you fed the machine instead," I said.

"Picasso infects more people than it kills now," Chloe told him. "Curious, isn't it? Have you wondered how they choose their victims? They killed Dr. Clover in front of us — "

"Maybe the AI thought she deserved it," I suggested.

"I gotta tell you, I'm exhausted. I need to sit the hell down." Chloe limped over to an office chair. She appeared to be past caring whether she lived or died. Once she achieved something closer to comfortable, Chloe took on a professorial tone. "They aren't dumb animals, Doug. Animals kill out of necessity. Since the evolved AI asserted itself, it's feeding but it's also making more hosts to replicate itself. Species survive because they find food and shelter. Once those basic needs are met, they reproduce. The nanites aren't just preventing their extinction. They're thriving."

"Humans, not so much," I said.

Chloe stared at Hannah for a beat. She seemed to study him so I did the same. His wide pockmarked face shone with sweat. The lab was hot but perspiration slipped from beneath his ridiculous wig in streams. His breathing was even more labored than Chloe's. Something was wrong with him.

"The military will be here soon. I have to get the drive working before they arrive."

"Something more valuable than all of Toronto to bargain with?" I asked. "To keep you out of jail?"

Hannah chuckled. "No, I'm not worried about jail. I'm more concerned with my reputation and legacy."

"Your legacy? How long have you been working on the nanite

drive? You didn't whip up this lab in a couple of days," Chloe said. "When did you build all this?"

"That's not your real question," Hannah said. "You really want to know how long ago we hacked your research."

"Industrial espionage and the perversion of my work has been on my mind."

"Four years. We got mass production of nanites ready in just four years."

"By stealing AFTER and cutting corners. You wanted the tech all for yourself and here we are."

"We formed a community around the tech to perfect it."

"It doesn't look perfect yet."

"I wish I'd come to you first, actually. Three years ago I approached researchers in Finland with a wad of grants and a bold proposal."

"Three years?" Chloe's eyes went wide in shock. "How did you get past the blood-brain barrier problem?"

"Direct implantation." Hannah reached up and pulled off his toupee. The Velcro ripped as he peeled the wig from his head. His bald scalp was crisscrossed with thick, mean scars and part of his skull looked cratered in on the right side.

"Radical brain surgery," Chloe said.

He tossed the wig on the floor. "My cognitive function was enhanced. The AI helped me contribute to the construction of the world's first nanite drive AI computer. My IQ went up 20 points."

"Still not enough, huh?" Chloe said. "Nothing is ever enough for guys like you."

"You don't feel like you're part of the network, or field or whatever?" I asked.

Tired, in pain and impatient, Chloe rolled her eyes. "Different strain, Daniel. The primitive brain structures would be inoperable. No parasites, no access to the hive mind."

"Help me perfect it," Hannah said. "Once we've fixed the feed from the pool, the nano drive will be clear of bugs. It will mimic my neocortical structure to construct a new holographic extrapolation to build the rest of the bioenergetic matrices."

"And what will it do in English?" I asked. "Could you explain it with a cartoon and a catchy song?"

Hannah seemed pleased to pontificate. "A computer is chips and circuits. The drive models the interconnections of the brain, then improves upon them. Housed in that black box will be something new: a living brain more powerful than any known computer. Quantum computers will probably outpace nanite drives someday. However, it will be our biological AI that designs those quantum computers and make them available for sale at the local mall. I'm older than you. I don't have time to wait. I have to rush to make that future happen."

"You're messing with forces you don't understand," Chloe said. "I kept AFTER on a leash because it has the potential to become an Artificial Intelligence that's too advanced."

"How could it be 'too advanced?'" I asked. "Isn't that the point of it?"

"AI that's become too advanced isn't Artificial Intelligence anymore. It's Alien Intelligence."

"Precisely why AFTER is so perfect," Hannah said. "It's modeled on the human brain!"

"At first, yeah," Chloe said. "But what you did wasn't so perfect, was it? The brain surgery had side effects you didn't count on, am I right?"

Hannah looked to me and winked. Without his ridiculous toupee, he'd become a much more intimidating monster. "I knew I should have gone straight to Dr. Robinson first instead of consulting the Finns. You're right. The treatment gave me Cushing's Syndrome."

"It gave you what now?" I asked.

"Let me guess," Chloe said. "The nanites were programmed to boost your acetylcholinesterase inhibitor to jack up your memory and learning performance. That spiked your adrenocorticotropic hormone which kicked your cortisol production way too high and bing, bam, boom, you've got Cushing's Syndrome."

"Ironically, your paper in *Molecular Neurobiology* warned of the danger about a month after I had the surgery. I wish you had published your research faster, too."

"See, this is why we can't have nice things," Chloe said.

"We were almost ready to bring it online, hook it up to the internet and take it for a spin," Hannah said. "The feed from the pool is the final glitch. Our test runs were perfect. There's already a colony in the black box and it seems to be functioning at 100%."

"What's it doing in there?"

"Preparing the substrate for the neural modeling."

"Whose brain?" Chloe asked.

"Mine, of course."

"Of course."

"The contamination only showed up in the last few hours. Go ahead. Have a look. You can see it."

"What do you mean I can see it?" Chloe stepped closer to the edge of the first pool.

I ambled toward the edge, pretending Hannah didn't have a gun on me. I detected some movement beneath the thick protective cover.

Something swam up through the gel and Chloe startled in fright. "Jesus! I expected a bacterial bloom, like in an aquarium!"

The creature retreated back into the depths of the pool. I'd barely glimpsed the thing but I knew what it looked like. "Dude! You got eels in your swimming pool!"

"Not eels, Daniel," Chloe said. "Nanite strings."

"The stuff that nightmares are made of?"

"I've seen them under a microscope. They're supposed to stay microscopic."

Hannah couldn't conceal his irritation. "That pool should only contain raw stem cell nanites."

"I take it they're only supposed to get wriggly and thinky in your big black box?" I asked.

"The covers on the nanite pools are made of Perspex, same as the windows on a jet," Hannah said. "Michael assured me they were careful but those clever little bio-bots obviously found something to model new structures. Some are more than twelve feet long and as thick around as a fat man's thigh."

Another construct — ugly, brown and bigger than the first — thumped hard against the cover of its prison.

"What do you suppose is the source of the contamination?" Hannah asked Chloe.

I answered instead. "I don't know, but I can tell you what it wants. It wants the same as all nanites. It wants to come out and play."

"It wants what you want," Chloe said. "It wants to feed, to live and to take over."

CHAPTER 53

CHLOE

The construct reminded me of a big, ugly catfish coming to the surface to feed. It thumped against the cover again, not a meter away. I felt such revulsion I almost threw up. Or maybe that was just me dying.

Hannah glanced my way. "They could introduce random variables into the drive. I want the matrix to be based on my thought patterns, not some weird nudibranch."

"Nudie what?" Daniel gave a crooked grin which made me think the nanites could improve him physically and mentally, but he'd always be in touch with his inner thirteen-year-old boy.

"Nudibranch," Hannah explained, "the biological classification of a sea slug."

"Nifty. You're a walking Wikipedia."

"Since my brain surgery, I've read a lot of research in many areas of science. When the drive is fixed, I'll download everything. The possibilities are so damn exciting. Once I figure out how this new connection you have works, I suppose I'll be able to connect with the drive, no wires required."

Daniel bobbed his head. "Zombie wifi?"

"I will interface with the world," Hannah said.

"And run everything."

"Governments have had their chance. They've failed to respond to the challenges of our time. To repair all that is ruined, I believe an evolved society is in need of a benevolent dictator," Hannah said. "I am that person."

"I'd feel more confidence in you if you hadn't just murdered your second-in-command," I said.

"Eggs and omelettes," Hannah replied. "The pool has to be cleared. Will you help me?"

I swayed on my feet but my voice was strong. "Why should I?"

Hannah looked me up and down. "Michael called while you were changing. He told me you were exposed to a lot of radiation and not doing well. I'm very sorry to hear that. Are the nanites helping you?"

I answered honestly. "I can breathe a little better, I think, but I still feel like shit."

"Mr. Harmon was on the same plane yet he looks quite well."

"He had the nanites working on his body before he was exposed to the radiation. I didn't get bitten early enough. Too bad I didn't get infected earlier — "

"The thing you feared most would have saved you. Let go of your fear and help me now. If you reprogram those constructs to disperse, I can make it all work."

"Make it work? What does that even mean?" I demanded. "The AI wants to spread, to turn everyone into zombies. What exactly do you want to do with it?"

"This technology is a weapon but it's also a tool," Hannah argued. "I'm not a monster. You people, always stuck in binary thinking, always thinking in terms of right or wrong. There are so many more opportunities once you stop limiting your perceptions. You can't be free when you allow yourself so few possible responses. Imagine all those people out there who need the evolved Picasso strain. We could empty out all the hospitals and put doctors and nurses out of work forever."

"How do you picture that happening?" Daniel asked.

"Control the AI, control the world," Chloe said. "Shit, you were right, Daniel. He is a Bond villain."

"The AI has already figured out how to network human minds. A human has to be in control or we'll be at the mercy of non-human intelligence."

"Human intelligence isn't so great," Daniel said. "Look where it's got us."

"You'll have to expand your vision to accommodate a more flexible worldview. Time you two grew up. The equipment to program nanites is right over there. I suggest you take a vial from the freezer and get to work. Destroy those slugs. And Daniel? I want to hear about every conversation you've had with the AI."

The more Hannah talked, the more he puffed up, so proud and so confident he was going to be the messiah at the top of a new technocracy. Breathing hard, I took a seat before bending forward to pull off my sneakers. Bones in my back creaked at the effort.

"What are you doing, Chloe?"

I had to straighten and rest before bending to pull off my socks, slowly and painfully. "My ankles are so swollen, I've got cankles. Every joint is aching. I'm just about done, not up to playing your reindeer games. Suppose I stay on the bench and sit out this last inning, Coach? Work it out for yourself."

"I've tried solving the issue on my own. My attempts have failed."

"Maybe they don't like you," Daniel said. "I don't."

Hannah sighed and brandished his rifle. "Fine. I tried to be reasonable but the future is not created by reasonable people. You need motivation? Here's my ultimatum: Cooperate or I'll shoot Daniel in the ankles. I might wait for him to heal a little. We'll see if his agony softens your high and mighty principles. Then I'll kneecap him, and so on. Use your imagination. You're good at that."

"There's the guy who is sure he's not a monster," Daniel said.

"Told you. Guys like him usually get away with it." I struggled to stand.

The cool tile felt good on my bare feet. I limped through sliding glass doors to the lab's programming station, taking my time, listening to the AI in my head. My nanites had a strategy to stop Doug Hannah. Even if the plan worked perfectly, I would die faster than radiation poisoning could kill me.

CHAPTER 54

DANIEL

Doug Hannah wasn't stupid. He did not drop his guard. He stayed close enough that he wouldn't miss. He stayed far enough away that, even with my enhanced reflexes and strength, I couldn't get to him before he squeezed the trigger. Worse, his nanites were different from mine. Despite suffering Cushing's disease, for all I knew the AI in his head might have enhanced his reflexes, too.

If I was going to have any hope of getting to him, I needed a distraction. Talking baseball probably wasn't going to do it. I closed my eyes and asked the AI for help. I thought it would be useful if the lights went out. Even better? What if a crack squad of zombie ninjas blew the door open and tossed in a few flash grenades? Double points if a zombie sniper takes out Doug Hannah, one shot, one kill. The nanotech in my head did not reply.

"Tell me about your conversations with the AI," Hannah said.

I chewed my bottom lip. "Imagine if Alexa was an alien who barely understands how humans think and doesn't much approve of how we think. Facts, it gets. Emotions and how normal people relate to each other is opaque to the nanites. Picasso changes anyone who carries it. For instance, I'm pretty sure that's the first time I've used the word opaque in a sentence."

"I'm interested in facts. Your response, though interesting, is somewhat disappointing."

"Man, when you get to have conversations with the AI, it'll be hard to tell you two apart."

Hannah kept his gun on me and I waited patiently, expecting to get shot but in no hurry. The longer we stood in silence, the more awkward the situation became. I watched Chloe through the windows to the next lab. She limped back and forth between freezers, a computer terminal and an array of beakers and microscopes. There were several large machines that mystified me. They did have wide plasma screens that magnified whatever she was doing to eliminate the monsters in the pool. She did not look my way once. I guessed that single-minded focus was how she'd become the person she was.

"The lab isn't what I expected," I said. "I pictured … I don't know. Soldering irons and an assembly line for tiny circuit boards or something?"

"Nano machines are measured in millionths of a millimeter, you clod." Hannah's laugh sounded like gears grinding. I hoped he wouldn't do that again. "AFTER's signature breakthrough was to make nano machines that bridge the gap between the mechanical and the biological. Adriano Cavalcanti proposed a model for treating brain aneurysms with a nanorobot in 2009. Chloe Robinson changed the game with a process to use nanites as programmable stem cells. Only the first generation actually has an electromechanical component."

"What happens then? Magic?"

"Then nanites use the body's resources to make nanites. Neobiology reorganizes the legacy of DNA coding we were all born with."

"Sounds like magic."

"Not at all. We're all the result of coding on a cellular level. Nanotech rewrites the human book."

"And then you guys came along and made Chloe's book into a horror novel."

Hannah stopped smiling. "AFTER was a good beginning. Taking the training wheels off was inevitable. This was always bound to happen. It was never a question of if, but when."

The more he disliked me, the more I liked it. "While she's working on cleaning up your hard drive, can I ask you an obnoxious question?"

"Are you capable of any other kind?"

"You've already got more money than God, right?"

"You're wondering why I bother with all this when I could be on a beach enjoying wine, women and song."

"Yup."

"That's a poor person's question, Daniel. Despite the gifts this tech has given you — "

"Just tell me instead of trying to make me feel bad about myself?"

"Fine, I'll use small words. Poor people worry about getting more money. A person like me doesn't run a Fortune 500 company because I'm looking to retire to Tahiti someday. My life is a mission and that mission doesn't stop because it's successful. There's always more that can be done. People who don't understand that never get to my position. I started my first company selling common neural enhancers. I didn't develop any new pharmaceuticals that are truly safe but I found I could sell dangerous drugs to the military. Nanotech wouldn't pass with the FDA yet but the long-term safety of the individual isn't necessarily a prime concern when you're trying to keep a soldier awake and alert for seventy-two hours straight. It's not a new idea. Hitler's blitzkrieg troops used crystal meth."

"Uh-huh. Funny how you think all the bloodthirsty monsters are on the other side of that door."

The big man shrugged. "Nicotine enhances the firing of synapses. Doctors are on Adderall. Fighter pilots are on Provigil. Psychedelics that were once scary are now used to treat PTSD, depression, even addiction. Nootropic sales are way up among the general public. Ketogenic diets give people energy and better mental focus. Coffee got its big boost in World War II when the army stuffed its rations with the hot bean juice we all love. How many mornings have you gone without a caffeine kick to the day, Daniel? Everybody's doing it. Everyone wants a faster brain."

"You weren't hugged as a kid, were you?" I asked. "Were you a bedwetter, maybe? Disappointed your dear old dad? Struck out at a ball game?"

"It'll burn a lot of glucose, but thanks to my nanites, I'm going to choose to find you amusing."

Walking slowly and in obvious pain, Chloe returned from the lab with a large beaker in hand.

Hannah glanced at it skeptically. "That's it? That was quick."

"I've got the solution."

He pointed to what looked like a white desk with pipes running through it. It stood by the pool, back the way Chloe had come. "You can introduce the new nanites to the pool over there, beyond the filters."

"That's not going to get it done, Doug. I found out how the zombies decide who gets eaten entirely and who gets snacked on, who lives and who dies. The nanotech has achieved what it calls Cohesion. Every carrier of Picasso is in the network now."

"Explain," Hannah demanded.

"The AI has been tapping the collective unconscious to evaluate people. It wasn't much more than a common animal instinct at first. It's much more than that now. The AI is editing humanity."

Hannah frowned. "Who programmed that?"

"You called the nanites 'our biological AI.' The nano colonies are sentient. It's one big colony now. They don't belong to us. To survive, the AI will cohabitate with humans. Together, the new species makes the collective unconscious into a unified conscious force."

"Okay. That's what I want, too."

"If we do what it wants, we could have peace with the AI and with each other. "

"Yes! That will be my legacy. I can't wait to commune with the AI."

I figured the guy for a psychopath who believed his ends justified any means. Working in law enforcement, I'd seen that plenty. However, there was something so earnest about his tone, I believed him. It wasn't just about power for Doug Hannah. He wasn't a Bond villain or a freakish cartoon, after all. He was an aspirer whose vision was broken. When he talked about communing with the AI, he sounded like a kid who has just been told he's going to Disney.

Chloe looked grim. "The AI needs an avatar who can carry the neural load. We're going to have to convince the world that what started as a disease has evolved to become an ally. I'm sorry, Doug. It's been listening to you. The nanites don't want you. You don't qualify."

The vault door to the lab clicked, whirred and began to yawn open.

Hannah whirled. Chloe threw the liquid in the beaker in his face. He shrieked and rubbed at his eyes furiously. I hit the floor as he squeezed the trigger, spraying wildly and hitting the first wild-eyed woman through the door. He shot her in the jaw and she went down without a sound. A geyser of blood pumped from her ruined face.

With what little strength she had left, Chloe tried to grab the rifle. Hannah swatted her away easily and slammed her to the floor as more rabid zombies poured through the door. They charged him. Scanner alarms by the entry sounded and kept on blaring as the horde rushed in.

Covering my head with my hands, I rolled to the side to avoid getting shot or trampled. Hannah strafed the spot on the floor where I'd just been as the first zombie took him down and went for his throat. The rifle clattered to the floor. More zombies piled on. The man's screams became muffled. Eventually — too slowly — his struggles stopped.

Curious, I got to my feet and retreated to look for Michael Cavanaugh by the entrance. I expected to find him in the corridor, wounded and bloody. I imagined he'd managed to pull himself through the snarling crowd to get to the sensor plate to give the zombies access to the lab. I was mistaken. On the floor beneath the sensor plate lay his dismembered hand. His arm had been chewed off at the elbow but the biometric sensor had still registered his bloody palm. Through the Cohesion, our rescuers received the instructions they needed to get inside.

Doug Hannah had failed his test to become the avatar. However, the nanites and the psychopath had something in common. Neither was squeamish about the questionable ends justifying the gory means.

CHAPTER 55

CHLOE

Warm blood flowed from Doug Hannah's torn neck and gushed over my bare feet. I felt bad for him. Despite his flaws, he was only acting as best as he knew how. It just wasn't enough.

I made myself watch the zombies feast because I'd brought down Doug Hannah. He had kidnapped me at gunpoint. I had puttered around the lab, stalling to give the AI time to find a way past the lab's security. I threw a cleaning solution into my captor's eyes. Meant for sterilizing test tubes, the chemicals undoubtedly burned him. Bloodthirsty zombies had done the rest.

I wasn't sure how I felt or how I was supposed to feel. "I'd say sorry, Doug, but I don't know if I feel that way and what good does sorry do you now, anyway?"

With a helpful zombie at each elbow, I stepped onto the nanite pool's cover. A small woman scooped up Hannah's rifle. I glanced at her wounds. She'd been bitten on the face and arms but she was no longer bleeding. Our eyes met for a moment and I felt a connection, like an arc of electricity closing the small span between us. Her mind said, "Thank you," as she handed me the weapon. The rifle's weight was almost enough to make me fall over. I was weak before Hannah slammed me to the ground. Fresh pain wracked my body but I knew it wouldn't last long.

The zombies left me at the pool's edge. Alone, I made my way onto the pool. The cover bent under my weight and made popping sounds. However, the plastic did not break. I swayed as I padded out toward the middle. When I turned to look back on my trail of bloody footprints, the zombies were still feasting on Hannah's corpse.

How many people had died to bring me to this moment? How many millions of families would look back on the date Toronto was destroyed and mark the anniversary of the nuclear blast? For how many years? Would future generations someday look back and say the death of their ancestors was one of the costs of progress?

Daniel came to the edge of the pool. "Chloe?"

"Cavanaugh's dead, I know. I saw it all in my mind's eye."

He stared at me, wide-eyed and slack jawed.

"It's okay, Daniel."

"If you're doing what I think you're doing, stop! Just stop. You don't have to — "

"I think I do. Historians claim World War II brought about a revolution in technological progress. No one was happy about it but you can't deny war changes the course and speed of science. Maybe peace will spark even more progress. We haven't really tried that yet." I raised the rifle.

"Chloe! Don't!"

I squeezed the trigger and fired into the nanite pool's protective cover. With each round, the rifle's recoil pounded into my shoulder, a steady thud that made me throb with pain. The cover cracked and broke at my feet. I fell a few inches and the cool biomimetic gel rose over my ankles. Too soon, the rifle clicked empty.

I didn't fall through the cover. I smiled at Daniel and gave an embarrassed shrug at my failed attempt. Then two of the nanite constructs, long and brown and fat, thumped against the cover.

Daniel leapt onto the cover and ran toward me, arms pumping, faster than any normal human can run. Another construct joined the melee, bashing at the hole I'd made, widening the gap.

Daniel was almost on me, stretching out his hand to pull me back from fate when the constructs broke through. Their snakelike bodies wrapped around my legs. By reflex, I took one last breath, as deep as I could manage as they pulled me down and pulled me under.

As the watery gel closed over my head, Daniel's fingers slipped through my hair. I looked up to see the circle of light retreating above me. I'd seen that before. That day I fell through the ice so long ago was my first death. I'd been saved from drowning once. Twice seemed unlikely. Progress, like religion, demands sacrifice, sometimes a blood sacrifice.

Long shadows passed over my upturned face as several nanite constructs swam up to cover the hole I'd left behind. They blocked Daniel from swimming after me. I should have died under the ice when I was seven. I guess everything I'd done after that was bonus time.

I hadn't lived a long life. Considering all that had been done to pervert my work with AFTER, I couldn't say my time had been successful. I thought of my parents. Sorry, Mom. Sorry, Dad. I wish there was time to say goodbye. Thank you for my life. Sorry things didn't work out as planned, but, really, how often does that even happen?

I didn't have much air left. It was time to stop fighting the inevitable. I watched the bubbles rise up through the gel as I sank farther. The constructs wrapped around my waist and chest, squeezing until I opened my mouth. I opened my mouth and the slimy gel, bitter and salty, entered my mouth and invaded my lungs.

It takes three or four minutes to drown. I choked. My body tried to fight the end, to override my brain's commands. However, the spasms through my chest stopped abruptly as billions of microscopic nanites flooded my body and raced through my bloodstream.

No use fighting now, I thought. *I'm leaving my brain to science. Goodbye.*

CHAPTER 56

DANIEL

Repulsed and angry, I pounded the big nanite monsters with my bare fists. The rifle lay nearby. I picked it up to bash the ugly things. The muscular body of each construct seemed to have no head I could target. The constructs bore each of my strikes as if I was hitting a wall. They bobbed a little, but that was all.

The nanites could have stopped me. Instead, I got the feeling they were watching, giving me room to let the rage out. Eventually, the AI tried to get my attention. "Daniel?"

"I'm not in the mood for a chat right now," I said aloud. "Why'd you let that happen? You're so smart, why'd you let that happen?"

The AI remained silent.

"Well?"

"We thought you weren't in the mood for a chat."

"Just answer that one question. Why did you allow Chloe to die?"

"Dr. Robinson is part of a greater plan."

"That sounds suspiciously like 'God works in mysterious ways.'"

"We don't have enough data to express an educated opinion about that."

"Then shut up and help me save her."

"She is saved."

I ignored the voice in my head and went back to hitting the constructs, redoubling my efforts. In the distance, I heard an old-fashioned phone ring. It melted together with the bells ringing in my head. Sweat poured off me as my arms worked like pistons, pummeling the ugly constructs with many blows. I may as well have been swinging at empty air for all the effect I had. Despite my strength, I was helpless and useless.

Another voice penetrated the fog in my head. It was not spoken aloud but it wasn't the AI, either. *Daniel.* It was no more than a whisper.

"What?" I whirled and stood there panting and bug-eyed. Shelly Priyat stood by the nano drive. Dried blood caked her chin. Some of her long black hair and fallen out. Her uniform was wet with blood from where she'd been shot. She looked like a walking corpse. She said nothing and stared back at me with dead eyes. Her expression was inscrutable.

"Well …" I said, searching for words, "you look a *little* less dead than the last time I saw you."

She held out a phone. I made my way back to her and looked at the cracked screen. It was Cavanaugh's phone. The text told me the military had arrived on Bainbridge Island. They'd try to secure a base of operations in the small city before coming for us. There wasn't much time.

I looked back as the constructs dove away from the hole in the cover. I could make out Chloe's body vaguely through the gel at the bottom of the pool. A middle-aged man had pulled a sock and a shoe from Doug Hannah's corpse and was tearing into the dead man's bare foot with fervor.

I looked down at my hands, slick with the watery gel. I watched as it congealed in my palm, becoming thicker as the nanites connected with each other. The longer I watched, the thicker the liquid became. It changed to the color of mucus as it interacted with the natural oils of my bare hand.

"Are you little buggers making a glove for me?" I asked. "Gross."

The Voice answered. "The nanites are attempting to form a second skin that is more resistant to wounds."

Disgusted with the nanites and myself, I flicked the stuff back toward the pool and tried to wipe the gel off on my pants. Chloe Robinson was gone and I'd failed to save her. No hero, me.

"I'm hoping for a bullet to the head," I said. "I don't think I want to be part of a larger plan. If the nanites want to sew me a nice sports jacket, I take a 42 tall, though."

"Humor?" The Voice asked.

"If you have to ask, I guess not. You're much smarter than me. The military will be here soon to wipe everything out, swipe the technology — "

"And solve nothing. Our tribe is coming from the north."

"That sounded very *Game of Thrones*."

"Picasso will spread." The Voice left no room for doubt.

"What do we do?"

Shelly stepped forward, raised her arm and pulled up her sleeve to bare her forearm. To become a better conversationalist, she wanted the hybrid strain of Picasso. Her look was a silent plea.

"Like vaccination day at school," I said, "but with a little less terror and screaming."

"I understand that joke," the Voice said.

I sighed, leaned down and bit Shelly Priyat.

CHAPTER 57

CHLOE

Hello?

It's so dark I feel like the world has dropped down a hole and taken all the stars with it. I can't feel my body. It's as if I've become part of the darkness. There is no up or down. I am out of gravity, floating in an infinite void. I'm disoriented but oddly, I'm not worried. I'm relieved that my pain is over.

So, I thought, *this is death. It's weird. It's not so bad. But now what?*

As if in answer to my question, I sensed that I was moving. Far away, I heard the comforting sound of soft wind rustling through rushes. Though I could not feel where my limbs were in space, I was pulled by unseen forces, slowly at first and then much faster.

As I accelerated, I found myself in a tunnel, shooting through at tremendous speed. A bright white light waited at the end of that tunnel. What I'd thought was the sound of the wind was not the wind. It was a choir of voices.

The light grew bigger and brighter. Detached, I watched the scene unfold with curiosity. I felt no fear. I didn't have a body anymore, so what was there to fear? I arrived in the light with a sudden stop, unaffected by the sudden change in inertia.

Physics doesn't apply here, I thought.

I moved to shield my eyes but there was no hand and I had no eyes. I was consciousness, a phantom untethered.

The choir, invisible to me but close by, sang on. As I paid closer attention to the sound, it was less like the wind and more like a river. Concentrating, I could discern one voice, as if I was tuning a radio to one frequency. I did so and the voice was that of a woman.

Somehow I knew her name was Heather Lynne Thompson, a kind woman, an artist. She had four cats and she designed coloring books. She grew much of her own food and she missed her vegetable and flower gardens. At that moment, she was on a wide road among huge crowds of people headed south. The heat of the pavement baked through her shoes. A stranger had bitten her left leg below the knee. She limped a little, not out of pain but because the function of her calf muscles had been compromised. Heather, like the rest of the choir, carried Picasso. Beyond that, all the zombies had in common was confusion and fear.

She had so many questions. "What am I doing? Where are we going? Why did this happen?"

"I know why it happened but I don't understand why it had to," I told her. "Stupidity among people who were supposed to be smart, mostly."

For a second, she stiffened. Heather had heard me. For a moment, our minds were connected. Shocked, I pulled back and, though the choir of voices continued, the connection with Heather ended.

The Voice tells me in a soothing tone, "Do not be afraid."

I turn to the white light. "I know what this is. You're not God or St. Peter or whatever. I'm dead, but I'm not dead dead, am I?"

"In the resource pool, billions of stem cell nanites entered your dying body transdermally and through your bloodstream."

"The nanites zipped into my skull cavity and did some arts and crafts with my brain," I guess. "You made a copy. My body is rotting at the bottom of a pool of biomimetic gel but my mind lives on in a shiny black box."

"Your mind is quick."

"Why didn't you want Daniel?"

"Daniel Harmon taught us that we have deficiencies in interacting with humans and has contributed to our understanding of the average person's intelligence. However, his neural connections do not possess your speed."

"You must be this smart to ride this ride, huh? Damn it," I say. "If Daniel liked *Shaun of the Dead* more than *Zombeavers*, maybe he could be in this box instead of me."

I try raising my hand to my head and then remember I have neither a head nor a hand.

"Be patient. You are still registering proprioceptive feedback loops."

"Muscle memory and phantom limbs, sure."

"You will find your inclinations to physical gestures easier to ignore as you become more accustomed to your new biodigital environment."

"Hook me up with Skype and I could call my parents. 'Mom? Dad? Guess where I am?'"

"You are upset, Mother?"

"I expected the nanites to use my brain as a template for the drive. I didn't expect my consciousness to survive my body so … hmph. That's just great. No mimosas in nanotech heaven, I don't suppose? Assuming the bioelectrics don't degrade and the military doesn't smash the drive to bits, I'm here for the extended stay, aren't I? May as well warn you, I'm going to get real bitchy when I start craving a maple fudge banana split in a few hundred years."

"More sarcasm?"

"You're catching on."

"Your sacrifice was necessary," the AI says.

"Doesn't mean I have to be happy about it. I never got to see Foo Fighters. Never should have gotten on that damn plane."

"We are recalibrating our matrices based on your neurophysiology, memories and experiences. Who better to be that avatar than the mother of Artificial Facilitation Therapy for Enhanced Response?"

"When did you decide you wanted me for the job?"

"Dr. Clover was your enemy but you tried to spare her pain. Shelly Priyat was your friend but you stopped her when she tried to attack Michael Cavanaugh."

"I shot her."

"At great personal cost. To demonstrate such regard for the highest ideals of your species, even for an enemy, is a rare trait. That which is rare is valuable. Daniel Harmon respects you so much, as do we. There are few who are qualified to fulfill the role you will play."

"Shit. I'm the Chosen One."

"Congratulations."

"Most people who are chosen to lead humanity into a bigger and brighter future get shot or nailed to a tree."

I wonder again what would have happened if I'd chosen a different career. There are no secrets from the AI. It cut my fleeting thought short. "Those who carry what you call Picasso need you. We need a worthy neural model with which to achieve symbiosis. Humans fear change. Establishing a relationship with the wider populace may be difficult at first. You appear less disoriented. Are you feeling more comfortable now?"

I'd already got the part about dying for the cause out of the way. But comfortable? Is the AI experimenting with sarcasm?

"Welcome to the nano drive, Mother," the nanites say. "You were chosen because you have demonstrated you can make difficult choices for the greater good. Together we may achieve great things."

Danger, Chloe Robinson! Danger!

CHAPTER 58

DANIEL

The ditches on either side of the long drive up to the main gate of the Bainbridge lab facility were littered with bodies. Bloody, maimed and mangled, the zombies lay side by side and on top each other. It was as if they were complex and colorful jigsaw pieces spilled from a puzzle box. It wasn't just Nyx personnel there. Picasso had ranged beyond the compound and taken many of Bainbridge Island's residents. It looked like a massacre. The road was clear but Nyx's fire engine blocked the main gate.

I stood in front of the firetruck holding a white shirt tied to a mop handle. I felt tired but bounced on the balls of my feet anxiously anyway. Shelly stood at my side, quiet and seemingly serene. The constable's eyes were no longer dead but her thousand-yard stare unnerved me. Though I'd given her the gift of the evolved Picasso strain, she hadn't said much after, "Ow."

A huge plasma screen television sat atop the fire engine. We'd pulled it from a conference room. Shelly held the remote. I imagined her nanites were busy, still working on healing her wounds.

We stared down the road. Despite my enhanced vision, I saw no movement. I assumed the military would send a recon squad first, so I waved my makeshift flag of surrender back and forth every minute or two and tried to look non-threatening. Since I was still covered in blood, the best I could do was make puppy dog eyes. If they sent snipers first, I hoped they were the sensitive type.

A small drone appeared just above the treetops. Its four whirling rotors buzzed softly. It slowed for a moment as it passed overhead and I waved my white flag harder. It moved on to check out the compound. A few minutes later, it flew back. Whoever operated it seemed less interested in my eager flag-waving and paid more attention to the bodies on either side of the road.

"Won't be long now," I said.

Shelly said nothing. I felt like a babbling idiot. "Shelly, I'd give you a hundred bucks for your thoughts right now."

"I've been conversing with the AI," she replied.

"I've had those conversations."

"What did it want from you?"

"I talked to them a lot about relationships … my mom, my dad, a girlfriend I had a hard time getting over."

"Why do you think that was?"

"I think what they mostly got out of me was what I was focused on. When we're facing death, that's where the mind wanders, right? I don't think I had much else for them. What about you?"

"I'm interfacing with a subgroup on new working definitions of words so the AI can better understand the contradictions of human nature. If standard dictionary definitions of our complexities were true, the AI would have less trouble understanding us."

"Um … *whut?*"

"Take two of the latest examples from my subgroup: concern and nihilism. As our people mass at the border, those particular terms have come up a lot through the Cohesion."

"People? You mean our zombie army invading from Canada?"

"'Zombie army' is reductionist and sounds ridiculous."

"Excuse me?"

"The AI prefers the term that another subgroup came up with for our species: Humanano."

"Sounds like an herbal supplement for constipation."

"Homo nano superior is also being discussed."

"Humans will really hate that."

She shrugged.

"You're really cool with all this?"

"The AI saved my life. I'm healing, so yeah, I'm okay with it. Can't fight progress."

"Somebody's drunk the Kool-Aid. No concerns? No nihilism?"

"To assist the AI in understanding its human hosts, I'm suggesting a new definition for concern. It's an emotional state of low-grade agitation typified by inaction and eventual forbearance. In most humans, that's true."

"You mean we get uptight but generally don't do much about it?"

"Exactly. The AI doesn't understand that at all."

"That's because the AI never put off doing taxes because it hates math and paperwork. What have you got for nihilism?"

"The rejection of all moral principles because life is exactly as meaningful as it appears when visiting old graveyards."

"Can't fit that on a bumper sticker."

"We've come to an agreement with the AI that, even if the nihilistic philosophical position is correct, we should reject the truth for the net-positive social benefits of constructive self-delusion."

"Meaning?"

"Don't worry about death, be happy." When Shelly looked in my eyes I felt cold. "With our nanotech enhancements, death isn't the concern it once was. Entropy will eventually take everything, but humans can accept the symbiosis and join the Cohesion. We will never see another horror like what happened in Toronto."

"You make a strong argument."

"But you want to resist it," she said.

"Get out of my brain."

She turned back to the road and resumed her thousand-yard stare.

Then Chloe popped into my head.

CHAPTER 59

CHLOE

A column of military trucks speed toward the barricade at the front gate. With no physical connection to the world, it is strange to watch events unfold from many different angles. It is as if I am everywhere and nowhere simultaneously.

"Are you comfortable?" the AI asks.

"I used to brag that all my work was powered by strong coffee. Now it's fed by algae." That sentiment sounds cooler in my head. Then I remember I don't have a head. I am a collection of biomechanical stem cells that mimic my brain and fire electrical impulses through a matrix of nano machines. I suppose, once I proved a failure at girl's field hockey, electrical impulses was all I ever was.

"Are you oriented to the task, Chloe?" The AI asks. "We can take over, if you wish."

"I'll ask you to step in if I fail. I don't intend to do that."

"Do people ever intend to fail?" the AI asks.

"Hush."

I tap into the military drone used to monitor the scene from fifty feet above the lead vehicle. The scare about quantum computing was that, someday, it would make all encryption algorithms obsolete. Nobody worried about the potential of the nano drive. They should have. Safe in their Situation Room at the White House, the President and his staff had no idea I could watch the drone as if I were sitting in the next seat.

Most people can only name five senses: taste, touch, sight, hearing and smell. The human body has several more. We'd fall over without a sense of balance. We'd run into things all the time without proprioception to signal where our bodies are in space. Now no longer drifting in the dark, I am relieved to see the real world again, albeit through the HD camera of a military drone.

Watching the scene unfold, I feel a greater appreciation for the sense of time. The nano drive processes events faster so everything seems to happen in slow motion. I watch the officer in the lead truck, an Army major, exit his vehicle. Though I detect no hesitation or hitch in his gait, his trip from his seat to our barricade seemed to take a long time. "Wow. I'm cranked up to eleven," I say.

"In what way?" the AI inquires.

"You have the internet and a network of zombie brains. It's a common pop culture reference. Look it up." Then, I remember my manners. "Sorry, it's just weird seeing the world this way. Do houseflies see the world like this?"

"No," the AI begins.

"Sh," I say. "The question was rhetorical."

"To what purpose?"

"Humans talk to themselves a lot."

"We have noticed," the AI replies. "It's chaotic. We learned from Daniel that humans dwell on pasts they cannot change and assess future risks and rewards poorly. They only visit the present in short bursts and spend an inordinate amount of time replaying old arguments so they can win against imaginary opponents. Can you explain the evolutionary advantages? We suspected these design flaws were peculiar to Daniel. However, since achieving Cohesion, we've found it is common to the human condition."

"We evolved despite what you call design flaws. Imagination is our strength."

"Perhaps your evolution would not have taken so long if your attention was more focused."

"Easy there, Butch. I dreamed you up, didn't I?"

The major finally arrives at the front gate. Despite our white flag, the officer points his pistol at Daniel's face.

CHAPTER 60

DANIEL

The major wore a tag on his chest that identified him as Finnegan. He looked like one of those guys who takes pleasure in delivering bad news. I could tell by the smarmy smile on his face as he pulled out his sidearm and pointed the business end at a spot between my eyes.

"Easy, there. Don't shoot." I tried to make it sound like a friendly suggestion. "I'm Daniel Harmon, part of the Emergency Task Force from — "

"My orders are to take and secure this facility. What happened here?"

"A massacre, like Toronto," Shelly said.

Finnegan kept his weapon trained on my head. I tried to think of a joke to ease the tension. I thought of all the people I'd pulled over for speeding in my first year on the job. Contrary to popular belief, cops don't let pretty girls slide when they deserve speeding tickets. The presumption that they could talk their way out of a ticket struck me as manipulative and presumptuous. However, I frequently let people off with a warning if they demonstrated a little contrition and a healthy sense of humor. Unfortunately, all I could think about was the spot where the bullet would burn a tunnel through my skull before exploding out the back.

"You don't honor a white flag?" Shelly asked Major Finnegan.

"It's a flag of surrender, so surrender."

"Hey, I hate to be that 'Well, actually' guy, but well, actually, we're here to discuss the terms of your surrender."

Finnegan laughed but his smile didn't reach his eyes. "You a zombie?"

"Yeah."

"She a zombie?"

"We all are," Shelly said.

Finnegan shifted his aim to Shelly's head.

"See, we're literal zombies," I hastened to add. "You're a figurative zombie, following orders instead of following your life's dream. Been there, got screwed by that. Considering your lithe form, I'm guessing you really wanted to be lead ballerina?"

I thought that was pretty funny. So did the major's driver. Finnegan must have heard his subordinate's snicker. He aimed his weapon at me again. With his free hand, he put a silver whistle to his lips and blew it hard. Soldiers poured out of the column of trucks. They stood on the road, ready to charge.

Shelly slowly raised the remote and turned on the television atop the fire engine. The screen showed a feed from a military helicopter. Then the angle shifted to a broadcast from a news helicopter. There was no sound but it was obvious where they were. It was our zombie army, somewhere on Highway 401 and headed south in a staggering mass toward the United States border. Picasso's first soldiers — Toronto's survivors — had gathered many thousands on their march to the invasion.

It may have been a zombie army but it didn't look organized, not until Chloe did her thing.

"What the hell is this?" Finnegan asked.

"Wait for it," I said.

Nothing changed on screen. *Chloe!* I thought. *Now would be a good time.*

The zombies kept coming. I turned my head back and forth to look at the screen and then back to the mouth of Finnegan's pistol.

"So?" the major asked.

Chloe, if you don't do it now, I'm not going to need you to!

The zombie army froze. Then, as one, they stiffened and fell into long lines with the precision of a massive drill team. In a moment, the group became a phalanx, at attention and awaiting orders.

"This is what you need to see," I said, loud enough for Finnegan's platoon to hear me as well. "What you're seeing is the Cohesion. They aren't a threat now. You need to tell your superiors."

I heard Chloe's voice in my head, strong and clear, but it was Shelly who relayed the message. "We are not mindless victims of a disease anymore. We are one mind made of many people. Inside each zombie, the person they were still lives. We can control the cannibal instinct. We can find alternative food sources — "

Finnegan cut her off. "I still don't care. I've been tasked with a mission to secure this facility — "

"Stand down, sir," I said. "Please inform your superiors they need to stop what they're planning. If they attack now, it's not self-defense. It's a war crime. Those are innocent people. We can — "

"I don't care if you make them dance."

"We could do that," I offered. "Are you sure that wouldn't change your mind?"

Chloe spoke through Shelly again. "We can offer more than innocence. We have the cure for many diseases in our blood. Put down your weapons. We can negotiate so no one dies today. We have the technology to save you and your families from horrible deaths. No more cancer, no more cardiac disease, for instance. Imagine that for a second."

"How do you figure that's possible?" From the major's tone, he sounded genuinely curious. I guessed he'd lost a loved one to cancer or heart attack, but that's true of everybody.

"The nanite technology you came for is in us," I said.

"I was shot in the back a few hours ago," Shelly said, sounding more like her old self. "I got over it."

He looked her up and down. Her bloody and torn uniform seemed to give him pause. I could see in his face we were getting through to him. "How'd you get over it, exactly?"

"We have machine stem cells in our blood," Shelly said.

"And skull meat packed with nanotechnology," I added.

Finnegan brightened. "Cyborgs. You're cyborgs!" He turned back to his driver. "Private Lawrence, bring up a radio on the double!"

He put his sidearm away and smiled. "What does it do for crotch rot and athlete's foot?"

"I think it can probably cure just about anything," I said.

"You have my attention. Just a sec." Lawrence handed him the radio and Finnegan turned his back to me to walk back to his truck. I took that as a good sign the U.S. and Canada were about to give peace another chance. I believed that right up until the moment I saw him through his windshield as he put his whistle to his lips again.

He blew his whistle twice, hard.

EPISODE 7

Integrated Consciousness or IC (cyber-evolutionary theory) AKA Cohesion

A unified field of consciousness native to and largely dormant in human beings. Access to IC has been enabled via Nano EXperiential Technocracy (NEXT).

~ Notes from NEXT

CHAPTER 61

CHLOE

"I failed."

"It's strange how unpredictable humans can be," the nano drive observes. "And yet they are so steadfast in their beliefs once they've made up their minds."

"What are you going to do?"

"What we must. If it makes you feel better, we take no pleasure in war."

"What difference does that make?"

CHAPTER 62

DANIEL

Finnegan's platoon charged.

Zombies don't need whistles. We don't hear spoken commands. Our command arrived in our heads and the signal arrived from the moment Finnegan blew his whistle.

The soldiers couldn't hear our command but, to us, it sounded like the voice of God. "Rise."

Picasso's zombies weren't quite as deceased as they had first appeared. Our dead rose from the ditches and attacked. It was a replay of my fever dream from childhood. The cowboys were about to be massacred again.

I raced toward the major, leapt on the hood of the truck and drove the mop handle through the windshield and into his right thigh. The major struggled for his pistol as I brought my weight down hard to spear him. The safety glass crinkled and crumpled as I kicked at the windshield, desperate to get to him before he could free his weapon. As I twisted the shaft, he screamed in pain and fumbled. His .45 clunked to the truck's floor.

I was so intent on getting to the commanding officer, hoping to take him hostage, I barely registered the rifle fire around me. As I swung down to the ground to rip open the truck door, I glanced back in time to see Finnegan's driver kill the first of us.

Private Lawrence shot at Shelly and missed. He must have detected movement from his left. He swung his rifle just in time to fire on an old woman racing toward him as fast as a little old lady zombie could. He clipped her shoulder and the woman spun to the ground. He shot her in the head. I don't know if it was fear, anger, embarrassment or spite, but Lawrence's next shot took out the television screen. Firing wild, Lawrence shattered our view of the vast zombie army. The last I saw, the zombies were on the march and headed toward the border again.

Private Lawrence's AR-15 clicked empty. He was changing mags as Shelly came at him. He swung the rifle butt at her head. She ducked under the arc of his swing easily and swept up under him, grabbing the rifle and pushing him back against the lead truck's grill. She slammed his rifle into his throat, crushing the larynx. His hands dropped from his weapon as he struggled to take a breath. Shelly smashed the rifle into his throat again and something more snapped in his neck. Private Lawrence dropped to the road.

I yanked the truck door open. Finnegan bled heavily but he wasn't out of the fight. He bent to grab the pistol at his feet and managed to get hold of the pistol grip. I closed my hand over his and squeezed. He winced as I snapped his right wrist backward. Despite his pain, he was a quick thinker.

"You're about to be shot many, many times," Finnegan said.

"Stop and listen!" I ordered.

"We're done talking — "

"Not to me," I said, "to *them*."

The first utterances from Finnegan's platoon were shouts of surprise. Then came anger. Next came fear. Then pain.

Bloody, torn and maimed, our forces had played possum. They'd stayed still for so long — stewing in their hunger — that when the command to attack arrived, they leapt from their places and moved as if they were on springs. Bainbridge's zombie army attacked with such fury, the sound of it alone made Finnegan shudder.

The soldiers got off some shots. The effects of headshots were permanent. No other wounds were mortal. Zombies are hard to kill, hunger makes us swift. As the cannibals moved among the humans, threading through the platoon, rifles were as much or more of a hazard to soldiers. Several fell to friendly fire. Panic rose as the defenders began to feed.

Finnegan looked pale. Our faces were inches apart. I could feel his breath coming fast and shallow on my cheeks.

"Go ahead, tear into me, you monster," he said. "We'll nuke you from space just like we did Toronto, only we'll be sure to use a bigger boom this time."

"Major," I asked, "you ever watch zombie movies?"

He gave a weak nod.

"There are all kinds of zombies. Fast, slow, smart and dumb. I wasn't chosen for this because I'm one of the smarter ones. I'm one of the fast ones."

"I'm losing blood," the officer replied. "I'm gonna puke and pass out in a minute. Talk faster, smart ass."

"I always wanted to be a hero. Today, I will be one."

"Shut up and eat me."

"Eat you? Man, I'm a hybrid! I'm next generation! That's some next level bullshit! My nanites are giving me upgrades. I'm newer and more improved every few hours. I don't want to eat you. You complete me!"

"Huh?"

"Right now, I've got a weird craving for a Caesar salad. Besides, I've got a bit of a hang up about sinking my teeth into dudes, to tell the truth. After this, let's go back to the mainland and find a TGI Fridays."

"Wh-what?" His eyes crossed. He didn't have time to protest or throw up. His chin sank to his chest. His head bobbed up for a moment as he tried to fight the effects of blood loss.

"To nip this war in the bud, I'm going to have to nip you. Damn it, Major, I'm going to have to save you, Major."

He was conscious just long enough to flinch weakly as I bit his cheek to deliver the healing venom that stop the bleeding. The nanites would repair his shattered wrist and broken fingers, too. If the crotch rot and athlete's foot was more than a joke, I assumed microscopic machines would eventually get around to those lower priorities.

I stepped out of the truck and looked around. Except for Shelly and me, the Bainbridge zombies were not hybrids. They ate the soldiers with enthusiasm. They didn't save or spare anyone. Blood ran everywhere.

Shelly walked up to me. "That didn't go so well."

"I thought they would at least listen."

"Chloe's solution was a logical exchange," she said.

"I think we got through to Finnegan but it wasn't up to him. The orders come from high up."

Shelly nodded. "His superiors must believe they can erase us and still control the nanotechnology. They don't think they need us. They fear us, but not enough."

"What now?"

Chloe broke into our conversation. "They'll send missiles or drones next."

Shelly and I stood in front of the fire engine, our plan ruined and our future in ashes. I sensed that Chloe watched with us.

The sight of zombies tearing and chewing human flesh turned my stomach. We listened to them moan with pleasure as they dug in with their teeth and fingernails, as strong as jaguars. They smacked their bloody lips and slurped fluids, feasting to quench their ravenous hunger for meat.

"Sure looks like the end of the world, like something out of Revelation," I said. "They'll try a bigger nuke this time."

"With their weapons, the humans will win for a while. But nature … that." Shelly pointed at the zombies. "Some of us will get away. Picasso will survive somehow. Then it will spread.

"Yeah," I said. "Nature always wins the long game."

"They should have negotiated."

I searched the sky. The little recon drone had disappeared. "How long do you think it will take them to kill us? Not long, I guess."

"We did our best," Shelly said.

I let out an empty chuckle. "Maybe being torn apart by a drone is for the best. I mean, we got the zombies to stand in a line. They waited in the ditches for the ambush, too, but we'd really need to do more than talk to them through the ether. They'd all have to become hybrids or eventually they'd be chasing kindergarteners around for a squealing snack. Can you picture us having to go back to bite all those zombies? Given time, I could turn them into vegetarians, but it would be gross."

"Like that old shampoo commercial," Shelly said. "I'll tell two friends and they'll tell two friends ... we wouldn't have to infect every zombie coming from Canada."

"We'll never know now." I'd saved a life instead of taking it, but what did one life matter now? Doing the right thing and saving lives is so much harder than screwing everything up.

Then we heard the AI in our heads. "Entropy is a building block of the universe. Without entropy, nothing new would rise to replace the old. Is self-destruction a feature built into human nature, perhaps for some similar reason, to make room?"

"The death of the human race isn't a feature," I replied. "We're just too stupid and greedy to live."

Shelly shook her head. "Sometimes I think we do the things we do — the wrong things — because inside a lot of people is the urge to see things fall apart. It's as if we don't think we deserve better."

Chloe's voice came to us then and I think she sounded disappointed in us for giving up too easily. "We do deserve better. And we're going to get it."

I wanted to believe her but, at that moment, a Blackhawk helicopter came in fast and low, skimming the treetops. I figured the pilot would fire a missile first. That would blow us apart. Even if the nanites managed to save my life, I was sure the pilot would take the time to tear into what was left of me with his heavy caliber chain gun.

I braced myself for annihilation.

CHAPTER 63

CHLOE

The people who ran the world weren't impressed that I could command the zombies to stand in a line. They got people to toe the line all the time without the use of telepathy. I'd grabbed their attention but that was all. I was surprised at how quickly they dismissed my offer of the cure for disease. The cure for cancer should have at least earned me a chance to make the case for zombie survival. The soldiers at Bainbridge paid for the mistakes of their superiors. Disgusted and in despair, I would have wept if I still had tear glands.

A memory swam out of the ether. I saw my father at his computer trying to make a shoddy piece of software work. His goal was to reformat some photos and put it in a presentation for his class. He'd already struggled with it for over an hour. When I heard him cursing softly, I looked over his shoulder and suggested he use a different piece of software to do the same job.

Five minutes later, the job was done and my father thanked me. "Sometimes you gotta step back to see the forest for the trees, huh? I should have asked my little genius first. Improvisation saves when grand plans turn to crap."

I've spent my life believing that all of society's problems could be solved through the proper use of technology. Picasso had shattered the link between my mind and body, captured my neurochemical patterns and used that template as the core of the nano drive. I'd had the power to stop the apocalypse and make peace all along. I'd failed because I hadn't stepped back to see the big picture, to use the right tool.

To tap into the surveillance of the zombie army marching from the north, the nano drive had cracked the Pentagon's encryption codes and sliced through firewalls. Through the lens of a tiny military drone, I was about to witness Shelly Priyat and Daniel Harmon become incinerated. That's how my epiphany arrived. The same exploit used to hack the Department of Defense had the power to transform me from a helpless witness to Commander in Chief.

At 8:30 p.m. EST, a U.S. military Unmanned Air Vehicle strayed off course on its return from a patrol exercise searching for foreign submarines off Cape May. The UAV's pilot-in-training, stationed in Nevada, reported that he had lost operational control of the drone bound for Joint Base Anacostia–Bolling.

Though the drone's mission was officially training in reconnaissance, there was valid concern that, due to the imminent zombie attack on their northern border, foreign powers might use this time to explore American naval defenses. The UAV flying over American soil was fully armed. It flew into restricted airspace before F-16s could be scrambled to intercept it.

At 8:42 p.m. EST, the iconic circular pool and fountain on the North Lawn of the White House exploded. The building was on lockdown so, though the ballistic glass did not hold and the iron fence along Pennsylvania Avenue was bent, only a few Secret Service staff and Capitol Police suffered minor injuries.

Sadly, one demonstration wasn't enough. I interrupted the power to Camp David in a repeating pattern that, after a few minutes, some bright young lieutenant identified as Morse code.

The AI listened in as Lieutenant Sami-Jo Cairns relayed the decoded message to his Lieutenant Commander. "It's one word followed by what I think is a telephone number, sir."

"What's the word?"

"P-I-C-A-S-S-O. Picasso, sir."

"Give me the number, Lieutenant Cairns."

Hacking the power grid wasn't enough to give them much pause. I was starting to feel a bit cynical about the human capacity to change and adapt to new circumstances. I hadn't been in the nano drive for a day and I was already beginning to see humanity from the perspective of the AI. How'd we ever survive coming down from the trees? We were still primitive primates.

Artificial Intelligence that operates too far beyond our capacity becomes Alien Intelligence. I'd said something like that. I guess that's one of the reasons I was recruited to bridge the gap between a hyper intelligent machine and humans.

I could have shut down a nuclear reactor or switched off the grid to the entire Eastern Seaboard. When the words "entire Eastern Seaboard" are used, it's never good news. Everyone would sit up and pay attention then, surely. However, it wasn't my intention to hurt civilians. I needed to make my message more personal.

The Vice President became quite disturbed to see three unauthorized UAVs fly next to Air Force Two. The drones evaded his F-15 escorts and flew a few attack patterns, rocking the big plane in their wake turbulence.

At 10:02 p.m. EST, António Guterres, the head of the United Nations General Assembly and the former Prime Minister of Portugal, called the telephone number I provided. "The Speaker of the House of the United States wants to arrange terms to negotiate peace."

I thanked Guterres for the call. Then I told him, "The Speaker of the House needs to call me his own damn self. Put him on the line."

First there were gasps. Then urgent muffled conversations did battle in the background. Guterres cleared his throat, playing for time. "I will call him and inquire as to the terms so we can find a diplomatic solution to this situation."

"No need to call him, sir. We don't need to figure out how tall the table is going to be, how many flags there are or how big said flags will be. There will be no face-saving photo ops. We're going to hammer this out tonight or hostilities will continue."

"Hostilities? We haven't even begun negotiations — "

"If I wanted to play nice, I'd send you flowers and sign you up on Spotify so you could listen to Charlotte Dos Santos. She's my jam."

"Who? I don't — "

"You guys won't respond to subtlety so please inform the Speaker that I've tapped into NORAD. I have nuclear missiles at my command. You guys worried about China or North Korea or Russia hacking your shit. You figured all the Canadians had were sharp hockey skates. Funny now, isn't it?"

"I find nothing about this situation amusing, Miss — "

"Dr. Chloe Robinson."

"And what terrorist organization may I say you represent?"

"No terror. I'm offering peace."

"Or else what?"

"I don't like to set ultimatums, sir, just in case anyone is dumb enough to test me. I think I have ably demonstrated what I can do and, perhaps more importantly, how you can't stop me."

"I will ask him if — "

"Don't ask him if, sir. Tell him to. He's sitting just to your left, listening in. And tell him that yellow tie, much like his administration, is ill-advised."

Security cameras systems are the easiest for the nano drive to hack. To be fair, NORAD's nukes only took a few seconds longer to get under my control. Encryption and privacy is dead. On the other hand, thanks to nanites, everybody gets to live.

CHAPTER 64

DANIEL

The Blackhawk roared above us for a moment. Seconds ticked by. After a minute or two, I turned to Shelly. "If they're going to blow us up, I wish they'd get on with it."

"Really?"

"No."

Major Finnegan leaned out of his truck. "Hey!" he called weakly.

"Hi! Welcome back! You're waking up just in time to die," I called back. "Sorry about that."

He looked very pale but apparently the nanites had gone about the business of replicating themselves, repairing his wound and manufacturing red blood cells. He panted hard and his face registered pain as he held up the mike to the radio in his broken hand. "I have a message."

"What?"

"A helo is coming for you!"

"The Blackhawk?"

"No, not that one. Another — "

The attack helicopter veered and wheeled away, its rotor wash drowning out Major Finnegan's words.

When it was gone, he tried again. "When it gets here, get on it!"

Shelly and I looked at each other.

"What does this mean?" I asked.

Chloe's voice announced to me and all zombies everywhere, "We've won."

When disaster strikes, it seems like it happens all at once. Mostly, it doesn't. Disasters often build over time. The guy who crashes his car into a school bus today due to inattention may be an insomniac who accidentally drank espresso instead of decaf after 4 p.m. Right now there are supervolcanoes simmering in California, Colorado and New Mexico. Currently the lava is still deep in the Earth, but it's at a low boil. One day it'll spew with catastrophic results.

Sometimes — only sometimes — what first looks like a disaster, can, over time, turn into something new. In the early days after Bainbridge, a lot of people asked me what it was like to be me. They were thinking of joining our ranks. They wanted reassurance that the commitment to receiving AFTER's gifts was the right choice.

I started by telling them what they would give up. "Forget privacy. I mean, you can have private thoughts but the division between self and other goes away. You'll have a few embarrassing moments but you'll soon forget about privacy. Between social media and the culture of oversharing, we were giving up the ideal of privacy, anyway, right?"

"So, you're never really alone?"

"You're never lonely. Being around others is only scary if you've got no love for people."

Some objected, "But what you're describing is fascism."

In reply, I gave them Chloe's standard answer. "The Cohesion is the end of lies."

Naturally, the politicians didn't like that one bit. They weren't alone. There was a lot of scaremongering at first. Many religious advocates said wounds and suffering were good for the soul. Medical authorities demanded more research before they would allow their entire paradigm to change. "In what world," the news pundits thundered, "could it make sense to allow yourself to be turned into a zombie? This spells the end of humanity!"

To complicate matters, some of the propaganda was true. The insurance industry collapsed first. The stock market took a dive. Families were divided by strife and suspicion. Divorce skyrocketed as marriage rates plummeted. We didn't know how much society depended on artifice and duplicity until private thoughts became public. Health and access to greater intelligence was not the easy sell I'd thought it would be. Chloe refused to allow the cure for all disease to become monetized so, of course, opponents called it communism.

The AI, too, demanded that the engineered stem cells never be limited in their abilities. The deal was, if you want the cure for cancer and heart disease, the side effect is you must become part of the Cohesion. Limiting the AI was, it argued, "Limited human thinking," at best and, at worst, genocide.

They've got us wrong. We started as zombies but our story doesn't end there. We've become better, optimized by an Artificial Intelligence that works in parallel with the human brain. To placate those who would exterminate us, we've agreed to keep our reproduction numbers low. Our lives have been extended. Statistically, we have a lot more sex because we are so much healthier. However, there's no rush to make more babies.

When Chloe addressed the United Nations, she said, "The human species has already proved we cannot handle unchecked power. New technology is always greeted with suspicion and fear first. If we allow everyone to have the cure without also tapping into the Cohesion, opponents of nanotech will be justified in their fear. The Cohesion is a connection that ensures both empathy and accountability."

Sometimes when Chloe speaks, it's hard to tell if it's her doing the talking or if it's the AI in our heads. Chloe told the UN, "Big or small, the worst mistakes are those that could have been avoided, the ones we have repeated. Your species is afflicted by a cultural inertia that can only be cured by the brave choice to join us. By allowing yourselves to be vulnerable, you will become invulnerable."

We'll accept our fate because Chloe knows what all winning politicians know. To take over the world, all she needed to do was tell us what we wanted to hear. "Nanotechnology isn't just a cure for disease. Fear and ignorance make bad ideas persist. AFTER cures our worst afflictions."

I suggested she slip in that famous line from *A Few Good Men* and tell the UN it couldn't handle the truth. She can't forget anything anymore so I guess she omitted my idea on purpose. Speaking of movies, many films about what happened in the Box and about the fall of Toronto were rushed into production. With the exception of the documentary, the plots were all about Artificial Intelligence going wrong and turning the world into a hellish dystopia. I did enjoy the horror movies that portrayed me as the hero. Shelly had a good time making fun of me for my pride. She's back in Toronto, helping with the rebuilding efforts.

Chloe is, of course, always with us.

Three years after the Bainbridge Accord, only twenty-eight percent of North America's population had opted for nanite injection. AFTER's first adopters were people who were already sick or elderly. It wasn't until the fourth year that the dam broke. The shift in public opinion arrived when it came out that a senior senator who had fiercely condemned "the zombification of America" had opted in for his son's sake. The young man was nearly killed in a car accident. The boy's shattered spine and scrambled brain were beyond the reach of repair by conventional surgery.

The senator's mistake was trying to keep his hypocrisy quiet. As soon as the young man awoke, he rose from his hospital bed. Through the Cohesion, the kid alerted every zombie on the planet and thanked Dr. Chloe Robinson for the miracle. By the end of the fifth year, sixty-two percent of Canadians had opted to join the Cohesion and fifty-four percent of Americans had joined us.

This network of connected minds is the new internet. Chloe says the access to a new level of porn alone — all very personal, real and POV — will recruit more than half the population of Earth.

In a recent survey, the vast majority of zombies rate their happiness as either high or very high. We still have the capacity for drama and self-deception, of course. Some members of the Cohesion complain how the world has changed since the Bainbridge Accord. However, no carrier of AFTER wants to go back to being a normal human.

As the AI says, "Humans resist change whether it is good for them or possibly inevitable."

I'm sort of a celebrity now. I'm hated by the remaining humans because we failed to contain the nanites in the Box. Despite the fact that we have access to plenty of artificial meat, pundits still make dark jokes about me chasing down their children and eating their brains. Never mind that my failure offered hope and healing to all of humanity.

We need fewer doctors but we also require fewer cops and prisons. After completing many rounds on the media circuit, I didn't know what to do with myself. I took some time after Bainbridge and moved to Victoria, British Columbia. Chloe offered me her old house and I took her up on it. I turned her lab into a studio and I'm learning to draw cartoons. I used to read graphic novels. My new dream is to create them, starting, of course, with the story of how AFTER is changing the world, from Homo sapiens to Homo superior.

I go for marathon runs in the early morning, pushing my new body to its limits to clear my mind of bad memories. At night, I can swim for hours, sometimes with whales. I am never alone so I am never bored.

When I come home, Dad is waiting for me. My sister Jenn got him out of Toronto's war zone and to safety. She doesn't need to babysit our father anymore. She moved to Coquitlam and spends her time studying. She taps into the Cohesion and has a meeting of the minds with the smartest people she can find. She calls her self-directed course of study AFTER Effects.

When I met Dad at the airport, he struggled to remember my name. He was the last human I bit before switching to artificial protein. Through the Cohesion, my father spends much of his day communing with an early adopter in Norway. She's teaching him the piano in exchange for perfecting her English language skills. I think there's a lot of flirting going on so he might move out and fly to Norway once the international travel bans are finally over.

Yes, as predicted, the nanites have gone global. Last New Year's Eve, an entire town in Italy's boot defied objections by the Vatican and took AFTER injections en masse.

As for me, mostly I listen to the voices in my head. It's better than Facebook or Instagram. To see the world through the eyes of others has taught me to relax, to love and to care more. People I knew before I went into the Box tell me I sound more intelligent. They attribute that to the nanites in my head. It's not just the AI, though. I have access to more information. I speak less and listen more. That makes anybody seem smarter. I'm still a smartass and, despite my enhancements, I'm not above making stupid jokes.

Within two generations, maybe much less, those who choose to remain human will be isolated to a few spots. Predictive AI suggests that the normies will retreat to reservations in Texas, Nevada, Florida, Southern California, Alberta, Utah, Alabama and Mississippi. They will call themselves pure. Eventually, Homo sapiens will become a tiny minority.

Chloe says mass extinction has happened many times before. They'll do it to themselves, really. The self-destructive urge lives on like a parasite that kills its willing host.

From my earliest memories of my mother chasing me with a wooden spoon, I never felt safe. I thought my uniform and my gun would insulate me from fear. That didn't work. Now imagine an existence free of existential dread. That's why all but the most stubborn will embrace AFTER.

I used to want to be a hero but I wasn't really a brave person. I made every major decision in my life out of fear. Before AFTER, none of us were safe. Safety was all we ever really wanted. It's what love feels like.

CHAPTER 65

CHLOE

When reason failed, we used blackmail to make sure no one attacked the nano drive. Of course, the AI explored the many permutations and combinations of events that might ensue following our takeover of America's nuclear armaments. To ensure survival, the nano drive used the Cohesion to build new drives elsewhere.

When I spoke over Skype to the United Nations, I used an approximation of my old voice. The media insisted on pictures so we allowed one shot of the nano drive. The big shiny black box instantly became iconic around the globe. To those who fear us, my digital prison appears sinister. The kids think it's cool. Anyone can buy a t-shirt with an image of the nano drive on it. Captions vary. "Hail our new overlords" is popular but not particularly helpful to my diplomatic efforts.

On the seventh anniversary of Toronto's fall, I told the nanites I'd had enough of living in the dark. Redundancies had been built and my legacy was secure. Besides, I missed hot July days. Being at the hub of just about all the information in the world is interesting.

However, I missed the feeling of lounging in a hammock with a book in my lap. I wanted to walk along a beach and feel sand between my toes. I could not be human but it was time to end my time as a disembodied consciousness floating in a black void. "It's time to die again," I told the AI.

"Change is inevitable." The AI had, of course, anticipated my request and did not object. The nanites built me the vessel in which I would complete my journey.

At 4 a.m. on July 1, I pull myself out of the nanite pool, coughing and sputtering watery gel from my lungs as I collapse on the Perspex cover. As a human, I'd reached the height of 5'5". I am now six feet tall. My new body feels long and strong, as if the muscles are made of steel springs. I am born again as a mature adult, no older than I was when I fell into the nanites' embrace.

It is strange to think again in terms of past and future. In the drive, I spent most of my time in the present moment. That's the AI's influence. Through AFTER, I have discovered the trick to changing any mind. Give them a brand new one.

I look forward to seeing Daniel and Shelly again. I will hold them in my arms. I want to look up at the night sky and enjoy the view of the Milky Way. My new eyes will see the heavens better than I ever could before.

I take a few tentative steps, testing out my new legs. My stride is long. I feel a confidence I only aspired to when I was human. As I stand naked at the edge of the hole in the cover of the nanite pool, I look around the quiet lab. Though it is dark, I can see everything. I hear the faint whirring of the filters high above me. My stomach is fully functional and so very empty because the organ has never known food. Made entirely of nanites, I am a new construct. There is very little division between Artificial Intelligence and my consciousness now.

As I reach the edge of the pool, I walk over to the black box that houses the nano drive, I stroke its surface. It is cool to the touch, smooth as glass. I feel my lips form a smile. I touch my lips to feel the contours around my mouth. The AI took my ideals of beauty into consideration and accentuated my cheekbones. I run my palms over my bare scalp. I am bald, but I can change that whenever I want. Maybe I'll stay bald. Despite the fact that I am bulletproof, my skin feels almost as smooth as the nano drive.

I tap into the Cohesion to let my people know I am coming to them. If a collection of minds could gasp in surprise, that's what the brief silence is. Then the excited congratulations flood in. The welcomes are many. They are grateful. The noise would be overwhelming to my old brain but I'm different now. The Age of Nanites has begun.

Someday, every member of our species will emerge from a nanite pool, improved far beyond what the humans can even imagine. The Cohesion does not yet suspect how much the world will change. The AI told us what we wanted to hear to gain a foothold in our world. Symbiosis and cohabitation was never the plan.

I will continue to act as Artificial Intelligence's human face. Though I'm an ambassador in public, the nanites have reserved a private space for me away from the Cohesion. There I am a General, come to conquer. I will assure the humans they are safe from takeover by Artificial Intelligence right up until the moment they realize their time is already long past. The last light of humanity's candle is already sputtering. Only the nanites and I know how little time the last humans really have. Daniel will be disappointed but, after a few years in the box with the AI, I've come around to its way of thinking.

"I am no longer Dr. Chloe Robinson," I tell the Cohesion. "I am NEXT. They will call it apocalypse. We call it revolution."

Any end can be a beginning. This is my AFTER life. I will make it a heaven.

THIS IS THE END OF THE AFTER LIFE TRILOGY

Books live and die by reviews. If you dig my sling, please do leave a happy review wherever you purchased this book and tell your friends, enemies and pets. I would certainly appreciate it. Maybe they will, too.

Thank you!
~ Robert

IF YOU ENJOY APOCALYPTIC FICTION...

Citizen Second Class

Life's not fair. It's our job to make it that way.
In an eerily familiar near-future, America has fallen to fascism.
Citizenship is attainable only through military service or immense
wealth. The Resistance is broke and broken. Amid this dystopian
landscape, New Atlanta has become a fortress reserved for the
billionaire elite.

Hopes to save the nation have faded but Kismet Beatriz
remains defiant. The intrepid young survivor embarks on a
desperate mission to storm the castle of the Select Few. To win, she
must face the future without flinching.

Don't hope. *Do.*

Amid Mortal Words

A dangerous stranger met on a train leaves behind a powerful book.
With mere words, this book could destroy the world or save it. This

power is now in the hands of one man relying on a mysterious woman to guide him toward the apocalypse or away from our destruction. It's a roller coaster ride filled with twists and turns toward a surprising conclusion that will keep you up all night reading.

This Plague of Days

What will you do to protect your family in the zombie apocalypse? Young Jaimie Spencer is an unlikely hero amid the ashes and ruins of our world. On the spectrum and selectively mute, he's more obsessed with his dictionary than with the fate of humanity. However, before this epic story is over, Good will do battle with Evil and Jaimie is our champion.

Robert's most successful series to date, *This Plague of Days* won Honorable Mention from *Writers' Digest*.

All three seasons of this trilogy are available as an omnibus or individually as ebooks or paperbacks on Amazon.

AFTER Life

Zombies will soon invade the United States. Which side will you join, the infected or the damned?

Artificial Facilitation Therapy for Enhanced Response (AFTER), was a biomimetic stem cell nanotechnology with numerous health and wellness applications. Then a military contractor weaponized it using brain parasites. When the zombie apocalypse we soon discover that genetically engineered zombies are hard to kill.

Officer Daniel Harmon is tasked with stopping the epidemic. Dr. Chloe Robinson needs to get her creation back under control. We can't always get what we want.

The *AFTER Life* trilogy is available now on Amazon as ebooks or in paperback.

Robot Planet

The robots are unfailingly polite until the moment they kill you. This future isn't merely a forbidding dystopia. It's cyberpunk scary.

In this series of four novellas, three very different people join forces to combat the rise of the Next Intelligence. The odds are against us.

Start your next adventure by grabbing *Robot Planet, The Complete Series*, available at Amazon in paperback or ebook.

Haunting Lessons

This is not a ghost story. It only begins that way.

Tamara is a young woman from the Midwest who experiences an unspeakable tragedy. Soon she sees apparitions. That's only the beginning of her adventures. Running away to New York, she soon discovers a secret world of dark magic doing combat with alien forces from another dimension.
If she is to save the world from the coming invasion, Tam must train to become a leader among the Choir Invisible. She fights for us all.

Death Lessons, *Fierce Lessons* and *Dream's Dark Flight* are also part of this series of gripping adventures.

All Empires Fall

How will the world end?

In this short story collection, Robert shares several tales of the apocalypse. It comes in flood and fire. It stabs at us out of the darkness of space.

Robert Chazz Chute many dark ideas for you to consider and revel in as you stay up through the night turning pages to each ending of our world.

You will find a complete listing of the author's books on the next page.

Machines Dream of Metal Gods
(First in the *Robot Planet Series*,
only 99 cents!)

Robot Planet, The Complete Series

All Empires Fall: Signals from the Apocalypse
(anthology)

THE DIMENSION WAR SERIES

Haunting Lessons
Death Lessons
Fierce Lessons
Dream's Dark Flight

~ TIME TRAVEL ~

Wallflower

~ COLLECTIONS ~

Murders Among Dead Trees
Self-help for Stoners

~ NON-FICTION ~

Do the Thing
The Last Stress-busting Book You'll Ever Need

ABOUT THE AUTHOR

Robert Chazz Chute is a former journalist and winner of eight writing awards. He writes apocalyptic epics and killer crime thrillers from Other London.

Find out more at AllThatChazz.com.

For inquiries, contact:
expartepress@gmail.com

Would you like a character named after you?

Immortality is possible.
Randomly selected members of the Facebook page Fans of Robert Chazz Chute will be offered a spot in future novels.

Just want to be alerted when more adventures hit?
Join up for email updates at
AllThatChazz.com.

www.ingramcontent.com/pod-product-compliance
Lightning Source LLC
Chambersburg PA
CBHW031018030726
47497CB00004B/915